I0614657

It had taken all his courage to pay a call to Elizabeth, only to find her with another man...

Jackson must have made a sound as the flowers tumbled from fingers gone numb. Beth looked up and all of the color drained from her face, making her white to the lips.

He gave her a nod with a jerk of his head. "I'm sorry. I came at a bad time." Drawing himself up as straight as possible, he clamped down on the pain and turned around, retreating out the door as fast as he was able. Down the driveway, out on the road, pushing his way home and he didn't look back.

There was the sound of an approaching car, its engine humming. Jackson wasn't surprised when the Coupe Deville pulled up beside him. "Son, let me give you a ride home."

He didn't stop. If he stopped, his back would give out and leave him a sniveling mess at the side of the road. Jackson would not give Hamilton Mason the satisfaction. "Thank you, sir. I'd rather walk. I need the exercise."

Beth's father wouldn't take no for an answer. It wasn't part of his make-up. "Jackson, please. I know how upset you must be, but I'm sure you see that Clyde is a better match for Elizabeth. He's going to be a partner at the firm." Silence for a few more agonizing steps. "Boy, if you don't get in this car, you're going to fall and be a frozen lump in the road. Your parents would never forgive me."

"With all due respect, sir, I wouldn't mind if that happened." Mason's words had stabbed him in the gut, nearly making Jackson double over. Elizabeth's father would have his way with an educated, white collar man courting his daughter after all. "I won't be bothering your daughter again, I promise."

On a blustery winter's afternoon, Casey Henry discovers her father-in-law's journal concealed in a cedar chest and shares it with her husband, Emmett. They sit together on their bedroom floor, mesmerized. Jackson Henry might have been a man of few words when it came to speech, but his devotion is faithfully committed to paper, echoed by the love letters of his wife. The young couple unearth the kind of love every girl dreams of while wearing her pillowcase veil and singing, "Someday my prince will come." From the day Emmett's parents fell in love until the startling conclusion, the young Henrys hold their breath and dab their eyes…

KUDOS for *A Man of Few Words*

In *A Man of Few Words* by Heidi Sprouse, Casey Henry finds her father-in-law's journal hidden in a cedar chest in the attic and shares it with her husband Emmett. As the couple reads the journal together, they learn the story of Jackson and Beth Henry, Emmett's parents, and the strength of their love in the face of horrific trials and tribulations. We get both the story of the elder Henrys and that of Casey and Emmett as the two stories are interwoven throughout the book. Sprouse's character development is superb and you can't help but fall in love with her characters, laughing and crying with them through the good times and bad, as a great love story unfolds. A compelling and heartwarming read. ~ *Taylor Jones, The Review Team of Taylor Jones & Regan Murphy*

A Man of Few Words by Heidi Sprouse is the story of Jackson and Beth Henry as told by Jackson in his journal, which is found in the attic by his daughter-in-law, Casey. Casey shows the journal to her husband, Emmett. Together Emmett and Casey read the journal, treating us to the heart-breaking and heartwarming story of Jackson's love for his wife Beth, and his steadfast determination to protect her and provide a good life for her and their children. But Jackson's task is made more difficult by an injury to his back that leaves him all but crippled. This injury is all the more devastating because Jackson is a horse farmer/trainer by trade, and his injury makes it difficult for him to make a living. As Emmett and Casey read the journal, the author also treats us to flashes of their current lives and some of the obstacles facing them. Sprouse has a fresh and unique voice that pulls you in and captures you in its spell. Her characters are fabulous, her plot solid and well thought out, with plenty of twists and turns that will catch you by surprise. Whether you are looking for a little romance, or just a compelling story of strong determined people facing almost insurmountable obstacles, you're going to love *A Man of Few Words*. ~ *Regan Murphy, The Review Team of Taylor Jones & Regan Murphy*

A MAN
OF FEW
WORDS

HEIDI SPROUSE

A Black Opal Books Publication

GENRE: FAMILY SAGA/ROMANCE

This is a work of fiction. Names, places, characters and incidents are either the product of the author's imagination or are used fictitiously, and any resemblance to any actual persons, living or dead, businesses, organizations, events or locales is entirely coincidental. All trademarks, service marks, registered trademarks, and registered service marks are the property of their respective owners and are used herein for identification purposes only. The publisher does not have any control over or assume any responsibility for author or third-party websites or their contents.

DEDICATION

To Mom and Dad.
You never needed words
to tell me I meant the world to you.
Thank you for showing me how to love—
With all my heart.

"Come live in my heart and pay no rent."
~ Samuel Lover

CHAPTER 1

To say that winter did not agree with her was an understatement. Cooped up in the house with too much time off, and Doctor Casey Henry was going out of her mind. She could easily self-diagnose her problem: a severe case of cabin fever. The remedy: physical activity and plenty of it. Restless for no reason and unable to sit still, she began a cleaning frenzy. After a year of marriage, the Henry House still held a fair share of secrets. Poking in all of the nooks and crannies would be an adventure.

Casey ran out of steam in the last room, their bedroom. Her rope of long, dark hair was heavy against her neck and clinging to her skin, irritating her as everything tended to do of late. She pinned the whole mess up on top of her head and sat down on the edge of the bed, blowing her bangs from her face and rubbing at the small of her aching back. Her mind became clouded with the image of her husband's strong, capable hands taking over the massage for her before moving on to some other choice areas.

As a horse farmer with a lifetime of experience gentling those large animals, Emmett had magic in his fingertips. Closing her eyes, she pictured the many times his touch had soothed her body. Her pillow beckoned, urging her to go to sleep and finish the fantasy. Perhaps Em would make her dream become a reality later that night.

Cracking an eyelid, Casey considered grabbing the quilt at the foot of the large, four poster bed when the cedar chest underneath caught her eye. Intriguing as Pandora's box, it was the one thing in this room she had never opened. She stood and reached her arms over her head in an ambitious stretch to shake out the kinks and knelt down on the floor, something that wasn't as easy as it used to be. The latch popped easily and the sweet scent of cedar rose to greet her as she lifted the lid.

Carefully emptying the contents one item at a time, the box revealed nothing out of the ordinary. Blankets, baby clothes, and photo albums mounded in a heap. Casey thought she hit bottom until her hand struck a loose board. Curious, she lifted up one end and found a gorgeous quilt, folded in a neat square, bound by a ribbon, with a sachet placed under the bow. Someone had packed away this blanket with care.

Setting aside the piece of wood, Casey lifted the quilt with hands that trembled, as if they knew the history of the heirloom. The needlework had been done with great attention to detail, a colorful assortment of small patches pieced together to create the famous wedding ring pattern that graced countless homes in America. Resting it carefully in her lap, she flipped one corner. *Jackson and Elizabeth Henry, September 4, 1957* was sewn in neat, small script.

Emmett's mother must have had a part in the masterpiece. Itching to see the full glory of her mother-in-law's handiwork, she stood up and undid the tie. A journal bound in leather, soft, lined and broken-in with wear, tumbled to the floor, along with a locket, letters, and a few pictures.

"Emmett! Em, come here right now!" she called out, breathless with excitement.

Footsteps pounded up the stairs, coming in a rush. Casey had never heard him move so fast before. "What, what's wrong?" He hesitated for only an instant to scan the room, yet still he managed to draw her eye, could draw every eye in a crowded room, completely at home in his own skin. Those GQ models couldn't hold a candle to him. Dressed in his typical wear—jeans, flannel shirt with a white T-shirt poking out, comfortable in his stocking feet, Emmett Henry was a marvel.

Dark hair streaked by the sun, regardless of the time of year, tumbled into amber eyes that gleamed like a jar of golden honey held to the light. They touched on her and glowed softly, flooded with relief that she was all right. He knelt beside her, his hand pressing on the nape of her neck, his touch tender. These days, he treated her like she was made of spun glass. "What is it?"

"I'm fine, but look what I found." Her gesture encompassed the small collection of keepsakes strewn in front of her.

He settled on the floor at her side and situated himself cross-legged, fingering the material of the quilt, his face going soft with wonder. "I haven't seen this since I was little. Mama," Emmett swallowed hard, eyes suddenly bright, "my mother used to gather it around Wyatt and me on rainy days or stormy nights. She'd stay and cuddle with us for hours."

Casey picked up the necklace and set it in his hand.

His fingers closed around hers, the chain entangled in between their palms as they warmed the golden locket. "She let me play with this. I used to make the heart spin in the sunlight, watch the sparkles on the wall." He cleared his throat and flicked the clasp with his thumb, revealing his parents on their wedding day.

"They're beautiful, Em." Casey wrapped an arm around his waist, giving him comfort or support, whichever he needed. Rigid at first, he went loose at her touch. Taking in the other treasures, she picked up the sachet and inhaled deeply. "Mmm. Roses…and rosehip, maybe?"

Emmett fingered the organdy packet and savored the scent. He rested it on his cheek and closed his eyes. "Mama loved roses. She used to make these all of the time from the bushes growing out in front of the house. My father must have saved this one. Funny, all this time and you can still smell it."

He set the sachet and the locket on the floor and sifted through the pictures, picking up one of a young couple standing with a horse in between, both looping one arm around the beauty's neck. They wore smiles from ear to ear. Jackson Henry dressed almost the same as his son, minus the heavy shirt, while Elizabeth wore a party dress. Emmett shook his head with a small smile. "I never saw my father when he was this young. Just look at them." He laughed softly and flipped the photograph over. Someone with sparing, tidy handwriting had written, *At my Beth's 18th Birthday Party, July 12, 1956.*

Casey traced the picture. "You really look like him, you and Wyatt, so handsome. Your mother, she was a real beauty." Emmett could only nod, his thumb stroking the old photograph. "What about this?" She set the journal in his lap, pulling him away from the undertow of his memories.

"I've never seen this before." He opened the book, found his father's name and the date inside the cover, *Jackson Henry, July 1956.* Flipping through the pages, hundreds, filled from front to back, he let out a low whistle. "No wonder my father didn't talk a lot. He put all of his words in here." His fingers stilled a few pages in. "Dad even pasted in letters from Mama."

Casey rested her hand on his and gave it a gentle squeeze. "You want to read it to me?"

After a year spent in blindness, reading was one thing Emmett Henry would never take for granted again. Something that gave his wife pleasure to no end was to hear his sweet voice as his eyes roamed over any kind of print. Indulging her, because he always did, Em gathered her between his legs, leaned back against the bed, and his rich, low voice rolled out softly in a river of words, his father's words.

"'I'm a man of few words—always have been, all my twenty years…as if that's so long. Get to the point, I say, don't waste your breath. Not much need for talk around the horses I've worked with all of my life. They're sensitive to moods and body language.'"

Emmett shook his head. "That's funny. It's like he's standing next to me or talking in my head. You don't know how many times he said that." Clearing his throat, he continued,

"'That's the way it should be, but I met the girl I'm going to marry today and I've got to get her down, get her right. Funny thing is, I've known her most all of her life, but I didn't really see her until today. Her name is Elizabeth Mason and she's got hair like the sunrise and eyes that shine as clear as a blue sky without any clouds to get in the way. Her eyes crinkle in the corners when she laughs and how she laughs…a lot.

"'She's a pretty little slip of a thing. Her nose could touch my breastbone, right in the center of my chest…perfect for tucking in under my chin. She's not too skinny. Elizabeth is soft around the edges. Looks like she'd be nice to hold on to. She enjoys eating, got right down to it at the barbecue, something I like to see. I can't stand a girl who picks at her food. What kind of cook would that kind of woman be?'"

Emmett stopped to nudge Casey in the ribs and give her a little pinch. "Sounds about right. Dad and I have the same taste in women."

Her nose scrunched up and she stuck out her tongue. "Enough from the Peanut Gallery. Keep reading."

"You're perfect." Emmett shifted slightly, gathering her in closer, and kissed the top of Casey's head before picking up where he had left off. "'She reminds me of my horses, shy one moment, ducking her head, turning all pink and frisky the next, her tongue wagging. Shoot, that girl can talk. Hmmm, that's not enough to put her on the page. There's so much more. Guess I've got to start at the beginning.'"

As Emmett became absorbed in the words in the journal, they both became lost in the past...

CHAPTER 2

July 4, 1956:

The annual Fourth of July barbecue was well underway at the Bradleys', a tradition that had been passed down for generations. Will Bradley claimed they could trace a shindig at their home back to the year the Declaration of Independence was first put on paper. Jackson didn't care how it started, simply that he and his younger brothers, Emmett and Wyatt, could enjoy a little piece of their own sweet freedom for the rest of the day and evening.

They'd all worked hard, alongside Pop, to get all of the chores done at home. Owning a horse farm meant their job was never really done, but Landon Henry said the horses would keep until morning. "Everyone needs to take time out on Independence Day. It would be downright un-American if we didn't!"

The picnic tables were groaning with every kind of picnic delight. Corn on the cob, salads of every sort, cold cuts and thick rolls for sandwiches, a medley of fresh vegetables plucked from someone's garden, luscious fruit, and meats cooking on the barbecue rounded out only the beginning. The ladies' pride and joy, their pies, breads, cakes, and cookies, would be brought forth when everyone could make some room, along with homemade ice cream. Fresh pitchers of sweet tea and lemonade were at the ready to wet a body's whistle, and kegs of beer were waiting for men who were willing. A veritable feast, created by the combined forces of the close-knit rural town, meant this would surely be another occasion to remember.

Jackson leaned against the pasture fence, listening to the cows conversing out in the field, enjoying the pleasant shade of a large oak tree and a gentle breeze giving him a cool down. The summer in upstate New York promised to be a real cooker, already hitting the ninety-degree mark for the past few weeks. While he loved working with the animals from sun up to sun down, the heat could really suck the life right out of him. This barbecue couldn't have come at a better time.

He scanned the crowd. All of Charlton's residents appeared to be in attendance as was customary. His brothers, twin hellions at sixteen, were getting into mischief, doing a tightrope act on Loretta Bradley's porch railing. She gave Wyatt and Emmett a good dressing down and a swat with her apron to chase them off. Their response— to pick up that fine lady, carry her over to a rocker, and plant kisses on their hostess's cheeks before they took off. The woman was blushing to beat the band, a pretty complement to her snowy hair.

Shaking his head, Jackson couldn't help but grin at their antics. He caught his father's eye and watched him shrug, while his mother blew him a kiss. They were nestled in together, taking time for each other, a rare thing in the busy lives of a farm couple. It did a son's heart good to see two people who could still love each other that way nearly twenty-five years, something to aspire to.

Landon looked very much like his son, tall, broad of shoulder, with a firm jaw, and dark hair that had a golden cast in the sun, a thread of silver interspersed here and there. The point of difference—his eyes were as green as the tall grasses swaying in the breeze. Jackson's mother had gifted him with espresso eyes, passed down from her Italian heritage. Ella's dark hair, usually a mess of curls run amok, was tamed into a tight twist at the back of her head, making her look exotic amongst the rest of the simple country folk. Every time he looked on his mother, Jackson couldn't fail to note what a beautiful woman she was. No wonder Pop had fallen for her, hook, line, and sinker. The first time they met, here at the Bradleys' one distant Fourth of July, he was a goner.

They were settled at a picnic table, beneath a majestic red maple tree, a queen amongst trees with her branches providing ample shelter for several other tables. More tables were in the barn, but most of the party-goers opted for the sunshine and fresh air. They'd head to the barn at nightfall when the band started playing.

Jackson's foot started tapping in anticipation of the dancing, something he enjoyed but didn't get much chance to do since graduating from high school three years ago. The wind picked up, carrying the scent of roses and other old-fashioned flowers from Loretta's garden, the kind that would make a return appearance for generations to come. Jackson tipped his head back, closed his eyes, and inhaled the day.

"Would you like a drink? It's sweet tea. I made it myself."

His eyes snapped open and he came to attention. A young woman stood before him, pretty as a picture in a yellow sundress. Her skin was already browned from being outdoors, golden hair pulled into a ponytail, sky blue eyes sparkling with good humor as she grinned up at him. It took a moment of flipping through pictures and memories in his mind to place her...*Little Elizabeth Mason, but she's not so little anymore! When did that happen?*

Elizabeth had been behind Jackson by about two years in school. He'd known her since her diaper days when their mothers would get together for quilting, baking, canning, and other such. He'd seen her many times over the years at local gatherings, always thought of her as that pesky, skinny, runt of a girl, gangly and stretched out like a colt.

None of those words did her justice anymore. This *woman* had beautiful proportions and everything had fallen right in where it belonged.

"Jackson Henry, you're not suffering from heat stroke are you? Do you want this drink or not?"

Giving himself a mental shake, he pulled out a smile and accepted the mason jar, taking a long draw before finding his voice. "Sorry. Woolgathering I guess. This is good, real good. You're looking well, Elizabeth. How have you been?" Looking well hardly even touched her. The girl was positively blooming with curves in all of the right places, a healthy flush to her cheeks, and eyes that glittered. Jackson's heart kicked up a notch and his mouth went dry, making him guzzle the tea. *This girl is mighty fine.*

"I'm very well, thank you." She sidled up alongside of him, giving him a whiff of something sweet—lavender and rosemary perhaps? Then the girl had to head him toward a heart attack as she pressed her lips to her own mason jar and all Jackson could picture was getting his own sample of that sweet mouth.

Turning around, he resolutely focused on the cows in the field. Nothing out there to get his blood pumping. Maybe that would help. Wrong again. When Elizabeth's arm brushed his and he felt a sizzle down to his toes that had nothing to do with the thermometer. *Somebody give me a cold bucket of water.*

"You're looking quite well yourself, Jackson," she said. "I haven't seen you in a while. What have you Henry boys been up to?"

He had a feeling she was only concerned about one Henry boy. His brothers had just jumped into the Bradleys' pond, clothes and all, taking the Bradley daughters with them and causing quite a ruckus, but Elizabeth didn't even turn her head that way. Her eyes were pinned on his, holding him down. Jackson swallowed hard and wished he could have her drink...or something much stronger. "Nothing much. Work, all the time. The horses don't know about clocks."

A grin tugged at the corner of her mouth, lighting her eyes, and she gave him a wink. "Well, I'm glad you escaped for today then. There has to be room for some fun. Life's too short." She took another sip of her tea, noted his empty glass, and handed over hers. "Finish mine. You look thirstier than I do." Thirsty wasn't the word. Hungry was more like it.

Jackson accepted with a nod and polished off her glass in a few swallows. "Thank you. That was downright refreshing." She took the glass jars and set them on the ground, leaving him empty handed and a tad lightheaded to boot. What if she expected him to do something?

Turning his attention back to the field, he gripped the fence hard enough to make the splinters begin to bite into his skin. Sending her a sideways glance as she stepped onto the bottom rung and rested her arms on top, he cleared his throat and tried to make conversation, something which had never been his strong suit. Horses didn't pay much mind to talk. They looked for a hand that could be firm, yet gentle. He often thought people should behave in the same way, rather than spend so much time yammering. "What have you been doing?"

"Nothing of great importance. Quilting, canning, go-

ing to choir practice. Perfecting the fine art of needle
work. Doing all the things a girl's supposed to do to prepare for a family of her own." She wrinkled her nose and
stuck her tongue out, calling to mind those younger years
that he still remembered. "I'd rather follow in Daddy's
footsteps, go to law school, but he doesn't think that's a
woman's place, says I should stay at home where women
belong and prepare for a husband."

Jackson turned to study her, saw the stubborn jut of
her jaw, her nose tipped to the sky. Freckles were sprin-
kled here and there, dusting her bronzed skin, tempting
him to stroke her cheek. Clearing his throat, he tugged his
mind back where it belonged. "You don't mark me as a
weak-willed person. Do you always do what your daddy
tells you?"

"Generally. I believe in respecting my elders and hon-
oring my father. He did raise me after all." Her arms were
crossed, her chin resting on her hands. How tempting it
would be to step up behind her and set his hands on her
tiny waist, feel the thrumming of her heart fluttering
against her ribcage like hummingbird's wings. Being a
gentleman, he did nothing of the sort, but he could dream.

"If you were mine, I'd let you do whatever you set
your heart and mind on. You could fly to the moon, I expect." On an impulse, he leaned over and gave her a kiss
on the corner of her mouth. After all, he was human,
wasn't he?

Her cheeks turned a bright pink and she tilted her head
his way. Jackson's innards began to tighten as Elizabeth
leaned in closer, anticipating a kiss in return, maybe a
slow, long, drawn out affair, when Loretta rang the dinner
bell. With a sudden start, the girl beside him almost lost
her footing, but he caught her and put her down on the
ground—no trouble at all, she was light as a feather—
setting them both to laughing softly.

"Would you like to sit with me while we eat?" He crooked his arm and she rested her hand lightly on his warm, tanned skin. Despite the scorching heat, her fingers were cool and soft, a balm that would soothe any soul. In that instant, Jackson realized nothing could compare to the touch of a woman.

They found a table tucked in the corner, away from the hubbub of the rest of the guests. Jackson's father stood with a cluster of farmers, flipping through his Farmer's Almanac, dog-eared with numerous pages turned at the corner, second only to the family bible in its daily use. His finger ran along key points of interest as his keen eyes scanned the columns, the lot of them talking shop.

Ella gave the illusion of being a young girl, dappled by the shadows of the leaves and sunlight filtering through from above as she helped the ladies to serve. A glance up in her son's direction and she tossed him a wink, nodding pointedly at Elizabeth. Emmett and Wyatt were raising Cain as usual, chasing after girls, poking their fingers in their plates of food and other nonsense.

Jackson could only shake his head in indulgent affection. *Boys will be boys.* Not enough that they had mischief for half the world over, they had to have a double dose in the form of twins. Heaven help his mother. He couldn't hold back a sigh watching them carry on, feeling much older. Someone had to be mature in the face of such antics.

The band began to play as Elizabeth tucked away the last of her samples from the sumptuous spread. Jackson pushed his around on his plate, more occupied by the sweet scent drifting his way from the girl beside him and the way a strand of her hair rested against her cheek. He itched to touch that lone curl and tuck it behind her ear.

"Do you want to dance?" he blurted out, mentally kicking himself. *You have to jump right in the thick of things, as usual. No finesse, no romance. Girls like that stuff.*

"I'd love to as long as you're my partner." He stood first and held out his hand, helping her rise from the bench. They made their way to the dance floor with his hand touching her lightly on the small of her back and his fingers tingled from that brief contact. An area of hardwood had been cleared off and polished to a high gloss, bales of hay situated around the borders to give people a chance to sit, rest, and enjoy the view. Taking Elizabeth Mason in his arms, Jackson had the best vantage point in the place. He didn't even want to close his eyes because then there'd be an instant of missing her.

One dance led into the next and the next as nightfall arrived. Several other young men attempted to cut in, but Elizabeth couldn't be bothered. Fireworks would light up the sky soon, but Jackson had his fill holding onto his dance partner, letting her rest her head on his shoulder, taking the steps slow to make the moment stretch. An uncomfortable prickling made the hairs stand on the back of his neck and he craned his head to catch a glimpse of Hamilton Mason, positively glaring at the couple from across the floor.

What have I done to earn such disapproval? There had never been any problems with Elizabeth's father before. Landon and Hamilton went way back, their families sharing many a meal over the years, yet in that instant, Jackson felt lower than a bug that had been squashed beneath the Mason patriarch's shoe.

Elizabeth looked in the same direction and grew stiff, a brilliant rush of color flooding her cheeks as her eyes began to snap. "Jackson, I think I need some fresh air. I'm feeling a touch overheated."

He didn't question her, simply took her hand and led her out into the star-filled night. The temperature had dropped considerably, as was typical on many a summer evening, providing a refreshing breeze after the stuffiness inside the crowded barn. Standing under the stars in the fresh air, he could breathe easier again but still felt the weight of Hamilton Mason's stare.

"What's got a bee in your father's bonnet?" Jackson couldn't help but ask as they leaned on the fence and watched the animals grazing in the field. The cows had been brought in and the horses were getting their chance to be frisky before being penned up for the night. Watching what he considered to be good friends managed to soothe his ruffled feathers from the razor-sharp gaze that nearly sliced him in two.

Elizabeth stared out at them, but did not appear to see the dark shadows roaming in the pasture. "I don't know. Maybe his dinner disagreed with him." Her eyes flashed in the moonlight, wet with the sheen of unshed, angry tears. Her hands grabbed hold of the railing in a fierce grip. She'd likely tear the old wooden plank clean off if given the opportunity.

"You sit tight, you hear? I'll be right back." He slipped away, returning a brief spell later with two, tall glasses of lemonade. "If you need cooling down, have I got the remedy for you. Mama's recipe. It's about even with your sweet tea." Jackson tipped his head back and relished the cool trickle down a parched throat. "Hmm. Might have to try the two together, half and half."

Elizabeth had hoisted herself up to perch on the top rung of the fence. She took a sip of her own glass and smiled appreciatively. "You're right. This is really good, just the right blend of tart and sweet."

She licked her bottom lip and sent a zinger straight to Jackson's heart. He joined her at a loftier point, a welcome spot for one of the horses to come and nuzzle their hair. They both started to laugh as Jackson fished an apple out of his pocket and let the dark beauty munch from his hand. "You know exactly what everyone needs." She tipped her head and scratched behind one pointy ear.

"Aw, making horses happy is easy. You just have to give them what they want. I always carry an apple or two." The stallion snuffled Jackson's shirt, begging for another treat. "Oh no you don't. You can't butter me up, handsome. I don't have any more tonight." He reached up and stroked the velvet nose, staring into huge, trusting eyes. They were so peaceful and uncomplicated, two reasons he loved spending his time with the gentle giants.

Elizabeth's hand brushed his as her fingers skimmed along the horse's cheek and pushed strands of his thick mane out of a noble face. "Jackson, have you ever wanted something so bad you could taste it, but didn't know how to get it?" She spoke in almost a whisper, making him strain to hear as her arms looped around the black stallion's neck and she rested her cheek against him. In that moment, she seemed vulnerable, as if the girl could break.

His hand hovered in the air, finally settling on her back and rubbing in a soothing, circular motion, one he'd used many times to gentle his father's herd. "I might have a notion of what you're talking about." His voice cracked and his stomach tightened painfully. He knew a thing or two about wanting and not having.

Elizabeth turned to him, her eyes opened wide, almost fearful. They were on territory that had never been trodden, after all. Her hand seemed to float and then her fingers were threading through his hair. "Maybe we can come up with a solution." A wink and she came in for a landing, planting a swift kiss on his lips, setting his system on overdrive. He closed his eyes, going loose, and starbursts exploded in his mind.

The night lit up with what promised to be a dazzling

show, yet it didn't compare to the girl by his side. "You're a firecracker," he murmured as she pulled away. She laughed, the mood broken, and set her hands on his shoulders. Taking the hint, he carefully grasped her waist and easily lifted her to the ground while sparks rained down from above.

"That would be the display that Will Bradley paid for, silly, not me." Her hand found a home in his and they wended their way to a picnic blanket spread out by the rest of the Henry clan, interspersed with the other townspeople. Mama was tucked under Pop's arm, both of them flat out and staring up at the sky with wonder. Fireworks never grew old, whether you were a young tyke or in a rocking chair.

Emmett and Wyatt were both chasing girls, flitting in and out of the rest of the crowd. It was highly unlikely that they'd ever come in and settle down. No one seemed to pay Elizabeth and Jackson any mind when they stretched out and tipped their faces to catch the show. Ella Henry patted Elizabeth's shoulder in welcome, passing both of the younger set a hearty slice of watermelon wrapped in a napkin. Soon, their mouths were dripping with the sweet, juicy treat that was synonymous with summertime.

Jackson's hands and mouth were sticky. Peeking at Elizabeth out of the corner of his eye, he could see watermelon juice staining her cheek. Kissing her seemed the best way to fix the problem. He leaned closer and her eyes locked with his, her lips parted slightly in anticipation. In and out like a butterfly, she made the first move. Jackson's tongue darted out, giving him a sample of watermelon that somehow tasted sweeter coming from her.

Wyatt and Emmett chose that moment to drop their pursuit of the fairer sex. Apparently, tormenting their big brother was a far better goal and more entertaining. With one threat to pound them both if they didn't cut it out, the boys behaved, but that didn't stop their whispers and jabs to the ribs.

Jackson didn't care. All that mattered in that instant was watching the color wash over Elizabeth's face, sparkles overhead reflected in her eyes. Each splash of light was like a birthday wish and every one held her name. Feeling her snug against his side as the evening chill deepened, he knew that he would marry Elizabeth Mason the earliest chance he could get.

After spending a night with her in his dreams, she was still on his mind when he found her note tacked to the barn door.

July 5, 1956
Dear Jackson,
Thank you for the best Independence Day I've ever had. You made me feel like I could sprout wings and fly...to the moon and back again. Today promises to be a hot one. Come join me at the swimming hole around noon if you can get away. I hope you can. Bring your trunks and nothing but yourself.
Beth

CHAPTER 3

July 5, 1956:

The heat showed no signs of breaking. What with the sweat dripping off of him, Jackson saw no point in wearing clothes. He shucked his t-shirt, wishing the same could be said of his jeans, and fought to keep his mind on the matter at hand. His thoughts kept wandering to Beth's invitation. Picturing her by his side at the swimming hole made his head start to spin, his mouth as dry as cotton.

He couldn't get Beth out of his head. It was like having a classic car parked in the garage, one taken for granted as it sat there forever. Until one day, that baby stopped a body in his tracks. That was Elizabeth Mason. Why had it taken him so long to appreciate what was right under his nose?

Wyatt and Emmett razzed him all morning long, chanting, "Jackson and Elizabeth sitting in a tree, k-i-s-s-i-n-g." Training a two-year-old stallion was more than enough horsing around without their aggravation.

Between the combined torments of kid brothers, record-breaking mercury levels, and the girl that clouded his mind, he was uncharacteristically miserable. A tumble off the horse made him sore, but his brothers put him in a

bad temper. When his father caught his eldest boy dousing his head under the water pump to cool off more than
his body, he grabbed Jackson by the nape of his neck and
gave a good squeeze.

"Why don't you get out of here for a little while? Take
a break. Maybe you'd like to take a dip in the ol' swimming hole, do something about that simmering temper…and whatever else is under your skin." With a wink,
his father headed into the house for lunch. *He saw the
note.*

Jackson shrugged into his shirt—didn't seem proper to
show up half-naked —and finger combed his hair. His
boots kicked up a cloud of dust for the entire walk on the
dirt road that ran between the Henry homestead and several other farms in the area. *Lord, bring us some rain. Not
only so we can beat the heat, but to give everything a
long, tall drink.*

The day began to work on him, making Jackson forget
about being out of sorts. How could a man complain
when the sun was shining, he had a roof over his head,
three squares a day, and people that cared about him? He
started to whistle a cheerful tune, his heart growing lighter by the second.

Venturing off the road, he ducked into the woods and
followed the footpath hidden beneath a great canopy of
trees and thicket of undergrowth. Anticipation and a
pinch of anxiety had him sweating even harder, gasping
for breath by the time Jackson finally broke through a
heavy stand of trees to find Elizabeth sunning on a rock
by the water.

His heart began to skip at his first glimpse of her. *Pal-
pitations…that's what they are, like my heart is going to
giddy up and go.* There was no help for it, the girl taking
him completely off guard wearing one of those two piece
affairs. She might be covered in all of the necessary plac-

es in a yellow bikini the shade of sunlight dripping down, but that only gave his imagination more than enough fuel. Giving her a wave, he took refuge in the icy waters of the swimming hole with a mighty jump, shooting to the top with a shout.

Laughing, Beth did a neat jackknife off of her perch and came up beside him, hair plastered to her head, rivulets snaking down her skin. *Wooee, this girl is something!* Jackson plunged down deep once more, staying put until his lungs were near to bursting. There was no choice when his heart was about to combust.

Hands took hold of his shoulders and he came back up, coughing and sputtering. Elizabeth moved in and looped her arms around his neck. "I thought you were going to try and stay down there all day. Didn't you come to see me?"

Flipping his hair from his eyes, he laughed nervously. "Oh, I can see you all right, more than I ever have. I'm surprised your daddy lets you wear a suit like that." Jackson could have bit his tongue on the last, watching the irritation in her expression. She dunked under water, managing to shrug it off.

"What Daddy doesn't know won't hurt him." She disappeared and seconds later, he gasped as her nimble fingers grabbed his ankles and gave him a hearty tug. Jackson went below the surface and stared into blue eyes that looked like they were laughing at him. An instant later and she shot back up with a splash. Jackson followed and some water frolicking ensued, innocent, clean fun as they splashed, tickled, and snagged each other's toes in the deep, dark water.

Finally they came up, breathing hard, taking a break and trying their hand at a game of look but don't touch. Dragonflies flitted across the water and a ladybug landed on Elizabeth's hair. Jackson carefully plucked the small bug out and watched the insect's progress into the forest. "Ladybug, ladybug, fly away home, your house is on fire. Your children are gone." Beth's voice was pure and sweet as she sang, drawing him in closer.

He wanted to hold her, maybe kiss her. To distract himself, his tongue started to wag. "That's awful, isn't it? Comes from an old nursery rhyme. Ring Around the Rosies has to do with the plague, and Rockabye Baby started when the colonists wanted to make fun of the Natives."

His words trailed off and the heat flooded his face, suddenly fighting a bad case of nerves. Jackson read often in his spare time, soaked up all of the stories that his family passed down, storing it all in a head chock full of knowledge. *Doesn't mean you have to bore the girl to death.*

"I think that's the most I've ever heard you say in as long as I've known you." Elizabeth spoke in a hushed voice and her hand rested lightly on his shoulder. She didn't want to spook him. A moment's hesitation and he looked up to find himself pinned by her gaze.

"You've always been like still waters. I knew you were deep, with a lot going on below the surface. I've watched you for a long time, Jackson, waiting for the right time to take a dip."

Her voice was husky, rough around the edges. He saw her throat ripple as she swallowed and moved in closer. Her breath dusted his skin as a prelude to a butterfly kiss, her lips brushing against his, making them burn. He closed his eyes tightly and concentrated on his breathing, afraid his heart would explode. Elizabeth's mouth touched both of his eyelids ever so lightly and then her hands hooked behind his neck. "Jackson, kiss me the way a man is supposed to kiss a woman."

He obliged, feeling her tug on him like the moon on

the tides, impossible to resist. His hands threaded through her hair and his head tilted to the side. Watching the mad fluttering of her pulse, beating at the base of her neck, he pressed his lips there first. She went limp and he thought Beth had fainted in his arms. Glancing up, her head was tipped back, her mouth slightly open, her eyes glittering.

Her hands tightened and she whispered. "Just like I thought. Show me more." Once again, he couldn't deny her. Jackson set his mouth on hers and the moment stretched. Only when they both had to come up for air did time resume. Holding out his hand, Elizabeth took it and they made their way back to the shore. He climbed out first and easily lifted her up, setting her down gently on the rock.

Chuckling softly, she wrapped her towel around both of their shoulders, allowing them to warm up after the chilly water. There really was no need. Her nearness could bring about instant evaporation. She grew quiet and he didn't fight it. Talk would come in its own time. Besides, he generally came up short on finding things to say.

Jackson stretched out and relished the warmth of the rock seeping in his skin. Elizabeth took his cue and stretched out beside him. They both stared up at the few patches of sky visible through the treetops, birds darting here and there. "Thank you for inviting me today. This is one of my favorite spots." Her fingers found his and gave a squeeze in answer.

She closed her eyes and her breathing leveled out. He thought Elizabeth was asleep until her voice broke the silence. "Remember when you asked about my father last night, what his problem was?" Jackson turned to look at her and saw her jaw tighten, color creeping from her chest up to her cheeks. He pressed her hand, hoping to calm whatever storm was brewing within. "My father's problem is you."

At the hurt he couldn't hide, Beth rolled on her side and rested a hand on his heart. "Well not you, personally, but men like you. Daddy thinks the world of you, but somehow he's got the notion set in his head that I should marry an *educated* man, a lawyer like him or some white collar, professional snob."

She practically spit out the last words and sat up suddenly, grabbing hold of her legs and driving her head into her knees. "The older I get, the more stubborn Daddy is, like a bulldog gnawing on a bone and refusing to let go. He doesn't know anything about a real man like you!"

Jackson hesitated, but couldn't resist. He slid closer to her and rested his hand on the nape of Elizabeth's neck. "I asked you this before, but hope I'll get a different answer this time. Do you always listen to your daddy? I really like you, Beth, but I'm not going to waste our time."

She picked up her head, her eyes wide with wonder, hope beginning to bloom. Her hands rested on his chest, vibrating with the thundering of his heart. "I do usually listen, but you, Jackson Henry, are an exception to the rule and worth fighting for, tooth and nail. I've just been biding my time, waiting for you to ask."

He didn't need to be a rocket scientist to take the meaning of her words. Holding her hand because it felt like the right thing to do, Jackson pressed a kiss to her fingers like men of olden days. One by one, he made the moment last. "Elizabeth Mason, will you be my girl?"

Were those tears in her eyes? He couldn't be sure when she blinked so fast but her smile trembled and her voice wasn't steady. "I've always been your girl, Jackson. That first kiss when you got here sealed it. You've just taken longer to figure this out."

Jackson stared into the endless sky of blue in her gaze, so calm and sure, opening his eyes for the first time. All these years, and he'd never seen the way Beth was like a puppy dog, tagging after him, always finding a way to spend time with him, even if she was like a planet circling around the sun. Every town gathering, all the school functions, each occasion their families had dinner together, turn around and she would be there, staring up with adoring eyes, hanging on the few words he would say, otherwise content to simply bask in his presence.

He nodded and pulled her close to him, tucking her head under his chin. *It's like I thought. She fits perfectly, as if we were meant for each other.* "I'm sorry I didn't know. I've got some catching up to do."

"That's all right. We've got plenty of time—a whole lifetime in fact." She gave him a smile of such sweetness, his heart squeezed in his chest. Jackson decided to make up for some of those lost opportunities right then and there.

He took her face in his hands, holding her as gently as the fragile baby bird he once rescued as a boy. His lips touched down lightly on hers, a hummingbird flitting in, finally settling in to claim its nest. Beth sighed and pressed her head into his collarbone. "That was a good start," she whispered softly.

His fingers trailed to Elizabeth's shoulders and started to knead her skin, warming her with his touch. A heartbeat or two and she raised her eyes, giving him the gift of one more kiss with her heart in it. Regretfully, Jackson pulled away and gestured to the pocket of sky above. "I hate to say this, but I've got to get back." She nodded and picked up her towel, wrapping it around her waist while he slipped his shirt over his head. "Can I see you tomorrow?"

Beth dipped her head and stared down at their feet. "We've got church. Family time, you know."

He pressed a finger beneath her chin and made her meet his eye. A tap of her nose and her smile lit a matching grin on his face. "I guess I'd start too much of a stir if I scooted in beside you," he said. "Don't let me fool you when I'm in my pew. You know what I'll be looking at and thinking about the whole time. Thanks again for today."

She took him by surprise, stealing one more kiss before streaking off into the woods toward home. Shaking his head, Jackson turned back toward the Henry House, whistling a tune to match the song in his heart and the words were *Beth, my Beth* over and over again.

That night before bed, he brought the horses into the barn. A note was tacked to the post on the gate.

Dear Jackson,
I can't get you off my mind. Yesterday was a mean tease. Whenever I get some time with you, I want more. It's like the addictions they warn us about in Health class. After church tomorrow, Mama and I are going quilting at the Daniels' place. I should be walking home around four o'clock or so. Perhaps we'll happen to be going the same way at the same time.
Your Beth
P. S. Thanks for the swim. It was…refreshing.

CHAPTER 4

July 6, 1956:

Church. Penance and torture for so many, especially the two little tykes squirming up at the front. Jackson amused himself watching as they kicked their feet, jabbed each other in the ribs, and slid down in the pew. He certainly could relate to them. Sitting in the tiny white building on a beautiful day was like keeping a lively horse trapped in a stall when the rest were prancing about the field.

On a spiritual level, Jackson could accept the need and merits of such an institution. That didn't mean he had to like being glued to a bench for two hours. Up. Down. Sing. Pray. Listen. Too many restrictions if you asked him.

Personally, he believed the best way to get close to God was to walk out in the Henrys' pastures and glory in some of His finest creations, the outdoors and horses. Sucking in air, taking it all in. Getting as close to nature as a man could be. That was neither here nor there as far as Mama and Pop were concerned. No shirking for the Henrys. They went to church on Sundays unless they were dying or dead, and even then, they might make an appearance.

The wooden pew was hard and unforgiving, more than likely a reminder of the burden our Lord Jesus had to bear. While Jackson's suffering was on a much smaller scale, he suffered none the less, accustomed to being on the move in the fresh air day in and day out. He sat with his arms crossed, fighting the urge to fidget like the children.

His father nudged him with an elbow and gave him a lop-sided grin. Landon Henry understood, being of a like mind with his son. Craning his neck, his father cast a glare at the twins, situated beside their mother. They were tapping their toes, shifting in obvious discomfort, not faring much better than the youngsters up ahead. Being restrained had always been a great challenge for them. Even at the age of sixteen, they had a tendency to rebel, but one look from Pop was enough to quell any signs of mutiny.

The pastor droned on about their weekly life lesson, something to do with humility and avoiding an excess of pride. Jackson blew a strand of hair out of his eyes and straightened a back gone stiff. His tie was strangling him and his long-sleeved shirt was scratchy. Ninety degrees outside and here he sat, covered up from head to toe like a mummy. No matter what the conditions, Ella Henry insisted that her boys, young and old, look presentable in church. Just because they worked in a barn with animals all day, there was no reason that they couldn't be proper in the house of the Lord. That meant spit and polish, decked out in their best clothes, no ifs, ands, or buts.

It didn't help any that Jackson spilled half of Pop's cologne all over. The whole place was probably choking on the fumes. He'd even used some hair cream to smooth out some wild tufts here and there. His brothers had teased him so unmercifully before leaving, they'd likely be the death of him—if Jackson didn't kill them first. To make matters worse, Mama had been watching him closely all morning. She was probably on to him. As for Pop, his mouth started to twitch several times and there was a mischievous gleam in his eyes. He was enjoying himself.

Clothing, seating arrangements, and his family's scrutiny aside, Jackson's closest thing to a crown of thorns was the view, giving him a sharp stab of longing each time his eyes wandered to the front of the church. Two rows ahead to the right, Elizabeth Mason sat on the end of the Mason family pew. Talk about temptation. She wore a rose colored dress that matched the flush in her cheeks and complemented the sun in her hair, which was done up in some fancy twist with a flower from the garden tucked on the side.

A few times, her brilliant eyes turned his way, drowning him in a sea of blue. What he wouldn't give to sit by her side. Only sheer force of will kept him in his place, that and an unwillingness to cause a public display or cast any shame on the Henry name. Jackson had learned long since that life was about making choices. Often, you did not get to do what you wanted. Obligations came first and preservation of the family ranked at the top of the list.

A hymn began and he rose to his feet, studying the set of Beth's shoulders, the fine line of her spine, her trim waist and the glimpse of perfectly shaped calves leading to feet perched on white heels. Glancing back up at her face, he eyed a strand of hair that lay against her cheek and itched to be that close to her. Beth gave him a wink and his father cleared his throat.

The mutual attraction of the young people had not escaped Landon. A rush of heat flooded Jackson's face as he caught Hamilton Mason's disapproving stare. Elizabeth's father had noticed as well. Jackson straightened his shoulders and resolutely leveled his eyes at the pastor, feigning interest in what the leader of the flock had to say. *You might keep me from looking at her right now, Mr. Mason, but you can't tame my mind.*

The last strains of music ended and the preacher preceded his congregation, the others filing out behind him. Beth passed and laid her hand on Jackson's arm as he stepped out of his aisle. She slid him a smile and moved on, but the heat of that brief contact branded his skin. Wishing for nothing more than to take her hand and go somewhere, anywhere, away from the confines of church and prying eyes, he tugged at his tie that suddenly felt tight enough to choke him and stepped out into the sunlight.

Taking a deep breath, he loosened the top button of his shirt, assuming that would be acceptable, and honestly not giving a hang at the moment. Offering the perfunctory greetings to their spiritual leader, Pastor Brian, Jackson made his way to the rectory, hoping to catch a minute or two with Elizabeth.

She stood at the refreshment table, pouring cups of juice for the congregation, wagging a finger at the little boys he'd noticed earlier. They were poking their hands in the frosting of the cake and making a mess of themselves. Jackson stepped up and accepted a drink, chuckling with her. "These two could compete with Wyatt and Emmett in their younger years."

"Their younger years? How about now?" Beth nodded in the direction of the twins. They could be glimpsed through a window, scaling a tree. She smiled and took up her own drink, making his heart flutter at the sight of that pretty mouth, lips pursed on the brim. Pulling his gaze in an upward direction, he caught the mischief in her eyes. The girl must have had an inkling of what she was doing to him. "I remember. I also remember the day you put a frog down my dress."

That brought out a belly laugh that made Jackson sputter and nearly spill his juice. "I forgot about that! The twins were only babies and I was acting up, feeling a bit of resentment maybe. You were sitting there in the same spot as today, your head bent down as you kicked your feet. You hated being cooped up as much as me, don't deny it! Anyway, when I saw the gap between your dress and your neck, I couldn't resist! I'd had that frog in my pocket since we left the house. The poor thing had to go free. Why not help it along with you? How you shrieked and danced in the aisle. If looks could kill, I would have been reduced to ashes."

Beth shook her head and returned to her duty of pouring as more people began to mill about. "My, Jackson, that tongue of yours is wagging double-time again. I never knew you had so much to say. You've always been so quiet."

He waited until a few members of the church cleared out before leaning in close to tell her in a low voice. "I never felt like having much to say before. You loosen my tongue." He raised his cup only to discover it was empty.

Looking up, Jackson found himself pinned by her stare, unable to move, watching the pulse fluttering at the base of her throat. A slight breeze drifted in, lifting the loose hair on her cheek. Swallowing hard, he reached out and slipped it behind her ear. Her eyes closed and a brilliant rush of color rose in her cheeks. Beth had always been one to show powerful feelings with her blush.

Heavy footsteps approached. Jackson glanced over his shoulder and saw Hamilton Mason, with thunderheads brewing in his eyes. The man was on a war path. "Come, Elizabeth. I'm sure the Henry boy has work in the *barn* to do." A sneer of contempt marred his handsome features as her father crooked his arm, his face smoothing when the pastor passed by.

Beth set her hand on his elbow, the tears welling up as she caught Jackson's eye.

Katherine Mason joined them at her husband's beckoning, and they headed toward the parking lot. Just as they were about to get in their car, another family stopped to talk. One of their sons pulled a flower from his jacket pocket and handed it to Beth, making her blush, the way she did for Jackson.

The young man was smooth, polished. Comfortable in church clothes because they were his everyday clothes. *Hamilton Mason's Mr. Right*, a cruel voice stabbed at Jackson's heart, made a tight band squeeze around it. It was hard to breathe watching the two families say their farewells and everyone departed.

With knees suddenly gone weak, Jackson dropped down on the steps and sucked in air. Seeing someone else interested in Beth's affections made jealousy rear its ugly head. There was nothing stronger than the power of a woman to wreak havoc on a man's heart and Elizabeth was definitely all woman. Jackson tipped his face to the sky and took another deep, restorative breath. *Lord, You knew exactly what You were doing when You made Eve...keeping us in line and on our toes! I understand why Adam would do anything for that woman.*

Warring with his feelings about Beth and potential competition was her father's marked disapproval, the man speaking about him as if Jackson was lower than the dirt beneath his feet. He had never been the target of someone's loathing before. He kept to himself, worked hard, and treated others with respect. He expected the same in return. During the drive home from church, Jackson was quieter than usual, face turned away from his brothers, his stomach churning. Completely out of character, Wyatt and Emmett left him alone.

Back at the Henry House, there were chores to be

done, a source of distraction. Horses didn't know anything about a day of rest. Jackson shed his church clothes, gladly exchanging them for a T-shirt and jeans because horses didn't care what people wore either. There was a mare that would be foaling sometime soon. Jackson kept a close eye on her, watching intently for first signs of labor. A few colts were frolicking in the field, a welcome diversion when the oppressing heat and the inner turmoil that had him in knots threatened to do him in.

He stood under the shade of a tree, arms draped over the fence, and watched the young ones prancing about in the pasture, all legs as they raced across the wide open space. Two of them were neck and neck, calling to mind his brothers and the many times they'd set challenges for themselves over the years. Jackson would have to be the final judge, announcing the victor, sometimes the sheriff to break it up, and still others he'd be the one to prove they couldn't top their older brother. Might as well not try.

Having rested long enough and not one to be idle, Jackson moved on to Charlie Brown next. The chocolate stallion needed attending to. The horse had been a gift from Pop when Jackson was knee high to his father, and the stallion held a special place in everyone's heart. He'd gone lame a week before, limping badly. Close inspection revealed an abscess in the soft portion of one hoof, resulting from a puncture wound, likely from a sharp stone.

Through a team effort that involved Wyatt, Emmett, and Pop, Jackson managed to drain the wound, apply an antibiotic ointment, and a dressing. The veterinarian came the next day with an antibiotic shot. For the space of six days, the wound had to be bandaged after a thorough cleansing and application of medication. Today was the first day Charlie Brown didn't limp. Jackson stood with his pet for a long time, stroking his neck and whispering endearments while the stallion snuffled his hair. Jackson's gratitude knew no bounds.

Finally, after what seemed an eternity, late afternoon arrived. Jackson showered, quickly washing away the sweat and grime, donning fresh jeans and a crisp white T-shirt. His hair was still dripping, refreshing rivulets of water running down his neck as he set foot on the porch to find his father seated on the chaise lounge while reading the paper, Ella at his side with her head propped on his shoulder, both resting their feet on the railing. "Hey, Pop, Mama. I'm going for a walk, maybe stopping by the creek for a while to see what's doing."

Ella's eyebrows crept up to her hairline, a grin tugging at the corner of her mouth, while Landon peered at him closely over the rims of his reading glasses. "Just make sure you're home for dinner. Your mother's been slaving all day over that hot stove to make us a delicious meal. The least you can do is have the courtesy to be at her table on time. Five o'clock, Jackson." There was a satisfied smile in his eyes and tone as well, like the cat who ate the canary.

"Yes, sir." There was no sense in arguing. No matter how old Jackson was, his father was the authority figure in their home. All due respect was in order. Walking down the dirt lane, headed in the direction of Kathy Daniels' house and a potential rendezvous with Elizabeth, he was plagued by the image of Hamilton Mason's scornful scowl, his obvious distaste. Beth owed her father the same respect. Pushing misgivings aside, Jackson determined to find a way to gain the man's approval. *All in good time.*

Sweet anticipation hummed in his veins, making his heart skip at the prospect of catching another glimpse of the girl. A brief interlude would not give Jackson his fill, but would have to suffice. Rounding the bend, she came into view and his mouth went dry. Beth Mason was definitely worth the wait.

She'd changed from her formal dress to denim clam diggers, white sneakers, and a sleeveless button-down of blue plaid, knotted at the waist. A matching bandanna formed a headband, holding back the heavy mane of her golden hair. One tug and it would rain down over her shoulders. She raised a hand in greeting and his heart slowed to a painful thumping. A heart attack, swift and sure, would be a blessed way to go if Beth Mason was the last thing he saw. "Jackson? Jackson, are you all right? What…has the cat got your tongue again?"

Somehow, she'd managed to close the gap between them and stood before him in the path, her head tilted sideways as she studied his face. She touched his cheek and his heart kicked back into motion. Jackson's hand covered hers, entwining their fingers together and they began to walk side by side.

"I just can't get over how pretty you are." The roses bloomed in her cheeks once more as they ventured down the lane that would eventually come out to her driveway. "How was quilting?"

"Oh, absolutely thrilling." She rolled her eyes and slid a glance his way. "All I could think about was you. I had to pull out my stitches three times and start over again because I kept making mistakes. Kathy said I had butter fingers or something. What about you?" Her hand tightened on his like her hold on his heart.

Jackson shrugged. "Nothing much. Worked with the horses, watched the colts. Tried to occupy my mind because the only thing I could see was you. You sure you weren't thinking about that fellow who gave you a flower at church?"

"Daddy works with his father. I don't even remember that *boy's* name. The only name that's written on my heart is yours, Jackson Landon Henry." Their footsteps slowed, trying to drag out the time and make the distance stretch, finally coming to a standstill. Elizabeth turned his way, tipping her face to his like a flower opening to the sun. There was nothing for it but to give her a kiss. Jackson took his time about it, his hands cupping her cheeks, marveling at the softness of her skin, watching her lips part and her eyes droop before his mouth sealed hers.

His own eyes closed and he gave himself to the moment when a flash of light illuminated his eyelids and a clap of thunder made them both start. The skies opened up, dumping a downpour on their heads, making them both laugh as Jackson grabbed her hand and ran with Beth into an abandoned barn at the edge of a neighboring field. They stepped inside, both gasping for breath, clothes and hair plastered to their skin.

The urge to laugh died as he stared at Elizabeth and felt her magnetic pull, drawing him in as close as two people could possibly be. She hooked her hands behind his neck and tugged hard, bringing his lips within range for a kiss that stole their breath away, surprising them both. Jackson held her close, wanting more, fighting his desires, willingly losing himself in her nearness and not caring if he ever found his way.

Eventually, they had to breathe and he propped his forehead against hers. "Beth, I know this is going to sound crazy, but I think I love you."

She let out a laugh that was nearly a sob, a tear running down her face. "Oh Jackson," she whispered, her voice trembling. "I've loved you since that day with the frog!"

Beth pressed her lips to his again, this time gently, giving him the sweetest kiss with a promise in it. She let out a little sigh and he tucked her against his chest, resting his chin on her head. He could feel her heart fluttering like a bird trying to get out of a cage and knew his own must be the same.

That night, sitting at dinner, he pushed his food around on his plate, unable to think about something as trivial as eating, picturing the moment when they reached the gate at the end of her driveway and Beth raised up on tiptoe to kiss him once more, her lips grazing his cheekbone, jaw, and finally his mouth, making him forget how to breathe. "Thank you for walking me home, Jackson," she said softly before running down the lane in the rain. Jackson stood watching her, making sure she made it to her door safe and sound, already in the grips of a painful withdrawal once she was gone.

"Jackson, is something wrong? You're awfully pale since you came home and you've hardly said a word. I don't think you've eaten more than a mouthful, a rarity when I make a roast. What is it, sweetheart?"

His mother's concern made the heat rise up his neck, toward his ears, and he couldn't look her in the eye. "Nothing's wrong, Mama. I've got a bit of a cramp from running in the rain, that's all."

She rose from her place and walked around to his side of the table, laying her hand on his forehead. "You feel feverish to me. Don't worry about cleaning your plate tonight. Go lie down for a while. Wyatt and Emmett can take care of the chores for the night." Ella's imperious gaze would brook no arguments. The younger Henry boys simply nodded their heads, not even letting out a customary grumble.

Jackson cleared his throat and stood, skimming his mother's cheek with a kiss. "That's not necessary, Mama, really. I'll do my part and then go to bed. Dinner really was delicious. I'm sorry I was out of sorts." He took his dishes to the kitchen and set them in the sink. Heading out to the barn to check on the horses for the night, he found another note tacked to the door. She'd slipped there and back without notice.

My dearest Jackson,
Hearing you say those three small, yet so powerful words, "I love you," has made me truly understand the verse in the Bible that states, "My cup runneth over." I feel like I could fly to the moon, run around the world and back again, do anything I set my mind to, which includes seeing you day in and day out. Until we can make that happen, I'll make do with whatever I can get. My eighteenth birthday party is on July twelfth at noon. Daddy says I'm finally old enough to invite boys and I have chosen you, whether he likes it or not. Please come, Jackson. Bring nothing but yourself and that heartbreaker of a smile. There's no need for a gift. You gave me the wonder of my first kiss. I hope you'll be the last boy I kiss.
Love,
Your Beth

That night, Jackson went to sleep with her note under his pillow, his hand resting on the envelope to reassure himself it was real. He made himself a vow. Waking and sleeping, she would be his. There was simply the matter of when and how. That night, his dreams did not disappoint, recreating the moment they stood together in the barn, both fighting for breath, letting the other steal it away.

❦❦❦

"Stop. I have got to take a bathroom break. I think little whatchamacallit has taken up permanent residence on my bladder and just gave me a good kick in the kidney."

Casey rubbed at her back, teeth clamped down on her

lip in frustration. Emmett massaged the offending spot with his competent touch. She often wondered how hands that held such power could be so tender.

"I can't wait to meet the tiny bugger." With a mischievous grin, he bent over her rounded belly and planted a kiss smack dab in the middle. In one fluid movement, Emmett was on his feet, pulling her up with ease. Casey missed being able to move like that.

As she waddled past, he stretched his hands over his head until his back popped. Too irresistible to pass up, Casey stepped in and grazed her lips along his jaw. He gave her a gentle swat on the bottom as she continued on her trek to the bathroom. "Hey, stop being so sexy. It's no fun when I can't play."

At the roll of her eyes, a deep laugh rumbled down low in his chest. "I'm going out to bring the horses in for the night. I didn't know it was this late already."

She could only smile to herself at the sound of his footsteps, taking two stairs at a time all the way. That was Emmett Henry, a full speed ahead kind of man, with so much energy his body could barely contain it. Lowering herself down on the seat with a groan, Casey wished she had one iota of her husband's pep. Right now, she felt somewhere between a cross with a beached whale and a sloth.

By the time she returned to the bedroom, her eyes were drooping and the bed looked too tempting to pass up. It seemed that all she did lately was sleep. Sinking down into a nest of covers, Casey drew up the blanket and pointedly ignored the journal on the nightstand. Emmett would never let her live it down if she read ahead. She closed her eyes and pictured that long ago summer when Jackson Henry fell hard for the girl who would become her mother-in-law. Sleep took her down fast.

She awoke with a start and glanced at the clock. *Mid-*

night?! There was no sign of Emmett. Thinking he might have fallen asleep on the couch, Casey huffed and puffed her way to her feet. With a flick of a switch in the stairway, she illuminated her way to the first floor. The house was pitch black. Emmett hadn't come in from the barn. He always left a light on over the kitchen sink.

A twinge of misgiving formed a knot in her stomach. Reflexively, her hands began to rub her belly protectively round and round, even as her heart began to race. *There's no need to panic. He probably fell asleep in the straw.* Devoted to their herd of horses, there had been many a night that her husband had drifted off when one of the majestic animals was ill or foaling. There'd been other times when he'd stayed away, afraid he'd disturb her rest coming in late. That galled Casey to no end. A woman's husband belonged in her bed. If his retreat to the barn was intentional, she was going to chew him out.

Beginning to stew, she shrugged into her coat, barely able to button it over her bulging midsection, and slipped on her husband's barn boots to avoid stooping over. Finding her feet was a major challenge. Casey hit the porch light and trekked out into the snow, shivering the instant she walked out the door. Old Man Winter certainly was making quite a stir this year. Her breath trailed behind her in a cloud as she plowed through several inches of fresh powder, her aggravation mounting with every step. A pregnant woman on the verge of popping shouldn't be expected to chase her husband to bed. It should be the other way around.

The barn door creaked loudly as Casey pushed her way in, slamming hard enough to make her jump when it was caught by the wind. *Good! Maybe he'll wake up!* Catching sight of a lone figure sitting on a hay bale, shoulders hunched with his head in his hands, her irritation immediately fizzled out.

She quickly closed the gap between them and rested her hands on Emmett's shoulders. His muscles were stiff as stone. "Another migraine?" He mumbled an affirmation, but did not look her way. She prayed her fingers were nimble enough as they began to work at the knotted column of his neck, the base of his skull, then up to his temples. "It's no surprise really. Staying up late. Reading all that time. You've got to try not to strain yourself."

Casey continued to knead at taut muscles until he let loose a deep-throated groan. "God, when are these going to go away?"

She winced to hear his voice gone raw. How long had he fought the monster of a headache out here by himself? "It's hard to say. Head trauma can cause side effects that last for years." She nearly bit her tongue. *That's it. Good pep talk, Case. Where's your bedside manner?* "Why didn't you come in?" She couldn't hold back her reproach.

His hands shifted to press against his eyes. "Didn't want to bother you." He still couldn't look at her. The light only made it worse, but Emmett turned to take hold of her and pull Casey onto his lap. He buried his face in the crook of her neck. "Should have known I'd need you to make it better. Please. Make it better."

Unable to resist his plea, she struggled to gain her feet and took his hand. "Come on, Em. I'll get your medicine, you'll lie down in our cool, dark bedroom, and you'll be good as new come morning."

He cracked an eyelid to catch a glimpse of her, squeezing it shut again to blot out the lamp hanging by the door. "All right, but you're going to have to be my guide. My head's throbbing so hard I can't even see straight."

A stab of fear ran through her, carrying her back to the time when her husband truly couldn't see. She forced

herself to speak lightly. "Don't worry. I've had practice."
She made sure the light was turned off and the door
locked as they made slow progress inside, helping one
another to get out of their outdoor gear in the entryway.
His efforts were clumsy, his fingers fumbling over everything, fighting with buttons and laces until he started to
breathe hard.

She laid her hands on top of his and he grew still. "It's
okay, Em. Wait here and I'll get you some of your pills."
Her own hands were shaking as she spilled out two pain
relievers and poured a glass of water. She returned to find
him with his back propped against the wall, palms
pressed to his forehead. "Here."

He swallowed both in one gulp and rested an arm on
her shoulders. Somehow they made it to the bedroom and
Emmett dropped on to the bed. Casey pulled off his boots
and slipped in beside him, turning down their bedside
lamp on the way. She reached out and began to run her
fingers through his hair, hoping to soothe, moving on to
stroke his temples. Being a Henry, he didn't complain,
but the crease between his eyes told a story of its own.

Gradually, his body went loose and his forehead
smoothed. He slowly exhaled and lifted a hand to rest it
on her hip. Clearly exhausted, it was all he could do to
make that small gesture. "Thanks...Case. That was a bad
one."

She didn't know how long her husband lay still. She
quietly watched the rise and fall of his chest. She almost
drifted away when his words tumbled out. "I can't sleep."
He peeked at her from under a half-raised lid, allowing
her to catch a glimpse of golden honey. "I want to find
out what's next."

"I think you already know the answer, Em. You're
here after all," she snorted. Seeing the longing in his
gaze, she leaned in to give him a kiss. "All right. I'll read

for a little while, but only until you fall asleep." She picked up the worn, leather book off the nightstand and thumbed through the faded pages. Wrapped in the silence of the Henry House, their bed, and her husband's arms, she continued the story of his beginnings...

CHAPTER 5

July 12, 1956:

Jackson took a deep breath in and let it out, gazing in the mirror over his dresser for a final inspection. He hadn't dated much, wasn't used to all this. New jeans. A crisp, white T-shirt. The green plaid button-down Mama gave him for Christmas—said the color brought out his eyes, whatever that meant. His hair was trimmed, the sun streaked strands blending into the darker ones were neat and didn't fall in his face. A splash of cologne made for a finishing touch. Jackson wasn't used to fussing, but thought he'd pass muster.

He closed his eyes, fighting the fire in his veins. Beth was like a fever and he couldn't shake her. She clouded his mind, set his heart to racing, made his blood start pumping. Sometimes, just thinking about her, his gut hurt and it was hard to breathe. He'd never felt that way about a girl before, figured it wasn't going to happen. Jackson had come to one startling conclusion. He had been waiting for her. An image flashed in his mind, of the more fitting suitor at church, a vivid picture that was squashed mercilessly like a bug beneath his boot.

He took one last turn in front of the mirror and clenched his jaw at the sound of whooping and general carrying on, announcing the arrival of the twins who proceeded to barge in without knocking. "Haven't you two learned what privacy means yet?" He grumbled, giving them a fierce scowl.

They ignored him, of course, circling round, wearing grins that were fit to split their faces. Wyatt reached out and straightened his brother's collar. "Ooh, check it out! Jackson's had a haircut and he's all prettied up." A pair of sea glass green eyes stared back at him, filled with mischief, hair tumbling in the way, nearly blonde from the sun. Wyatt shook it back and gave the uncomfortable center of attention a wink.

Emmett's dark, unruly mop of curls, so like Mama's, bounced as he nodded with enthusiasm, his deep brown eyes revealing a glimpse of the wild child that could not be tamed as he patted Jackson on the cheek. "I think our brother is sweet on someone. Elizabeth Mason, perhaps?"

Quick as the strike of an adder, Jackson had both boys in a headlock, giving them a sweet smile, pinning them with a gaze that told another story. "Listen up, you two. I am older, bigger, and stronger than you. No matter how old you get, you'd do well to remember that and to respect your older brother. Understood?"

"All right, all right," Wyatt called out, struggling to break free. As soon as his brother's grip loosened, both boys popped up, bouncing on the balls of their feet. With a devilish grin, Wyatt tossed Emmett a wink and leaned in close. "It's just you smell *so* good, Jackson!" Following his twin's lead, Em stepped in as well and they both planted a sloppy, wet kiss on their brother's cheeks before taking off, carrying on like banshees.

Jackson stood still, hands on his hips, shaking his head. Tempted to give chase, he thought better of it. After all, he was supposed to be the mature, level-headed son. Besides, after making such an effort to clean up, Jackson was not about to allow those two rascals to make a mess of him and that was exactly what they hoped for. They'd like nothing more than to lead Big Brother on a wild goose chase that would end in disaster.

Out in the barn, Beth's birthday present was waiting for him, all saddled up. Lucy was a four-year-old mare the color of deep chocolate. Quite a beauty and spirited in nature, she was well suited to Elizabeth's personality. He'd braided her mane and tail with red ribbon entwined and tied a bow around her neck, clearly marking her as his gift. She was his horse, one of several that he'd raised from a foal and trained, his to keep, sell, or give away. Jackson knew she was a generous gift, but he wanted to leave no doubt regarding the depth of his feelings.

Twenty minutes into his ride to the party, he began to question his delivery method. The ninety degree plus sunshine was beating down, making the sweat pour off of him. Jackson was thankful for the forethought to put on cologne and hoped it would be enough. Dust kicked up from the roadway since conditions had been dry the last few days. Needless to say, *he* was probably not going to make a grand entrance. Lucy's good impression would have to make up for him.

Beth was waiting at her gate, a vision in her party dress fluttering in the breeze, sucking the breath right out of him. She stood propped against the post, wearing something filmy over a shimmering, white material, covered in delicate, pink flowers. Her hair was done up in some kind of fancy braid with a rose tucked in the strands, looking very grown-up, making him wonder when that happened. A glance down at her feet and his mouth went dry. Where did she get pink heels and how did women walk in those things? Impractical they might be, but they did show off her tiny calves to their advantage and Jackson's heart began to flutter.

Don't you dare fall of the horse! "Happy birthday, Beth," he told her weakly, sliding down to the ground and holding on to the saddle pommel for some extra support. Pushing down the butterflies that suddenly rose up in his stomach, he pulled out a smile from somewhere and gave a little bow. "How do you like her?"

She pushed away from the gate, her eyes bright, jaw dropping at the sight. Circling around the horse, Beth finally came to a stop next to him and threw her arms around his neck. "I've never had such a wonderful present in my life! How did you know that I've always wanted a horse?"

"Doesn't every girl want a horse?" Face hot from the mad rush of color at her touch, Jackson cleared his throat and took up the mare's reins with one hand, Beth's hand with the other. They walked slowly down her lane, her smile shining brighter than the sun and nearly blinding in intensity. He had to look at the ground before him in order to find any words. "Her name's Lucy. My stallion, Ricky Ricardo, is missing her already. They had a thing for each other, both raised at our place since they were foals."

Sliding her a grin, he opened the gate to their pasture and let the horse wander. "Go on now, girl," he told her amiably when she hovered. "This is your place now." The couple stood side by side, arms hanging over the railing, watching the horse nose the grass for a minute or two before she began to prance, making them both laugh. "She's a playful one. I figured you'd have room for her in the cow barn. They'll get along well enough."

Beth rested a hand on his arm and kissed his cheek. "I love her. Thank you, Jackson. You *weren't* supposed to get me a gift." He bobbed his head, inexplicably shy as she took his hand once more and gave a little tug. "Everyone is out back on the patio. Daddy should have the grill all fired up by now. I hope you brought your appetite because he'll make enough to feed an army."

Tossing him a wink, she drew him into the back yard. The trees and shrubs were dressed with colorful streamers and balloons, a giant banner announcing, *Happy 18th Birthday, Elizabeth!* A large table was laden with food, set up like a buffet, while the guests were seated at another table, which was covered in a rosebud tablecloth. Everyone held a mason jar, brimming to the edge with ice, pink punch, raspberries and lemon slices. For one brief moment, fear that another boy might be there was a tightened knot in his stomach. A quick scan only revealed an *older*, small select group in attendance. None of the younger set, no friends. The knot drew tighter and he sucked in hard.

Everyone looked completely at home. Jackson shot a questioning look at Beth and got a shrug in answer. "This is a family party. Did you expect other guests?"

He shook his head even as his stomach sank to his toes. He'd planned on being nothing worth taking notice of, lost in a sea of friendly faces. Swallowing hard, he took his place next to Beth and made nice to everyone. A small woman with snowy white hair and dark blue eyes that twinkled reached across the table and shook his hand, introducing herself as Elizabeth Mason the first, setting off a round of laughter.

Her husband, Jonathan Mason, was a rather robust looking man with rosy cheeks, steel gray hair, and eyes of a stormy gray. It gave Jackson a start when the older gentleman pinned him with a penetrating stare. *Like father, like son.* An instant later, the comparison ended when Beth's grandfather gave Jackson a hearty clap on the back and smiled in welcome. Uncle Jon Mason sat beside his father, proving that they shared the same blood, similar in build and feature although his eyes were a deep blue and his hair was as white as his mother's who made a point of noting hers had turned to snow at the spry age of fifty as well.

While Beth's uncle grumbled good-naturedly about his age, his wife, Janet, rounded out the group. She was rather plump with her dark hair in a stylish bob. She had a warm smile, but her most remarkable feature were her green eyes that flashed like gemstones. A regular chatterbox, she took over the conversation, allowing Jackson to do what he did best—be quiet.

Hamilton Mason stood at the grill, his khaki pants and pale blue shirt covered with a large apron, steam rising around his head, a younger version of Beth's grandfather except his hair was still salt and pepper. One glance at Hamilton's slate eyes filled Jackson with a sense of foreboding. There was no doubt that troubled waters lay ahead with Beth's father.

Katherine Mason stepped out of the house with a dish and flashed their newest arrival a fetching smile with nothing but friendliness behind it. Very much like her daughter, her curves were a bit more ample, her hair an absolutely stunning silver, and fine lines surrounded eyes of the same sky blue as Beth's. Jackson thanked her for welcoming him to their home, standing up and taking her hand in appreciation. She blushed prettily and gave him a brief glimpse of what Beth would look like in years to come, something to anticipate with pleasure.

Hamilton called out, "Soup's on," setting a platter of meat on the table, everyone's signal to fill their plates. Jackson pulled out Beth's chair and hung back at the end, staying out of the mix, relieved when her father joined his wife at the table. Beth stood at the end of the line and patiently waited for her guest, giving him that sweet smile that started his blood to singing.

Jackson didn't even know what was on his plate or

what he ate, as he was too aware of the girl beside him, the scent of her perfume like spring flowers, the way her eye would catch his, casting him adrift in an endless expanse of blue. Beth brushed his hand when reaching for her punch and his fingers convulsed, nearly knocking her glass over. "Sorry," he told her hoarsely, draining his own cup to appease a throat gone dry.

She took his hand and the heat bloomed in his cheeks. He tried to look away, but she wouldn't let him. "Jackson," she spoke softly so that the rest of the conversation continued to flow over them like a river. "Don't be so nervous. You're doing just fine, more than fine."

Entwining her fingers with his, she raised her head, apparently unruffled by direct contact, responding to a question from her uncle, and joining in the discussion. Jackson focused on his breathing and regaining a sense of control, not an easy thing when Beth Mason sent him for a tailspin.

Dinner passed uneventfully, Jackson fielding questions and comments directed his way, otherwise embodying the old adage meant for children, "Only speak when spoken to, otherwise be seen and not heard." Most of the conversation revolved around childhood memories for Beth and the older set as well. Jackson sat back and listened, laughing or smiling as was fitting, giving no one reason to find fault with him.

Eventually, Hamilton appeared to relax, even exchanging some pleasantries with his daughter's young man. Perhaps he was only on good behavior due to the presence of company. Jackson would take what he could get. The two kept their distance like opposing generals, scoping out the lay of the land, waiting to make a move. For one day, a tentative truce was in place.

Katherine outdid herself with a confectionary delight in the form of a double layer cake, frosted in white with tiny rosebuds in pink, matching her daughter's dress and complexion. Jackson joined in the singing with his deep baritone of a voice, one the church choir had tried to recruit. He'd declined, not wishing to stand before everyone, being more of a behind the scenes kind of man. Beth's gaze met his and she wore a secretive smile as she blew her candles out, making him blush once more. Did she wish for the same thing as he did?

"Jackson, I'm plumb full up to my eyeballs what with Mama's cake and Daddy's cooking. Would you mind taking me for a walk?" The rest of the party remained on the patio, catching up on the latest doings, digging up more old memories.

"I'd like nothing more." He offered her his arm and she set her hand in the crook, strolling slowly by his side away from the colonial style home, which was painted a deep red with a white trim. Beyond the rolling expanse of the backyard, a long white fence line surrounded spacious fields. Their tails flapping at the flies, cows were grazing peacefully, some lying under a shade tree, others taking a drink at the pond.

Lucy caught sight of Jackson and her dark head raised up high. She trotted to the fence to greet him.

"Aw, did you miss me, sweetheart? Don't you worry. Miss Beth is going to be really good to you." Rooting in his pocket, he pulled out an apple and handed it to the birthday girl. "She loves these. You give her one every time you come out to see her and she'll follow you every step of the way."

Beth giggled as the mare's lips brushed her palm, making quick work of the crunchy fruit. She rested her palm on the soft velvet of her horse's nose and gently stroked it in a soothing manner. "That's a girl, an apple a day keeps the doctor away. You sure are a looker. I want to ride you. Can I?" She turned the power of those baby blues on Jackson with a pleading pout. He was gone without her even trying.

"Have you ridden before?" At a reluctant shake of her head, he climbed the fence and helped her to sit on the railing. "Then you'd best let me go with you. You'll have to sit sideways. You're not dressed to sit any other way in a saddle."

He put his foot in the stirrup and swung up on the mare's back, patting her neck and speaking softly to her all the while. Bullying was not his way when dealing with horses. His philosophy was to treat them the way he wanted to be treated. When he was good to the animals, they were good to him. An easy pull on the reins and he had Lucy up alongside of Beth.

"Now you stay, girl," he told the mare softly and she planted her hooves firmly in the ground, turning her head to watch the activity with open curiosity. Jackson set his hands on Beth's waist and lifted her on to the saddle, perching her securely in front of him. He had one arm firmly wrapped around her waist, the other holding the reins. "You all right?" he asked her.

Beth smiled at him, not nervous in the least, brimming with excitement about her gift. "Never better. Show me what this baby can do," she teased, making him shake with laughter.

They set off at an easy pace, venturing far out into the field as the sun dipped lower in the sky and the heat of the day finally broke.

She leaned her head against his shoulder and let out a contented sigh. "This is nice, Jackson. I still can't believe that you gave me a horse. I asked Santa and Daddy for years."

"Don't you know? All good things come to those who wait." He held her close, relishing the warmth and weight of her against his chest, the way her dress fluttered in the breeze, how soft she was to the touch. He could get used to holding on to this girl. "Another day I'll come over and teach you about riding, when you're dressed in something more…casual. You look very pretty in that dress. You've been making it really hard for me to think straight."

She turned and looped her hands over his neck. "Is that so? I thought something was wrong or you were bored." He pulled up on the reins, bringing Lucy to a halt. When he released the reins, the mare dropped her head to munch on the sweet, green grass, allowing him to give the birthday girl his full attention. Lifting a hand to cup the back of her golden head, he pressed a kiss to her lips and she seemed to melt in his arms.

"I could never be bored with you, Beth Mason. I've just been thinking how much I wanted to give you the rest of your present. How about I finish part two?" Seeing her eyes light up and the smile that answered him, he didn't think she would argue about one more kiss…or two.

They took their sweet time riding back to the barn, Jackson slipping off of the saddle first, lifting Beth down. She seemed light as a feather and his hands lingered on her waist for a moment, reluctant to let go. Lucy swatted him with her tail, making them both start to laugh, and he attended to the mare, showing Beth how to undo the girth of the saddle, letting her feel the weight of it.

Reaching into the saddle bag, he pulled out a soft cloth and a curry comb. "She really likes a good rub down after a ride." Jackson demonstrated on her right side, speaking to the horse softly as his hands ran over her body. He allowed Beth to take over on her other side and found it hard to breathe once more, watching her body sway and her fingers playing with Lucy's mane. Right then, he'd have been happy to be that horse. He showed Beth how to use the curry comb next.

They finished up by feeding the mare apples and oats from the second saddle bag. Beth led the way to an empty stall that was already prepared and she turned to him with her hands on her hips. "How?" She simply asked.

Jackson shrugged. "I have my ways." She shook her head and let him go in before her where he stopped to put his arms around the mare's neck. "I'll miss you, sweetheart, but if you love Beth half as much as I do, you'll be the happiest you've ever been." Planting a kiss on Lucy's cheek, he ducked out of the stall, certain he saw tears in Beth's eyes when she passed him to say goodnight to her horse.

After her family left, she walked him to the end of her lane under a sky filled with so many stars, it made him dizzy to look up…or perhaps the company he kept had something to do with his condition. Beth held his hand and slowed her steps, drawing out the time when he would have to go.

Her pretty little heels dangled from her other hand as she padded along on bare feet that were sore, barely making a sound.

At her gate, she rose on tiptoe to kiss his cheek. "Jackson, thank you for making my day perfect."

"You're welcome. Thank you for having me," he whispered, staring down at the flash of her painted toenails in the moonlight. Even her feet were pretty. Her finger rested beneath his chin, forcing him to meet her eye. He became lost for a heartbeat or two before he took hold of his courage. "Beth, I'd like to see you again. Would you like to go out on a date?"

She smiled, her eyes shimmering brightly and squeezed his hand. "Any time, any place, as long as I'm with you, Jackson."

He felt her magnetic pull drawing him closer and gave in, ending their night with a kiss to tide her over. Her shoes fell to the ground as her hands came up to take his shoulders and he wished she'd never let go.

The rest of the walk home, Jackson was sure his feet didn't touch the ground because he felt like floating up to the clouds. Stepping on to his porch, he patted his pocket and heard a crinkling of paper. Somehow, Beth had managed to write him a letter and slipped the note in before he left her driveway. Sitting down on the chaise lounge, he read by the porch light.

Dear Jackson,

My birthday was beyond belief...what you did was too much. I guess I'll have to take a lifetime to repay you, something I won't ever mind doing. Lucy is absolutely beautiful and I'll cherish her always. I look forward to going riding on her...with you by my side.

If anyone asked me what I wanted more than anything else on God's green earth, I'd have to say that it is you. You're my best present of all and I think you know what I wished for when I blew out the candles on my birthday cake. I love you. When I go to sleep tonight, I know my dreams will be filled with you. I hope yours are just as sweet. I can't wait to see you again.

Love,
Your Beth

CHAPTER 6

July 15, 1956:

W hat did they do now?" Jackson felt an instant headache coming on as he stood in the kitchen, pinching the bridge of his nose. He'd stopped inside to suck down a tall glass of ice water, parched from another scorcher of a day. Mama was out hanging clothes, and Pop was working in the pasture. That left him to intercept a call from the town sheriff. "I'll be right down."

Squashing the aggravation that threatened to boil over, he headed to the bathroom and slicked back his hair. A quick inspection proved a change of clothes was in order. Jackson made a swap for a fresh T-shirt and clean jeans before heading out the door. "I'm running an errand, Mama. Be right back."

He cranked up the old pick-up and rumbled to town, thankful he had a fifteen minute drive to cool his head. He'd dropped the boys off earlier that day with some equipment that needed repairs and expected them to walk home. *Don't you know better? You can't expect anything with the twins. They'll surprise you or pull the rug out from under you every time.*

Jackson parked in front of the small, unassuming police station on Main Street. For a sleepy town, business was generally pretty slow. A drunk would spend the night from time to time to sober up or there might have been a fight. Stepping in the door, he took one look at his brothers and let out a long, low whistle. Fight, indeed. Wyatt had quite a shiner, a towel with ice pressed to a nasty bump on his forehead. As for Em, his lip had swelled two sizes and tissue was stuffed up his bloody nose.

"What was it this time, Sheriff? Defending Miss Hillary's honor again?"

Both boys had taken a shine to the new librarian in town. Wyatt was especially gone on her.

Rob Maxwell shook his head with a long-suffering sigh. It wasn't the first time these two trouble makers had graced his jail. "Oh, they mixed it up with the Peabody boys. Wouldn't tell me why. It happened over at the diner in the middle of ice cream sodas. Made quite a mess. Louis Peabody already rounded up his sons. Gave them the what for, too."

Jackson gripped the back of his neck and gave it a good squeeze. A tension headache was running from his temples all the way down to his shoulders. "Thanks for calling, Sheriff. There's no need to bother Pop about this. They'll make amends at the diner *and* with the Peabodys. You have my word." He hitched a thumb to the door. "Let's go."

Glowering, the twins slouched as they shuffled past, grumbling and mumbling apologies to Sheriff Maxwell on the way out. Once everyone was settled in the truck, the doors were slammed hard enough to rattle the whole truck. Jackson turned and stared his brothers down. "All right. Spill it." The twins eyed each other, reluctant to make a peep until their older brother growled at them, "Talk or I'll tell Pop."

Emmett broke first, blurting out, "Joey Peabody, the

little pip squeak, had the nerve to say that you weren't good enough for Elizabeth Mason—" He broke off and crossed his arms.

Wyatt took over, the blood rushing up to his hairline. Jackson wouldn't be surprised if steam shot out of his ears. "Then his brother, Carl, the idiot, said about the only thing you *were* good enough for was a mat to wipe her feet on."

An instant knot formed in the pit of Jackson's stomach and gave a good twist. No one liked hearing such hateful words, especially when he couldn't think of why the Peabodys would have any reason to talk about him in such a way nor did he know how Carl and Joey knew anything about his feelings for Beth. Gripping the steering wheel, he mulled it over. Then it hit him. They'd tried to dance with her on the Fourth of July, but she wouldn't give them the time of day. Worse yet, their older brother, Clyde, was the one who gave her the flower at church.

Counting silently to ten, Jackson let out a long, slow breath and dredged up some patience. He turned to his brothers and spoke slow and steady so there would be no misunderstandings. "Listen, boys. I appreciate you sticking up for me, but I can handle my own battles. Now, we're going to the diner and then the Peabodys and you are going to make this right."

Emmett smacked the dashboard and cursed, getting a jab in the ribs in answer, while Wyatt waved his hands in the air, sputtering, "T—The Peabodys! T—They should be apologizing to *you*! Why make us face those little worms again?"

Jackson reached across and grabbed hold of his brother's neck, turning the pressure on. "Because you are not going to give anyone a reason to speak poorly about a Henry. Do you understand me?"

At the look in their big brother's eye, they knew better than to argue.

Their sentence at the diner: washing dishes that weekend. Jackson personally escorted them to the door and shook hands with Louis Peabody, expressing his regret for his brothers' actions. The man was gracious, calling his boys out to receive apologies and give them as well. Once the Henry boys were back in the truck on the way home, Jackson couldn't help cracking a grin. "At least the Peabody boys look worse than you do." The twins became animated, reliving their every move in a spirited recounting of the fateful event for the rest of the ride home.

eↄeↄ

A sense of déjà vu came over Jackson as he checked his reflection in the mirror and straightened the tie Pop lent him, along with a suit jacket. His good pair of pants and a white button-down shirt completed his get-up. Except for church and funerals, he never dressed up. His palms were sweating and he had to wipe them on his pants—*again*, followed by a good tug at the knot at his throat because he was about to choke. He couldn't stop thinking about Clyde Peabody. Always dressed in his best with his pants pressed, a spotless shirt, jacket, tie, and not a hair out of place, Jackson came in second in the fashion department when compared to the Peabodys' eldest boy.

Tonight would mark his first real date. Sure, there had been school dances and football games, a hayride or two, but Jackson had never taken a girl out for a sit-down dinner in a nice place. What if Beth found him lacking? He hoped that his clothes looked all right and that he didn't do anything embarrassing. It made him uncomfortable to go to a fancy restaurant with a crowd of people. Too many stares. Too many tongues wagging. Better to be around the horses. They accepted him for what he was and left him in peace.

Taking one last deep breath, like an inmate about to meet the executioner, he went downstairs to find his family gathered at the dinner table. Jackson wished he could strip off his finery, get back into normal clothes, and join them, but the prospect of seeing Beth burned brightly enough to keep him heading to the door, Clyde Peabody be damned.

"Woo-wee! And we thought he was done up the last time. Wyatt, I do believe our brother is completely gone on Miss Beth Mason," Emmett nodded emphatically, his lips curling up in a devilish grin. He passed a bowl of potatoes to his mother. Good thing or Jackson might throw one at his brother.

Wyatt, chin propped on his hand, eyed his older brother up and down and let out a long, low whistle. "Yes sir, Em, I do believe you're right. Hook, line, *and* sinker. This boy has been caught. There's one less fish in the sea."

Jackson couldn't resist. Reaching across the table, he clamped down on the twins at the nape of their neck with a firm squeeze. "You just remember, boys. What goes around, comes around. My memory is long and your day will come, so I'd watch it if I were you."

Mama pushed away from the table and stood up, straightening her oldest son's collar and pushing his bangs away from his eyes, fussing like mothers tend to do. "I think you look very handsome. You make me think of your father when we were dating."

She rose up and kissed Jackson's cheek, her eyes bright. Behind her, he could see the twins pretending to gag. He gave them a glare that could set the place on fire and cleared his throat meaningfully, while his father started to laugh. Ella glanced over her shoulder at her husband and tossed him a smile. "Doesn't he look nice, Landon?"

Pop nodded and rose from his seat, giving his son a good clap on the back. "Very nice, Ella. Now let the boy go. Can't you see he's sweating bullets?" His father gave Jackson a quick hug and a sympathetic wink. "You know it's serious when your stomach's in knots and you're lightheaded just thinking about her, the same way I felt about your mother some twenty years ago. I can see it all over your face. Try and relax and have a good time, Jackson."

They resumed their places, Wyatt and Emmett echoing Landon's words in sing-song voices that made Jackson chuckle in spite of himself. Incorrigible hellions that they were, he couldn't love them any more in spite of the way they tormented him. One day, they'd get their due. The plotting would have to begin now in preparation.

The screen door squeaked open and shut just after he walked out. Wyatt caught up to him and grabbed his shoulder. All signs of humor were gone, his green eyes dead serious when meeting Jackson's gaze. "You *are* good enough for Miss Elizabeth Mason, more than good enough. Don't you doubt it for a minute."

Jackson gave him a crooked grin. "Thanks, Wy. I'll tell you two all about it later. I'm sure you'll need pointers." His kid brother gave him a wink at that and loped back inside.

The farm truck, a forty-five Chevy in a dark green, had seen its better days since Pop bought it as an indulgence at the end of the war. There were some dents, a fair share of scratches, and rust spots, but like a Henry, it got the job done. The pick-up chugged down the lane at a steady pace, announcing their arrival with the loud rumble of the motor. She might not be the prettiest vehicle on the roads, but this baby would get a body where it needed to go, come snow, sleet, rain or shine. Passed down from his father, Jackson was honored with ownership upon his graduation from high school.

He drove the venerable pick-up with pride. Belle, as he called her, had character. Whether Beth would appreciate her personality or not remained to be seen. Slamming the heavy door with a thud, he yanked on his tie one more time, carrying two bouquets from Mama's garden with him. His heart thumped in anticipation of seeing his girl. Only three days had passed, yet they felt like an eternity.

Approaching the front door, he was brought to a standstill by the shiny, brand-spanking new Coupe Deville sitting next to the house. Its black paint was sleek, polished to a high gloss. The white top and white-wall tires capped off the ride, making him feel completely inadequate. The oldest Peabody boy could buy Beth a car like that. The thought came unbidden and he squashed it down.

"Jackson, it's good to see that you are punctual, a good virtue to have. Elizabeth will be down in a few minutes. How do you like my baby? I just picked her up in Albany today." Hamilton Mason stepped up to the Cadillac and affectionately patted the roof.

Jackson swallowed hard and gave a sharp nod. "She's a real beauty." His hand started to tremble, but he held steady. *Cut it out, now! You're a Henry. You don't need a car to prove your worth.*

"Why don't you sit down and we'll have a talk?" Beth's father gestured to the white wicker chairs on the porch. Jackson felt like an unsuspecting fly about to be trapped in a web. Remembering his manners, he allowed Hamilton to sit first.

As Jackson sat the farthest distance possible from the man, he had the sinking sensation that Mr. Mason truly meant, "Welcome to my parlor, said the spider to the fly." What he wouldn't give to be sitting in his truck with his girl, anywhere but here where he was completely out of his element. As a lawyer, Beth's father was accustomed to formal wear, dressed in three piece suits on a work day, wearing *slacks* and a button-down shirt when being casual at home. Jackson felt underdressed, as his clothes were obviously of a lesser quality than his host's, and began to squirm inwardly.

The two men were like night and day. If there was work to be done around his place, with his wife's cows, or their vehicles, Hamilton hired out. He wasn't a man who liked to get his hands dirty, and yet the knot in Jackson's stomach suggested Mr. Mason could muck around in a person's life without ever lifting a finger.

"Fine evening we're having, isn't?" Curse his voice for cracking, betraying his nerves. Not one to avoid a situation, no matter how bad, Jackson sat up straight and met Elizabeth's father's eyes. What he saw in their gray depths sent a shiver down his spine. *You are not welcome,* whispered a voice in his head.

Hamilton leaned forward, resting his elbows on his knees and forming a steeple with his fingers. "Yes, Jackson, it is a fine evening, fine indeed, perfect for someone like yourself to take my daughter out and show her a good time like she deserves. However, I want you to keep one thing in mind. Don't plan on having serious intentions with my daughter. You are a nice young man and I respect you and your family. However, I intend for Elizabeth to marry a man of learning, an individual with wealth and position, one with prospects. You simply do not fit the bill."

You're not someone like Clyde Peabody. Jackson

would have preferred it if Hamilton had spit at him. At least that filth could be wiped off, while those hateful words left a stain on his heart that was spreading and making his blood boil. No one had ever made him feel so low. Picking his spirits up, he reminded himself of the pride he carried for his father and their family farm. How dare Mr. Mason have the gall to belittle such a thing? He attempted to collect his thoughts for some form of response, but Beth saved him the trouble.

"I'll date who I please, Daddy." She stepped out on the porch and let the screen door swing shut with a bang, blue eyes flashing, on the brink of angry tears, her cheeks crimson. Her chest was heaving, yet she showed remarkable restraint. "I could do much worse than Jackson Landon Henry. He's a good man and you ought to be ashamed of yourself. You've known him since he was a baby, watched his growing up years, know what he's become. Why don't you give him the same benefit of a doubt as defendants in your court room, allow him to prove his mettle?"

She was very close to tears, angry above all else. Jackson took her hand, forming a united front. They could go or stay. It was her decision.

Katherine stepped out then, her silver hair pulled back from her face in a tight bun, making her look more severe than usual. Her gaze fell on her husband and her disappointment was obvious to everyone. "I couldn't help but hear your words, Hamilton. I must say I'm surprised and not a little disappointed in you." She stepped forward and took Jackson's hand, kissing his cheek as he rose to his feet, ready to snap. "You have a nice time, Jackson, and try not to let Elizabeth's father ruin your evening. He's not dealing very well with the fact that our little girl is grown up and can make up her own mind about who she'll spend her life with in the future."

Jackson cleared his throat, avoiding Hamilton's stare and handed her one bouquet of flowers, setting the other in Beth's empty hand. "Thank you, Mrs. Mason. I hope you have a nice evening." Giving Beth a gentle tug, he drew her beside him, off the porch and to the truck.

No time to dawdle with two sets of eyes watching from the porch, each taking up the flag of different sides of a war about to ensue. Jackson opened the passenger side door and held Beth's hand, allowing her to step up, reaching across to secure her seatbelt, brushing her hand once more and giving her a smile, even though he felt terrible. No one had shown outright disrespect to him in his life. It was not an experience that he would choose to repeat.

He climbed in the truck and glanced in the rearview mirror. Hamilton had returned to his car and was polishing the spotless surface, rubbing in the entire exchange even more deeply. Jackson cranked the engine and stomped on the gas, pulling out and leaving a cloud of dust behind.

By the time they pulled out of the Masons' driveway, the dam broke and Beth's angry tears started to rain down. Jackson reached across and patted her shoulder, pushing his hurt feelings aside to deal with hers. He pulled over once they were out of the line of sight to gather her in his arms. "It's all right. Your father wants what's best for you. He doesn't mean to be hurtful, he just has tunnel vision concerning you. Perhaps I'll feel the same way when I have children of my own."

She buried her head in his chest and cried herself out. When the storm abated, she accepted a handkerchief with a shaky smile, wiping her eyes. Her hands were in fists as she banged them on her lap. "He makes me so mad, Jackson! How dare he talk to you that way or try and make such a decision for me?! This is my life and I *will* be the one who chooses my partner, not Daddy. The days of arranged marriages are dead."

She turned to study him and her face softened as she set a palm on his cheek. "I am so sorry my father treated you like that. I was just mortified. I absolutely wanted to fall through the floor. I was actually hoping a pit would open up and swallow him whole for being so dreadful. Never in a million years did I dream he could be so nasty."

Jackson shrugged, setting his hands on the wheel. "Are you sure I'm worth the fight? If not, I can take you back right now. We can walk away, consider this was not meant to be." The words were hard to say. The cut would run deep if she wanted to end it, but swift. His eyes remained trained on the dashboard. Otherwise, he might break.

Beth slid across the seat and took his face in her hands. "Jackson Landon Henry, I don't ever want to hear such nonsense come out of your mouth again. You are Fort Sumter, Bull Run, and Bunker Hill all rolled into one, worth every trial and tribulation if I have you at the end of the war." Nodding once to give emphasis to her words, she sealed her proclamation with a kiss.

The knots in his stomach finally loosened and he hugged her tightly. "All right then," he murmured gruffly. "Then we'll let this roll off of our backs and figure it out as we go. Let's get on with enjoying our night."

He started the engine, thankful it fired right up and gave the dash an affectionate pat. "Belle might be old but she's a faithful chariot. Hope you don't mind her. I know she's not that pretty anymore, but I like her well enough."

"Jackson, I don't care where we go or how we get there as long as I'm with you."

She looked at him with those amazing eyes and he tumbled into the blue, his forehead resting on hers. His heart did a little dance because he knew exactly how she felt.

The Olde Inn and Tavern opened its arms to the young couple, drawing them inside a building that had been functioning in a similar fashion since colonial times. The place had character with wooden floors that creaked beneath their feet and thick, dark beams high overhead. To the right, a festive crowd enjoyed the tavern with seats at the bar, booths, and tall tables.

The young couple was ushered to the main dining room to the left and a table tucked in the corner, away from the hubbub. Tiny, white lights were strung over the windows, across the mantle, and adding accents to the walls, like a firefly's flicker. A candle wavered at the center of their table while a lantern hanging overhead cast a dim glow. The main dining room was quiet with only a few more couples interspersed throughout the room, giving their newest arrivals some welcome privacy.

"You look beautiful tonight, but then you always do." For the first time that evening, Jackson had the opportunity to study the girl across the table and her cheeks flushed becomingly at his compliment.

She'd chosen a dress in pale blue that fell from her shoulders, hugged her upper body and flared out at the waist. Her golden hair was loose, falling down her back, shimmering in the lamplight. A signature flower, this time one in a deep shade to match her dress, was tucked behind her ear and all he wanted to do was take it down for an excuse to touch her. Exhaling slowly, he fought to keep his mind on the straight and narrow. "So tell me, how's Lucy?"

Her face became animated talking about the horse, so expressive as her words bubbled up in a rush and overflowed. "Oh, she's wonderful! I think she was a little homesick at first, moping in her stall. I sat with her and talked to her for a long while, brushing her with the curry comb. As soon as I let her loose, she pranced around the field, tossing her head. She's quite a flirt. I took her for my first solo ride, with Daddy's help. I know you wouldn't believe it from his behavior, but my father's taken quite a shine to her and he's impressed with your generous gift. I think that's what pushed him over the edge about your so-called *intentions*."

She rolled her eyes and reached across the table to take his hand. "By the way, you look amazing tonight. I've never seen you like this."

It was his turn to blush, the heat blooming in his cheeks as he glanced down at their hands. "Well, I figured the least I could do is try to look decent if I was going out with you, though I must say it's a lost cause. You are out of my league."

She drew herself up to argue with him, but he raised a finger, gesturing for her to wait. "Before you spout off about something we both know is true, let's go back to what you said about Lucy. What do you mean? Did your father think I was giving you a horse in exchange for taking you as a wife? It's not like the old days. Livestock does not mean marriage, although I wouldn't mind," his voice trailed off at the end and he stared at the candle, afraid to see the expression on her face.

"Fathers can forget about common sense when it comes to daughters. Did you ever see 'Father of the Bride' with Katherine Hepburn and Spencer Tracy? Spencer went off the deep end when Elizabeth Taylor was about to get married." She laughed softly and quiet fell between them.

The waitress came and went, taking their orders and leaving drinks. Beth took the opportunity to take his other hand, forming a connection that seemed invincible in that moment. "As for the thought of marriage, I have been imagining my wedding day since I was about four. I've tried to picture many different grooms, but they always turn into you."

How did a guy concentrate after a girl turned his world upside down? The food was a distraction, as well as the bottle of wine that loosened her tongue. Now that she was eighteen, Jackson figured they should indulge in her first legal drink together. They shared a piece of cake and then the music started to play, setting her toes to tapping.

"Jackson, dance with me." Not one to turn down a girl's requests, especially this girl, he took her hand and led her onto the flagstone patio out back. Lanterns were strong along the awning, providing enough light to see by as they slowly began to sway back and forth. Changing it up a bit, he gave her a spin and reeled her back in, making her tip her head back and laugh. God, how he loved that sound! "Jackson, where did you learn how to dance? You have to teach me your moves."

He moved to the steps, dancing her down on to the grass, allowing the night to close in around them, broken only by moonlight and the tiny beacons of the fireflies. "Oh, Mama said it was becoming a lost art and I'd best learn, said I'd never know when dancing would come in handy. She taught all of us." He shook his head at the memory. "You should have seen the twins. They were hysterical, trying every trick in the book to get out of their lessons. They underestimated the power of our mother."

Beth laughed with him, only to take hold of his shoulders in order to grab his attention. "Let's save the dance lesson for later. How about we continue our lessons in the art of kissing?"

She didn't have to ask twice. A little tipsy from the wine, she nearly stumbled and he had to hold her firmly at the waist to keep her on her toes. He found himself caught in a wave of dizziness as well, but he'd only had one glass of wine. Alcohol wasn't to blame. Try the power of a woman once again. Giving himself to the kiss and her warm, inviting arms, Jackson couldn't help but smile. His Beth was something else.

They'd danced three songs only to come to a standstill, caught in each other's arms and the magic of when their lips touched. Eventually, He came to his senses and pulled away. If they came home too late, Hamilton Mason would be sending out the dogs. "Beth, I'd better take you home, before I do something I shouldn't."

Reluctantly, she agreed. They held hands for the entire trip home, Jackson driving with one hand on the wheel. Keeping his eyes on the road took a supreme force of will. He had the best intentions of getting her back early, but Elvis Presley crooned on the radio, blasting out "Hound Dog."

Beth leaned forward and turned up the volume, her eyes glittering with excitement as a rush of color planted roses in her cheeks. "Oh, I just love him! Let's dance!"

He couldn't deny her. The old Chevy rolled to a stop on the side of the country lane. There wasn't another person in sight as they danced in the middle of the road, moving with exuberance as rock and roll pumped into the night. Jackson held on tight to Beth and swung her round, drawing her in close at the end. Both of them were breathless and the longer they stared at each other, the less either wanted to move.

She moved into him, her hands linking behind his neck. She rose up on tiptoe and his mouth found the way home. A breeze kicked up, ruffling her hair, carrying the sweet scent of meadow grass and the hum of the crickets. He didn't hear anything but the pounding of his heartbeat in his ears. She broke the kiss first. "I'm sorry, Jackson. I have to go home."

He gave a slow nod and took her hand, opened the door, and handed her inside. The sound of the engine broke the silence as they completed the short journey. Pulling into her lane, his heart sank.

Hamilton Mason had resumed his place on the wicker chair on the porch. Casting aside the guise of casually reading the paper, he deliberately set it down and crossed his arms over his chest. The older man leveled a contemptuous glare that was intended for one target only.

Jackson set his shoulders and raised his jaw, walking around to the passenger side and handing Beth out of the truck. He walked her to her door, her arm in his, and accepted a brief kiss goodnight. Only on the cheek would have to suffice, due to her father's close scrutiny. Hamilton rose from his seat and extended his hand. "I apologize for how I behaved earlier, Jackson. It was uncalled for." His daughter lit up at his words, giving him a hug and kiss before bidding both good night.

Jackson quietly accepted the apology and drove back home, all the while his mind returning to one burning realization. *Beth's father lied to me.* Most likely forced by her mother, the gesture meant nothing if not sincere. The man did not want Jackson seeing his daughter. A dark cloud hovered over their relationship. The heavens must have agreed because the skies opened, bringing one of the sudden thunderstorms that were common in the summer. It didn't sit well.

After a restless night, tossed between worry over Hamilton Mason and the wonder that was Beth, Jackson took refuge in the barn, long before the rest of his family was up. Greeting the horses, feeding them, giving them water, giving each some individual attention helped to ease the tension that had been with him since he left Elizabeth's house. Her note, pegged to the entry gate into the pasture, finished the job. She hadn't slept well either.

Dear Jackson,

I couldn't get you out of my head from the second I closed my eyes until the instant I awoke, many times over. I didn't want our evening to end. That song, "I Could Have Danced All Night,"...I know exactly how the singer felt. Once you took my hand, I don't think my feet ever touched down again. I might still be in the clouds right now.

Don't worry about my father. I'm sure he'll come around. Even if he doesn't, I'll find a way to see you. Thank you for a wonderful date. One isn't enough. I think I'll do something desperate if I don't get a steady dose of you.

Love,
Your Beth

ℯↄℯↄ

Emmett rubbed his hands together and blew on them. Man, but it was cold. Mid December and they were caught up in their first serious cold snap. *Gotta love the great Northeast.* With the thermometers plunging fast, he wasn't about to put the horses out. Mucking out the stalls warmed him up some. Pitching fresh hay to each occupant and tossing blankets on their backs finished the job. He was thinking about heading inside to find some heat in the warm and willing arms of his wife when the door creaked open.

Casey gave him a little wave, shivering, cheeks already rosy from the short trek between the house and the barn. The wind caught the door and practically pushed her all the way in with a yelp of surprise. She held up a thermos and a small sack. "I thought you could use some refreshments." Her endearing smile was enough to bring a thaw to the North Pole.

"Just what do you think you're doing?" Emmett strode forward, happy to see her, aggravated as all get out at the same time. At the hurt in her eyes, he took her hand and reeled her in for a kiss. "Case, I appreciate you thinking of me, really I do, but have you paid attention to the weather? It's absolutely freezing out there and the path is icing over. I don't want you falling."

She kissed him on the nose, effectively banishing all traces of anger. "I was really careful. Now, what do you say? Is it a date?" Her hand gestured to the bales of hay in the corner.

"Remember our first date?" Emmett snorted and drew her along with him, settling her on his lap while she filled the cap of the insulated thermos with steaming cocoa. They passed it back and forth, welcoming the hot trickle that hit just the right spot. A poke in the brown paper bag revealed fresh, chocolate chip cookies, still warm from the oven. One bite and he squeezed his eyes shut in pure ecstasy. "Heaven. Must be why we had more than one date."

Casey rested her head on his shoulder while he happily tucked the entire contents away, waving off offers to share. "I ate my fill while I was baking. I'm going to pop. What do you consider our first date, by the way? Lunch at Sonny's or that dinner at your house?"

He rested his chin on her head as he thought back. "Well, they were both great, but the dinner, that would be my pick. We spruced up for that one, you know? Prepared for it. Though, they can be spontaneous, like right now. This is perfect."

They sat quietly for a while, simply enjoying holding on to each other, listening to the sounds of the wind as it buffeted the barn and the horses quietly eating.

Eventually, she brushed his cheek with her lips. "Hey, Em, do you think we could go in now? My feet are numb and I think my nose is about to fall off from frostbite."

"Oh, I think I can warm you up." He proceeded to give her a dose of tickling that nearly had her rolling off of his lap.

"Emmett Jackson Henry, you are insufferable! Stop it before I go into labor and have this baby in the barn!" That was enough to make him stop. He gathered up the thermos and paper bag, giving his horses a pet on their way out the door. Two steps and her foot hit a patch of black ice, nearly sending her flying. His stomach clenched hard even as he scooped her up in his arms and held on tight.

The rest of the trip to the house was uneventful, the couple peeling out of their coats, gloves, hats, and boots when they walked through the door. Casey threw her arms around Emmett and held on tight, still frightened. Her heart fluttered like a bird trying to escape its cage. Like his.

He rested a hand on the back of her head and murmured, "Now, do you see why you shouldn't have come out there, Superwoman? You think you're invincible. Pretty close, but not quite."

"I know, Superman." Walking through the house with her, hand in hand, he built up the fire and sat down in his favorite recliner, allowing his wife to ease down with him. She sighed and leaned back against him. "So, what do you want to do now?"

He shrugged, mesmerized by the dancing flames and the comforting weight of the woman at his side. "We could watch a movie, pop popcorn, take a nap or read a book. Your call." The combined effect of the hearth and his wife's presence was making him sleepy. Wouldn't take much to go under.

She shifted and dug in the pocket of her sweater, pulling out his father's dog-eared journal. "How about this?"

He burst out laughing. "What? Were you planning on reading in the barn or something?"

Casey turned red at his teasing. "Well, each time we stop it's like freezing a movie at the best part. It gives me a chance to know your parents better, Em. Please, can we read it?"

He smiled and leaned back, kicking out the foot rest. With a little maneuvering, she was actually snuggled up against his side in the large, oversized chair. Secure in the knowledge that his wife and unborn child were secure in his arms, Emmett resumed the journey into the past.

CHAPTER 7

July 30, 1956:

My God, Wyatt! You just about took my head off with whiplash! You have got to learn the meaning of the word coast!"

Jackson's foot nearly went through the floor boards as he tried to apply an invisible brake, his hands itching to take the wheel. Of the twins, Wyatt was the only one without a license. Emmett couldn't stop gloating about it. Being the older brother, Jackson felt sorry for the other twin. Besides, a driving lesson was a good distraction. He hadn't seen or heard from Beth in two weeks. Jackson was going out of his mind.

His kid brother moved on through the intersection, grinding his way through the gears, making Jackson wince. At this rate, they'd need a new transmission. The old Chevy picked up speed on the back country road and Wyatt got a shot of confidence. Cruising along, he took a turn that nearly had his big brother sliding into the driver's seat.

"Wy! Do you think you can keep it on four wheels? I don't know how you are ever going to get a license if you don't settle down for once in your life!" He smacked the dashboard in emphasis, at his wit's end.

Sullen expression in place, jaw clenched tight enough to make the muscles twitch, Wyatt quietly coasted to the side of the road and turned off the engine. "Listen, Jackson. If you're just going to scream at me, I might as well go with Pop." Their father had completely lost patience with his impetuous son. While Landon generally found the twins' antics to be humorous, he had a serious turn of mind when it came to driving. "It's just…I get mixed up with the gears and I'm afraid I'll stall, so stopping and shifting down are tough—"

Jackson reached out to grip his arm. "You're right. I'm sorry. I've got a lot on my mind. You just need to go easy. Let the clutch out nice and slow, let the stick glide into place. You get us into town in one piece without running anyone off the road, and I'll buy your breakfast."

Wyatt took to the road once more, sitting up straight, focusing so intensely he started to sweat. Jackson couldn't hold back a grin watching him out of the corner of his eye. "Breathe, Wy. You're doing fine."

Taking that same advice and setting aside his role as driving instructor, Jackson took a deep breath and stared out the window, soaking up the beautiful day, wishing Beth sat beside him.

The rest of their ride was uneventful to the point that Jackson's hold on the door handle finally relaxed. Home free, the old pick-up rumbled to a stop in front of the diner. Wyatt glanced out the window and let out a long, low whistle. "Woo-wee! Will you take a look at Miss Hillary? Now that is not your typical librarian."

The young brunette, dressed in red with matching high heels and a rose in her hair, definitely did not bring scholarly thoughts to mind. Wyatt lifted his foot off the brake, the truck rolled forward, and BAM! Smack dab in the back of a shiny, black Coupe Deville. Jackson sank down and covered his eyes even as he heard Hamilton

Mason bellowing at the top of his lungs. The tirade and sputtering continued while Wyatt sat frozen, gone completely white, his hands shaking on the wheel.

Jackson let out a pent-up breath and nudged his brother on the shoulder. "Go on now. Get out there and talk to him. You want to be treated like an adult, get the privilege of driving? Then you have to take responsibility. I'll be here if you need me. That's what brothers do."

Wyatt pinned Jackson with sea green eyes gone wide with fear. An audible swallow and he got out of the truck, sweeping a hand through his sun-bleached hair to smooth wayward ends, checking the buttons on his shirt to make sure they were all done up. He shouldn't have bothered. Elizabeth's father was so hot, he only saw red.

"Do you see what you've done? This is my brand new car and that back bumper is about to fall clean off." The man was flustered, hat knocked to the ground in his agitation, salt and pepper hair poking up. For someone who was usually so put together, he'd come undone today.

"I'm sorry, Mr. Mason. I truly am. I just took my foot off the brake for a second. I'll make good on it sir." Wyatt was stammering so, he hardly got the words out. A body couldn't help but feel sorry for him. He was definitely finding out about consequences for his actions.

Hamilton stepped forward and jabbed Jackson's brother in the chest. "I should have known the roads wouldn't be safe with you *Henry* boys behind the wheel. When are you young pups going to grow up? You *boys* don't have the sense God gave a rock. There's no way you should have a license and if I have something to say about that, you won't!"

Jackson had enough of the tirade, especially when the older man's tone suggested his brother was scum of the earth. He shot out of the truck and gave the door a slam, walking purposefully toward the altercation. He gripped

Wyatt at the nape of his neck. "You go on and get us a table, you hear? I'll be in shortly."

With relief washing over his face, his kid brother made a hasty retreat. Jackson waited until he was gone before turning to the patriarch of the Mason family, head held high, shoulders back. "With all due respect, sir, you are being insulting to my brother and, worse yet, my family. If you have a problem with me, that gives you no right to take it out on Wy. He's learning how to drive, something you might vaguely remember. I promise he'll pay for your repairs. You call over when you have the bill. Good afternoon, sir." With that, he proceeded to buy his brother breakfast. Within the hour, Hamilton Mason called with his repair bill. The man didn't waste time.

෩෩

"One hundred dollars? I can't give Mr. Mason that kind of money. I'll be cleaned out!" Wyatt banged a hand on the table in aggravation. The Henry men had come in for lunch. Mama and Pop had already been brought up to speed about the driving incident. They were in complete agreement. The culprit would have to make amends.

"Yes, you can. I know you have a stash in the cigar box under your socks. Go get it." Jackson couldn't even sit still. He was still boiling after the encounter with Beth's father. He'd projected calm for his brother. Wyatt needed steady and Jackson would be his rock. That didn't mean he'd stop simmering. Pacing back and forth with his hands on his hips, he held out his hand for the wad of bills when his kid brother dragged his feet back to the kitchen. Meanwhile, Emmett sat at the table happily munching his sandwich, clearly amused.

"Hand it over. I'll take it to Mr. Mason."

Wyatt muttered his thanks under his breath and sat

down to eat, jabbing his twin in the ribs along the way. Jackson counted the money and stuffed it in his pocket. "I'm going now, Mama and Pop. Elizabeth's father will be home for his lunch and I don't want to miss him."

Landon eyed his oldest closely. "Shouldn't Wyatt be doing the delivery to complete his punishment?" Ella squeezed his hand and nodded in agreement.

Jackson's face tightened at the memory of Hamilton's explosion. "I'd rather do it. Let's just say Mr. Mason wasn't *nice*. I see no need for Wyatt to feel like he's being dragged through the dirt again. He's paying up. That's plenty for now."

Seeing something in his son's eyes, Landon rose from his chair. "You want me to go with you?"

One thing you could count on in a time of trouble was a Henry. They had your back.

"That won't be necessary, Pop. I can handle it." Somehow, Jackson pushed down the anger inside and found a smile, hoping it would be enough to reassure his father.

Ella stood up quickly and squeezed her son's arm. "Just a moment. I've got a quilt I just finished for Katherine. You can bring that over. Give her my best."

He walked. Figured it would do him good, maybe shift the rock that had settled in the pit of his stomach the moment they rolled into Hamilton Mason's car. Truth be told, the rock had been there since Beth stopped talking to him or leaving him notes. Today just made it grow bigger. Ever since their date, she was occupied or unavailable when he called, her continued silence gnawing at him. The last time Jackson called, he did the unthinkable. He hung up when her father answered. Otherwise, there might have been an eruption. Maybe he'd see her today. Unlikely, but that slim chance kept his feet moving, even as the oppressive heat tried to press him down.

At the Masons' place, things looked annoyingly cheerful and it irked him to no end, the flowers blooming, the yard meticulously kept, sun shining bright. As if all was right in the world. Resolute, Jackson tucked his annoyance away, the picture of courtesy when Beth's father answered the door. "What do *you* want?"

"Here's your money. You can count it if you want. Make no mistake. It's Wyatt's." Jackson thrust the stack of bills in the older man's hand and waited. Surprisingly enough, he pocketed it without a blink.

"Why isn't your brother here instead of you?" Hamilton's level stare would have had a lesser man quaking in his boots. Small wonder those slate eyes intimidated the accused in court.

"I think you dressed him down enough at the scene of the crime. He's paid his dues. Consider it done, sir." Jackson raised his chin up a notch and squared his shoulders, waiting. Beth's father continued to stare at him intently, making that rock in his stomach start to roll. Jackson turned to go, then remembered the other part of his mission. "Sir, I also have a blanket for Mrs. Mason."

"I'll give it to her. Good afternoon." Mr. Mason reached for the quilt, killing all hope of seeing Beth until Katherine Mason joined her husband at the door.

"Hamilton, where are your manners? I think the heat must be getting to you. Jackson, come in and have a refreshing drink out on the veranda before you go. How kind of you to bring the money and this quilt. Come in. Let me see this creation."

She took the blanket from her husband and shook it out, blue eyes sparkling brightly as she gazed at the fine work in wonder. "Magic. Your mother has magic in her hands, Jackson. This is a work of art. Now you go on out. It's quite pleasant in the shade and Hamilton—" She took his arm and gave him a pointed stare. "*Be* a true host."

The two men stepped outside, Hamilton settling on a chaise lounge with a thick cushion, crossing his arms. Silent.

That was no problem for Jackson. He didn't like talking anyway. He turned and glanced out on the perfectly tended backyard and immense flower garden that won prizes every year. The sight grated on nerves worn raw. There should have been horses and fields that stretched on as far as the eye could see, rather than this prim and proper place where he didn't fit.

A quiet footstep sounded behind him, ice cubes rattling in glasses from unsteady hands. Jackson turned around and he couldn't breathe. Beth stood before him, holding a tall glass of sweet tea, holding his heart. It was the Fourth of July all over and he couldn't see anything else except those big blue eyes that looked like a slip of the sky, her sweet, full lips, and that fall of sunshine in her hair. He itched to reach out and touch her, but her father had gained his feet and was approaching. Beth's finger grazed his as she handed him the drink and he swore it burned. "Thank you," he told her softly even as his pulse began to skitter.

She handed the other glass to her father and stepped back, hands at her sides, head down. A blush crept up her cheeks as they all made an effort at a fitful conversation about the weather and other inconsequential, safe topics. In less than five minutes, Jackson bid the Mason's goodbye. Walking home, the rock in his stomach had turned to a solid block of ice. Seeing Beth, being so close but only allowed to look and not touch...it was worse than not seeing her at all.

∽ೲ∾

"Quit messing with my coffee!" Jackson shouted at his

brothers, slamming his fist on the table and making everything jump. Playing his typical tricks, Wyatt had dumped half the sugar bowl in the mug, remarkably recovered after the driving incident. Emmett finished the job, pouring creamer to overflowing, prompting a blistering glare and a tongue lashing.

Their eyebrows shot up in unison. "I think I hear Pop calling," Emmett muttered as both twins wrapped sausage in a pancake and gave their mother a kiss on the cheek. "Thanks for breakfast, Mama," they called over their shoulder as they cleared out of the kitchen to give their older brother his space.

Ella busied herself with tidying up while Jackson dumped his coffee into the sink and poured another cup, sucking the hot brew down black, wincing when he burned his tongue. Setting the cup down, he pressed his fingers to his forehead in an attempt to ward off the headache that had started to bloom the moment his eyes opened. Not a good sign for the day.

Mama sat down across from him and raised her own coffee cup, only her eyes visible over the brim and he knew—a mother's intuition was poking at her and there'd be no avoiding her. "Jackson, what has been bothering you? You've been very short tempered of late and that's not like you. You never bite the twins' heads off that way either. As a matter of fact, you usually indulge them more than the rest of us. I've often said you have the patience of a saint when it comes to Wy and Em. You proved that when you faced Mr. Mason yesterday. What's making you so miserable?"

"It's nothing," he mumbled, pushing away from the table. Time to head to the barn to avoid a full blown interrogation.

Jackson downed a few aspirins at the sink as his mother stepped up behind him and pressed his shoulder. "I know you've never been one to say much but what needed saying and you don't ever complain, but I hope you know something. No matter how old you get, I'm here to listen to what's troubling you. I might even be able to help."

He turned and hugged his mother, pressing a kiss to the top of her head and finding the smile that had been scarce of late. "You help just by being there, Mama. I've got some things to figure out on my own right now. If I can't manage, I know where to go." She patted his cheek, accepting his answer, and his heart lifted a little on his way out the door. Mothers had magic in their touch.

Jackson decided keeping to himself would be best, give him the chance to mull things over and avoid another outburst. Two dilemmas circled round in his mind: the need to see Beth and finding a way to deal with her father's opposition. He *would* have her in his life, if she wanted him, but hated the thought of defying Hamilton. The respect of one's elders was ingrained in Jackson since he was a little boy. The past two weeks had been spent trying to circumvent Mr. Mason's disapproval. The fact that he hadn't been successful only made him more determined to find an answer, yet cantankerous at the same time.

Everything had been brought to a head when he saw Beth the day before and she didn't say a word.

Pushing his problems aside, Jackson focused on what he did best—working with his horses. He chose breaking a group of young stallions because it would take all of his attention and was hard work.

Disdainful of the term breaking, he found training or acclimating to be a better way of referring to the process. Jackson used patience and a gentle approach, beginning with a thorough rub down and brushing to soothe a young animal, attaching a lead line next and simply walking the stallion, allowing him to have more freedom little by little in an ever-widening circle.

He'd already gone through the introductory steps with his six students, making them comfortable with his presence, introducing them to tack, getting them accustomed to the bit and saddle. Riding was in order today. The lunch hour came and went, yet Jackson remained in the pasture, determined to ride each one. He took several hard falls for his efforts, received some bumps and bruises, yet always picked himself up again. When the last one took a turn around the fence line and his rider's patience was starting to fray, Jackson removed the tack, set the stallion free, and mounted up on Ricky Ricardo.

The horse had been rather forlorn since Lucy left, poking around the fields, not showing much spunk. Jackson could sympathize and chose to let the black stallion have his head. One good nudge to the ribs and they took off, fast enough that he had to hold on tight or fall off.

"Seems like you've got the devil on your tail, old boy," he whispered softly in the horse's ear when they came to a stop at the pond and Ricky took a long drink. Leaning over the pommel of the saddle, Jackson looped his arms around the warm, sturdy column of the stallion's neck and rested his head a moment. It was still throbbing. Likely, only Beth was the cure.

When Ricky blew hard through his nose and touched his muzzle down to the ground, his rider patted his cheek in understanding. "You're missing her something terrible, aren't you? I know exactly how you feel. We'll have to do something about that, something that will work for both of us."

Taking his time going back to the barn, he noticed the others had already migrated inside, cleaning up for dinner. Jackson slid to the ground and fished an apple out of his pocket. He let Ricky Ricardo munch and then pro-

ceeded to rub him down with a soft cloth, the way any
rider should after giving a horse a workout. These animals deserved absolute respect and appreciation. If they
could give their service and bear the burden of a human
being, Jackson owed it to them to make them feel comfortable and loved.

Once inside, he didn't dawdle, or his family would
have more cause for suspicion. Faking sick wouldn't do.
Mama would be wrangling Doc Smith away from his
own supper table to make a house call. Jackson changed
into a fresh T-shirt and jeans, relishing the feel of the cool
floors on his bare feet. Summer continued to be a cooker.
He looked forward to the cooler days of fall.

His family was gathered at the picnic table under a
grand maple tree in the yard. He took his place as his father said grace. Pop closely eyed his oldest, but otherwise
didn't say a word. The twins monopolized the conversation, filled with energy and one hare-brained scheme after
another. Jackson was relieved when no one paid him any
mind, one of the benefits that came with being known for
being quiet.

His mother gazed his way on occasion, but he stayed
under the radar. Wy and Em seemed to have forgotten his
crankiness that morning, passing dishes his way, asking
him questions about the horses he'd worked with that
day. Pop complimented his progress, lighting a soft glow
within. No matter how old he was, his father's approval
would always mean a great deal.

As was the custom, the three Henry boys made quick
work of clean up for their mother. Rounding up dishes,
carrying them in heaping piles, Wyatt and Emmett always tried to take more than was practical. Many a broken dish and scolding had resulted over the years, but not
that evening. Jackson manned the sink, up to his elbows
in steaming, sudsy water. Washing and rinsing without

comment, he set everything in the rack. His brothers turned the next chore into a game as well, racing to grab each dish the moment it hit the drain board, drying, and putting them in their place. A game of football toss followed and Jackson joined them to keep the peace.

He went to bed early that night, not unusual considering the hours they kept on a farm. By nine, everyone turned in for the night, although Jackson could hear the sound of a television turned down low in Emmett's room. The twins were probably watching a movie. Jackson passed the time doing what had become the norm of late, staring at the ceiling until he became dry-eyed, turning things over in his mind, flipping through mental pictures of Beth. The house finally fell silent around eleven-thirty, except for the soft sound of his father's snoring, the whirring of the fans attempting to cool the place down, and a hoot owl outside his window.

Fully dressed, Jackson slipped out of his room and down the stairs, avoiding the steps that creaked, and out the back door. The stars and moon were bright enough to guide his way as he took the quiet, country road that passed between the Henry and Mason homes. All the while, his heart pounded. What if she didn't want to see him? It didn't bear thinking on. *Cross that bridge when you come to it. You can always jump off if you have to.* Smiling at that grim turn of thought, he actually began to jog, eager to close the gap.

No lights were on when he went down her lane, a good thing. He hadn't thought about a contingency plan if anyone was awake. Scooping up a handful of pebbles, he shimmied up an oak tree by Beth's room and gently tossed rocks at her window. On the fifth try, she poked her head out, eyes and smile gone wide at the sight of him. "*Jackson*! What are you doing?"

His relief was so strong, he nearly toppled off of the

branch. "Remember how you wanted to go on that second date? How about now?"

He held his breath and a heartbeat later, she nodded yes, holding up her finger to wait a moment. He caught a glimpse of pajama shorts and a button-down pajama top, her golden hair pulled back in a ponytail, cute as a button. Two minutes later, she returned with cut-off shorts and a T-shirt. One glance down at the ground and she couldn't hide her fear. He slid a little closer on the branch and held out his hand. "Trust me."

"Always." Her teeth flashed in moonlight's glow and her hand caught his. Making sure he had a good grasp of the branch, Jackson helped her to cross over, seating her firmly in front of him. They slowly progressed down the tree, his hand securing her anytime she began to wobble.

As soon as they were on solid ground, her arms were around his neck and a rainstorm of kisses fell on his face. "That's for two weeks overdue. My account's paid up. This is so romantic, like Romeo and Juliet."

A hush fell between them as they crept away from her house and back on to the road. Only when they were a good distance away from anyone's eyes did he stop and return payment on her kisses.

He was breathing hard when she tucked herself in under his chin and his forehead touched the top of her shining hair. "So you *did* want to see me. I was beginning to worry."

She pulled back and pressed her palms to his cheeks, tears in her eyes. "Oh, Jackson, I haven't thought about anything else but you all this time. Daddy had a conniption of sorts the day after our date, a family conference about his wishes and that he expected them to be followed. My mother doesn't agree, but she doesn't want to go against him either. She's felt terrible every time you called. Then when you came yesterday, I was simply dying. I wanted to hold on to you so bad. I just don't know what to do!"

Jackson gave her a smile, shaky as it might be, and gave her one more kiss. "Well, you know what they say—two heads are better than one. We'll figure it out. For now, let's make the best of tonight."

He took her hand and they crossed over neighboring fields, listening to the tall grasses swishing against them and the wind shaking the trees. Eventually, they came out by the swimming hole. Bathed in moonlight with fireflies dancing in the air, it looked like something out of a fairy tale.

Beth's eyes were lit with wonder as she took her fill. "It's like magic. Maybe if we make a wish, it will come true." She turned to him and set her hands on his shoulders. "I know what I'll wish for." She gave him a smile of such sweetness, he thought his heart would stop.

"I've heard that if you catch a firefly, your wish will happen when you set it free." Beth was game, enthusiastically joining in the pursuit of the elusive creatures. Countless times she came close, only to squeal in disappointment. He had years of experience in a favorite pastime the Henry boys had indulged in many a summer night. Using patience and speed, he quickly snatched one from the air and held it in his cupped hands.

They knelt down side by side on the large rock next to the water and Beth leaned in close to get a peek, her breath skimming across his skin, her pulse fluttering at the base of her neck in all of the excitement. He swallowed hard and prayed for the strength to adhere to the morals he'd been taught when it came to a young lady. Talk about temptation. "I made my wish. Did you make yours?"

She nodded. "Wait a moment before you set it free," she whispered breathlessly, brushing the top of his hands with a kiss for good measure. "All right, you can let it go." He did as she wished and they both held their breath, watching the tiny light, carrying their hopes, floating off into the night until they could no longer distinguish their wish maker from all the rest.

A long sigh escaped from the girl beside him and she slipped her sneakers from her feet, poking her toes into the water. "The water's nice, Jackson. Dip your feet in too and get cooled off."

There was no chance of a drop in temperature when Beth Mason was in his proximity. She slid him a sideways grin and he wondered if she felt the same way. Happy to oblige, he kicked off his shoes only to hear *kerplop* as one went tumbling into the swimming hole. Shrugging because there was no help for it, he rolled up his jeans and waded in, retrieved the sneaker, and tossed it on the bank. "You're right about the water. Come in with me."

Her grin bloomed into a full-blown smile and she proved to be adventurous once again, stepping in with a little squeak when he couldn't resist sending a splash her way. "Jackson Henry! You are a devil in disguise!"

Beth kicked as hard as she could, soaking him, proclaiming war. They both did an utterly thorough job of drenching each other, sending them into fits of laughter. He bent at the middle, laughing so hard he couldn't breathe and she wasn't far behind him. The minutes passed and they wore themselves out, falling silent, providing the perfect opportunity to marvel at each other in the moonlight. She took one step closer, and another, reaching out with fingers that trembled to push his dripping bangs from his eyes.

"You're cold," he told her hoarsely. "Let me warm you up." He took her in his arms and her head tipped back, eyes shimmering, lips starting to part. His hand shifted to cup the back of her head and he tucked a wet strand of hair out of her face. There was no help for it but to kiss her again and again. He could do this world without end.

With the sense of the passing hours, the young couple gradually came back to earth and began the trek home, holding hands and dripping dry. Goosebumps rose up on their skin and Jackson would give anything to indulge in some more hugging and kissing to make them go away, but they both were very aware of how easy it would be to cross the line. Maintaining restraint, as hard as that may be, sharing each other's company in the wee hours of the morning on a sleepy, country road would have to be enough...for now.

A turn into Beth's lane and their bubble of happiness evaporated. The porch light was on and Hamilton Mason sat by the door, in his bathrobe and slippers, a thunderous expression on his face. Jackson squeezed her hand as a lump of ice formed in his stomach. There was one thing to be thankful for—her father didn't have a gun, although the possibility of finding one didn't seem too far-fetched. He rose to his feet, drawing himself to his considerable height of six feet, bringing him eye to eye with his daughter's suitor. Jackson had no doubt the man would level him if such a thing was within his power.

Beth's gaze darted back and forth and she placed herself between the two. "Daddy, it's not what you think. We went for a walk and waded in the swimming hole, that's all. We just wanted to spend time together. It wouldn't have happened this way if you hadn't been so unreasonable." She stepped forward, pleading their case. As a lawyer's daughter, she was skilled in the art of argument. It came naturally.

Hamilton was an expert and at the moment, would be judge and jury as well, doling out the sentence for the crime. "Elizabeth, go to your room." His voice was low and cold, turning Jackson's blood to ice. Being reasonable was not in the cards tonight either.

"But Daddy…" Beth reached out and took her father's arm only to pull back at his angry scowl as his face began to turn crimson. Give it a few minutes and steam might start shooting out of his ears. Jackson stepped in and took her hand once more, offering his support, preparing for the blast.

"Elizabeth, I gave you an order. As long as you are living under my roof, young lady, I expect you to do as I say. *Go to your room now!*"

The volume was gradually rising until the man's voice shook and he was quite formidable in appearance. She turned to Jackson, the tears streaming down her face, slipped him a kiss on the cheek, and whispered good night. The door banged shut behind her. Only willpower kept him from jumping.

Slinking off with his tail between his legs seemed like a favorable option, but Jackson never took the coward's way out. He stood his ground and straightened his shoulders, looking Hamilton Mason in the eye, taking the brunt of his gray, stormy gaze. "Mr. Mason, I apologize for sneaking your daughter out of the house. I would've preferred to do things the conventional way, but you wouldn't allow it."

Beth's father closed the gap between them, practically nose to nose with the young man on his porch, his breathing becoming more labored by the minute. A full blown fit was fast approaching. "I told you once that I have other ideas for Elizabeth's future and they don't include someone like you with few prospects in life." He practically spit the words through clenched teeth, his contempt like a wall, pushing Jackson out. "I don't want you to see her anymore. Don't show hide nor hair on my property again." He turned to go, his proclamation delivered, but Jackson wasn't finished, not by a longshot.

"Mr. Mason, with all due respect, I don't agree with your opinion of me. As for seeing your daughter, I snuck her out because I have to see her, the same way that I need air to breathe or water to drink."

The anger and frustration of the past two weeks was rising up and it took everything he had not to unleash a rant on the man before him.

Beth flew out the screen door at that moment and took Jackson's hand, creating a united front, her chin raised to face the force that was her father. "I had a higher opinion of *you*, Daddy. I thought you were the most honorable man I know, not one to judge someone by their position in life or learning, or their social graces. You couldn't find a better man than Jackson and I *will* see him, with or without your approval. I'm an adult, Daddy. If I have to run off, I will."

Her eyes were snapping with blue fire, like the center of a flame when it reaches its hottest temperature. She was so angry, her cheeks flushed, her breath coming in short, fast pants like she'd run a marathon. Jackson had never seen her angry. He rather liked to see her so feisty, but right now couldn't give into distractions. He smiled at her in gratitude for her support and held her hand tightly, borrowing its strength.

"Mr. Mason, I've never felt this way about a girl before. I'm twenty years old and I know my heart and my mind. I know my place in this world, where I belong, where I'm going, and I picture Beth by my side. I love her." He paused, gathering his thoughts, driven by the need to get it right because there might not be another chance. "I don't want to see her family torn apart or come between you, but I intend to change your mind. I've known your daughter all of her life and you held me on the day I was born. You've watched me grow up, seen the man I've become. You need to give me a chance to prove you wrong, sir."

Hamilton's gaze passed from his daughter to Jackson and back again. Katherine, also wrapped in her bathrobe, eyes red-rimmed from crying, stepped out and wrapped an arm around her husband's waist. She said nothing, but her wishes were clear. His jaw tightened and his eyes became slits. "I've expressed my wishes and my mind's made up. Elizabeth, to your room. Jackson, leave. *Now.*"

Beth's father had the last word, sending Jackson home in darkness. At four in the morning, heavy steps carried him down the lane of the Henry House. He headed straight to the barn.

Wyatt came out to find him at six o'clock to announce that breakfast was on the table. As Jackson made to follow him in, he handed him an envelope. "Beth dropped this off at the front door." There were no jokes this time, only an arm around his shoulders. The paper shook in Jackson's hands as he opened the envelope, fearful it was over between them.

Dear Jackson,

I am preparing for a showdown at high noon...or whatever happens next. I have complete confidence in your abilities to convince my father of his lack of wisdom, to tear down this wall that he has built around his heart. Just remember that I love you and I'm with you no matter what he says, even if it means choosing you over him.

I found this four leaf clover on the way over this morning. Keep it for luck. The sunrise was absolutely beautiful. Did you see it? I think it means the world is smiling on us. Please...don't give up on me.

Love,
Your Beth

CHAPTER 8

July 31, 1956:

Jackson stood side by side with his father, providing a united front against a particularly difficult stallion—a troubled case from one of the neighboring farms. The new owner feared the handsome steed was the victim of abuse. Scars on the chestnut hide, on the back haunches, and around his mouth were strong indicators. He had a skittish nature and was quick to lash out with his hooves or teeth, whichever came in handy. The Henrys would do their best to make him civil. If they couldn't, Landon had agreed to keep him. He couldn't stomach letting a beautiful animal be destroyed. If someone didn't have the sense to treat God's animals well, the horse shouldn't pay the price.

Landon was talking softly, a comforting rumble, moving in a slow, measured way. When Hercules calmed enough, he began to stroke his neck. The male had been given his name for his impressive height and strength, something that had to be held in check in order to be safe. With a barely perceptible nod, Pop nodded at his son. Jackson took his cue and eased a saddle onto the horse's back. Hercules tossed his head, snorting hard, but didn't pull away. Progress at last.

Jackson took a deep breath, tightened the girth, and gripped the saddle horn, intent on going up and over for the first time. He was half way there when the loud blast of a horn sent the panicky horse packing, shooting across the field, nearly dragging his prospective rider along with him. Jackson let go in the nick of time and cursed inwardly. So close. They'd almost made it to the first step toward taming the stallion.

"What on earth is Hamilton Mason doing here now?" It was only six in the morning, not the usual hour for social calls, nor did they expect the Cadillac kicking up a cloud of dust as it raced down their lengthy driveway. Wailing on the horn one more time, Elizabeth's father screeched to a halt and burst out of his car, fuming. The rock in Jackson's stomach became a boulder.

"Landon Henry! I need to talk to you right now!" The man was crimson, so livid with anger he was hoarse from his bellowing. He would have knocked the pasture fence down if the Henrys didn't come out to meet him.

Landon, unruffled, poked his hands in his pockets. "I'm here and there's nothing wrong with my ears so you can stop your shouting. What is the problem, Hamilton?"

Beth's father pointed an accusing finger at Jackson in answer, face twisted in distaste. "Why don't you ask your boy? Your son snuck my Elizabeth out last night, and I want to put an end to this. I've already told him that I didn't want him seeing my daughter. If he can't get it through his thick skull, then I'll ask you to do it for him. Elizabeth is not wasting her time on a *horse farmer!*"

One look at the steel in Landon's eyes, and Hamilton's face drained of color. He stepped back instinctively even as Jackson's father moved in closer. When Landon spoke, his voice was deceivingly quiet and glacier cold. "Because of our friendship all these years, I'm going to forget the way you just spoke about my livelihood, Hamilton. If you are even suggesting that what I do is beneath you, you would be dead wrong. I put in an honest day's work with my sweat, back, and hands. My son is cut of the same simple cloth. I think you and your family had best come here for dinner tonight, come see exactly what I do—what my sons do in our world—before you pass judgment. When you can act like a civil adult, we'll talk."

Showing remarkable self-control, Landon put a hand on his old friend's back and steered him toward his car. Jackson knew his father was a powder keg about to ignite. One spark and BOOM!

⸙⸙⸙

"That puffed up, bag of hot air! Hamilton Mason thinks *my* son isn't good enough for his daughter?" Landon practically exploded, throwing a bale of hay into the barn with more force than necessary and latching onto another.

At this rate, the truck would be unloaded in record time. The family had not welcomed the news at breakfast when the head of the family informed them of the invitation he'd extended to the Masons and the reason behind it, taking Hamilton's stance as a personal insult.

The twins had been up in arms. God love them, they wanted to go to war for their big brother. Jackson could picture them in days gone by, wearing armor, raising their swords and giving a great battle cry before heading off on their noble steeds. Wyatt would lead the charge, fired up since Jackson had taken the heat for the encounter with the Masons' Coupe Deville.

Ella had been quiet, but there was a glint in her eye and set to her jaw that spoke of defiance. "It would appear that Hamilton needs to open his uppity, tiny, little mind. I'll see what I can do to help him along." If Jackson knew his mother, she'd be revving into rare form, a whirlwind of activity as she planned for the perfect meal down to napkins folded in decorative patterns and an intricate centerpiece created from her award-winning garden.

His father hefted another bale of hay that hit the barn wall with a resounding thud. "Hamilton and I have been friends since school days. We come from the same place and the same kind of people. It looks like too many days spent in a fancy office, behind a big desk in those three-piece suits have made him too big for his britches, maybe made him forget his roots. I'll have to give him a refresher along with a piece of my mind when he gets here later this afternoon. I was so furious earlier, I couldn't even think straight. It's a wonder I put two sensible words together."

"Pop, I don't want you and Mama to do anything. This is my problem, not yours. I knew Mr. Mason was pretty hot under the collar when I snuck Beth out last night. I never thought he'd drag you into it." Jackson tossed a few more bales, trying a bit of extra force himself. It was a good release, venting some of the frustration that had been simmering ever since the confrontation with Hamilton.

Landon stopped and wiped the sweat from his face with a bandanna, finally cracking a smile. "Shoot, we all snuck a girl out a time or two, Hamilton included. That just proves that you're alive." He winked at his oldest and gave him a hearty thump on the back. "My old friend should have taken it as a compliment for how beautiful his daughter is."

His father walked to the water pump in the barn yard and doused his bandanna, running it over his neck, cheeks, and head. Jackson took the remedy a step further, plunging his whole head underneath the icy flow. His head was pounding and fuzzy from lack of sleep. He had to do something to clear his mind before the Masons arrived. A strong arm wrapped around his shoulders while he braced his hands on his knees and watched the water dripping to the ground.

"He'll come around. If you can't make it happen, then I'll step in, even if I have to knock him on his backside. It wouldn't be the first time." Pop gave Jackson a grin that set them both to shaking with laughter. They took a moment for a cold drink and went back to work because the horses would always need to be cared for, no matter what life threw at them.

Later in the afternoon, Jackson studied a young filly with a dark red coat named Cinnamon. At three years old, the American Saddlebred still acted like a baby. While most of their horses were born and bred on the Henry farm, this one had come to them as a problem child from a neighbor. Cinnamon had been aptly named. She was as spunky as an overdose of the favorite spice could be, yet sweet-natured as well. When anyone spoke of breaking horses, they laughed warily about her, saying it was more likely the young girl would break them.

Jackson had been handed the responsibility of training the filly, a task that proved to be difficult, not only thanks to her personality, she should have started her training a year ago. Waiting this long meant dealing with a horse that was more set in her ways. His father had given her a go, only to surrender after too many failed attempts. Wyatt and Emmett had been bucked off of her like a bronco in a rodeo. They turned to Jackson for hard cases like hers because he had the personality for it. Patient beyond measure with the animals with a gentle manner that drew them like bees to honey. Everyone recognized that training horses was his calling.

Cinnamon was no different from the rest when it came

to Jackson. If she was out to pasture and he walked across the field, the filly would trot over to greet him, nuzzling at his pockets for the apples that were always there. Sometimes, she'd be his shadow, tagging along behind him when he was working with another horse. Jackson had used that to his advantage, getting her acclimated to the tack, his commands, and his touch. She was comfortable with him and that was half the battle.

Today he'd ride her. Getting her to take to the bit and saddle had taken every ounce of Jackson's patience, many trials, and nearly a bushel of apples. The filly was a bit smaller than average, just under fourteen hands and about 800 pounds of pure energy. He was counting on her size being to his advantage. She'd seen him from the ground and at eye level on a fence. He'd managed to sit on her for about five minutes or so before she'd had enough and sent him packing. His right hip and shoulder were still protesting from that last round. Today, he hoped to charm the shoes off of the spirited, little thing.

Like any lady, Cinnamon appreciated being wooed. He rubbed her down, working his way all over her body with a soft cloth, hoping to hypnotize her or at least bring out the tame demeanor of a mare, aged four and beyond, a mellow side that remained to be seen. Jackson tucked the cloth in his pocket and moved to her head. Stepping in close, he pressed his head against her nose, letting her breathe in the scent of him while he stroked her neck. The saddle, bit, and reins came next, eased on slowly with a lot of coaxing and sweet talking.

"All right then, Little Bit." The nickname had been given affectionately as a testament to her tiny stature when compared to the other young horses in the herd. "I'm getting up on your back and we're going to go for a nice, easy ride. No tricks, no stunts, no showboating. Think of it as a Sunday drive. I'd really appreciate it if you didn't hurt me." Giving her a final pat, he moved to her side, gripped the saddle horn and swung up until his rear end was firmly planted. Taking up the reins, he took a deep breath. *It's now or never. Look out world. Here we come.*

Forget about easy. Cinnamon glanced back at him, gave a toss of her head, and was off like a rocket. There was nothing for it but to hold on tight and say his prayers. Jackson decided he wouldn't fight her, but rather would let the girl get it out of her system. Leaning down close over her neck and squeezing his legs around her as hard as possible, he couldn't help but let out a whoop of pure exhilaration, not without a pinch of fear.

This baby could move! To the far reaches of the pasture and back again, through the open expanse of green grasses that went on for acres, she finally slowed to a trot and then a leisurely amble. Jackson's heart stopped pounding and he made good use of the calm moment, getting her to respond to the reins for direction, guiding her back to where they started.

He slid off of her back, his legs a little shaky, and handed her another apple. "Good job, Cinnamon. We'll have you behaving like a lady yet. Go on now with the others. I'll give you a good rub down and brushing later." She bobbed her head as if the filly understood every word he'd said and nudged his cheek in farewell before prancing off to frisk about with two young fillies. Jackson couldn't help but laugh. She was something else.

"Well done, Jackson!" Beth's voice called out behind him and there was a quiet round of applause.

The Masons had arrived. Settled under the shade of one of the property's many grand red maples, everyone was taking refreshments already, Ella Henry playing hostess. Each guest had a mason jar in hand, filled to the brim with sweet tea or tart lemonade and ice. An appetizer tray sat on the table, no doubt filled with delectable delights crafted by Mama's skilled hands.

They had the perfect vantage point to see the Henry men at work. Wyatt and Emmett had just herded some of the horses back in, making preparations to join their guests, while Pop was already seated beside Hamilton, his amiable expression masking his aggravation from the skirmish earlier in the day. Apparently, no one had wanted to disturb Jackson—or they couldn't catch him, what with Cinnamon's pace.

He gave a wave, conscious that he was dusty and covered with sweat, not overly presentable at the moment. But Jackson had to remind himself that the whole point had been for Elizabeth's father to see him in his element. The young lady in question pushed open the gate and set out to greet him. She was a breath of fresh air and sunbeams rolled all into one, wearing a yellow blouse, knotted at her midsection, accentuating her fine lines, a pale blue skirt billowing around her.

He had to smile when he glanced at her feet. She had been a little more practical this time, choosing flat sandals that would not turn an ankle when crossing the field. Her eyes shone brightly and her lips were turned up in an exuberant grin as she dashed forward to meet him, unable to contain her enthusiasm.

"Jackson, you were wonderful! We saw everything, from when you gentled that beautiful horse to the moment you took off like a shot. My heart was pounding fit to leap from my chest. If Daddy isn't impressed by that, the man is made of stone."

"Thank you for that vote of confidence." Jackson couldn't resist. He grabbed hold or her and swung her around, finally letting her touch ground and burying his face in her golden hair that was blowing in the summer breeze.

Her face tipped up his way, open and welcoming, a homecoming every time. Kissing her was a necessity, no matter how many eyes were watching. His lips touched hers long enough that he forgot to breathe when Jackson heard a shout. Hamilton had risen from his chair, a crimson flush staining his skin, and he was intent on one destination: the pasture. Jackson barely had time to acknowledge Beth's father when opposition came from a totally unexpected source in the form of a loud whinny of protest.

Cinnamon came barreling toward them, snorting hard through the nose, head and tail held high. Her gaze was focused on Jackson, only one destination in mind. He didn't think she had a mean bone in her body, but the filly did think of Jackson as hers and if any other horses joined him, Cinnamon would butt her way in to get into the middle of things. One of the other animals could take a nudge from the young horse, even at a gallop. Someone as delicate as Beth was another thing entirely.

"Beth, get out of the way!" he shouted and gave her a push just as the spirited horse arrived on the scene, snorting and pawing the ground. Thinking to calm her, he grabbed hold of the reins to give her a firm tug, and Cinnamon did the unthinkable. She rolled, taking them both down while he went under. Jackson's head smacked the ground hard and he saw nothing but horse. He couldn't breathe or move and then everything went black.

"Jackson? Oh dear God, please…Jackson! Can you hear me? Wake up, Jackson!"

He slowly became aware of the little things first. A stone digging into the back of his head. Grass scratching at his cheek. The whinny of one of the horses. The wind tugging at his hair. His whole body hurt, but the worst thing was the crushing weight on his chest. Cinnamon stood off to the side but it felt like she was sitting on him.

When he tried to gasp for air, pain stabbed at him like a sword ran him through and his lungs wouldn't fill.

Droplets of water were raining down on his cheeks...a storm? No, tears, and someone had him by the shoulders and was gently shaking him. "Jackson, please be all right!" Beth was unraveling beside him, her voice heading toward hysteria.

That wouldn't do. The sky was spinning when his eyes opened, making him slam them shut. He shifted slightly and licked his lips, searching for words that had become like slippery fish, hard to hold onto. Finally, "I'm okay," slipped out weakly, sounding like the words came from someone else. Jackson tried to suck in a deep breath, but that only set him to coughing and the pain jabbed at him hard enough to bring tears to his eyes.

That was all that was needed to set Beth off, sobbing her heart out and burying her head against his chest, only aggravating his condition further.

He slowly lifted an arm to pat her back, but couldn't manage anything more. He'd started to pant, making a terrible crackling noise with each short intake of breath and just couldn't get enough air. He could hear running footsteps and his eyes fluttered open again to see Emmett taking hold of Cinnamon. The mare reluctantly allowed him to lead her away.

The Masons, Pop, and Mama were at Jackson's side, his mother kneeling down to take his hand, tears running down her face as well.

Landon was white-faced, obviously shaken as he pushed the hair from his son's face, reassuring himself that his boy was alive. Hamilton rested a hand on his old friend's shoulder, all signs of animosity wiped away, while Katherine wrapped an arm around her daughter.

Uncomfortable under all of their scrutiny, Jackson struggled to speak. "I can't—I can't—catch my breath."

Fear was rising, threatening to make him panic. His father's grip on his hand helped to squash it.

"Wyatt! Run to the house and call Doc Smith. Ask him if he can get here as fast as he can." Landon took hold of his son's shoulders. "Ella, move behind him and hold his head. Maybe if we prop him up it will help."

Jackson's mother nodded, brushing her oldest boy's cheek with a kiss as she did her husband's bidding.

Hamilton knelt down on the other side to help. At the count of three, they gently shifted Jackson until his back was resting on his mother's knees. He couldn't help but let go of a moan out of pure agony. His chest felt like someone was jabbing him with a hot poker. So dizzy he felt sick to his stomach, Jackson squeezed his eyes shut even as Wyatt's voice carried across the field. "Doc Smith is playing golf!"

For the first time in Jackson's life, he heard his father cursing up a blue streak, words he hadn't even heard before. "Wyatt, you bring the truck and—"

Hamilton grabbed hold of Landon's shoulder. "The keys are in the Coupe Deville. Tell him to drive it out here on the field."

Landon didn't miss a beat, holding on to his son's hand even as he shouted at the top of his lungs. "Get the car, Wyatt! Get it out here now! Your brother's turning blue! Emmett, open the gate and chase back the horses if you need to." Suddenly, his father squeezed Jackson's hand hard enough to make his eyes spring open. "You listen to me, Jackson. You stay with us! You hear me? You stay with us!"

There was a dull roar in Jackson's ears as a dark fog rolled in over his eyes. It was getting even harder to breathe. The women were crying, his mother whispering brokenly, "I love you, Jackson. I love you. Don't you leave me, Jackson."

There was the sound of an engine roaring to life, the peeling of rubber, and the slamming of doors.

"In the back seat. We can lay him down, Landon. Let me help."

Hamilton sounded frantic. Vaguely, Jackson wondered why. He'd never heard Elizabeth's father sound that way.

"Boys, get his legs. Ready, lift him up."

The pain was a monster, taking him in its teeth, shredding him to pieces. Jackson screamed.

☙❧❧

Bright lights. Strange Voices. People in masks standing over him. Wave after wave of excruciating pain on top of pain, cresting when an incision was made in the side of his chest and a tube was thrust between his ribs. Mercifully, Jackson blacked out.

"Jackson? Sweetheart, can you hear me? It's Mama. Pop and I are here, Wy and Em too. Beth's right in the hallway. Come on, honey. Come back to us." His head was fuzzy and the voices sounded like they were really far away. Slowly, Jackson rose up out of the darkness, something pressing on his face. He lifted a hand to try to brush it away. Landon caught it.

"You've got an oxygen mask. Leave it be, son. You're connected to all sorts of things." His voice broke and Jackson could hear him swallow hard before he went on. "You're going to be all right, but what a scare you gave us."

Jackson finally opened his eyes. He was lying in a hospital bed, a needle in his arm, machines making noises, oxygen hissing. He sucked in a shallow breath, wincing. It hurt all over. "What happened?"

His mother smothered a sob and buried her head in his shoulder. Helpless, he rested a hand on her untamed curls. For once, Ella Henry was not put together. Landon sat down on the side of the bed and squeezed his oldest boy's hand. "You got a collapsed lung when Cinnamon fell on you, that and a concussion. They've got a chest tube in your lung to drain the air and inflate it again. You're going to be here a while, a couple weeks or so."

Emmett and Wyatt came forward, unnaturally subdued, their anxiety obvious. They gave him tentative hugs, fearful of hurting him, and backed away.

After a few minutes of reassuring everyone he would live, Jackson whispered, "Do you think I could see Beth?"

They all took their leave of him, promising to be back shortly. The door pushed open quietly and a rainbow entered in the form of a girl. Beth was a medley of pastels, her long hair hanging loose, her eyes red from crying and she was the prettiest thing he'd ever seen. She ran across the room and wagged a finger at him in mock anger, only to have her face crumple as she ducked in close to kiss his cheek. "You really frightened me, Jackson. I love you."

"I love you too, more than anything." He stroked the curtain of her hair and drew her in close, oblivious of the pain. Holding her was worth it.

"Jackson, if you're up to it, I'd like to talk to you," Beth's father said in a voice that was so low, one had to strain to hear him, standing in the doorway. She moved to go, but he stepped in and gently pressed her back down. "You stay put, Elizabeth. I'm sure you'll want to hear this too."

Hamilton cleared his throat and waited until the patient's eyes were upon him. "I want to thank you for what you did for my Elizabeth, putting yourself before her when she was in danger. Her mother and I are in your debt." Beth's father didn't wait for a response. He simply patted Jackson on the shoulder and turned to go. "Don't be long, Elizabeth. Jackson needs his rest."

"Well, that didn't seem to hurt too much. Maybe your father is coming around." Jackson's eyes drooped shut as he slowly dragged in another painful breath. He was tired. So tired. "You—you should go, Beth. Don't want to push it, make him mad."

She held his hand between both of hers and pressed a kiss to his fingers, calling to mind their day at the swimming hole, the day he discovered what his heart already knew. He rested his free palm on the top of her shining hair. "Too close, Jackson. I came too close to losing you. I don't know what I'd do." She was shaking, the sobs threatening to rise to the surface again, her tears splashing down.

Moving gingerly, trying not to jostle anything, he pulled her down and slid his mask aside, brushing her mouth with his. His head started to throb and his chest was aching something fierce. He didn't care. "I'm not going anywhere and I've figured something out since we've been apart." His voice dropped down to a whisper, his breath drifting out in a sigh. "I have to be with you. I've never wanted anything so much in my life."

Mercifully, he fell asleep after she left, the memory of the weight of her sitting beside him and the touch of her soft fingers a comfort. Almost immediately, a dream grabbed hold of him, of his girl falling asleep by his side. Waking up to her every morning. Knowing she would be with him every night. Somehow, he had to make it come true.

⌒⌒⌒

"Pop? Where's Mama and the boys?" It was a term of endearment for the twins that continued to stick. Hard to picture them as grown-ups. Jackson wondered if it would ever happen.

"In the cafeteria. The bottomless pits can't stand another minute without food or they'll keel over." His father scraped a hand across his face and fought back a yawn. It had been a very long day, starting with Hamilton's angry confrontation early that morning. "Is there anything I can get you?"

Shifting slightly, Jackson winced as the tube in his chest gave him a jab that stole his breath away. "Hmm…I really…*really* have to go to the bathroom and I am *not* using that bedpan. Can you give me a hand?"

His father sat back and crossed his arms, jaw set. "I don't think that's a good idea, son. Let me go get the nurses—" He stopped at his son's heated glare. "I know. I know. They'll make you use the bedpan. All right, I'll help, but I still don't like it."

Placing his son's hand on the rolling IV stand, Landon let him grab hold of his shoulder for leverage. An excruciatingly slow inch at a time, Jackson pulled himself into a standing position. One step forward and a lightning bolt jolted down his spine, making his legs give out, taking him to the ground. A swirling darkness came for him again, his father calling to him as if standing at the other end of a long tunnel, and Jackson knew no more.

❧❧❧

"What—What is it?" His back was on fire and his head felt like it was full of cotton. Nausea rose up and Jackson choked it down. One attempt to move and electricity crackled down at the base of his spine, ripping through him. It took everything he had not to scream. "Mama? Pop? Somebody—somebody tell me something." The pain—in his chest and his back—threatened to swallow him whole. His hands tightened into fists and he squeezed his eyes shut.

His mother was crying again, her head pressed to his hand. His brothers were sitting in chairs at the foot of the bed. All in all, Jackson felt like he was at a wake, surrounded by mourners. *Being dead would hurt a lot less.*

Someone squeezed his shoulder. It was Landon Henry. "In all of the excitement over your collapsed lung, the doctors overlooked your back. You broke four vertebrae below the waist. They performed a spinal fusion. The broken bones have been permanently fused to the vertebrae around them. It was the only thing they could do. That or you'd be a cripple. The doctors said you might have to live with pain, but you can still lead a productive life."

Pain? The way his back felt, Jackson wondered if he'd ever walk again.

CHAPTER 9

September 2, 1956:

Four weeks, completely bedridden in the hospital and Jackson thought he'd go out of his mind. The pain pills didn't even touch his back.

He'd never known suffering like this in his life. He couldn't eat, couldn't sleep, could find no peace. When the doctors came in, they eyed him piteously and shook their heads, murmuring about the extensive damage to his spine, hopeful that time would heal him. He had his doubts.

He told the nurses at the desk not to allow visitors in, unfit to see anyone. Only family came, and even then, he didn't want them either. Lying on his side, he poured his agony into his journal.

No one else needed to hear it. When he slipped into an uneasy sleep, Beth walked beside him in feverish dreams, jerking him awake and back to his tortured reality. Alone. Jackson wanted to be left alone.

It was like being trapped in a nightmare, unable to wake up. Even with a back brace, his brothers practically had to carry him to his room at his homecoming.

The doctors told Jackson he should walk as soon as possible. He couldn't even get out of his bed.

 erscn

"Jackson? Jackson, your mother sent me up." Her
voice was quivering. The sound of it, knowing Beth was
there after he'd longed for her so much it hurt, sent a
shudder through his body and lit the fire at the base of his
spine. His hand tightened on the edge of the mattress as
he lay on his side, face turned to the wall. He squeezed
his eyes shut. Jackson would *not* let her see him this way.

"Beth, you need to go. Really. I'm not up to company.
I'm sorry." Damn his voice for breaking. *Why, Mama?*
She knew he didn't want to see Beth, yet disregarded his
wishes and there wasn't a thing that he could do about it.

"I'm not leaving." She walked around to his side of
the bed and dragged a chair as close as it could get. Her
palm was cool on his cheek, the smell of her perfume so
sweet and familiar it nearly set him to crying. Jackson's
hand tightened on the side of the bed and he swallowed
hard. "Jackson Landon Henry, you look at me. Tell me
what is going on inside that head of yours. Now is not the
time to keep your thoughts to yourself."

He opened his eyes and took his fill of her—because
this might be the last time Beth was at his side. Dragging
in a deep breath, Jackson met her clear gaze and felt as if
he was tumbling into the sky. If only she could carry him
away. "Beth, you need to go, to forget about me."

She gasped as if slapped and took hold of his shoulder,
giving him a little shake. Even that slight movement hurt
and had the air hissing between his clenched teeth. "I
think you must be out of your mind with pain. I will *never* forget about you."

His hand shot out and snatched hers, squeezing hard.
"I can't take care of you the way I am now. I don't know
if I ever will be able to, which means I definitely will not
be the kind of man your father would want for his daugh-

ter. Neither would I! I won't have you putting your life on hold for me! I just won't!" He tried to sit up to shake some sense in her and couldn't hold back the groan that came all the way from his toes. Jackson slowly eased himself down and breathed out from his nose. His voice was so low it was practically a whisper when he finally spoke. "Please. Leave me alone."

She dropped a fleeting kiss on his cheek and her retreating footsteps sounded down the stairs, her sobs drifting behind her. The slam of the door made him jump. A few minutes later, his door opened again. "I said to leave me alone. That means you too, Mama."

Emmett rounded the foot of his bed, a glass of water in one hand, his horse-pill sized pain medication in the other. "I thought you might need this." His younger brother's espresso eyes were troubled, face drawn, marred by dark shadows. Jackson's injury had taken a toll on the entire family.

With a hand that trembled, Jackson took the pill and choked it down, the water sloshing around. "Thanks, Em," he whispered. When the twin wouldn't go, he gritted his teeth. "Just go now. Please. Leave."

The door closed softly behind him. Jackson's frustration welled up and he flung the glass against the wall. It's shattering couldn't disguise his broken heart.

CHAPTER 10

October 25, 1956:

J ackson, it's been nearly three months. Enough of this. I won't stand for it." Doc Smith had just been in for his weekly assessment. Mama hung back during his examination and said little, taking away the chamber pot to empty it. She did not return with it. It was time for a long overdue dressing down. "The doctor says you have got to get out of this bed and, by God, you'll do it if I have to drag you out by your ankles."

Jackson shifted with a wince. The doctor's poking and prodding had irritated his lower back to no end, stirring up the painful beast that never went away. "Mama, do we have to do this now? I'm not feeling so hot." In truth, his stomach was churning. He might need that chamber pot for an entirely different reason.

His mother sat down in the same chair Beth had used. She took her oldest boy's hands and stared him down. "You are going to listen to me and you are not going to scare me away. You have forgotten who you are. You are a Henry, Jackson, and a Henry doesn't let anything keep him down, not for long."

His eyes were burning, but he could not evade Mama. All this time, he'd been trying to hide, but she wouldn't let him. "The pain, Mama. I can't stand the pain. I thought I could handle anything, but not this. It hurts too much."

She nodded and the tears rose up. "I know, baby. You think I don't know that, how much it's eating you up inside? It's tearing me up too, and your father, the twins." Her fingers began to run through his hair, soothing him, gentling him the way she did when he was a boy. Slowly, his insides unwound and, as he relaxed, the pain ebbed some. "That's it. Let it go, Jackson, just let it go."

When his breathing had dropped into an easy rhythm, the knot in his forehead smoothing, he managed to find a ghost of a smile. Something that had been quite rare of late. "Mama, what do I do?"

She kissed him gently on both cheeks, then between the eyes. "You start with baby steps, just like you did when you were little, and I'll be here to catch you if you fall. We all will be." His mother stood and held out her hands. "And the first thing you are going to do is use the bathroom."

Stubborn. Jackson didn't think he knew anyone with an obstinate streak that ran as deep as Ella Henry's. *Marrying a Henry must have worn off on her.* Taking a deep breath, he took hold and hitched himself up, all the air leaking out of him like a popped balloon the instant he gained his feet. He began to sway and she ducked under him. Tough. His mama was like steel.

On legs that trembled like they were made of jelly, Jackson made it to the next room down the hall, sweating and inwardly cursing all the way. The instant he stepped through the door, he was on his hands and knees. Throwing up came next…in the toilet.

The first week of Operation Recovery was spent walking from the bathroom to his bed, then to his brothers' room. In the second week, Jackson made it down the stairs to the kitchen table. He was shaking, his reflection pale in the kitchen window. When his father looked up, he cleared his throat and blinked back tears as he pulled out a chair. "Well, it's about damn time." In the third week, Jackson walked out to the barn, his father gifting him with a cane carved like a horse's head to remind him why he needed to keep going. One day, he made it to the end of his driveway, some of Mama's hardy mums tucked under his coat. He kept on walking.

ಆರಾ

"Jackson! Good Lord, You must be half frozen!" Katherine Mason took his arm and pulled him into her warm, bright kitchen.

The temperature had dropped dramatically and the air had a bite to it. Snow would be coming soon. Jackson's teeth were chattering by the time he reached Beth's door. The thought of her warm smile kept him going.

"Can I get you a cup of tea or coffee?"

He shook his head and fought to control his shivers. "No, thank you, mam. Is Beth here?" His hand tightened around the grip on his cane, steadying him. If he'd gone all that way only to hear no...

"Yes, she's in the parlor." With that, he gave a nod and continued on, struggling to walk at more than a hobble. His body would drop if he stopped. Beth's mother called after him softly, "Wait, Jackson!"

He pulled up short in the doorway. Hamilton sat in the corner, smoking a pipe and scanning the paper. Beth was on the loveseat, a caller at her side. He was dressed in a suit and tie, his hair neatly trimmed and slicked back with cream, everything about him polished and professional. The man was holding her hand. *Clyde Peabody!*

Her companion leaned in closer and gave her a peck

on the cheek. A brilliant rush of crimson bloomed in her cheeks and Jackson thought he'd be sick all over the Masons' floral carpet.

He must have made a sound as the flowers tumbled from fingers gone numb. Beth looked up and all of the color drained from her face, making her white to the lips.

Jackson gave her a nod with a jerk of his head. "I'm sorry. I came at a bad time." Drawing himself up as straight as possible, he clamped down on the pain and turned around, retreating out the door as fast as he was able. Down the driveway, out on the road, pushing his way home and he didn't look back.

There was the sound of an approaching car, its engine humming. Jackson wasn't surprised when the Coupe Deville pulled up beside him. "Son, let me give you a ride home."

He didn't stop. If he stopped, his back would give out and leave him a sniveling mess at the side of the road. Jackson would not give Hamilton Mason the satisfaction. "Thank you, sir. I'd rather walk. I need the exercise."

Beth's father wouldn't take no for an answer. It wasn't part of his make-up. "Jackson, please. I know how upset you must be, but I'm sure you see that Clyde is a better match for Elizabeth. He's going to be a partner at the firm." Silence for a few more agonizing steps. "Boy, if you don't get in this car, you're going to fall and be a frozen lump in the road. Your parents would never forgive me."

"With all due respect, sir, I wouldn't mind if that happened." Mason's words had stabbed him in the gut, nearly making Jackson double over. Elizabeth's father would have his way with an educated, white collar man courting his daughter after all. "I won't be bothering your daughter again, I promise."

He kept moving, even though it felt like there was a

mortal wound deep down inside the heart of him, slowly bleeding out. Hamilton Mason was not content to let things lie. He made sure the ailing Henry boy made it home. His obligation fulfilled, he turned the car around. He didn't see Jackson drop inside the door.

ℰↀℰↀ

Freezing didn't even describe it. Jackson felt like his entire body had turned to ice. Sitting on the back porch, wrapped in a blanket, he stared out at the horses prancing in the field. A fresh snow had fallen in the night, making them frisky. He tried to remember how it felt to be happy like that. Ever since he saw Beth sitting with that shirt and tie a week before, Jackson felt like a heavy weight was pressing him down, driving him into the ground. He didn't care what happened now. Didn't care about anything. He leaned back against the glider, his back protesting fiercely, and closed his eyes. Why not embrace the pain? It was all he had.

"Jackson Landon Henry, you and I have to talk." His head snapped up and he started to stand when Beth stomped across the porch and pushed him down. "You just stay put. I think we need to get something clear once and for all." She grabbed hold of his shoulders and pressed her lips to his, long enough that they both became dizzy. "*You* are the only boy I care about. Can you get that through your thick skull?"

He shifted, fighting a grimace as he did. Would it ever be easy to move again? None too gently, he pushed her away, his jaw set. "I saw Mr. Fancy Pants kiss you, saw you blushing. You didn't look like you minded too much."

She set her hands on her hips and stomped her foot. "You didn't stick around to see what happened next. I slapped him! Clyde Peabody turns my stomach! I would have run after you, but Daddy wouldn't let me, said he'd see to you himself. I'm sure he told you something comforting, like I was better off or something, right?" She whirled around and slapped the post. "That man makes me so mad! I'm going to give him a piece of my mind for once and for all!"

With that, she dashed down the length of the porch. Then calamity struck. It all seemed to happen in slow motion.

Her shoe hit a patch of ice on the top step, and she pitched down the stairs, her head whacking against the railing before she landed in a heap on the cold, snow covered ground, blood trickling from her nose, gushing from the slash on her temple. Scarlet splashing on the backdrop of white, making Jackson sick with fear.

"*Beth*!" He lunged from the glider and a white-hot streak of pain shot through him, taking him down. He crawled the rest of the way, pulling himself down the steps, heedless of the cold or snow as he gathered her still form into his arms. Fishing for a bandanna in his pocket, he pulled it out and pressed it to her forehead. "Beth! Beth, wake up! Beth!" A gentle shake was useless and his breath came out in a sob. He called out raggedly. "Mama? Pop? Anyone! Help me!"

෴

Pressure…on her brain. A swelling so severe, they'd had to drill a hole in that beautiful skull to insert a shunt and drain off the fluid, blood, whatever awfulness it was. Jackson barely made it to the bathroom when he heard the doctors break the news to her parents. Spilled his guts and nearly passed out himself.

Fighting off the black fuzz that threatened to cloud his

brain, he splashed cold water on his face and straightened up. Time to pull it together…for Beth.

She looked so small in the hospital bed when they finally brought her to a room. Turned on her side, a tube running from behind her ear, the sight of it turned his stomach again, but he held his ground. Standing at the foot of the bed, hands gripping his cane, the carved horse's head digging into his skin, a constant reminder. *You're a Henry. You're steady and strong. Your back can carry any weight…yours and hers. Even damaged as it is.*

Beth's mother sat at the side of the bed, head pressed to her daughter's still hand as she prayed softly, interrupted from time to time by her crying. In the hallway, Hamilton's voice carried from far away as he shouted in anger. "You need to do more for my daughter! Do you know who I am? I want the best of care for her! You bring me the best doctor in the country and you bring him *now!*"

A moment later, he burst into the room. One look at Jackson and he held the door open wide, livid with anger. "Out! You get out of here now! We do not need you here!"

Jackson didn't budge, hanging on tight, breathing through his nose. If he had to club Mr. Mason with his cane, he'd do it. "I'm not leaving and you need to calm down. She might hear you."

Hamilton turned to take in his daughter's still form, and his eyes filled with tears. He closed the door and took a step forward, only to stop as if afraid to touch her. He grabbed hold of the bed frame and bowed his head. "You pushed her away, told her to leave you alone." His tone was accusing.

"Because I didn't want to burden her with my troubles, but I've learned something about myself. I'm strong enough to shoulder my load and hers. That's what being a

Henry is all about. What about your young lawyer? The
only thing I see is a bouquet of flowers. I'm here and I'm
not going anywhere until she wakes up."

If she wakes up.

The unspoken words hung in the silence between
them. Hamilton's face crumpled and Jackson opened his
arms, drawing on his heritage to be like the mighty oak.
Unshakeable.

ↄ৵৹৻

They kept watch. Katherine at the head of the bed,
holding her daughter's hand or pressing her forehead to
her shoulder, Hamilton and Jackson at the foot of the bed,
each holding on to a leg.

It was as if by maintaining a physical connection,
they'd make her stay. The rest of the Mason and Henry
family paid visits as well, offering support, relief, food,
anything to ease them.

Five days after the fall, five days of anguish and tor-
ment, Beth opened her eyes. It was Thanksgiving Day.

Assured she was out of danger, Landon drove his son
home for some badly needed rest.

Silent for the trip, Jackson pulled a slip of paper from
his pocket and opened it with trembling fingers.

My dearest Jackson,

*I asked my mother to write this for me. My head still
hurts too much to do it myself—but do not worry. I will
be myself soon. Waking up, seeing you waiting for me, I
thought my heart would burst. I need you to know that I
never gave up on you, even when you shut me out and
this is the reason why.*

*You could never give up on me. I've always known we
were meant to be, Jackson Landon Henry. You just take a*

little longer to come around. Maybe we've gotten over our bumps in the road. I love you.

Love,
Your Beth

CHAPTER 11

December 24, 1956:

Slowly, Jackson and Beth walked the path through her garden, admiring the white lights that glistened on the trees and gazebo out back. What with his back still acting up and her lingering dizzy spells, the young couple wasn't too lively yet. They leaned on each other, mounting the steps. When Jackson faltered at the top, it was Beth who steadied him.

Laughing softly, he drew her in close and kissed the side of her red wool cap. Her cheeks were flushed from the cold and her eyes sparkled. She was irresistible. A lingering kiss gave him enough strength to ease his way down onto the bench, his knuckles going white as he gripped his cane. Sitting and standing continued to be a challenge, but progress was happening bit by bit. He was a far cry from lying in bed all the time. A deep breath in and he patted his knee, settling her on his lap. "I don't know about you, but I was starting to think we were like Romeo and Juliet, star-crossed lovers or something. You?"

She shook her head emphatically, wincing as she did. Headaches had plagued her since her fall. At Jackson's frown, she brushed his lips with a kiss. "Never, not even once. You and I are like peanut butter and jelly, meant to be. Problems came our way when you tried to deny it and we let anyone or anything else get in the way."

He held her for a moment, gathering his courage. Gritting his teeth through the pain, Jackson knelt before her on one knee. *Got to keep with tradition if it kills me.*

"Beth, I'm sorry I took so long to get this through my head. That day, when I saw you fall and I thought I might lose you, I prayed to God that I'd have one more chance to get this right. I've never been more certain of anything than how I feel about you. Since the accidents—mine and yours—I've learned we can't afford to waste time. You are my heart's content." He fumbled with the ring in his pocket, a small, unassuming emerald that flashed with the reflection of Christmas lights as it slipped on her trembling finger. "This belonged to my great-grandmother. She gave it to me for safekeeping until I found its rightful owner. It's meant to be yours. I've known you all of your life and I don't want to miss another minute. Elizabeth Katherine Mason, will you be my wife?"

There were more tears, but a smile was attached this time around. Speechless, Beth wrapped her arms around his neck and kissed him until they both had trouble breathing.

To say that the family was stunned was an understatement. The couple hurried in as quickly as possible and pulled up short before the group seated around the table. Everyone was chatting, relaxed, sipping coffee while Katherine cut generous slices of cake. Beth forgot all restraint and pushed forward, holding out her left hand to reveal the ring on her finger. "Jackson has asked me to marry him and I've said yes."

Eyes were popping and jaws were dropping. Hamilton rose to his feet and took Katherine's hand, the knife slipping from fingers gone numb. Both appeared a little shell-shocked. Jackson raised a hand imploringly and hoped that he could properly express what needed saying. "I know I should've asked you first, but the way I see it, this is the natural order of things. We already know all about each other, know our minds and souls. I hope you're not upset. After all we've been through, I can't let her slip away. What better Christmas gift could I give her than my heart?"

There was a moment's hesitation and Beth's father gave him a nod. "I have already come to the conclusion that there is no standing in your way, not for either one of you. I misjudged you when this all began. I realize now that no amount of book learning could teach the kind of character that has been instilled in you. You are of a stronger mettle than most. It's not the kind of man you are or even what you do that I have a problem with. It's your health. Will you be able to withstand the rigors of a horse farm on your own to take care of my daughter? You can barely walk now."

Jackson drew himself up to his full height and extended his hand. "Come spring, if I'm not back in full form, I'll break it off." At Beth's exclamation, he tucked her under his arm and caught her hand, running his fingers over his great-grandmother's ring. "Don't worry, Beth. I'll do it and that's a promise I plan to keep."

Hamilton met his eye as Jackson raised his chin, his determination clear. Their hands met, her father's grip firm. "Let's shake on it." Applause broke out as everyone became animated, their happiness bubbling over.

Katherine was first to extend congratulations, followed by the rest of the Henry family. The women laughed and cried, Landon patted his son on the back, and the twins pumped their brother's hand until it nearly fell off. The rest of the evening, Beth remained at Jackson's side, her hand in his. She would not let him out of her sight...and would not let him off the hook, pressing her ring into his palm, leaving its imprint, an unspoken reminder.

Settled on his bed that night, propped up by pillows as he waited for the aching in his back to die down, Jackson read Beth's Christmas letter one more time.

December 24, 1956
Dear Jackson,
Merriest of Christmases to you. Nothing can make me happier than being here to share this day with you and knowing you are by my side, both of us getting stronger every day. I hope you know that I would not care if you never got out of that bed. I'd be with you, holding your hand, watching every breath you take. It would be enough...but being a Henry, you won't settle for less than your best. I'll take it and promise to give you mine. I have complete faith in you. Come spring, we'll be together. I love you, Jackson Landon Henry.
Love,
Your Beth, the future Mrs. Henry

❧❧❧

The old forty-five rumbled down the road, decked out in holiday finery with a pine wreath and white lights on the grill. Lovingly preserved as part of the Henry heritage, Emmett only brought the old girl out for special occasions—parades, car shows, or to appease an extremely pregnant wife.

"I'm sorry. I know. I'm miserable. Impossible. Insufferable." Casey bit down on her lip, the heat creeping up in her face and her eyes beginning to sting. She'd been particularly sharp with her husband after dinner. His response? Firing up the pick-up, unceremoniously bundling her in a warm coat and boots, practically dragging her out the door. "I don't know what's wrong with me."

Emmett tilted his head her way, a grin tugging at the corner of his mouth. "Gee, maybe it's something to do with raging hormones or the fact that you've been carrying around something the size of a bowling ball for nine months? Not to mention you will be pushing said bowling ball out of your body all too soon, something I hope you will forgive me for once the dust has settled."

"Thanks for those words of encouragement." She stuck her tongue out at him like a brat of a child. Exactly how she felt at the moment, ready to sit down, throw a tantrum, and whine her head off. Her husband merely handed her one of his irresistible smiles and reached across to knead the tightened muscles of her neck. She dropped her head and closed her eyes. "So good. That feels so good. I don't know why you put up with me, Em."

A low rumble of a chuckle made him start to shake. "You put up with me when I was at my most cantankerous after my accident. I think I can manage." The truck chugged along, reliable and steady as Old Faithful. Or a Henry. Music drifted over the old radio, Alabama's "Dixieland Delight."

"Rolling down a backwoods Tennessee bi-way, one arm on the wheel, holding my lover with the other, a sweet, soft Southern thrill, my Dixieland Delight…"

Casey hummed along and turned her head to catch Emmett staring at her. "Sounds like Jackson and Beth," she told him softly, sliding in closer.

"Sounds like us." He hooked an arm around her shoulders, the other hand resting on the steering wheel. They took a turn off the road, down a dirt lane, coming out by the shore of a lake. Off on the other side, a lone pine stood by itself, covered in twinkling lights of white. He shut off the truck and they sat in silence as big, fat flakes began tumbling down.

"It looks like a prayer," Casey whispered. She rested a palm on the mound of her belly, pulling her eyes away from the evergreen to watch the wonder as her stomach rolled with the baby's movement. Emmett threaded his hand in the thick curtain of her dark hair and kissed her softly, without urgency, simply cherishing her.

Heart rates kicking it up a bit, he pulled away and turned his focus to the shining beacon on the other side of the frozen surface. "I've been thinking a lot lately about our fathers, especially since I found out how Grandpa Mason was with my dad. How do you think your father would've handled me?"

It was strange, the uncertainty in his voice when he'd already won her, proven a thousand times over that he was a man of worth. She took his hand and pressed it against her heart. "My father would've been over the moon about you, Em. First, he'd have wanted to spend a day trying to do what you do and learn from you, soak it all up. Then, he'd sit you down and share his top picks of fine literature."

He laughed at that one, even as shadows darkened his golden eyes. "That would've been fine by me, but your mother wasn't exactly thrilled when we first met. Remember?"

Talk about an understatement. Their first encounter had been a disaster. Casey reached up to brush the fall of hair from his eyes. "She was as soon as she got to know you." She stole a kiss, bringing out a sweet taste of honey in his gaze. "What about your father? How was he about dating?"

Emmett's face softened at that one. He was silent for a

moment. Gathering his thoughts? Revisiting the past? "Oh, Dad pretty much let us have our heads, just like he did with the horses, but made sure we found our way with our hearts. He also taught us that we'd have to be responsible for our actions. There's one lesson he taught me well—to hold on to the right girl when you find her and never let go. I knew from the first, that you were the one."

"Me too." She brushed his lips with hers and rested her head on his shoulder. She didn't know how much time went by, but the truck had cooled, giving her a chill. She drew closer, relishing his warmth. Solid. Steady. Hers—a true Henry in every way. "Now I really understand why you've become such a man. You couldn't help it, not with your parents. They were steel strong."

He kissed the top of her hair, his breath warming her face. "They were something, eh? I'd no idea what either one of them went through. Wyatt and I never knew. If either of them was hurting, they didn't show it."

Casey squeezed his hand and couldn't hold back a catch in her voice. "Just like you." A few minutes more and she shivered. "Hey, Em? I'm getting cold. Can we head home now?"

He grinned. "What? You just want to read that journal, don't you? How will we occupy ourselves when it's over?"

She closed her eyes and laid her hands on her belly once more in benediction of the miracle of life growing within. Her smile bloomed as Emmett wrapped his large, work-hardened hand over hers, closing the circle. "Oh, I'm sure we'll think of something."

CHAPTER 12

May 25, 1957:

J ackson thought he knew the meaning of hard work. Until it meant reclaiming his body, bringing it back to the way it used to be, hurting all the time and accepting that as his lot in life. Over the long winter months, he put himself to the test, taking on more and more each day. Shoveling. Mucking stalls. Grooming the horses. Doing repairs out in the pasture. Anything that needed doing, he didn't shy away. At first, the pain was so bad his back was screaming and many a night was spent soaking in a hot tub, followed by ice and a heating pad until exhaustion finally won out.

He learned to adapt, to make accommodations. Lifted with his legs. Didn't twist and bend as much as before. Made the pain his own and tamed it. He acknowledged his chronic companion and adjusted. As he became stronger, it became more manageable. His family helped him every step of the way. With words of encouragement. A hand up. A shoulder to lean on. His brothers carrying him when he couldn't go on. Each improvement brought him a step closer to his ultimate goal: leaving the cane behind. Jackson would walk down the aisle without it, or not at all.

In the midst of it all, an old-fashioned courtship continued with Beth. They'd gone full speed ahead before. This go around, the couple would try slow and steady. Jackson shared many dinners at the Masons' table, sat in the parlor under Hamilton's watchful gaze, walked Beth round and round her frozen garden. Took her for drives in Belle. Went to the movies and the diner. Waiting out the changing seasons, their bond became unbreakable.

On a warm day in April, Jackson mounted Ricky Ricardo for the first time in nearly a year, the pain at a bearable level. Finally, able to do what he loved. Ride. Beth was waiting for him, sitting on her pasture fence. At the sight of him back in the saddle, sitting straight and tall, she was brought to tears. He reached out and swung her up, settling her snug in front of him. They galloped full tilt across the field, pulling up short as her mother and father stood up in the gazebo and approached the fence.

Hamilton looked up at the young couple and met Jackson's gaze. His arm came up around his wife. "Well, Katherine. It looks like we're planning a wedding."

୧୬୧୬

Everyone gathered round the patio table at the Henry House. Ella had baked a dream of a strawberry layer cake to celebrate Jackson and Beth's official engagement. Once the dishes were swept away, Landon stood up and lifted a glass of wine. Everyone raised theirs to join in his toast as he spoke his piece. "This is a very special day, indeed. It does a man proud to see his sons prepare to marry and make lives of their own."

His voice became hoarse with emotion and he took a sip from his glass before he could continue. "I know that Hamilton and Katherine may not have believed our son would be well enough to take care of their daughter. Ella and I knew otherwise. Jackson has always been a determined sort. Once he sets his mind on something, that's it. I think in part due to the fact that he's the oldest—that, and his accident have really strengthened his resolve. I couldn't think of a better choice than Elizabeth. We've always been very fond of you, watching you bloom like a flower all of these years. I guess we should have had an inkling that day in church, the one involving a frog."

Everyone chuckled while Beth blushed and dipped her head, holding on tightly to Jackson's hand. He thought Pop was done until Landon cleared his throat and leveled his gaze on Beth's father. There was steel behind his smile and his green eyes had darkened, serious in a way that was not the norm.

"I'm very glad that you came to the realization that you were wrong about our son, Hamilton. When you came tearing in that morning before Jackson was injured, spouting off that you didn't think he was good enough, Ella and I were quite hurt. We've been friends a long time, and I consider your feelings to be a slap in the face." It was Elizabeth's father's turn to flush and he began to stammer an apology, but Landon raised a hand for silence.

"We live well here and lack for nothing. It might not be the high life, but it's a happy one." Landon stepped forward and pressed a hand to his oldest son's shoulder. "We also take care of our own. Even if Jackson needed our help, we would have made sure he was taken care of. Being the kind of man he is—being a *Henry*—he'll manage to give Beth a good life."

Hamilton stood at this point and approached his childhood friend, extending a hand as a peace offering. "Landon, you're absolute right. I was completely out of line. I hope that you'll accept my sincere apology and realize that I questioned their relationship simply because I'm crazy—crazy for my daughter. I know now that the best has been right in front of me all the while. Your son stood by my Elizabeth when we feared she would slip away from us. I'll never forget that." He had to look down as a sheen of tears covered his eyes.

Jackson's father accepted the handshake and smiled, mischief glinting in his eyes. "I'm really glad you realize that, Hamilton. You'd best sit down while I explain to you just how good my son's prospects are." Mr. Mason obliged, easing himself back down slowly beside his wife, waiting for the other shoe to drop. He didn't have long before it came down with a bang.

Pop motioned to the young couple and had Beth and Jackson join him, putting an arm across their shoulders, his smile getting wider by the second. Any bigger and it would split his face in half. "You probably don't realize that my parents' house on the property next door is intended for Jackson. Now that they've relocated to Florida, they have signed it over to him."

Jackson's mouth fell open and he became light-headed once more. It appeared to be a day filled with exciting news for everyone. As the group began to chatter, his father stopped them again. "That's not all. They've put money in trust for each of our sons for their wedding day. Ella and I have added some as well, not to mention the savings that Jackson has faithfully been building up all these years whenever he sells horses that are his own or performs training services for others." There was one more pause while everyone held their breath. "Jackson has about $20,000 to get started. I'd say that's a pretty good nest egg, wouldn't you, Hamilton?"

Jackson had to sit down then, the strain of the day catching up to him, compounded by the bomb his father had dropped. He almost wished for his cane for a support system. Beth sat in his lap, giving into sobs while everyone congratulated the couple and Hamilton fell over himself to apologize, stating, "Never again will I judge a book by its cover. I will take the time to read the pages, front to back, and discover everything they hold."

That night, after everyone left and the dust settled, Jackson sat on the porch and took Beth's latest letter from his pocket. When she had time to write, he did not know, perhaps when she helped his mother in the kitchen. She'd slipped the note in his pocket as the Masons prepared to leave. The moonlight was bright, illuminating her words. The thoughts running through her head made his heart begin to thump.

Jackson Landon Henry,

You are my heart and I could not live without my heart. Ever since we both were hurt, I've only thought about how short life is and being with you.

I keep thinking about you and your horses. You are magic with them, like the Pied Piper. Who can blame them? I've been following you for as long as I can remember. I can easily picture what our life will be like together and I can't wait for it to start. You stuck it out and didn't give up. Because of the man you are, we will be married soon. Because of the man you are, I love you.

Love,

Your Beth, One Day Closer to Mrs. Henry

CHAPTER 13

September 2, 1957:

Thanks to Emmett, Wyatt, and Pop, Jackson's horses were installed in the barn on *his* property. Every time he realized his grandparents' place had passed into his hands, Jackson felt near to bursting with pride. The ladies of the church, Beth, and their mothers had descended upon the place, cleaning it from top to bottom, adding decorative touches, setting up house from a woman's perspective, and planting cheerful red blossoms, a tribute to love, in the flower boxes out front.

Jackson had already moved in to take care of his herd. On their wedding day, only two days away, his future wife would join him. His arm was bruised from pinching himself. He kept waiting for the moment someone would tell him this was a dream or the instant Clyde Peabody would appear and take her away from him. "Hello, earth to Jackson. Are you in there?"

Beth sat straight and tall, at home in the saddle. She'd taken to riding Lucy with ease since he gave her the mare the year before. One would think the little horse would be tired after the journey from the Mason homestead, but the opposite held true as she shot forth with a burst of energy at the first glimpse of Jackson and Ricky Ricardo. The riders let the horses take the lead, galloping across the pasture at an easy lope, the wind tugging at Beth's hair, a golden banner unfurling behind her.

She never failed to take Jackson's breath away, looking more beautiful each time that he saw her. The air had cooled, adding a hint of crispness with the approach of fall. She had dressed appropriately in jeans, tall boots, and a plaid flannel shirt in a medley of reds. What he wouldn't give to undo those buttons—*Two more days. Behave.*

Lucy finally slowed by an apple tree on the far edge of the property, munching contentedly on apples that had fallen to the ground. Ricky Ricardo apparently believed in the philosophy, "If you can't beat them, join them," taking his fill beside his mate. Jackson was happy to have them together again.

He'd missed Lucy, but not as much as Beth. Each time the thought of being without her crossed his mind, it nearly tore the heart from his chest. Thank God Hamilton Mason came to his senses. "You're looking awfully serious," she told him, reaching over to take his hand that was resting on the pommel.

He gave a little start and a sheepish smile. "Just thinking how much I want the next two days to fly by so you'll be here all the time, so I can make sure this is real." He lifted his chin and gestured to the horses. "They're happy."

She leaned in close and kissed his cheek. "Almost as happy as us." That was all the encouragement he needed to let go of the saddle and hold her precious face, brushing her lips with a hummingbird kiss, settling in for more.

"Jackson," she whispered, her eyes drifting shut as the color rose in her cheeks.

That pulse in her neck was doing a mad dance, fluttering wildly by the unbuttoned collar of her shirt. She licked her lips, a move that drove him to distraction, and held onto his waist for support.

"Jackson, we'd best stop or I'm not going to be able to wear that white gown in good conscience. How about you get me some of those fresh apples so I can make you an apple jelly for our honeymoon breakfast?"

No matter how many times he'd offered other options, she insisted they spend their honeymoon in their new house. She wanted to start their new life right away.

Proving to have considerable strength of will, he set his forehead on hers and waited for his breathing to settle down, along with his heart. A swallow and a grin later gave him the ability to slide out of the saddle and climb up a tree. He congratulated himself on the fact that his back hardly gave him a twinge, that he *could* climb a tree once again. He started loading apples in his shirt, reaching for an elusive sample of rosy perfection, only to lose his balance and tumble onto the ground.

"Jackson!" She was down in a flash, kneeling beside him. He'd had the breath knocked out of him and his back was throbbing, but Jackson still managed to snort with laughter. She swatted at him and pelted him with an apple. His response—to pull her down for another kiss.

Eventually, they came to their senses, gathered the fruits of his efforts, and filled the saddle bags for a leisurely journey back to the house. Dutiful as always to the horses, Jackson and Beth rubbed them down, finishing with a thorough brushing. Shutting them in stalls side by side where they could cheerfully whinny to each other or brush noses allowed their owners to walk to the house, light at heart.

"I must be a mess. Are you sure you know what you're getting into?" Jackson held Beth's hand while she giggled and pulled grass from his hair. He shrugged and dipped in for a kiss. She set her hands on his waist and gave a few more practice runs at a skill that was coming along quite well.

"I wouldn't want anything else." She leaned her head on his chest and they stood quietly on the porch while the breeze made their ladybug wind chime sing. Beth's father had hung the gift himself, wishing them blessings upon blessings.

"Come on now, we'd best get you cleaned up and presentable for dinner at my parents." They were supposed to do a rehearsal of sorts, but Jackson didn't need to practice what his heart already knew how to do without any instructions, saying "I do" with every beat.

He humored her and opened the door, giving a little bow. "Ladies first," Jackson told her with a wiggle of his eyebrows. Unable to resist temptation, he gave her backside a little swat on the way in, making her giggles rise up around them. Stepping inside, he picked her up and swung her in a circle, nearly dropping her as a loud shout rang out, "Surprise!"

The entire town, or close to it, appeared to be crammed within the new Henry house. Men and women alike, as well as children of all ages, surrounded them, bearing gifts, lifting their glasses, calling out congratulations. In one corner, a small band began to play in celebration. Both sets of parents, as well as Wyatt and Emmett, stepped forward to greet them with arms and hearts wide open, Beth's grandparents, uncle and aunt right behind them.

"Happy Jack and Jill Party!" Katherine called out, kissing the couple on the cheek. "You all did this so quickly, we needed to come up with something fast. We thought it would be easier to get everyone in on the act so we could put our heads together to get you what you needed."

Stunned, neither Jackson nor Beth knew what to say.

They were ushered into the living room and planted on the couch. From there, guests passed by to wish them well, bring them drinks, and deliver heaping plates of food. Next came a mountain of gifts. The community humbled them with their generosity, proving how much everyone cared. The music continued to play and couples started to sing along or dance. It was a down home celebration, helping a young couple to set off on the right foot in their married life.

When the last guests had left, except for the immediate family, Katherine wrapped an arm around her daughter's shoulder and gave her a squeeze. "Don't worry about the mess, sweetie. A crew of us will take care of everything tomorrow." She kissed the top of her daughter's head, then Jackson's cheek. "You kids are so blessed and rightly so. You're father and I will be waiting outside while you say good night."

Jackson's parents and brothers said goodbye next and joined the Masons outside, leaving him alone with Beth. The two stood in the middle of their living room, gazing at the pile of gifts that were beyond belief. "I just can't believe it. Did you know anything about this?" He pressed a hand to his forehead, unable to believe his eyes.

"Not a thing. We have such good friends and neighbors." She stepped into his arms and simply let him hold her. Her heart beat was fluttering against this chest. Protective, he grazed her forehead with his lips and ran his hand down her hair. She looked up at him and he fell into the blue, drifting for a minute or so until Beth gave him a kiss and brought him back to the here and now. "Good night, Jackson. Only one more after tonight." She turned and walked away, blowing him one more kiss before stepping into the night.

He found himself at loose ends after all of the excitement died down. Being a quiet person didn't mean he

liked living a solitary life. He missed the twins, their mischief and crazy schemes, Mama's attentive ways and her
cooking, Pop's commentary and company. Add the anticipation of making his home with the woman of his
dreams, humming through his veins and filling his brain,
and settling in was long in coming.

He cleaned the place up the way a woman would like,
storing the gifts in the spare room. Beth would want to
have a hand in finding a permanent place for them. Poking in the refrigerator didn't tempt his taste buds. There
was nothing good on television. In the end, he set the radio on low to fill the emptiness. His back troubled him,
probably due to his stint with the tree. He took a hot soak
and turned in for bed. Sleep came for him reluctantly, a
dream of Beth by his side shaking him awake just before
dawn. Might as well get to work.

Working with a herd of ten didn't take much time.
While there was the added challenge of taking care of all
of his horses by himself, Jackson had his routine down
like clockwork, thanks to Pop teaching them all so well.
By mid-morning, all of his chores were done. He stood at
the fence and gazed out at his prize possessions—Lucy
and three young fillies in one pasture, and Ricky Ricardo
and four stallions ranging from ages two to four in the
other.

Rounding out the group was none other than Cinnamon. Jackson had taken a shine to her, even after all of
the commotion the day the Mason family came to call.
She'd make a good balance to a steady, male bloodline.
All in all, he had a fine start for a man starting out on his
own. Counting his blessings, Jackson's thoughts turned to
his family. He'd best show his gratitude and lend a hand
back home.

Emmett was mucking out stalls when Jackson
emerged from the quarter mile path that connected the

two pieces of property. His younger brother did so with the same enthusiasm that he felt for most everything in life, whistling a cheerful tune while working at a rapid pace. Wyatt had one of their stallion's hooves held against his thigh while he treated a sore spot before putting on a new shoe. Glancing up at the sound of footsteps, his face broke out in a playful grin. "Aww, look who's back already. What's the matter, Jackson? Did you miss us?" He tossed him a wink while Emmett came up next to his brother, hooking an arm around his neck and puckering up.

"Will you two cut it out?" A bit of a wrestling match ensued while Jackson laughed all the while. "Get off of me! I came to see if you needed any help, and yes, I'll admit I missed everyone even though you two won't let me live it down. Where's Pop?"

Emmett poked a thumb in the direction of the field. "Breaking Blackie. Pop could probably use you. That rascal already proved to be cantankerous this morning, got Pop's dander up." As Jackson turned away, his brother caught him once more around the shoulders for a bone crusher of a hug. "We missed you too, Big Brother. Place isn't the same without you."

Before anyone put on an emotional display, Jackson headed out to the pasture, wearing a smile that he couldn't shake. His father was leaning against the fence, red-faced and out of breath while a two-year-old, black stallion munched contentedly at the meadow grass, tail flicking away the flies. Blackie appeared to be completely unperturbed. Landon Henry was another matter.

"Want me to take over, Pop?"

His father huffed in exasperation, his patience worn thin. He cast a glare at the horse that could strip paint off the walls, but managed to keep his counsel, giving his son a pat on the back instead.

"Be my guest. That...*animal*...is full of spit and vine-
gar." He winced and began to massage his stiff hip.
"That's the third time he's argued with me, forcing me to
get off and mount again. My bones don't want to move
that way. Three strikes and I'm out. Getting too old for
this."

Jackson couldn't help but grin as he squeezed his father's shoulder. "You could never get too old, Pop."

He turned to the horse and set his hand on Blackie's
back, giving him a chance to become accustomed to his
presence. Without appearing to take notice, the stallion
continued to graze. Jackson took his sweet time, running
his hand over the great shoulders, down the strong column of his neck, and began to scratch between the ears. If
Blackie was a cat, he would have purred in contentment
as evidenced by the way his head pressed against Jackson's fingertips.

"That' right. I'm not so bad, now am I?" He moved
down to stroke the velvet on his nose and pulled out an
apple which was devoured quickly while Jackson moved
on to give the same attention to Blackie's other side.

His father shook his head. "Your bribery must have
something to do with it. All of the horses around these
parts know that you are a regular Johnny Appleseed."
Jackson nodded, humming softly all the while, and taking
hold of the pommel. Closing his eyes, he took pause and
listened to the rhythm of the horse's breathing. Sensing
no change and heartened by how relaxed Blackie remained, he decided to go up and over.

In one fluid movement, practiced and mastered after
countless times since he was a small boy, Jackson seated
himself firmly in the saddle, pushing down the pain that
threatened to take his breath away with the sudden
movement. He *would* continue to do everything that
needed to be done to be a horse farmer, back be damned.

His legs pressed in hard enough to ensure his security, loose enough in order to avoid panic in the horse. The stallion snorted and tossed his head, glancing back at his rider. Jackson gave him a nod, took up the reins and gave a slight nod in return. Blackie's response—to set off at an amble, like this was old hat. Jackson was grateful—a gallop, and he'd feel it in every hoof beat.

Pop took off his hat and threw it on the ground. "Unbelievable! I don't know how you do it, son, every time. You're getting a reputation as a miracle worker for all of the lost and hopeless causes in this town."

Jackson shrugged looking back at his father and couldn't help but grin. "What can I say, Pop? I had the best teacher ever. You taught me everything I know." His father waved off the compliment, not one to boast or brag. His son wasn't either. Rather than talk about his accomplishments, Jackson would rather concentrate on the animals. He let Blackie have his head and rode off across the fields, a good way to keep himself occupied. All the while, his heart continued to count down. *One more day.*

Mama was only too pleased to include her son for lunch. A stretch of good weather continued with blue skies and sunbursts dazzling the eyes, perfect to eat outside. A brisk breeze blew, making the leaves swirl, dance and skitter across the yard as the family sat at a picnic table and enjoyed fried chicken, fresh potato salad, and the tail end of the greens from the vegetable garden. Conversation flowed easily like a river and Jackson basked in its warmth, comforted by the nearness and familiarity of his family. He didn't say much himself, but didn't need to. The Henrys were accustomed to their oldest son's ways. His presence at the table was enough.

"Jackson, why don't you stay over tonight and sleep in your old bed? I know you must be lonesome and truth be

told, I've missed you something fierce." His mother set a
generous slice of chocolate cream pie in front of his
place, a great temptation. How could he deny any request
from the woman who bore him, especially when accom-
panied by his favorite dessert. "Em and Wy can take care
of your horses for you in the morning, right boys?"

Wise to the ways of her children, Ella held two plates
under their noses as she made her request, entrancing
them with her culinary powers. She hesitated before setting them down, giving the twins the eagle eye. Wyatt
jabbed his brother in the arm, making him jump.

"What? Oh, yes, of course we will." Emmett's smile
grew and his eyes widened as she set the pie down for
both.

"No doubt about it." Wyatt plunged his fork into his
ample slice and opened wide for a big bite before pulling
up short with a puzzled expression on his face. "Wait a
minute, what will we do?" Laughter spilled out from everyone as their mother swatted her youngest sons on the
head and settled down to enjoy her own piece of pie
along with her husband.

As soon as their plates were empty, Wyatt jumped up
and thumped his twin on the back. "Let's go check on
those horses now, make sure Jackson is doing everything
right." They disappeared, making themselves scarce to
avoid clean up committee.

Used to their ways, no one hounded the boys. Landon
said they'd be tamed soon enough, let them be young,
before heading back to the barn. Jackson helped his
mother to bring everything in the house, volunteering for
dish duty while she put things away. At one point, he
turned away from the sink to catch her burying her face
in a dish towel, trying to contain her tears. "Mama,
what's wrong?" He stepped toward her, concerned. Ella
rarely cried.

She flapped her hands and let out a laugh that could easily become a sob. "It's just so hard to believe my baby will be leaving the nest for good tomorrow. I'm so proud of the man you've become, so very proud." Choked up with emotion, she could only smile at him while the tears kept coming.

He took her in his arms and set his chin on her dark mess of curls. So strange to switch roles this way. Only yesterday, she had been the one to tuck him on to her lap and sing him to sleep, songs that still played in the corners of his mind. "Mama, I'll only be across the way, just the next house over. I'll likely be over here so much, you'll want to get rid of me."

She lifted her head to take his face in her hands. "Never, Jackson. Until my last breath, I will never grow tired of looking on this beautiful face and those of your brothers. I love you with all my heart, baby boy."

"I love you too, Mama." His voice went hoarse and his eyes were smarting. He had to swallow hard to keep from embarrassing himself, although that wasn't possible in front of his mother. His brothers, on the other hand, were a different story entirely, bursting into the kitchen at that vulnerable moment of all times, pretending to cry their eyes out, blowing their noses in their sleeves, holding on to each other for support. Mama batted at them both with her dish towel, laughing just the same.

When Emmett could finally settle down, he stopped carrying on long enough to pull an envelope out of his back pocket. It was pink with doodles of flowers covering the front and back while a giant heart graced the center with the words, 'Beth and Jackson Henry, forever and ever, amen.' Wyatt took the note away from his brother, running the paper beneath his nose and sighing dramatically, a hand pressed to his heart.

"My oh my, I do think this is a love letter. It looks like

a love letter. It smells like a love letter. Perhaps I should open it up to confirm that it is filled with mushy, sentimental nonsense." Jackson lunged to snatch the letter away, only making matters worse. Emmett grabbed hold of it next and the boys took off, in rare form. The only recourse? To go after them.

In recognition of this being a last chance to involve their big brother in hijinks, the twins really gave him a run for his money. Out to the barn, up to the hay loft, pouncing from one bale to the next only to slide down the rope that hung from the window. Off to the pasture next, over the fence and up a king of an oak tree, one they'd climbed many times over since childhood.

Emmett made his way out on a large branch and hung upside down, dropping it to Wyatt below. A devilish grin lit his face as he ripped one corner ever so slightly. The old Jackson could move quick as a wink when he had to. Ignoring the fire that flared up at the base of his spine, he shot forward, hooked an arm around his brother's neck, and stole his note away. Huffing and puffing, everyone took a breather.

When their hearts stopped galloping, Wyatt pressed a hand to his brother's shoulder. "You know we were just messing with you, right? We wouldn't read your mail. Beth left it on your front door." The twins headed back to the house, intent on giving the groom-to-be a little privacy. "By the way, the horses were fine. We'll check them again tonight and in the morning."

"Thanks, boys," Jackson called after them, a smile creeping up as they walked away. Yes, he would miss them. Once certain he was alone, he held the envelope to his nose. The scent drifted up and said, *Beth.* Picturing her taking care with her note, drawing doodles and spraying perfume, he took his time to open the envelop. Butterflies fluttered in his belly, as they always did when his girl came to mind. Sucking in hard with the bone-deep ache that had taken hold since his stint chasing after his brothers, it was a moment before he could focus on the words on the page. Once he did, his back was the last thing on his mind.

Dear Jackson,

I'm sorry that I took so long getting this to you. I had my final dress alterations today. Grandma's dress seems like it was made for me. My mother wore it too and I've only needed the length taken in a bit, otherwise, it's perfect. The veil is so beautiful, like angel's wings, floating around me when I walk. It has to be since it will be carrying me to you. When I stand in the mirror and look at myself, in my mind I see the little girl who put on her mother's slip and a lace tablecloth on her head, imagining that Jackson Henry would be the one to say, 'I do.' Maybe I knew then what is coming now.

Tomorrow is the day that it will become real. I don't think I can sleep a wink. Otherwise, all of this might be a dream or just a memory from long ago. Tonight, when I'm counting every heartbeat, staring out my window, I'll be thinking of you. After tonight, there will be no more lonely nights and I will be a Henry. I feel like I should hold my breath—or pinch myself black and blue. This is going to be the longest night of my life. I love you, Jackson Landon Henry.

Love,
Your Beth

CHAPTER 14

September 4, 1957:

The very first day of the rest of his life. Unable to sleep, Jackson got up early, lingering over his horses, waiting with the dawn to meet the sun. Bathed in its warm light, it felt like a baptism. His back hurt, more than usual, payment for horsing around with his brothers. Fearing he'd wrenched it, a long soak was in order and he prayed. *Please God. Help me make it through this day.*

Time seemed to stop that morning. Sitting at Mama and Pop's for a huge breakfast, watching the hands tick on the kitchen clock, he swore they actually started to go backward until Pop pulled Jackson into his parents' bedroom so they could all get dressed in their rented tuxedoes.

His brothers continued to ham it up. After all, this was not the most important day in *their* lives, just an opportunity to put on a display, dance with some pretty girls, and find some sort of mischief or another.

Pop finally shoved them out of the room and locked the door, shaking with laughter. "I'm sorry, but *I* need some peace and quiet, even if you don't." He took the opportunity to adjust his tie and did the same for the groom. "There now. You look good, Jackson. You remind me of myself on my wedding day."

Landon cleared his throat and shifted his attention to combing his hair, a distraction from a well of emotions that ran deep. "I still can't believe my boy is getting married. It seems like yesterday that I held you for the first time. Not long from now, you'll do the same with a little one of your own."

Jackson followed his father's lead, smoothing his hair, adjusting the front of his jacket, adding a splash of cologne as a final touch. His reflection gave him a start. Today marked a true rite of passage into adulthood. A grown man stared back at him with no trace of the boy. The muscles in Jackson's lower back tightened into a knot, the pain rippling across his face, making him look even older. Landon saw it before he could hide his discomfort.

"You've been overdoing it, haven't you? Stay put." His father stepped out, returning with a glass of water and two pills. "Take these. You have a long day ahead of you. You'll need all the help you can get."

Jackson was grateful for his father's foresight as he waited at the front of the church, able to stand tall as he waited for his bride. Breaking tradition as his best *men,* Emmett and Wyatt acted like saints for once after threat of bodily harm if they didn't. The wedding would be a simple affair with no pomp and circumstance, what with only a short time for preparation. Beth's best friend from early school days, Sandra Roman, was her attendant in a plain dress of robin's egg blue with a bouquet of snowy carnations in her hand, her flaming hair pinned back and threaded with blue blossoms. On a normal day, Jackson would have noticed how pretty she looked, given her compliments, but he only had room in his head for one girl.

The pews were decorated with white ribbons. The ladies of the community had outdone themselves, combining forces to dress the place with flowers galore, the last of their gardens gladly donated for the cause. The church was packed to bursting. An open invitation had been extended to the members of the small community, family and friends. They were only too happy to join in the celebration.

As Jackson scanned the crowd, he saw Mama dabbing at her eyes while Pop wrapped an arm around her in comfort. His surviving grandparents, Grandma and Grandpa Henry, flew up from Florida to join his parents in their pew. His neighbors, the shopkeepers in town, and all of his teachers from grade school on up were here to share in his day, not to mention many of his classmates. On Beth's side, he could see the Mason grandparents, her aunt and uncle, and an assortment of friends. In a town of their size, everyone knew everyone.

Many of the women were pulling out their tissues in preparation for the ceremony, waving at the groom with tremulous smiles. The men were giving a thumb's up or staring at their feet, reluctant to show any displays of emotion. All in all, the town sent a wave of love his way and Jackson couldn't be more grateful that everyone could be with him.

The first strains of the Wedding March began, humming through the floorboards, strumming through his veins, drawing all eyes to the central aisle. The congregation rose to its feet as Wyatt, standing closest to the groom, jabbed his brother in the ribs and Emmett let out a low whistle. Jackson's mouth went dry and his heart began to skip. For one instant, he thought about fainting dead away, but stood his ground because missing a single second of her walk to him was unthinkable.

His Beth looked like something heaven sent, a vision

in lace and satin in a gown that could have been custom tailored for her. A long, film of a veil covered her face yet could not hide the flush in her cheeks or the sparkle in her patch of sky eyes that were pulling him in. He knew in that moment that this was the reason he had been born.

Forever and a day later, Hamilton brought her within the groom's grasp, but not before he lifted her veil and kissed her cheek. She was crying a little, smiling brightly at the same time. As one hand reached out to take Jackson's, the other let her father slip away in a symbolic changing of the guard. She turned to give her full attention to the groom and he brushed her cheek with his lips, tucking her in close and setting off a ripple of laughter amidst the congregation. She tossed him a wink and Jackson held on to her even more tightly. He would never let *her* slip away from him. She tilted her head, her gaze locking with his, and neither of them could move.

The pastor began to speak, but he didn't hear the words or see anything but the woman beside him. *Amazing. She is absolutely amazing. How did I end up with her?* At some point, Sandra stepped in for the bride's bouquet so that they could exchange rings and vows. *Do you take this woman, to have and to hold, to love and to cherish, in sickness and in health until death do you part?* Her beautiful face, still in that hospital bed, counting her every breath, flashed in his mind and his hand tightened on hers. *I will NOT let you go.*

Her words rang out in the church, echoed, and circled round his mind. When Jackson said "I do," he made the most solemn, unbreakable promise of his life and Beth gave it in return.

The haze didn't lift from his brain even when the pastor told him to kiss the bride. Dipping her down until her hair brushed the floor, listening to the thunderous applause of those gathered, Jackson was only aware of her—the slight weight of her in his arms, her scent encircling him and making him dizzy, the warmth of her touch as her breath skittered over his skin, her lips brushing his as her eyes set his soul on fire.

He didn't remember walking outside or all of the people they received except for their families and the bittersweet moment when Mama congratulated them both. Breathtaking in a deep blue, her dark curls pinned up with flowers woven in between, Ella Henry was a wonder. With the exception of his bride, Jackson had never seen a woman who could compare. She gave Beth a hug and kiss first, reserving her son for last.

Mama took pause with Jackson before the guests poured out of the church. She held her son's hands, pinning him with her dark, glistening gaze. "Let me just look at you." Her eyes filled and her lip began to tremble. "My baby is truly a man. I wish you only blessings upon blessings, Mr. Henry." Pop handed her his handkerchief and led her away before they all were a sniveling mess.

The pictures, the reception, the toasts, and the dances were all a blur with one constant: his Beth. She was like a torch, burning brightly beside him, and he was a moth consumed by her flame. He had to stay close to her, to touch her, brushing her with his arm or his fingers, his eyes never straying. The last dance began to play and everyone cleared the floor as the bride and groom took center stage.

He swayed round and round, her head tucked under his chin, his eyes closed as he felt her heartbeat fluttering against his chest. If only they could stay in each other's arms forever. The whole world could go away. As long as they had each other, it would be enough. The final strains of the song died out and their feet ceased to move. His bride tipped her head back to look up at her husband, the tears spilling from the corners of her eyes. He wiped them away ever so gently, as if he held something as fragile as spun glass, and pressed his lips to hers. "It's time to go home."

"I can't wait." When they walked out of the hall to let their honeymoon begin, their hands remained linked and she was equally attentive to him, rising on tiptoe to brush his cheek with a butterfly kiss. Both were taken completely by surprise to discover a horse-drawn carriage waiting for them. Wyatt and Emmett wore top hats and treated the couple like royalty, opening the door to the white carriage, offering the bride and groom a hand, bringing them to their destination in style.

Jackson climbed down first, Em grabbing hold of his shoulder as he did and passing him a grin. "Don't you worry about your horses tomorrow. We've got you covered. You've got some important business to take care of."

Jackson dipped his head, his eyes burning as his throat thickened. "Thank you, fellas, for everything," he called out to them. Wyatt gave him a pat on the back and pointed to his *wife*, spurring the groom to step forward, gather her in his arms, and carry her over the threshold. His back argued with every step and Jackson argued right back. He *would* carry his bride to their room. The door closed with a resounding click and they made their way through the house, up the stairs, and to the bedroom, kissing and giggling the whole time—until they stepped inside.

A hush fell over the room, except for the sound of their breathing. Jackson wouldn't have been surprised if Beth could hear his heartbeat, thundering, fit to leap from his chest. Someone had come up ahead and lit a soft lantern. Rose petals were strewn across their bed and champagne sat chilling on the bedside table. A negligee—a sheer, white slip of a thing—waited on Beth's pillow.

"Excuse me a moment. I have to go freshen up."

Blushing furiously, she picked up the delicate garment
and went to the bathroom to change. Funny. God willing,
in a few minutes, they'd both be stepping out of their
clothes, but modesty won out first. He didn't have long to
wait. Thirty seconds later, she stepped out and turned her
back to him, flushing a deeper shade of crimson. "Can
you please help me with my buttons?"

He took his time with each tiny, delicate pearl,
fighting tremors in his fingers. When he reached the last
one, he bent his head to kiss her delicate, white neck.
"Don't be long now." She nodded and flitted to the door
in her stocking feet, her shoes in her hand. Turning the
knob, she looked back over her shoulder to blow him a
kiss before disappearing.

That brief glimpse of the fair skin of her back and the
fine hair trailing down her neck really cranked the anticipation up a notch. To stomp down an attack of nerves that
was rising fast, he slowly and methodically removed his
shoes, his tie, his coat, and his cufflinks, unbuttoning his
shirt last and leaving it loose. The bathroom door closed
with a click and he heard her breath come out in a rush.

Turning around slowly, his did the same. She wore her
gift from their mothers, a white sheath that fell to the
floor while clinging to her body, revealing curves that he
didn't even know she had. As if that weren't enough
cause for temptation, her negligee fell low on her chest,
giving a tantalizing hint at what lay beneath the delicate
material. A slit up one side showed her leg to her advantage, and a lacy robe draped over her shoulders,
transparent and hiding nothing, a tease to say the least.
He glanced down, fighting to catch his breath and stop
his head from spinning to see racy pink toenails gleaming
up at him. Would this woman ever stop surprising him?

She stepped in front of him and lifted her chin. There
might be a glimpse of nervousness in those eyes, but no

fear. "Jackson, show me what it is for a woman to truly know a man." The words were a whisper. He nodded once and swallowed hard. Denying her anything was not possible.

He began with her hair, freeing flower buds and her curls from hairpins, allowing them all to fall and trail down her back. His hands ran through their shining glory, lifting them high and letting them rain down.

"Oh, Jackson, touch me," she begged, tipping her head back and exposing her milky throat. He pressed his lips to the fluttering pulse at the base of her neck, but couldn't stop there.

He scattered kisses across her shoulder, earlobe, jaw, and cheekbone, eventually skimming across her lips. He took his sweet time, drawing out the moment. "I don't know everything myself, being this is my first time and all, but I think we'll figure it out together."

He removed her robe and she slipped his shirt from his shoulders with fingers that quivered. Jackson leaned in to press a palm to her chest and could feel her heart racing. He pressed one kiss over that steady beating, let her warm to him, and scooped her into his arms. A few steps and they tumbled on to the bed together, surrounded by pillows, covers, and petals.

Together, they discovered what it meant to truly know each other, and he felt no pain.

Dawn tiptoed in, waking Jackson. He turned his head to see Beth sleeping, roses blooming in her cheeks, hair mussed, breathtakingly pretty. Beside her, a note was on his pillow.

Shaking his head, wondering when she got up to write it after their eventful night, Jackson read her letter.

My dear husband,
Oh, I love the old-fashioned ring from days gone by. I

want to lay claim to you and let the whole world know that Jackson Landon Henry is mine. It's four-thirty a.m., and I woke up, afraid I'd fallen into a dream and you weren't really here. I spent a long time simply watching you as your chest rose and fell and your breath kissed my face. I'm selfish. I want to wake you and have more time with you, but I'll be patient and wait. I was right about having our honeymoon here. There is no place else on earth that I would rather be than here in the home that we will make ours.

Thank you for being mine, for making me yours, for the wonder of last night and the wonder that you are. I know that there will never be enough years, days, hours or minutes to spend enough time with you, but I vow to try. Before last night, I couldn't breathe, hear or see. Now everything is in brilliant color. For the rest of my days, I will gladly give you all that I have and all that I am, even though it won't be enough to do you justice. Let's get started right now. I'm sure you will be a very good teacher when it comes to all matters related to love—and I will be your eager and willing student. I love you, Jackson Landon Henry.

Love,

Your Beth, otherwise known as Elizabeth Mason Henry the First (and Last!)

Jackson felt eyes watching him and set the note down to discover that his bride had awoken. He skimmed his fingers over her hair, smoothing it from her face, and dropped a hummingbird flurry of kisses on her jaw, her cheekbone, her forehead, and her nose. He left her lips for last to give them their due. Her breath came out in a sigh.

"Good morning, *husband.*" Her mouth tugged up in a smile as her words made him grin right along with her.

God, he liked the sound of that.

"Good morning, my bride. Did you sleep well?" She nodded and lifted her head so that she could return the favor of his kisses. His breath trailed out and he rested his forehead on hers. "Is there anything I can get you?"

She shook her head and her hand entwined in his hair, drawing him near. "Maybe a little bit more of what we had last night. I don't know about you, but I could use some more practice. I need to perfect a few things that I noticed."

Her laughter was close to the surface. Dip down and they'd both be shaking. He hooked his hands on her waist and kissed the warm, sweet skin on her neck. "You know what they say. Practice makes perfect and this is one thing I don't mind putting time and energy into if it makes you happy."

Beth touched a finger to his lips to silence him. "It makes me *very* happy. Stop talking, Jackson, and show me how it's done." They didn't get out of bed until well past noon. Both were a *little* tired and a little sore, but they were glowing as if alight with candles from the inside out.

છબળ

"Casey, call the vet. Tell him I need him now. Ricky's worse." Not waiting for a response, Emmett turned and ran back to the barn, as if rushing would make any difference. He felt like the sand of an hour glass was pouring through his fingers, too fast for him to make it stop. He'd been watching the stallion for the past several days, paying close attention to a cough. After a lifetime of working with horses, Emmett had it pegged as influenza. He wouldn't let his father's old stallion out of the barn, brought in an electric space heater and humidifier to make him comfortable, kept fresh water on hand. For a young horse, equine flu usually worked itself out. Ricky wasn't young.

At over thirty, the old boy was in trouble. Early that morning, Emmett went out to check on Ricky Ricardo. The stallion was struggling to breathe, coughing with a terrible rattle in his lungs. The only thing to do now? Call in the expert, get some powerful meds, and hope for the best.

A half hour after Casey's call, Doc Pearson rolled into the drive, trudging directly through the snow to the barn. Bundled up to his nose with a heavy coat, scarf, and hat with ear flaps, he resembled Elmer Fudd. At any other time, the elderly man would've been comical. Emmett couldn't find humor in anything today. He offered his hand in welcome even as he drew the good doctor to the horse's stall. "Thanks for coming out, Doc."

He nodded, his snowy eyebrows drawing together in concern as soon as he saw the old stallion struggling in the straw. "Wouldn't think of doing otherwise for Jackson Henry's favorite horse."

Ed Pearson had treated Landon Henry's herd for years, then Emmett's father's. His expression softened for a moment as he gave Em a nod. Doc Pearson understood why this patient in particular meant so much.

Lowering himself down on knees that creaked, he didn't beat around the bush. His stethoscope made an appearance in short order and then he pressed his ears to the broad, heaving chest. A wince and Ed pulled back. "Lot of fluid in there. Might be a bacterial infection. I'll do what I can."

That sent a stab of fear through Emmett, making his heart throb painfully. Bacterial respiratory infections were a concern for a youthful horse in top form. For Ricky, it would be a battle for life and death.

Doc Pearson made a valiant effort, injecting a powerful combination of antibiotics, including penicillin. He took his measures to the next level, pulling a mask out of his bag to give the ailing stallion something similar to a nebulizer treatment, forcing more intense doses of medication directly to the lungs. He stayed all day by his patient, alongside of Emmett, listening to the wheeze that wracked the horse's body. Come late afternoon, as the sun headed for the horizon, he set his hand on Emmett's shoulder. He didn't say a word, didn't have to. His red-rimmed eyes told the truth.

It didn't take long after the veterinarian left, walking slowly, as if he'd aged ten years during that visit. It felt like only minutes. By nightfall, the great black was gone. Resting his head on the horse's neck, still warm, Emmett understood how his father felt some ten years ago when they lost Lucy. That first gift to Mama, the mare had been a precious connection to their beginnings. It was the only time he saw his father break.

Emmett closed his eyes, hand on the muzzle that had turned white over the years, and let the sobs take him. They shook him to the core for in letting go of Ricky Ricardo, another piece of Jackson Henry went with him.

He didn't hear Casey come in, didn't even notice her fighting her way down to the straw, until her hand rested on the nape of his neck. She was quiet, just sitting beside him. Her presence eased him, the fact that he didn't have to explain it to her. As a doctor, as someone with personal losses of her own, she *knew*.

He was stiff, the bitter cold setting in, turning him to ice. He felt his wife shiver and that pulled him away from the sharp edge of pain that stabbed him in the gut, making it hard to breathe. Wordlessly, he stood and pulled a horse blanket over Ricky's still form. Arrangements would have to wait. Fighting tears that threatened to blind him, his hand reached out and waited. His wife latched on, allowing him to give her the leverage she needed to get to her feet. A small cry escaped her when she saw his face and she wrapped her arms around him, holding on tight.

He took what she had to give. When his lungs would finally fill with air again and his feet would listen to the command to move, he made for the house with Casey tucked under his arm. She helped him out of his winter clothes. He stood there, swaying, unable to figure out what to do. She slipped off her coat and boots, took his hand, and gently led him to the chair that was a refuge when he was hurt. It continued to be a haven. He sank down and gathered her warm, full body into his arms, the need to hold her strong enough to set him to quivering. She picked up the journal from the table, understanding how much he needed that link to his father that night. As her voice broke the silence, Jackson Henry's words brought him to life.

CHAPTER 15

November 24, 1957:

Jackson came in with a chill in his bones, shivering. With the cold, the persistent ache in his back kicked it up a notch, wearing him down. As if overnight, the air had turned, losing all remnants of a fall that had lingered long. All the signs were there, the trees practically bare except for a few brown, dead leaves rattling in the wind.

The animals had scattered, squirrels making last minute preparations to hole up, the rabbits gone, the geese sending up their mournful farewells.

He could smell the snow coming. Winter was about to settle in. He hoped for a doozy, one that would slam them hard and make them button up inside for hours on end. Shorter days and longer nights meant all the more chances to cuddle up close to his heart's content. Maybe she'd give him a back rub.

The thought of her, never far from his mind, made him smile. Fighting the last of the tremors running through his body, he took off his coat, gloves, and boots, going slow because his body wouldn't let him do otherwise. He looked forward to getting warmed up with some coffee, a hot meal, and the arms of his wife.

Forget about everything but the last. He could live on her sweet kisses and only ask for more.

Padding on silent, sock feet, he followed the sound of music to the kitchen. Beth was humming along to the radio, swaying while cooking at the stove. Something smelled heavenly. His eyes drifted closed and his mouth began to water. His wife was one heck of a cook and lunch was so long ago, he could barely remember it. Propping his hip against the door jamb, Jackson stood still and simply gloried in watching her.

Her hair was piled up somehow. He liked when she did that because he could pull it down and run his fingers through the strands of sunshine as they fell around her face. It wouldn't take much to get entangled as she snagged him for a kiss. He might even need some artificial resuscitation and knew someone who could take over the art of breathing for him. His heart started to trip and he had to clamp down on that train of thought or his hyperventilating would give him away.

Beth wore his flannel shirt, an old green one that was her favorite. He'd catch her holding it to her face and inhaling his scent when he dropped it in the laundry. Jackson wasn't even sure she washed the thing. Early in the morning, when she built up the fireplace, she'd slip the shirt on over her nightgown or when visiting him in the barn. Too bad her clothes were not what a man would wear and too small for him. If Jackson could carry a piece of her all the time, he would. His heart would have to do the job for him.

Her sleeves were rolled up to her elbows, the tail hanging down to that delicious dip behind her knees. His mouth went dry when he realized she wore nothing else. Following a long stretch of legs to her bare feet, her red nail polish set him to grinning. Shaking his head at the marvel that was his wife, he stepped up behind her and set his hands on her waist. "Mmm. You are nice and toasty, the best thing I've seen all day."

She gave a little squeal and a jump, spinning around to playfully slap his chest. "You sneak! I didn't even hear you come in and your hands are like ice. I can feel them right through your shirt."

She caught both of his hands in hers and rubbed them fast and furious, finishing the job with a kiss. They moved back to resume their position while her hands moved up to stroke his cheek.

She tipped her head back to kiss him. "I can smell the cold on you. You're wearing winter. How was your day?" Beth waited for him to skim her lips with his before turning around to stir the pots on the stove. The steam danced up around her face, making her flush and causing tendrils of hair to curl up against her cheeks.

Jackson couldn't resist pushing them behind her ears, getting a little nibble when he did. She gave into a fit of giggles and turned around to burrow against his chest. "Here, I'll be your heater. Now answer my question, Mr. Tall, Dark, and Quiet. How was your day?"

"Long. Hard. Good. Like all of my days with you waiting at the end of them. Lucy's pregnant." She pulled back, her eyebrows creeping up to her hairline while her blue eyes lit up with a glow that couldn't be contained. "I had a feeling. Soon after you brought her here, I noticed how she settled down and that's not Lucy. She wouldn't take any advances from Ricky Ricardo either. I've been keeping an eye on her and noticed she's missed her cycle for a few months now too. Ricky Ricardo seems very proud of his accomplishment. He's quite the doting mate. That old boy won't let her out of his sight. I think we should see a foal come sometime in June."

His mouth clapped shut before he rambled on more. Jackson didn't know how, but Beth always loosened his tongue. He'd said more in his time as her husband than in an entire lifetime.

She looped her hands around his neck. "That's wonderful. We should celebrate. How about a hug and a kiss?" She looked up at him, her head tilted to the side, eyelashes fanning out against cheeks that were turning brighter by the second.

"Oh, I think that could be arranged." Reaching around her, he turned all of the burners down on the stove. "They can wait. I'm not that hungry, not with you to fill me up." He ran his hands up her sides, to her shoulders, finally cupping her precious head, marveling at her neck as fine and fragile as the stem of a rose. Her jaw tipped up, breath rushing out in a sigh, lips parted. He lowered his mouth to hers, taking his time to come in for a landing and stay a while until his breath caught in his throat and he froze. Damn his back for flaring up now.

Beth broke off the kiss, hands on his collar, and eyed him with reproach. "Your back is bothering you. Go stretch out on the sofa and I'll get some of that liniment that works so well."

Jackson didn't argue. He'd learned his wife had some magic of her own in her touch. She pulled up his shirt and went to work, rubbing the ointment in, filling the air with its minty scent. Pressing hard enough to make his hands tighten into fists, she murmured an apology. It always hurt more before she eased him. Her deft fingers kneaded at the knots and sore bones until the muscles finally went loose. He could breathe again. Jackson tucked her in under his chin. His arms wrapped around her and she did the same, letting him soak up her warmth. His wife was better than a blanket, a hot bath, or the longest of summer days.

"What did you do all day?" He murmured with a voice gone hoarse, lips skittering over her golden head.

"Cooking. Oh, and I almost forgot. I painted my nails." She held out a hand like ladies did in days of old. He tilted his head to kiss her fingers, flipping them over to get to her palm and then leaving a trail that went all the way to her shoulder. He marveled at the music of her laugh. "You charmer you. What about these toes?"

She wagged a foot in front of him, making the polish flash in the last of the sunlight streaming through the kitchen window.

"I'm not kissing your toes." He couldn't help but chuckle at her pout. "Now, you must have been up to more than that. What about…let's see…what did you say on the Fourth of July? Something about choir practice, canning, quilting, and the fine art of needlepoint. Did you perform all of your womanly duties?"

"Oh, I did those first thing this morning after you headed out to the barn. I'm a fast learner. I've got this running a house business licked." She kissed him once more and glanced at the stove. "Unless you want my masterpiece of a dinner to be ruined, you'd best let me get everything laid out. You go on and clean up. No dirt at my table. Now git!"

She gave him a playful swat on the bottom and turned back to the stove. Jackson took the stairs with just a twinge of stiffness, humming all the while in anticipation of sharing her meal and company. After a quick dousing under a steaming shower, he pulled on his pajama bottoms with a long-sleeved jersey. He still couldn't quite shake the chills. Best to get down to the table and let Beth do some more of her magic.

She began with grace, bowing her head to give the simple blessing that started every meal at their table. He found himself staring at her, first at her shining crown, and then her beautiful face as the dishes were passed between them. If anyone asked what he ate, the only honest answer would be something good. His wife made him forget everything but the pleasure of her company. From time to time, she reached out to skim his hand with the tips of her fingers and her eyes touched on his, burning with the same need.

They spoke little throughout the meal, making quick work of cleaning up when they did the task together. Beth lit a candle and set the flickering jar on the table. Turning to him, she held out her hands, the invitation clear, and they began to sway. Many a night had closed with the two of them dancing in the kitchen. Jackson couldn't think of many better ways to top off his day, although every alternative involved his wife. "You look better in my shirt than I do. Maybe you ought to keep it."

She smiled up at him, her eyes flashing in the candle's dim glow. "It smells like you and feels like you. When you're outside, it almost seems like you're here. I missed you. I do every day. "

"I missed you, too." He gave her a long, lingering kiss that made her go loose in his arms. He picked her up, snuffed the candle with one breath, and shut off the music. "Looks like we have some catching up to do. Let's make up for lost time then."

He carried her up the stairs against all protests. She was worth any discomfort. Watching the frenzy of her pulse, fluttering at the base of her neck, his heart was doing the same dance in his chest. Pushing the door open with his foot, he crossed the room and laid her out on their bed, stretching out beside her.

She rolled into him and kissed him again and again, as if there would be no stopping. Eventually, her head dropped beside him. "Do you think this missing each other will wear off? Will it ever grow old between us?" There was a little tremble in her voice, as if she was actually afraid he could stop feeling the way he did.

Jackson took her hand and pressed her palm against his chest. "Feel that? As long as my heart keeps beating, you will be on my mind and if we're not together—a minute, an hour, or a day—I will miss you. You're my other half. I need you or I'll never be whole."

He'd gone and done it, turned on the water works. That was something he could remedy, kissing her cheeks, drying them as his fingers wandered over her smooth skin. Beth rose up, bracing her arms on either side of his head and gave him a kiss to set his head to spinning. Sleep was a long time coming, but the late hour was well worthwhile.

სახ

"*Beth*?" Jackson awoke with a start and came up quick, his breath hissing between his teeth as he did.

Fast wasn't doable anymore. His heart was a trip-hammer, doing a mad flutter in his chest. Something wasn't right. He reached across the bed for his wife's reassuring warmth. She wasn't there.

Swallowing hard, he attempted to calm his breathing and get his pulse to stop skittering. Straining his ears, he listened for sounds of movement in the bathroom. Nothing. Sliding out of bed, cursing his back for making him go slow like an old man, he checked the second floor and went on to the first. Maybe she couldn't sleep, got up to get a drink. There was no sign of her in the kitchen—and the front door was ajar.

Now his heart was at a gallop as he slipped on his barn boots and shrugged into his coat. He stepped outside, shuddering with the bite in the air. Big, fat snowflakes were fluttering down and enough had fallen to make it easy to follow her small foot prints—*Dear God, she's in her bare feet!*—out to their front yard. Moving forward at a jog, ignoring the pounding at the base of his spine, he peered through the darkness to see a still figure in white clinging to one of the mighty oaks that towered over the lawn.

Putting on a final burst of speed, he reached her, peeling off his coat with hands that shook. Beth had no jacket and trembled like a leaf, her toes turning blue in the moonlight as her cotton nightgown fluttered around her. She didn't like to sleep in flannel, said Jackson was more than enough heat for her. Touching her now, she felt like ice. "Beth, honey, come into the house. You're freezing, sweetheart."

She stared at him with unseeing eyes, tears streaking down her face. "Jackson! I can't find Jackson anywhere! I've got to find him! He needs me!"

Her voice rose up in a piercing wail and the sobs weren't far behind. She was sleep walking again. It had started soon after she came home from the hospital. Doc Smith said it was likely caused by the day she hit her head.

Jackson wrapped his coat around her and scooped her up in his arms, even as she fought against him. "Please! Put me down! Help me find him! *Jackson!*" Her scream ripped through the night and made him freeze. Her arms began to flail and she kicked. It might as well have been a hummingbird fluttering against him. At wit's end, he pressed his hand to the nape of her neck and clamped his mouth down on hers. *Beth, come back to me. Please!*

Finally, she went limp in his arms, even as he took big strides toward the house. Had to get her inside, get her warm before she caught her death. As they stepped into the welcome heat of the house, she looked at him with a sleepy smile and murmured, "Jackson? This is quite a wakeup call."

Pushing down the panic that had seized him from the

moment he awoke in an empty bed, Jackson managed a grin even as he headed straight for their bedroom. "You took a little trip, love. You were out wandering in the snow."

Her eyes widened in alarm, her lip trembling and she was shivering so hard her teeth chattered. Her arms tightened their hold around his neck as the tears started once again. These nighttime episodes frightened her, bits of lost time when she had no idea what happened.

Small wonder they terrified him. Kicking off his boots, he didn't even take his coat off of her, just pulled it closer around her body. He set her down and grabbed more blankets, piling them on top of her and slid in beside her to wrap his body around her. Small sobs rose up as she continued to shake. Inside, he was quaking just as hard. "Shh. It's all right. You're all right. I've got you and I won't let anything happen to you." He willed his words to be true.

Gradually, the shivering eased and her breathing leveled off, her head pressed against his chest. He hoped the hammering of his heart wouldn't wake her. What if one day she wandered so far away—physically or mentally—that he couldn't bring her back? The rest of the night, he lay awake, staring at the ceiling. As the pale light of dawn washed over her face, he kissed her in the middle of the forehead and she snuggled closer, a contented sigh slipping out. *Please God. Help me to keep her safe.* Finally, badly needed sleep took hold of him.

The next day was Thanksgiving. Beth beat him out of bed. Normally, she would lie with him until he went in the shower, sometimes joining him although that tended to distract them both from the things that needed doing. Once again, Jackson considered those days worthwhile. Today, she was already preparing in the kitchen.

He could hear cabinets, pots, and pans banging. This

would be her first, large family feast that she would play
hostess and she wanted to get it right. His parents, brothers, her parents, grandparents, uncle and aunt would all
be sitting at their table. Jackson had put the extra leaves
in the night before and brought down the table cloth. The
table looked a mile long and his wife planned on filling
every inch with one tasty dish after another.

Shaking off a lingering fear from her nighttime escapade, he smiled in anticipation of her incredible cooking.
He would enjoy watching her pull off a great success. He
hummed in the shower, pulled on his long johns, jeans,
heavy socks, and her favorite flannel over his t-shirt. Had
to make it smell right according to her. Jackson came
downstairs, whistling all the while, pulling up short when
he heard the sound of retching.

By the time he rushed into the kitchen, Beth was
standing over the garbage can, hanging on until her
knuckles went white. Her eyes were watering and the
color had washed out of her face. He stepped up close
and wrapped an arm around her, only to feel her trembling. "Are you all right? Is it anything to do with last
night?" There were times when her episodes left her with
a nasty headache and made her sick to her stomach.

She waved him off, smiling shakily. "No, no. Don't
you worry about that. Lots of people sleepwalk. Just
makes things more interesting, right?" She attempted to
laugh it off, but he knew underneath it all she was scared.
Like he was.

She set a hand on her stomach. "It's jitters, I'm sure.
My stomach is flip flopping, thinking about today. I hope
everything goes all right. I'm so afraid I'll mess up at
something." Her breath came out in a rush as she blew
her bangs away from her face. "Phew. I think it's over
now."

He rubbed her neck and against her protests, scooped

her up in his arms. He carried her to the table, sat down, and pulled her teacup in front of her. "Everything is going to be just fine. You're amazing." Sliding his plate of toast that she'd prepared across the table, he gestured toward it with his chin. "You have a little bit to eat to settle your stomach and some tea. Mama always used that remedy when my stomach was queasy and it worked every time."

Her mouth turned up in a grin and Beth did as she was told, taking a few nibbles and sipping the hot brew. Slowly, the color came creeping back to her cheeks. When she'd finished everything, he breathed a little sigh of relief. "Feel better now?"

She nodded and hooked her arms around his neck. "You are such a good man, Jackson Henry. Now it's your turn. Be a good boy and eat your breakfast." She poured him a steaming cup of coffee from the carafe in the middle of the table, adding cream and sugar last.

Taking the cup, he couldn't help but steal a kiss before drinking it down to the last drop. He scalded his tongue, but that was nothing compared to the heat that rose up between the two of them. She picked up a piece of toast and held it to his mouth, her eyes closing half way as her smile grew while she watched him eat. "Don't you let any go to waste, you hear?"

He obliged her, getting to the last bite and kissing her palm in the process. Jackson pulled her close, burying his face in her neck. "Do you think...will your dishes be all right for a few minutes?" His voice had gone deep and throaty, the sound strange in his ears.

In answer, she stood and went to the stove, turning all of the knobs down to low. He was waiting for her at the door, his hand palm up, calling for her. She caught it and let him draw her along. "What about the horses? Can they wait?"

"They'll be fine. I'm the one who can't wait."

He pulled gently and insistently, to the top of the stairs, across the threshold of their room, to the bed that was still unmade. Good thing because they were about to mess everything up all over again.

Dinner was an absolute smash. His wife was positively glowing, wearing a new red dress that hugged her curves and only made him want to peel the pretty fabric from her body.

Everything was perfect, from the fall mums that decorated the table, to the napkins folded just so, and the beauty of their wedding china!

As for the food, everyone left the house groaning, filled nearly to bursting from one delectable dish after another. It was a small wonder anyone could move. Every member of the family couldn't compliment Beth enough and Jackson was flooded with pride to think that she was his.

That night, after the door swung shut for the last time, she stretched out on the couch in her pretty dress, groaning softly. He sat down and began to massage her bare feet, making her groan louder, but this time in pleasure. "Thank you for an incredible day. You were absolutely amazing. You'd think that you did this every day. I couldn't picture any other way I'd want to spend Thanksgiving."

Beth sat up, brushing his lips with a butterfly kiss. Then lying flat once more, she curled up in a ball with her head in his lap.

Jackson knew the instant she fell asleep when her body went soft and loose while he stroked her hair. His heart was full to bursting with gratitude. He didn't need a day to be thankful. Every day was Thanksgiving with her.

The next morning, his letter was tacked on the barn door, like the first notes she'd given him. Somehow, she had slipped out before he woke up.

Sitting down on an old, wooden stool, her words lit a fire and warded off morning's chill.

Dear Jackson,

You kept thanking me yesterday, but it is I who should have thanked you, a thousand times over. If every fish in the sea were to land at your feet in gratitude, they wouldn't be enough, or every blade of grass, or every grain of sand...you get the picture.

I am so grateful that you are mine, my husband to have and to hold. Because of you, I look forward to every minute in every day and whatever is coming next. I know that this life will be wonderful with you in it. Even when hard times come, as they must come in every life, with you by my side, I can make it through. Thank you for every day that you share with me. You are a gift beyond measure. With every breath that I breathe and every beat of my heart, I will say the words that make me most thankful of all—I love you, Jackson Landon Henry. Thank you for always helping me to find my way back when I am lost.

Love,
Your Beth

CHAPTER 16

December 15, 1957:

Something was different about Beth. A little rounder around the middle and softer, like the mares when they were ready to foal. She'd been tired too, falling asleep earlier and lingering in their bed. Thank God, there'd been no more episodes of nighttime wandering. More often than not lately, Jackson found her curled up in a bundle of covers when he came out of the shower. She'd give him a sheepish grin when he woke her, pulling him in for kisses and cuddling.

But one thing had been troubling him—her throwing up every morning, either first thing or mid-morning when he came in to check on her. He set his journal down and pushed the bathroom door open. He'd started writing to steady himself, to stomp down the worrying that came each time he heard her retching. His being sick or tired was bearable, but not his Beth. If he could trade places, they'd swap in a heartbeat.

She was kneeling on the floor, shaking as another spasm came over her. He grabbed a washcloth and doused it in cold water, pressing the refreshing coolness to her forehead as he rubbed her back. "Hey, you all right? This has been happening a lot lately."

She gave him the ghost of a smile and stood up, leaning on him for support while he handed her a glass of water. She rinsed her mouth, took a few sips, and brushed her teeth. "It's over now, I think. Maybe I'm allergic to you!"

Her eyes crossed and she stuck her tongue out, but at the hurt he couldn't hide, she stepped in close to hug him hard. "Oh, Jackson! Don't look at me that way! I was only teasing. I'm right as rain now, really. I think I overdid it shoveling the walk. We got six inches or so in the night."

Reassured by the sparkle in her eyes and the color creeping back into her face, he wrapped an arm around her as they walked downstairs. "Beth, you didn't need to shovel. I've got that covered." He pulled out a chair for her and gave her a demanding look that said *Sit or else!* Within minutes, her first cup of tea was placed in her hands and a plate of toast was waiting for her.

He busied himself at the counter, making a cup of coffee and a few slices of toast for himself, worry gnawing at him about his wife. Turning around, he caught her nibbling half-heartedly at her breakfast. Seeing his scrutiny, she tossed him a smile and made more of a dent, tucking away one slice and sipping at her tea. Everything appeared to be staying put. He leaned closer and kneaded the nape of her neck, making her eyes close in pleasure and her body loosen. "Next time, let me worry about the snow."

She waved a hand at him in dismissal as he cleaned his plate and slugged back his coffee to get started on his day. "It's only the path, for Pete's sake! I knew you'd have your hands full with the driveway. Don't think I didn't see you leaning on that shovel a while ago. Your back is troubling you, but you won't stop."

She caught his hand as he moved to clear the table,

pulling him in for a kiss. "Thank you for helping me. So many men would say this is women's work. That's why I wanted to help you with the shoveling. This is *our* work. I don't expect you to do it all and you feel the same way about me."

Jackson set down the dishes so he could devote a little more time and energy to his wife. Cupping her face in his hands, he set his mouth on hers and a little zing went straight to his heart. Happened every time. "It doesn't feel like work if it is for you or with you. I'm heading outside now. You take it easy and I'd better not see you trying to single-handedly run this entire place. I need to feel like I'm useful for something."

She stood and tucked herself in his arms, inhaling his scent and making him a bit unsteady on his feet with her proximity. "I won't, promise. Do you think we could play in the snow later, when your work is done? Maybe make a snowman and get our Christmas tree? I know it's early, but I just love the scent of pine and doing the decorating. Christmas can't come until the tree is in the living room. I already know where I'll put it, right in front of the big window."

What a kid at heart! His fingers trailed through her hair, giving a little tug so that he could catch her lips one more time. Oh baby. Going out to the barn was getting harder by the second. "You know you've got me wrapped around that itty, bitty, pink painted pinky. If you asked me to hand you the moon, I'd be looking for a way to toss a rope up there and bring it on home to you. Let me get out there and we'll go out after lunch."

She grazed his lips with hers and started his blood to humming. His eyes slammed closed and he couldn't help but growl a bit. "Elizabeth Mason Henry, you are a mean tease. You let me go right now or I'm not getting any-thing done today. I expect one of your best back rubs tonight, all right?" He carried her smile with him out to the barn and stayed warm even as he cranked the tractor and took care of the plowing. All the while, there was a song in his heart named Beth.

The snow was fluttering down in huge flakes, turning the world into a giant snow globe, when Jackson let the horses out into the pasture. They'd eaten, had their water filled, and just like the little girl peeking out of his wife's eyes, were feeling frisky with the change in weather. Only Lucy took everything in stride.

The mare was downright sedate, ambling out into the middle of the field, Ricky Ricardo beside her. A few times he nudged her with his nose and she rested her head against him.

Jackson leaned against the fence, taking a breather and waiting for the ache in his back to ease. He studied the pair, noticing how the mare was getting a full belly.

The veterinarian had paid her a visit at the beginning of the month, cracking, "She's healthy as a horse!"

All humor aside, everything looked good for Lucy. Her calm demeanor, the fact that she was taking it easy, and all outward signs were common for a horse preparing to foal. Jackson's mind turned to Beth, comparing her symptoms of late. Could she be—

"Jackson Landon Henry, get in here for some lunch before you turn into an icicle!" His wife stood on the back porch, once again wearing his flannel shirt. Her cheeks were rosy in the cold, her blue eyes snapping as the wind caught her hair and whipped a golden cloud around her face. She didn't have to ask him twice.

Lunch was a short, cheerful affair and they were back outside, his wife so bundled up in winter gear, it was hard to tell where the clothes ended and she began.

She ran ahead of him, but he caught up in a burst of speed, bringing her down in the snow, where they both rolled until she was over him, pinning him down. "Now I've got you. What should I do with you?"

He shrugged and poked his tongue out to catch a snowflake. "I'm sure you'll think of something."

That was all Jackson needed to say and her lips were on his, heading them both toward a meltdown. Panting and feeling overheated, he struggled to form words.

"Listen, we're going to do something scandalous and dangerous if you keep this up. We're talking hypothermia and I really don't want anyone to find our frozen, naked bodies out here in the snow."

Snorting with laughter, Beth pressed her head against his chest. In a flash, he switched positions with her, his hands holding on to hers while he stared into her bright eyes.

"Not so much fun now, is it?" He playfully dipped down and rained kisses on her face, watching the color come up in a rush, melting the snowflakes away.

"Oh, I'd say it's the most fun I've had all day." She positively purred at him and craned her neck to give him another kiss that stole his breath away. He pressed his forehead against hers and heard her chuckle softly. "Okay, Mr. Henry. I think you're right about getting up. Besides, my drawers are getting wet!"

He rolled off her and froze, his breath coming in a hitch. "One problem. I *can't* get up." He closed his eyes and gritted his teeth. Why did his back have to be difficult now of all times? He pressed his forehead to the ground and waited for the pain to ebb. "Just need a moment and I'll give it another go."

Her answer? To roll up his coat and slip her tiny, nimble hands under his shirt. She started kneading and rubbing, making him groan. She paused and he reached back for her, squeezed her arm. "Keep at it. You don't know how good that feels."

Slowly, the worst of the kinks worked their way out.
Beth stood up and extended her hands to him, her feet
planted. Surprising him once again with her strength, she
gave him the leverage he needed to stand. They continued
on across the field, Jackson moving stiffly, but he kept
moving. She wanted a snowman. By God, his girl would
have one.

They set to work. She was excellent at rolling and
packing. She even helped supply the muscle, sparing
Jackson a hernia or worse when he had to get the middle
in place. She went a little easier on him with the head.
Pulling a carrot, scarf, and colored stones from her pocket, she proceeded to give their creation a face. Standing
back to examine her handiwork, he gave a little bow and
pulled his knit cap off his head. "There, Frosty. You're
looking good."

Beth held onto Jackson's shoulder, grinning from ear
to ear. "He is, isn't he? Our first snowman together, as
husband and wife. The ones we made as kids don't count.
This one was born at our house. Let's make snow angels." Like quicksilver, she was onto the next thrill, making it near impossible to keep up. Helplessly, he shrugged
and joined in.

Several angels later, a few choice snowballs sailed
through the air, and they ventured into the woods, examining one tree after another. "No, not that one. That's a
spindly tree, and although I love all of God's creations, I
want a big, fat tree for our first Christmas, one we'll never forget. Besides, our living room is huge with that high
ceiling. We have to do the space justice."

His wife discounted a few more selections, finally
clasping her hands together and jumping up and down
before a fine specimen of a blue spruce. "Oh, this is the
one! This tree is perfect, don't you think?"

Jackson looked her selection up and down with a critical eye. "Looks like a back breaker to me." He grumbled until her face fell and he gave her a wink to make up for his poor choice of words. "I'm just teasing. I can picture it on Christmas morning. You've picked the right one."

Pulling the saw off of his back, he set to zipping back and forth, making the teeth sing as they bit into the bark and the chips began to fly. Gradually, he made his way farther and farther into the trunk. And all the while, his back was screaming. No matter. His Beth had to have her tree.

"All right now, stand back! Timber!" He'd always wanted to say that. The beauty fell with a thud, the scent of pine rising up around them. She clapped while he ran a sleeve across his forehead, thankful he wasn't a lumber jack. Tying a rope around the trunk, they managed to drag the tree back to the house between the two of them, sharing the load. A few times, Jackson stumbled. He feared the pain was going to get the best of him, but he stomped on it and pushed on.

Beth was in rare form when they muscled the evergreen into the living room. Peeling off her heavy clothes, she flitted through the house in her sock feet, bringing out the tree stand, boxes of ornaments, and hot cocoa, in that order. Once Jackson had the tree in place, she pushed him into a chair and handed him a steaming mug while she had fun. He didn't have the heart to tell her how much he hurt and didn't let on, but the longer he sat, the worse he felt.

He had no clue how long his wife spent in her decorating flurry. Every minute was paid for in pain. He made appropriate noises and smiled at her efforts. If she asked him to move, there'd be a better chance of moving Mount Rushmore.

He tipped his head back and dug his nails into the arms of the chair, praying he'd find the strength to get up.

If he could just get in a hot shower, maybe round up the heating pad, take some pills—

"Jackson Landon Henry, what is wrong with you? You're white as a sheet and you're trembling." Beth's palms were pressed to his cheeks. He looked up at her to find her blue eyes dark with shadows. "Why didn't you say something? I can't help you if you don't talk to me!"

Angry tears glittered as she flounced away. He could hear cabinet doors slamming and the sound of water running. He made to get up and had to bite off a curse. Nope. Moving was one luxury he couldn't manage, not yet.

His angel of mercy returned with a tray laden with all sorts of odds and ends. Liniment. A heating pad. A towel that had been soaked in boiling water. A glass of water and some of his horse pills. She set it down with hands that shook and gave him the medicine first. "Take it. Next time, maybe you should have some *before* we go out—or maybe we shouldn't go out at all. You try to do everything, Jackson. Maybe you just have to admit there are some things you can't do anymore."

He slammed the glass of water down on the end table and moved forward with a jerk, snatching her hands. "Don't say that! I can do anything I set my mind to, anything I have to do. You didn't marry an invalid!" His teeth clamped together as the pain reared up and nearly broke him.

She shook her head and set a butterfly kiss on his lips. "I know—I know that, Jackson. It's just—you don't have to be so tough all the time. Now lean forward a bit."

He did as she asked, jaw clenched so tight he thought his teeth would be ground to powder. She rubbed the liniment in first, then set the hot towel at the base of his spine. The intense heat felt so good he almost cried. Given enough time to get fired up, she set the heating pad on his back next.

Beth kneeled before him, hands on his knees, anxiously waiting. Sweet relief finally came for him. Jackson took her in his arms and propped his chin on her head. "Thank you for taking such good care of me. I'm sorry I bit your head off."

She sniffled and brushed at her cheeks. Somehow, her lips still turned up in that beautiful smile that lifted his spirits more than anything else. "You're welcome. I think your middle name should be stubborn. Now you listen to me. I am going to run a hot bath for you. You *are* going to take a good, long soak, and then to bed. No arguments."

She stood up and offered her hand. Slowly, struggling through the stiffness, Jackson gained his feet. He looped an arm over her shoulder and pressed his mouth to the shining curtain of her hair. "I won't argue if you go with me." As usual, they found the way to each other.

In the next week, his house underwent a transformation. Each afternoon or evening, he would come inside to pick out her latest addition to the holiday decor. Besides the main attraction, a tree that absolutely dazzled the eye in the full splendor of tinsel, ornaments, and lights galore, Beth truly exemplified the phrase, "Deck the Halls."

She draped pine garland across the mantel, over the doorways, and up the railing along the stairs. Delicate white lights gave the impression of fairies' glow, tucked within the pine needles of greens dressing anyplace imaginable. Snowmen, Santa, and other figures appeared as if by magic while candles lit a beacon throughout the house. Many times, Jackson would walk in to hear Christmas songs playing while tiny flames flickered softly to light his path.

The kitchen was under siege as well. While Mama was doing Christmas dinner, his wife cranked into high gear

to make Christmas cookies, cakes, and pies. She also prepared a turkey for their Christmas Eve because they
needed to have a feast in their own home to celebrate the
day. Besides, that would mean leftovers. The bird had
been thawing for days in the refrigerator and would be
ready for roasting when the time was right.

Beth was a complete whirlwind, setting his head to
spinning as she seemed to be everywhere at once, out to
the market to do the shopping, back at home knitting a
Christmas present, or lost in a pile of paper and ribbons
during a wrapping extravaganza. Jackson stumbled upon
her in the midst of the latter endeavor and couldn't resist
having a little fun. He placed a ribbon on her head and
gave her a kiss. "You know, I wouldn't mind unwrapping
this package to get a look at what's underneath." Her
packages were abandoned as she led him upstairs to their
bedroom and they both did a bit of unraveling.

In the midst of all of the preparations, he would catch
himself watching his wife, wondering at his good fortune.
He didn't know what had made him deserve her, but he
must have done something right. While she was busy
with her latest project, he ventured off to his parents' to
work with Pop on Beth's present. They'd been at it for
weeks, tucked in his father's wood shop, building a rocking loveseat for their front porch. Two days before
Christmas, they finished the final touches, sanding it
down until it was smooth as a baby's bottom, saving
staining for last.

When the job was done, Pop poured a cup of coffee
from his thermos and handed it to Jackson. "You've done
fine work, son. She's going to love it. Trust me, after
nearly twenty-five years with your mother, I know what
makes women tick. A girl like Beth will love this more
than jewels, furs, or anything fancy. It will mean the
world to her because you made this with your own two

hands. I'll bring it on Christmas morning, all right?"

Jackson nodded, sipping at the hot brew while his father did the same. "That's fine, Pop. I can't take all of the credit for this. You really helped me a lot."

Landon stood and wrapped an arm around his son's shoulders. "That's what fathers are for. I'm just so glad to see you as happy as you are and Beth too. I bumped into her at the grocery store the other day and she was positively glowing. Marriage looks good on the two of you. Now come inside and let your mother spoil you some. She made an apple pie with your name on it."

Jackson couldn't help but laugh as they stepped outside and were hit by a wall of cold air. Old Man Winter was here to stay and hanging on tight, digging in for the duration. "Well, I can't let that one get away. Thanks again, Pop."

His mother greeted her men at the door, taking their outerwear and giving them both her warm smile and kisses. Landon caught her up in his arms and danced her into the kitchen, dipping her in a bow and stealing a kiss when she came up. Hanging back and grinning hard enough to make his face hurt, Jackson knew why his marriage was so good. His parents had set the perfect example.

Christmas Eve finally came, a crisp but clear day. The wind whipped through the trees, making them sway and sweeping the snow into the air until it swirled or rushed away. Jackson hurried with his chores, keeping the horses in to stay out of the bitterness. All the while, he kept thinking about his present to Beth, hoping she would be happy. There was nothing more for her to give him.

He couldn't ask for anything more than his wife...or so he thought until he came in for dinner and found a note on the kitchen table, sitting next to a flickering white candle while Christmas music played softly in the background. He sank down in a chair and picked up his letter, his hands inexplicably beginning to tremble. As he started to read, his wife stepped up behind him, her arms looping around his neck and her chin propped on his head.

Dear Jackson,

I didn't want to say anything to you until I was absolutely sure. I had a feeling and I talked to my mother, didn't know for certain, so I dropped by Doc Smith's when I went shopping the other day. His exam and blood test confirm what I suspected. Sometime around July, you are going to be a daddy.

When I thought about all the things I could give you, none of them seemed good enough until the doctor gave me the news. This one is the greatest gift I will ever know and I'm so glad I can share it with you. I wish we could open it now and find out what's inside. It will be a long wait, but worth it in the end—like you. I love you, Jackson. Merry Christmas.

Love,
Your Beth

Jackson bowed his head as a few, fat drops splattered down on the paper. He could feel the flutter of his Beth's heartbeat against his back. To think that there was another life growing inside of her. He turned around and wrapped his arms around her waist, pulling her close and pressing his head to her middle. "I don't believe it. Already, you are giving this miracle to me. What did I do to deserve you?"

She laughed softly and kissed the top of his head. "I've asked myself the same question about you many times." They remained still for a few minutes, soaking up each other's love until she took his hand. "Jackson, won't you dance with me?"

To the ends of the earth, to the top of the mountains, to the bottom of the sea. He'd go anywhere with her and do anything.

෴

"I hate shopping!" Emmett sat on a bench in the mall, arms crossed, positively glowering while the holiday hubbub, crowds, and music swirled around them.

Casey blew out a great puff of air as she sat down beside him and tried to find her feet. They ached like the dickens and small wonder. They were the size of balloons. She rested her hands on her stomach, startled as the form within rolled from one side to the next in a giant heave. *Quiet down in there!* "We have to, Em! It's Christmas!"

"I don't need any presents. I've got you and little it will be here soon." He rested his hand on her belly, a grin chasing away his grouchiness as the baby moved under his touch. "There's a wildfire of a boy in there, wait and see." He sighed, grazed her cheek with his lips. "Sorry I'm miserable. I just don't like this. The crowds, the commercialism. Why couldn't everyone keep it simple?"

She smiled and kissed him back. "That's what I love about you." She winced at a jab down below. "Oof. Question Mark is tap dancing on my bladder. I need to find a bathroom—*again.*"

Emmett stood and helped her up. They worked their way to the opposite end of the mall. After that trek, Casey was beginning to agree with her husband's assessment of the situation. She went in the Ladies' Room, settled in, and just finished going for the hundredth time that day when a sharp pain nearly took her breath away.

Closing her eyes, she blew out slowly through her nose. Waited. Thought she was in the clear when another one hit. Realizing Em was probably about to hit the panic button out there, she left the stall and washed up, hands shaking. Another pain hit and she gripped the sink.

"You all right honey, want me to get someone?" An elderly woman stood at her side and touched her elbow.

Casey stared up at her white reflection, eyes gone round. "No," she said faintly. "My husband's right outside."

The woman smiled. "I'd say. He's chomping at the bit, about to come in."

Casey made her way out, had to hold on to the wall when another one shook her. Em was at her side in an instant grabbing her hand. "It's time?"

She shrugged. "Could be. Guess you don't have to shop anymore." He ushered her out to the truck within minutes, through a snowfall that made the whole world look like a snow globe. He helped her in, went around, and blasted the heat. "Hospital or doctor's office?" The hospital was forty-five minutes away, their local clinic about a half hour. "Your call, Case."

"Home. They're too far apart to go anywhere yet." He was white-knuckled the whole ride home, watching her closely. When they pulled in, she let out a long breath and gave him a shaky smile.

"False alarm. They're gone." She patted her belly, reassuring herself and her little occupant that all was well.

"Stay put." Em told her abruptly. He jammed the truck in park, killed the engine, and got out with a slam of his door. He walked around and scooped her up in his arms

"What are you doing, Em? I'm not an invalid. I can walk." Pushing at his shoulders was like trying to move granite.

"Don't argue with me." He fought with the door and kicked it shut with his foot. A few long strides and she was on the couch, her husband down on his knees, tugging her boots off with a yank, grabbing her coat next. "Now. You *are* going to put your feet up and you'll stay on this couch. Do you understand me?" His eyes flashed and he bowed his head. His grip on control was slipping.

She reached out and set her palm on the top of his tousled hair. "It's all right."

He shot up fast. "No, it's not! You're so damn stubborn, Case! You think you can do it all. You'd work in that clinic until you dropped the baby right there on the floor, pick it up, and return to business as usual. Thank God Paul and Sharon made you start your leave." The husband and wife team of pediatrician and OB/GYN specialist completed the trio at the Charlton Medical Clinic. They'd come to the consensus that there was no need for Casey to have her baby while on duty.

Pacing back and forth, Emmett raked a hand through his hair. "Good thing it came from them. Lord knows I certainly couldn't make you."

"You're one to talk, Emmett Henry!" She sat up fast, the heat rising through her body in a rush. *Great! A hot flash!* It wasn't the first in her pregnancy. Aggravation didn't help any. "I've seen you dead on your feet and you're still out there from dawn to sundown, so don't you tell me—ouch!" She winced, gripping her right side, and held her breath.

He dropped down beside her and laid his hand on hers, all irritation gone. "What is it? Are the pains back?" '*You catch more bees with honey*' drifted through her mind as Emmett pinned her with his golden eyes. They had snagged her from the start.

"No, it's just a cramp." Slowly, she let her breath out. "The muscles right here, over my pelvis, must be stretched to the limit." She grimaced with another twinge and started to rub.

Emmett took over, first the right, then the left hip. As

always, her body responded to his warm, strong hands. She dropped back against the pillow on the end of the couch and closed her eyes. "You always know what to do."

"Not right now I don't." He leaned forward and pressed his lips to her belly, then her mouth. His hand came up to stroke her hair. She met his gaze and saw that equilibrium had been restored. "I've never handled a pregnant wife before. I'm not doing a very good job."

He buried his face in her neck and she began to massage muscles that had probably been in knots from the instant she walked out of that bathroom. "You're doing fine."

"What should I do now?" He looked up at her expectantly, grinning in anticipation.

"First, take off your coat and boots. They're making a puddle on the floor." She got a rueful grin for that one. "Next, bring me herbal tea and make yourself a stiff drink." Casey gave him a wink. "Finally, relax and don't forget to breathe."

When both had finished herbal tea and they were wrapped up in a cocoon of a blanket, Emmett sighed. "I don't think I've relaxed in nine months."

She kissed him on the cheek. "Tell me about it. Read to me. Maybe that will help." He didn't argue, squeezing in beside her, rubbing elbows and sharing body heat as his voice filled the room.

CHAPTER 17

February 14, 1958:

It's a good thing you love horses so much because I'm going to look like one, soon." Beth rolled over, tangled in a mound of covers and wrinkled her nose as she peeked under the blankets. "No, make that a cow. What are you doing sitting there with that goofy grin?"

Jackson leaned over and braced his hand beside her head on the pillow, his other hand coming up to rest along her cheek. "Thinking about how crazy in love I am with you, wondering what I did to deserve an incredible woman like you, thanking my lucky stars for whatever it was." He'd been up since four in the morning, watching her sleep. He couldn't get enough of her. He dipped in to steal a kiss. "Happy Valentine's Day, Beth."

"Happy Valentine's Day to you." She grabbed hold of the lapels of his flannel shirt and drew him in for another sample of his lips, closing her eyes and humming a bit in pleasure as she did. "Mmm. I love the way you smell just out of the shower, that blend of soap, deodorant, and after shave, all mixed in with the scent that says Jackson. When you come in from the barn, it's even better because you carry the snapping cold with you. It makes me feel alive."

She smiled and winked at him. "Mmm-hmmm, I think I'm the one who should be saying thank you for a man like you to wake up to. You're toasty, like a heater, and your hair's still damp. Why don't you come back to bed and share some of that with me?" She flipped back the covers and opened her arms wide when her stomach protested with a loud grumble, making them both laugh. "Oh my, I guess that's my cue to make breakfast."

"Oh no you don't. You stay put and let me make it for a change." He rested his palm on the slight mound of her belly, his mouth curving up at the corners playfully. "Looks like we've got a demanding little critter in there. Get back under those covers and I'll be back in a jiff." He pulled the blankets back to her chin, tucking her in with one more kiss. She played along, closing her eyes.

He took his time, making her eggs the way she liked them, over easy. Two, golden slices of toast with butter, freshly sliced apples because his wife believed in getting as many fruits and vegetables as possible. Said if she was eating for two, might as well be healthy. Orange juice and tea because she couldn't take coffee, said the caffeine made her stomach do flip-flops.

Jackson set his coffee and toast on the tray as well, finishing the job with a long stem, red rose. He'd picked up a dozen the day before at the florist's and hid them, planning on doling them out one at a time. He took the stairs slow. Couldn't spill her breakfast on Heart's Day, now could he?

Stepping in their bedroom, his wife brought him to a standstill once again. She'd fallen back to sleep wearing a smile, a secret smile he'd caught many times as her hand rested on the precious gift hidden within. Her hair was strewn across the pillow in a golden curtain, a splash of sunshine, thicker and shinier. The flush of her cheeks never went away and they were fuller, making her even more beautiful than before. Right under his nose all that time, she'd showed so many signs, like his mares. How had he missed it?

He crossed the room and quietly set the tray down, sliding into bed and fitting himself against her body, spoon style. His arm wrapped around her middle, protecting her and the gift she carried. Beth let out a sigh and settled in. It looked like breakfast and the barn would wait for a little while yet.

Eventually, he slipped outside, content that they both had full bellies, but more importantly, enough time spent with each other to tide them over until later. He lost himself with his work in the barn, letting the horses out in the pasture so that he could muck out all of their stalls and fill the hay bags with fresh, sweet hay. He took his time and went easy. No letting his back get in the way today. Lucy kept nudging him from time to time, looking for an apple. Good thing he filled his pockets, making sure Ricky Ricardo got some for good measure.

He stood in the open door of the barn, watching his horses. Snow was coming down in a fine powder and a cold blast was picking it up and forming tiny cyclones that danced across the fields. Cinnamon pranced here and there, trying to catch the little whirlwinds, while some of the young stallions joined in on their side of the fence. *What a flirt!*

"Brrr! It's cold out here. I brought you some hot chocolate before you catch a chill." Beth was wrapped up in a red coat, cap, and gloves with a white scarf at her neck, a rose tucked behind her ear. Holding onto his shoulder, she stood on tiptoe to kiss his cheek. "I found a rose in the breadbox, on the mantel, and in the pantry. Any more surprises?"

Jackson shrugged. "Can't say. Then it wouldn't be a surprise." Feeling her shiver, he drew her away from the door and pulled it closed. They moved to the back of the barn where the fresh hay was piled up. If they leaned back against the bales, the bitter winds couldn't reach them.

"Thank you. I was just thinking about something hot." He hooked a hand at the nape of her neck and grazed her cheekbone with a kiss. "Oh, thanks for the drink, too." He wiggled his eyebrows and got another kiss for his efforts.

She sipped at her own cup of cocoa, the steam rising up around her face and making her cheeks even rosier. "This tastes so good on a day like today." He finished his cup and settled his wife on his lap, making her smile. She looped her arms around his neck and rested her head on his chest. "I'm here for another reason, a little buttering up. When did you want to exchange presents?"

Jackson kissed the top of her head and inhaled deeply. "Presents? Who said anything about presents? I don't need any." She looked up at him with such a pitiful pout, he couldn't keep up the tease. "I was thinking dinner time, so we could enjoy the rest of our evening without interruptions."

Beth pressed her lips to his. "Sounds perfect, although I don't mind any interruptions involving you." Her husband proved to be of a like mind when he spent a good while perfecting his kisses. It was one job you could never do too well. Practice was always in order.

When he closed up the barn and headed in that night, the lights were turned down low. The fireplace was burning bright, a blaze crackling merrily and putting out plenty of heat. Music was playing in the kitchen and the table was set. She'd found the rest of the roses and put them all together in a vase. A candle was lit at the center, making a pretty table with the beautiful china, but nothing was as lovely as his wife.

Beth wore a simple dress of pale blue that wrapped

around her middle and fell loosely to the floor. She had
done her hair in some kind of intricate braid wrapped
around her head like a crown with Baby's Breath woven
in the strands of honey. Heels were on her feet. Singing
softly to the radio, she swayed with the music as the last
of her dinner preparations were finished. He moved in
close, mirroring her moves as his arms wrapped around
her waist and her hands rested on his. "You look absolutely amazing."

She turned into him and stuck out her tongue. "I look
huge. Can you believe this baby belly already? This dress
is supposed to have a tiny waistline." Beth shook her
head in regret at the loss of her trim figure.

"I like having more of you to hold on to." His lips
brushed her neck and the wild pulse beat that always
kicked into action when he was near. His mouth found
her cheek and then her lips next when there was a tiny
movement under his hands. "Did you—I think—yes, that
was a kick!"

Ignoring arguments to the contrary and her protests,
Jackson picked her up and sat down at the table, laying
his hand on her belly once more. "Now hush! Maybe it
will happen again." They both waited, eyes opening with
wonder when there was another small fluttering. He slid
out from underneath his wife and knelt beside her, kissing
her stomach. "Hello Little Whatchamacallit."

Her smile was shaky, but she hung on to it as her fingers threaded through his hair. "Why don't we call it
Wyatt? Won't that be much easier?" They'd batted
around boys and girls names, but no definitive answers
were agreed upon. "Even if it's a girl, that name will
work, don't you think?"

Jackson couldn't speak. Too moved by the thought
that she'd choose one of his brothers for the name of their
first child, he could only bury his face in her middle and

hold on tight. They remained that way a long while, Beth running her fingers through his hair and whispering sweet nothings.

She served a delicious meal and they set the dishes in the sink to wait for once, moving out to the living room to sit before the fire on a pile of blankets on the floor. "Are you ready for your present?" He asked her as she leaned against his chest, her shoes kicked off in the corner and her hair falling loosely around her face now that he had set it free. She smiled up at him and nodded, excitement lighting up eyes that could not be any brighter. He reached in his pocket and set a small box in her hand.

With fingers that trembled, she lifted the lid to reveal a heart locket made from gold. He lifted the necklace out and popped the latch to reveal a picture from their wedding day and the words, "My Always and Forever," inscribed on the other side.

Beth bowed her head and he slipped the necklace over her shining hair when she caught his hands in hers. "Oh, Jackson. It's absolutely beautiful. Thank you." She gave him a kiss and reached behind a pillow on the couch to hand him a package. "Here's yours. It's not nearly as special."

He carefully unwrapped the tissue to reveal a chamois shirt in a deep, rich chocolate, the material so soft he couldn't resist putting it to his cheek. "I made it for you because I'm always stealing yours. I looked everywhere for a color that would do justice to your eyes. It's close."

He set it aside and cupped his wife's head in his considerably larger palm to kiss her thoroughly. "I'll think of you every time I wear it and that alone will keep me warm. Thank you." He made sure his affections proved his point.

They both gave into the warmth of the fire, their bodies becoming heavy and mellow. They stretched out on the blankets, staring into the flickering flames and he began to stroke her belly, whispering to the tiny occupant within. Not satisfied with that, his hands moved on, massaging her body from head to toe, working from her shoulders to her arms, down to her hips, her thighs, and finally giving each delicate foot their due.

Beth shifted and let out a tiny moan. "Oh Jackson, do you know what you're doing to me?" Her hand reached out and he caught it, kissing her fingers, her wrist, and traveling up to her lips. He could feel her shuddering at his touch.

"The same thing that you're doing to me. Let's call it a night, Mrs. Henry." He stood in one fluid movement and pulled her to her feet next, lifting her into his arms. Up the stairs they went like they had on their first night as husband and wife. His back protested, but he didn't care.

On this Valentine's Day, their first celebrated in matrimony, Jackson planned on paying homage to his Beth if it took all night long. Laying her down on the bed, he peeled her dress from her body to find her wedding negligee underneath. He couldn't help but smile in the middle of a kiss as a flurry of movement ran across her middle, making her laughter bubble up. "My, someone's active. Let me see if I can settle things down."

In the wee hours of the morning, he awoke to find moonbeams streaming through the curtains and a puddle of white light on the pillow beside him, illuminating another letter from his wife.

Dear Jackson,
I have had Valentines in my life, quite a few to be sure, but none mattered to me like you. None were my true love or my Always and Forever. Every day spent by your side, my heart grows bigger and my love is deeper for you. I feel like it is a river running through me, flooding to the

banks and overflowing, threatening to carry me away.

How I can have room for a little one too, I don't know, but I can't contain my happiness at having a tiny person that carries a part of you. That will make me love the both of you beyond bounds.

I hope I can give you just a morsel of the joy you bring to me each day, Jackson Landon Henry. For the rest of my days, I'll be trying to show you how very much you mean to me. I hope we have at least fifty more Valentine's Days together. They won't be enough, but it's a start. Sometimes, I feel like every minute is sand running through an hour glass, slipping through my hands, and time is running away from us. I wish I could stop the clock so I would never live one second without you. I love you.

Love,
Your Beth

CHAPTER 18

May 24, 1958:

Running a horse farm on Jackson's own was challenging. He was used to being part of a team, he and his brothers working with his father as part of a well-oiled machine. Em and Wyatt lent a hand from time to time, but Jackson wasn't one to shirk or pass off his responsibilities to others. Some days, he was bone-tired. Add the aching in his back that was a constant companion and his feet would start to drag.

Beth would be there, waiting with a cold drink, something to eat, or the gift of her smile. He would catch her often throughout the day, arms propped on the fence, slipping away from her duties to offer moral support for his. Somehow, she could sense when he was running on empty. One shot of her, a hug, a kiss or a wink, would give him a badly needed refill.

Her mother had taught her the art of housekeeping well. His wife was amazing, a whirlwind of activity from dusk to dawn. She made a point of getting out of bed while he was in the shower, making sure his coffee and breakfast was waiting on the table. Their house was neat as a pin and she was always caught up in the midst of one project or another—painting, adding stencils for a special touch here and there, sewing, or making additions to the nursery in preparation for their anticipated addition only two months away.

The closer the time came, the more frenzied Beth was to make sure everything was ready. Jackson helped to lighten the load as her date grew closer and the baby took more of a toll on her. Hanging clothes. Carrying laundry. Washing dishes. Doing any request. She rarely asked.

Late afternoon and he was turning in for the day. Tired didn't do justice to the way he felt, coming up his walkway, when he was stopped in his tracks. Weariness wasn't to blame. It was the sight of his wife. She was putting in flowers. She'd already done the entire length of the pathway leading to the house and was finishing up with the beds that lined the porch. *She does too much.* Shamed by his own inner grumbles, he resolved to make no more room for self-pity and do more for her.

Moving closer, he couldn't help but enjoy the view. She wore a dress in a sunflower print, her hair pulled back in a twist. From the rear, no one would know the advanced stage of her pregnancy. Her gloved hand came up to push a loose strand of gold out of her eyes, leaving a smudge of dirt on her cheek that made her impossibly cute, like a kid making mud pies without a care in the world.

Jackson stopped beside her and stared down at the sweet spot where her hairline met her neck. How he longed to press a kiss there. She tipped her face his way, giving him a glimpse of the lovely flush to her skin and the new fullness to her face that stole his breath away. "God, you're beautiful," he told her in a voice gone hoarse with awe.

He held out his hand and she tugged off her gloves, leaving them on the ground, accepting a boost up as his lips kissed her cool, soft fingers. Standing on tiptoe, she

brushed his cheek with a butterfly kiss and let out a sigh
as her free hand pressed the small of her back that tended
to ache all of the time. Jackson winced in sympathy. He
knew the feeling well, but wished he could spare her.

"*You* need your eyes checked. My cheeks are puffy,
I'm as big as a cow, *and* I'm dirty!" Taking pause in the
midst of her litany of woes, one and the same for every
expectant mother, she reached up and placed a hand on
his forehead. "I think you must be delirious. You'd better
go lie down a while. I'll be only too happy to join you.
My feet are swollen to the size of balloons and they're
killing me—I can't even wear shoes!"

Jackson lifted a hand to knead at her neck, watching
her exasperation evaporate as her lips curved up in a bow,
the perfect time to steal a kiss. "I'll take care of your feet
and you can inspect my eyes. How's that sound?" She
wrapped an arm around his waist and leaned against him
as they took their time heading inside. "By the way, the
flowers look really nice. You shouldn't have done all of
that in one day."

She flipped her hands in dismissal. "If you can do too
much in a day, so can I." She wiped her soles on the
doormat, giving him a glimpse of her poor, swollen feet.
Beth leaned back against him and he ran his hands up her
sides, cupped her stomach to give attention to the little
one, getting a quick jab in response, and moved on to her
shoulders. She closed her eyes and let loose a long, slow
sigh. "I'm hot. I'm sweaty. I *need* a shower."

"I've a better option. I'll run you a bath. I could use
one myself." Holding her hand all the way up the steps,
he left her sitting on the side of the bed while he filled the
tub nearly to the brim, going heavy on her favorite suds.
A throwback from bygone days, Beth had insisted on
keeping the old, claw foot tub even though Jackson offered to update the bathroom and bring in something new.

The tub was large and deep, spacious enough for the both of them, a fixture that had given them much pleasure, beginning with the morning after their wedding. Whether they were treating aches and pains, or feeling romantic, a hot bath was something to look forward to any day of the week.

Giving his wife the tenderness that was her due, he lifted her dress over her head and kissed her blooming belly, making her giggle as her underwear slid to the floor. He took her hand once more, determined to catch her if she fell while taking the big step in. She'd do the same for him. Quickly shedding his own clothing, he joined her.

He turned to face Beth so both could press their backs against the sides and tip their heads to the ceiling, basking in the warmth of the soothing waters. "There is a God," he murmured under his breath and let a good soaking take away all of the kinks and aches acquired during his daily labors. The heat eased into all of his bones, especially the damage done to his spine. *Need to do this every day. Good therapy.*

Eventually, her feet found their way to his lap. Jackson devoted plenty of attention to both, emitting a groan from his wife that must have come from her toes and caused a stirring deep down in his innards that would have to be placed on hold. This was her time, not intended for his pleasure although the sight of her come undone was almost more than he could bear.

Once finished, he took up a cup on a small shelf and began to rinse the wet strands of her hair gone dark, shampooing and adding conditioner, making her groan once again. He finished by gently soaping her legs, her midsection, her chest, and finishing with her arms. He took her hands in his, so small and delicate by comparison.

He felt her penetrating stare and looked up, drifting in an endless sky of blue without a cloud in sight. "What?"

"Your eyes. They're incredible. Like a river of melted chocolate, so warm and rich. They make me want to dive in." She cupped his face in her hands and continued to stare at him intently, making the heat rush up to greet her touch.

"So, they pass inspection?" He asked, his voice a low rumble in his chest, a teasing grin tugging at the corner of his mouth. Beth set her lips on his, making his insides begin to liquefy.

"They'll do." He nodded and dipped his head toward hers, settling in for a long, slow kiss, the kind that made them both forget how to breathe, the stuff that dreams were made of. Drawing the moment out, time stopped, and the world went away for a while. They climbed out of the tub when the water became cold and the bubbles were all gone, their skin wrinkled like a dried up, old prune.

She had a simple meal waiting when they went downstairs. A platter of cold chicken, sliced thin, rice with some kind of savory sauce, and some fresh greens. Her baking powder biscuits, heavenly with their light, fluffy crust, rounded out the perfect combination. Jackson ate seconds, he was so hungry, and thought about thirds while his wife watched him. Her smile stretched wider with each bite he took, her chin propped on her hand. "My goodness, Jackson. I won't have to wash any dishes what with the way you're polishing your plate."

After dinner, he stayed in the kitchen with his elbows propped on the table, mesmerized by his wife. His duty of washing accomplished, Beth finished the job of drying and putting dishes away, humming to herself as she did and making his mouth go dry.

With each passing day, the more her pregnancy progressed, the greater his attraction grew to the point that the woman was irresistible.

If only he could quench his thirst—but that was not possible in the advanced stage that she was in. It didn't seem right. That didn't mean he wouldn't keep dreaming about her with his eyes wide open.

She was swaying on her bare feet, wearing a summer night gown in white that came to the tantalizing dip in her knees and seemed to float around her as she moved. Her hair fell in a curtain to the small of her back, tempting him to thread his fingers within the thick strands and draw her closer to him.

Suddenly, she turned to him and beckoned with a smile in her eyes. "Jackson, dance with me." He obliged, tucking her under his chin. Her heart was aflutter against his as her arms wrapped around his waist and they took a few turns around the kitchen. Her humming stopped and she whispered, "Jackson, take me to bed."

"My, my, Mrs. Henry, rather demanding tonight, aren't you?" The baby gave a hearty kick, the hard, warm mound of her belly pressed against him, a reminder of the life blooming within. His palms slid to her stomach to pay homage to the little one that waited to greet them. "Since you're carrying our child day in and day out for nine months, I'll indulge you." He dipped down, hand coming under her legs, and he lifted her into the air, secure in the cradle of his arms.

She swatted at his head playfully, grinning from ear to ear. "Jackson Landon Henry, put me down! You'll hurt your back! I'm heavy as a house!" He continued up the steps, shoulders straight, without any signs of complaint. It *did* hurt, but she'd never know it. At the top, he grazed her cheek with a kiss.

"Darling, the day I can't carry my wife is the day I don't deserve the title of husband." He nodded to the door and she pushed it open, allowing him to cross the room and set her on the bed.

He made haste to join her, shucking his clothes, putting on pajama bottoms, deciding against a shirt. The summer night was hot and his temperature was skyrocketing anyway, considering the prospect waiting for him in the next room. He brushed his teeth, washed his face, and combed his hair because a woman like his Beth deserved a man who would make an effort. Stepping into the doorway, he leaned against the jamb and simply watched her. She still had the power to steal his breath away and make his heart race in anticipation.

"Jackson, come to bed." That was one request he would never deny her, no matter how tired, sick, old or feeble. They'd have to put him in the ground first.

The next morning, the sun was streaming in across his pillow. Rolling over, he found one of the yellow and orange roses from his grandmother's garden on his pillow. Inhaling its sweet scent, he picked up her note.

Dear Jackson,

Happy Memorial Day. I know that doesn't sound appropriate, but being with you fills me with such joy that I feel near to bursting. It's like I have this bubble of happiness growing inside of me and it's swelling, bigger and brighter every day—and no, I don't mean the baby! I often pinch myself, afraid that I'm dreaming. I expect I'll wake up and find out that it is the night after that Fourth of July when you finally saw what was right beneath your nose. What if you'd never opened your eyes?

I let you sleep in today because you never do. You don't complain or ask for help. You simply get up and put one foot in front of the other because there is no other option. I've watched you go white with the pain in your back that never goes away, know that you suffer often in silence. Today, I decided to give you a badly needed rest. I fed and watered the horses—no, I didn't hurt myself or push it. I took it slow and did a little at a time. They were patient, too. Lucy was especially understanding. I can see with the size of her swollen belly that her foal won't be long in coming. I wonder who will go first.

I've been sitting here at the table, the sun tiptoeing in our bright kitchen, warming my face while a cool breeze lifts the hair from my neck. While I wait to see how long you will sleep, I've been thinking about the meaning behind this day. Now that I am married and expecting, I truly understand this holiday for the first time. I picture all of the women who have lost their men, all the mothers who have lost their sons, and I do not know how they go on after the ultimate sacrifice. Without you, my life would not be worth living.

This Memorial Day, the first of which I am married, I carry gratitude in my heart. It is because of those who went before me that I have my home and country. Because of the brave who fought for our flag, I have this beautiful life. Because of the blood that has been shed to preserve this land, I have you. That is all that I could ever ask for or want. I could not bear to go a day without you. I love you.

Love,
Your Beth

A footstep sounded at the door and dishes rattled on a tray as his wife entered the room. She carried coffee, a plate of hot food, and a grin that touched her eyes. He held out his hand, inviting her in. "Put that down. I need my fill of you first."

She obliged, setting the tray on the dresser, allowing him to snag her in his arms and draw her into the nest of covers. He pressed a kiss to her shoulder, her collar bone, and the sweet skin of her neck while Beth tipped her head back. "Jackson," she murmured, "your breakfast is going to get cold."

He shrugged. "No matter. All I want right now is you." Her kiss made him forget any more words, food, or his surroundings. His mind only had room for her.

❧❧❧

How much more snow could they get? Emmett didn't really want to know the answer to that question. Plowing for the umpteenth time in the past two days, he'd turn into a block of ice if he stayed out any longer. He fought his way through gale winds, peeled out of his frost-crusted outerwear, and made a beeline for the fire place. "Case?"

Usually, she'd be waiting for him with hot tea, coffee, or cocoa. Better yet, his wife would lend him her body for a while. As the pregnancy came to a close, she blasted off heat like a furnace. A shudder ran through him as he shook off the chill and he called out again, "Casey?"

"Up here," she answered breathlessly. Did he hear a note of anxiety in her tone? Emmett was paranoid these days, reading something into everything. He took the stairs two at a time and burst into their bedroom only to freeze. A kiddie pool sat at the foot of their bed, steam rising up, while Hawaiian music filled the air. There was no sign of his wife.

"Casey, you're not planning one of those water births, are you?" His heart gave a lurch. Emmett knew the day was coming soon. That didn't mean he'd ever be ready for it. Belatedly, he saw the pair of swim trunks on the bed and had to fight the urge to laugh.

"No. I thought after our eventful trip to the mall, you could use a mini vacation. Put on your suit." A moment later, she stepped out of the attached bathroom wearing a dark green bathing suit that brought out her gemstone eyes and hugged her body, showing off every ounce of her swollen baby belly. Her dark hair was wrapped in a knot at the top of her head to keep it out of her way, a grin tugging at the corner of her mouth. "Look! I even brought the beach ball." She patted her belly, making him laugh.

She took his hand and carefully stepped over the side of the pool. With his help, she lowered herself into the water with a long sigh. "Mmmm. This feels like heaven. Come on in. The water's really nice."

He could only shake his head at the wonder that was his wife. He sank down beside her and drew her up against his side. "My God, you're right. I feel like I've melted inside. You're a lot of help. Your body is a furnace." They leaned back against the bed, holding hands and he started to laugh again. "Remember our first trip to the beach? That was a good one too. No matter where I go, it's good with you, Case."

She pressed a palm to his cheek and gave him a kiss, one that stretched out and reeled him in closer. His hands settled on her belly, roaming round and round, then upwards. The heat of her body lit a blaze that was burning him from the inside out. He felt like an inferno.

"Em. Please." She whispered raggedly as his lips ran along her neck and stopped at her jaw.

He pulled back to see her eyes glistening, the pulse in her neck fluttering madly. Like his. Emmett cleared his throat and contented himself with holding her hand. They both closed their eyes again, waiting for their heart rates to go down, to remember how to breathe again. The minutes ticked by, sliding into a half hour or more. A fine shiver ran through his body. The cold that had seeped into his bones was back, brought on by the cooling water.

Casey was shivering as well. He gave her shoulder a squeeze. "Let's get out. You're cold."

Tenderly, he helped her up. Everything was a struggle these days. Emmett dried her, pulled a warm, flannel nightgown over her head, and pulled back the covers. Casey slid in with a sigh. He wasn't far behind her. He turned on his side and threaded his fingers through her hair. "I'm sorry about before. It's just...it's been so long." With an inward groan, he realized he'd have to resign himself to wait a while longer.

She gave him a fleeting kiss on the nose, her tone playful. "Maybe this will occupy your mind." She shifted to pick up the journal from her nightstand and hand it over.

Emmett propped himself up with pillows and settled her by his side, his thumb stroking the cover of his father's book. He brushed the shining cap of her hair with his lips. "No matter where I am or what I'm doing, you are always on my mind. Nothing else can take your place." He was rewarded with a smile with her heart in it. He began to read...

CHAPTER 19

June 23, 1958:

Jackson was tired. They'd stuffed themselves silly and stayed up too late at the Masons. His in-laws had them to dinner once a week, anxiously keeping up the baby watch. Who could blame them? No one was watching more closely than the father to be.

He and Beth walked home beneath the stars, holding hands, listening to the leaves rustling in the wind. His wife was so weary by the time they reached the house, what with the extra weight she had to carry all day long, that he swung her up in his arms, carried her upstairs, and laid her down in bed.

Now that the warm weather was setting in, his back was much more cooperative, thank the Lord. She was still sleeping when he headed out to the barn and he was not about to wake her.

Before heading out to do his chores, Jackson brushed her golden hair with a light kiss. He walked away, only to stop in the doorway and stare at her. He'd thought she could never be prettier than the day when the sparks first started flying between them on Independence Day. Then, he saw her on their wedding day and realized he was mistaken, a marvel beyond compare. Wrong again.

There was nothing more beautiful than the woman who was carrying his child.

He started his day the same as any other day, watering and feeding the horses, letting them out in the field. Keeping a close eye on Lucy, there was no doubt today was going to be a long day. The pregnant mare was getting ready. The signs were clear, ones he had seen many times over growing up on a horse farm. This would be the first foal on *his* farm. The thought made his heart start to thump painfully, near bursting with pride, as he watched the horse in the field.

She was moving slow as molasses that morning, Ricky Ricardo shadowing her, nuzzling her when Lucy's head would droop. Glancing down, Jackson could see that her udders were very full, the teats especially swollen. Following the lines of her body and distended belly, he could see the tell-tale hollows by the root of her tail. Her body was preparing for the little one's arrival, just like his Beth.

Lately, his wife's every move had been slow and deliberate. Getting up was a real challenge. He loved watching her, her belly blooming with life inside her. Often, he'd catch her rubbing her midsection, standing still and devoting her attention to that inner world. She'd sing a lullaby softly under her breath with a far off look in her eyes and little smile. He wondered what went on between them.

As for Lucy, the mare had been restless for the past few weeks, unable to settle, walking round and round the pasture, then pacing some more in her stall at night, with Ricky Ricardo mooning after her. Today seemed no different, but she was wandering away from the rest of the horses, keeping her distance.

Approaching slowly, humming softly under his breath, Jackson sidled up alongside of her and rested his hand on her flank. She was covered with sweat and warm to the touch.

"There, there, Lucy. It's all right, girl. Your baby will be here soon. Don't fight it, sweetheart." He felt her shuddering under his hand, her nose nearly pressing against the ground. A space of a minute or so and she started walking again. What a marvel—a horse's contractions.

Jackson continued to work with the other animals, keeping the laboring mare in his sight. Ricky Ricardo was vigilant as well, nickering softly, watching his mate's every move. Soon. Her time would come soon. The hours of the afternoon passed uneventfully until he looked out in the field in the early evening and saw the fluid gushing from her hindquarters.

Time to get her in the barn. Grabbing a halter and lead rope, he eased his way across the pasture. There was no need to startle her. Lucy had enough on her mind. He needn't have worried. Her head was bowed and she stood still, quivering in the grasp of a powerful contraction. His presence, and the halter, was not even noticed. A hard exhalation and she raised her head once more, her large, chocolate eyes clouded with pain.

"Come on, Lucy girl. Time to go in, honey." He looped the strap over her head, and she went without a fight. The mare knew.

Bringing her to the largest stall he had, Jackson penned her in to give her some peace and quiet, a little privacy. Ricky Ricardo hung his head over the fence, pining after his mare. Did all fathers have that same pitiful, helpless look on their faces? Now the waiting game would begin. It could be a matter of a few hours, it could take all night. God willing, everything would go off without a hitch.

All the preparations were in order—the long gloves,

the antiseptic solution, a new horse blanket. Jackson pulled off his flannel shirt, sweating like the dickens. In his focus on the mare, he'd forgotten his heavy shirt to ward off the chill of early morning. Lucy went down on her side, making him think she was getting somewhere.

He climbed over the gate and started rubbing her neck and her side, murmuring soothing nonsense. Just when it seemed she'd relax and get down to business, the mare fought her way back to her feet and started pacing. Rubbing at the tension in the back of his neck, he let out a deep breath of his own. This was going to be quite a stretch.

"Jackson?" Beth pushed the barn door open to find them both flat out in the straw. Lucy was breathing hard, the contractions wringing the strength out of her, while Jackson stretched out beside her and rubbed her flanks, her hips, and her spine. He picked his head up to see his wife treading softly across the barn floor, peering through the dimly lit building. He'd hung a light over Lucy's pen, but the other lights were far and few between. "How is she?" She stood outside the stall, her hands pressed to the top railing.

"Not much change. I felt the foal earlier, reached up there with my gloves. It's pointed the right way. The little bugger is just too comfortable in there, needs to give his poor mother a break."

He stood up and stretched his arms over his head, listening to his bones crack, kneading at his neck. His body was starting to droop and his back was getting stiff. Imagine how the horse had to feel. Glancing at his Beth, Jackson had a new appreciation for what she was going through for nine months. No sense in complaining about one drawn-out night.

He climbed the fence and dropped down beside her, pressing a kiss to her lips and resting a palm on the mound of her belly. He received a hearty kick in answer that made them both laugh.

"Well, hello to you, too," he whispered, ducking down to press a kiss to the offending spot.

He looked up at his wife and saw the smile in her eyes, even though she was tired. That was enough for him to forget about himself. Glancing around the barn, Jackson grabbed a chair and set it down for her, easing her down and stroking her hair along the way. "How about you, little mother?"

Beth's cheeks grew pink at his attention and she took his hand, pressing his palm to her cheek. "I'm fine, but I wish you could come in. I tried to go to sleep, but our bed is too lonely without you. Do you know it's nearly midnight? How much longer can this go on?"

The mare snorted in discomfort as if on cue and he gave the other expectant mother a kiss. "Maybe things will finally get a move on now."

Receiving a fleeting kiss in return and scrambling quickly into the pen, Jackson resumed his post.

The mare was tired, moaning slightly each time the contractions took hold, the sweat soaking the straw beneath her. When another hour went by, with no amount of massage or words of comfort helping, he knew something had to be done. Lucy needed a little nudge. "Beth, see those gloves over there, the new set? Will you dunk them in that bowl of antiseptic and hand them over please?"

She obliged, passing them through a space between the boards, her eyes shadowed with concern. "What can I do, sweetheart? Should I call your dad or the vet? Do you want me to get in the stable with you?" She moved to climb on the fence and he gave her a paint-peeler of a glare.

"Don't you *dare* get in here! You could get hurt. I'm going to reach in there, see if I can help her. If this doesn't work, we'll get Pop, okay?" Giving her what he hoped was a reassuring grin, Jackson dipped in and dropped a kiss on her nose, making Beth giggle.

Assured his wife wouldn't do anything foolish, he turned back to her horse and knelt down in the straw. Making sure the last contraction had passed, he plunged his arm deep within the birth canal, surrounded by the heat and moisture, reaching around the foal that had moved a few inches since before. This wouldn't do at such an agonizing pace. Feeling this way and that, he worked on easing the baby farther along when another contraction came on.

"Holy Mother of God!" He called out, biting off a string of curse words as the mare's powerful muscles clamped down with a pressure intense enough to break his arm. His back chose that moment to give him a good jab that stole his breath away. All that was left to do was press his forehead to the horse's side, grit his teeth, and wait.

"Jackson, are you all right?" He could hear the edge of fear in Beth's voice. An explanation was in order before the stubborn woman intervened. A glance over his shoulder and he could see her with her face pressed to a gap in the fence, tension written all over her.

He tossed her a weary smile. "In a bit of a predicament here. Have to wait until the contraction is over. This girl is strong!" He set his head down, waiting for what felt like an eternity, until the muscles finally relaxed.

Sighing in relief, he moved fast, ignoring the mare's fussing, poking, prodding, shifting the foal. Sensing the next powerful tightening of her body, his arm was spared another crushing blow as he pulled out. There was a sudden shifting and an instant later, the forelegs emerged, the head following. "Atta girl, Lucy. Beth, toss me the blanket!"

A click of the gate and she was by his side, flushed with excitement, her weariness forgotten as she handed him the thick cover. "Oh my goodness! Lucy girl, your baby's here! A little more pushing, sweetheart. Just a little more!" Beth pressed a hand to Jackson's shoulder, holding on tight. "I've never seen a mare foaling before. This is...it's absolutely..."

He glanced up at her and kissed her cheek. "I know. Listen, I need you to back up. There's no telling what could happen. Even after all of that hard work, she could kick or manage to get up. I don't want anything happening to you."

His tone was gentle, imploring her to do as he asked. Beth obliged, retreating a few feet behind him and kneeling in the straw, hands on her protruding belly. Her fingers began to rub round and round, as was her habit. How could she help thinking about the approach of her birthing day?

The horse gave a great grunt, pulling his attention back to the matter at hand. He set the blanket beneath her hind end and grasped the foal carefully. With an easy tug, the tiny colt slithered out, the membrane cover breaking along the way. "Lucy, it's a boy! You have yourself a brawny, young stallion!"

The young couple began to laugh and cry at the same time, Beth leaning her head against Jackson's shoulder, while the new mother began to clean her baby. A thorough washing, a nudge with her nose, and the little one stood, knock-kneed on shaky hooves. A few minutes later, and the mare decided to finish the birthing process with ease, expelling the placenta and rising to her feet. She dipped her head, her nose brushing gently against her foal's forehead.

"Lucy looks like she's checking to see if her baby has all of its hooves, ears, and tail," Beth whispered, her tears

making silver tracks down her cheeks in the moonlight
streaming through the window. Jackson tugged off his
gloves so that he could touch his wife, skimming his fingers up her back, to her shoulder, finally cupping the
back of her head to come in for a needy kiss. "We'll have
to inspect later," she mumbled softly, her eyes drooping
shut in surrender to weariness and his touch.

He felt her sag and took her hands, keeping her away
from him. "I can't hold you now, baby. I'm filthy. We'll
go in, I'll get washed up, and we'll get to bed. Just let me
clean up."

He made quick work of disposing of the placenta and
tossing fresh straw in the stall, a heightened awareness of
his wife's presence urging him to get inside and share her
bed. She needed her rest and Jackson was nearly past the
point of no return. Wrapping up his efforts, he stroked the
little foal, marveling at the new addition to their barn, finishing off with a kiss on Lucy's forehead. "Goodnight,
sweet girl. You've had the first baby at a place of my
own. Rest up. You two deserve it."

Beth stood by the open barn door, waiting patiently for
him, her belly appearing to protrude even more as she
turned to the side, rubbing at her aching, lower back.
Jackson's throbbed more just watching her. He could
hardly see straight, he was so tired, yet the glow in his
wife's eyes was clear and the smile that greeted him. He
peeled off his T-shirt and tossed it in the garbage.
There'd be no salvaging it. She took his hand as he shut
the barn door and they walked slowly to the house.

The stairs seemed to stretch on before him forever, but
she tugged insistently, drawing him forward one step at a
time. Beth held a finger up to him and stepped inside the
bathroom, the sound of running water and steam drifting
his way. Jackson started to sway when she ducked beneath his shoulder. A few more steps and he dropped

down on the edge of the tub. Nimble hands were unbuttoning his pants and sliding them down his legs, his underwear following. A small push and he tumbled into the sweet glory of a hot, sudsy bath. A sigh came up from his toes and he closed his eyes, his body finally calling it quits.

Soft hands were running through his hair, giving him a shampoo, rinsing and repeating the process with conditioner. A washcloth came next, running over his skin from head to toe and he let out a low moan. "God, woman. If only I had enough energy to do something about the way you make me feel. Your hands feel so good."

He fought to open his eyes. His wife was kneeling beside him, her sleeves rolled up, a hair clinging to her cheek. He reached out with fingers that trembled and tucked a strand behind her ear. "You are the most beautiful thing I've ever seen."

She snorted, catching his hand and kissing his knuckles. "And you are delusional. Come on out of there before you're a prune." Jackson did as he was told, standing slowly, surprised his bones didn't pop. His girl held up a towel, wrapping the thick terry cloth around his waist. Her palm pressed to his lower back, prodding the most sensitive spot in question. At his sharp intake of breath, she went to the medicine cabinet and returned with the liniment that had helped him through many a tough night. He pulled out a grin from beneath the weariness and held out a hand for the tin of ointment. Gesturing for her to turn around, Jackson applied a healthy dollop to her bowed back. He wondered how she could bear it, what with the strain of the baby's weight day in and day out. It was his Beth's turn to groan.

Forgetting himself, he dressed and brought his wife to the bedroom. He lifted her dress over her head, running his fingers through her hair that trailed to her shoulders like a waterfall of sunlight, stopping to press his lips to hers. He took her hands and held her arms out to her sides, stepping back and gazing at her body. The blush crept up in her face and her eyelashes brushed her cheeks as he took his fill, turning her to the side to see her profile.

He let go of her hands to cup her belly, sinking down on his knees and kissing her bulging belly button. "No, I'm certain." Jackson whispered hoarsely. "I've never seen anything more beautiful than you." Her hands rested lightly on his shoulders yet he felt like she was his tether, keeping him earthbound when his spirit wanted to soar. No matter how tired he was, Jackson Henry would never be too exhausted to appreciate the masterpiece that was his wife.

"Jackson, let's go to bed. I need to sleep for a week." He looked up at her and saw the smile in her eyes, but the dark shadows as well and the way her skin was growing pale. The day had been too long for his Beth. He gained his feet once more, took up her nightgown, and slid it over her head. A tug of her hand and she slowly sat down on the side of the bed. He joined her, hairbrush in hand, and he began to run it through the heavy strands of her golden hair, relishing its weight and thickness, as well as the glossy shine. Pushing the mass to the side, he leaned forward and kissed her neck, feeling her shiver.

She turned, took the brush away, and framed his face with her hands. "Jackson Henry, you were amazing tonight, the way you took care of Lucy and her little foal. I have never loved you more, my man of many talents." One more kiss and she stretched out, her eyes never leaving his, her message clear. A husband's place was by his wife.

He laid his head on the pillow and tumbled off into sleep the moment his eyes closed.

Jackson found her letter tucked in his shirt pocket the next morning when he first ventured out to the barn.

June 21, 1958
Dear Jackson,
I have always thought you had magic in your touch, the way you handle God's wonderful creatures, big and small. Seeing you last night, I was in awe. Your patience, your gentleness, your instincts. The way you cherished both Lucy and the baby foal. Watching you bring a new life into the world, I think you could do anything. I would trust you with my life—any time or place. Soon very soon, I will entrust you with the greatest gift I have ever known—the life blooming inside of me. I can't wait to share this baby's arrival with you. I love you more each day.
Love,
Your Beth

CHAPTER 20

July 5, 1958:

I'm not going to the hospital! I want my baby to be born at home, like you and your brothers. This house and farm should be a part of our little one from the very start." Leave it until now for Beth to reveal her obstinate streak and dig in her heels. Her water broke conveniently, first thing in the morning when she went to the bathroom. Her contractions had been relatively mild at first, ten minutes apart.

Jackson kept a close watch on her as she walked through the rooms of their home, touching things, carrying on a conversation when the pains hit, laughing them off and proceeding to cook him a large breakfast, do the dishes, and even fold laundry! Exasperating woman! No matter how hard he tried to get her to stop doing anything but focus on labor, she wouldn't pay him any mind, dismissing and downplaying his concerns.

She'd never been more lovely to him. Like a sunflower opening its petals to the sky, stealing his breath away. Her rounded belly was full and drooping low like a Georgia peach, sweet and ripe for the picking. Her face was a dusky rose from labor, her blue eyes sparkling, her hair shining with a gloss that made him want to wrap his hands around it and lose himself. She was a distraction that made it hard to concentrate on the matter at hand, the fact that shortly, God willing, his wife would be bringing a little person into this world. *Lord help me to be up to the task.*

Things continued relatively uneventfully through the afternoon as she prepared his lunch and sat from time to time, rocking back and forth in the rocker he'd built on the porch, allowing him to rub the small of her back that was severely bowed with the size of her belly. A short rest and she'd be back up again, taking his hand and wearing a track in the floor.

Late afternoon and there was a shift. The contractions moved closer together, to a space of five minutes. Beth no longer talked or made light of the pains, often stopping to grab hold of something—a counter top, the table, a chair, his hands—as she bent at the waist and closed her eyes, breathing hard through the nose, her jaw clenched. She didn't complain, but her hurting was obvious.

A particularly rough one hit and her hands moved to cup her belly, a small cry slipping out. Jackson rubbed her shoulders and smiled encouragingly. "Come on now, Beth. I don't know anything about delivering babies, only foals. You need—*I need*—the hospital. Doctors, nurses, *experts.* I couldn't live with myself if something happened to you or the baby."

She took his hand and squeezed hard enough to nearly grind his knuckles to dust, her gaze turned inward, focusing on the natural process that was taking over her body. Her eyes closed and her face was tight as she forced another breath through her nose. When the pain finally let up, her blue eyes were clear, leveled with his.

"You can do this. I watched you with Lucy. These amazing hands can do anything. Your mama did this three times at home with all of you and Pop was there to help her. I know that you'll have no trouble handling this on your own, but if it will make you feel better, call your mother and she'll come. I'm *not* going anywhere, Jackson." Beth raised her chin and crossed her arms, daring him to defy her.

"Fine! I've never met such a stubborn woman. Would've been nice if you could've let me in on your plans a bit sooner!" He threw his hands in the air and stormed off to the kitchen, taking a deep breath of his own and fighting to keep his temper while waiting for his mother to answer the phone.

He continued to keep his wife in his line of sight, watching her move around the living room, nearly bent in half with the next pain as she grabbed hold of the arm of the couch, her hands balled into fists, fingers gone white, and a surge of panic threatened to shake him. He swallowed hard and stomped it down. "Hello?" Jackson felt dizzy with relief at the sound of a familiar voice.

"Mama, it's Beth. The stubborn woman is in labor and she's got the notion in her head that the baby should be born at home. Yes, her water broke. They're five—make that three minutes apart. What? Okay. Just hurry, please. Love you," he managed to say, even when distracted by the flash of pain on his wife's face, making her body go rigid.

He felt so helpless. If only he could do this for her. He crossed the room to take her in his arms and Beth drooped against him, tiring. "Listen, Mama said to sit on grandpa's old milking stool for a while, said that will help move the baby into position. When you're ready to lie down, say so. She's gathering some supplies and will be on her way. "

His wife didn't argue, an unusual event, sinking down with his help on the sturdy wooden stool until she was in a squatting position. She rested her palms on her knees and let her head drop, waiting, resting before the next contraction had her in its grip. The tension in her whole body and labored breathing were the only indicators when the pains hit. No screaming for this one. Steady as she goes.

Two minutes apart now. A cold sweat broke out on Jackson's forehead and ran down his back. Unconsciously, he began to pray. *Please Lord, keep her and the baby safe. Help me to help them.*

A low moan sounded from her toes and he kneaded at the nape of her neck, murmuring soothing words of comfort. Finally, her body went loose with a sigh. "Jackson, I need to lie down now." Beth spoke in a whisper, her weariness plain.

He kissed her cheek and gave her neck a squeeze. "Okay. Just a minute. I've got to get our bed ready. Don't move." She looked up at him, her eyes heavy with pain and exhaustion, yet a grin still teased at the corner of her mouth.

He hustled, grabbing a heavy, plastic tablecloth from the closet, along with a ratty old blanket. Beth didn't need to worry about the state of her sheets. Taking the steps two at a time, he quickly stripped the bed down and covered the mattress. Overcome by the heat all of the sudden, he stripped off his t-shirt and doused his head in cold water, his heart thundering in his chest and head.

A shriek rose up from down below, striking him with fear, and he didn't hesitate to head into the fray. An instant later, he was at her side, clamping down on his own anxiety, seeing hers looming in eyes gone wide. "What? What's wrong?"

She shook her head. "Nothing, nothing. They're closer. I'm going to need to push *soon*, I know—" She bit off the last of her words and grabbed hold of her bulging belly, moaning softly.

That was enough for him to spring into action. Jackson swept her up in his arms and carried her to their bedroom, stripping off her underwear and dress, leaving her in her bra. He set her on the bed only to have her lean forward, gritting her teeth, gripping his hands until she shook. Finally, she fell back and breathed again in short pants.

"How are you kids doing in here?" A cheerful voice chirped from the doorway. Ella Henry bustled into the room, a clean apron covering her clothes, hair tucked up in a bun, dark eyes filled with warmth, excitement, and a hint of tears. Moving swiftly to the side of the bed, she kissed her oldest boy on the cheek and flipped the sheet up to survey the situation. "Oh yes, you're moving along quite nicely. How close are the pains?"

Jackson scraped a hand through his hair even as Beth nearly ground his knuckles to powder, tensing up again. "A minute and they're hanging on for a minute. How much longer, Mama? It's been twelve hours. She's worn out."

Ella nodded in sympathy and patted his back. "It could be another twelve, could be an hour. It could take another twenty-four. First babies usually take their sweet time. Don't worry, honey. You two are doing just fine." She moved to the head of the bed and pushed Beth's hair from her face to lean in and give her a kiss on the cheek. "Keep doing what you're doing, little mother. That grandbaby will be here before you know it."

Twelve more excruciating hours and Beth was screaming. Each one sliced through Jackson, doubling him over. The pains had not let up, yet nothing was happening, no reassuring movement down the birth canal. Mama thought a warm bath might help.

Between his and her efforts, they helped the exhausted girl to climb into the tub. She'd proceeded to tell her husband in no uncertain terms to get out. He had an idea why. Each time she screamed, he couldn't hide the pain on *his* face.

Another shriek and he couldn't stand it anymore. Jackson barged in and climbed in the tub with her, heedless of his jeans, thinking of nothing but helping his Beth. His back chose that moment to remind him of his limitations, the pain rearing up and sinking its teeth in, snatching his breath away. *Not now, you hear me? Not now!*

Pushing past his own discomfort, he focused on his wife. She was on all fours, her head hanging low, drooping until it almost touched the water. The pain was pounding her in such forceful waves, one after the other, and she couldn't take it. "Oh, Jackson," she murmured as the next one rolled in.

He wrapped his arms around her and began to rub her belly, then her back with warm oil that Mama handed him, hoping to soothe her in some way, to do *something*. As his hands ran over her belly again, the baby gave a healthy kick that nearly made his heart stop. Closing his eyes tight, he prayed. *Lord, please let me be wrong.* Beth sagged as the contraction let go of its hold on her and Jackson stroked her hair, pressing a kiss to her cheek. "You're going to be all right. This baby is just being stubborn, likes it too much safe and warm inside of you. Besides, it's a Henry. Stubborn runs in our blood."

He glanced up and caught his mother's eye. The crease in her forehead, one that formed when she was worried, dug in deeper. She reached out and set a hand on his shoulder, questioning the concern that he could not hide.

"You try and relax. I think it's almost time, got to make sure everything is ready." Jackson climbed out of the tub, breathing hard through his nose as he fought to straighten up. He grabbed a towel and motioned for his mother to join him in the hallway. He waited outside the bathroom, listening to her reassure his wife before joining him. "Mama, I think—I *know* the baby is breech. He just kicked me while I was holding Beth way down low on her belly."

Ella's face became pinched with concern and she covered her mouth for a moment, her fear—the same fear that he felt—evident. A breech birth could lead to complications, something they did *not* want during a home birth. Shaking herself visibly, she set her shoulders and squeezed his hand.

"That's all right. We can do this. It just might mean a little more time and effort. I want you to go call Doc Smith as a precaution." Beth's wailing cut off any more conversation. While Mama attended to his wife, Jackson did as he was told and his heart sank. Doc Smith was out of town. Making the sign of the cross, all Jackson could do was pray that Beth would be all right and if not, that help would arrive in time.

"Jackson, I need to lie down," Beth called to him weakly when he returned. Meeting his mother's eyes and seeing her nod of approval, they worked together to get his wife in the next room and up on the bed. He tied rags to the headboard and set them in her hands.

A heartbeat later and he listened to the voice of authority when it came to birthing babies, shoving the pillows out of the way, clearing a spot behind his wife. Barefoot, bare chested, in an old pair of jeans pulled on hastily after his stint in the tub, he climbed up behind her even as his spine fought him every step of the way. If his wife could suffer through the agony of labor, his pain was nothing. He hooked his legs around hers, and pressed the small of her back while she waited for the next spasm to pound her body. She was completely spent at this point. If Beth was going to get through this, she'd need to borrow his strength.

A grunt and she leaned forward. He willingly gave her everything he had, from his strong, able arms to the support of his aching back and the power of his thighs. The whole process went on, drawing out for another hour, and he started to panic. How much more could she take?

Kissing her cheek and her hair, he rested his forehead against hers. "Listen. You hold onto those rags and pull as hard as you can when the pain comes. Go ahead and scream your head off. Mama just took a look and she said you're ready to push."

Beth's eyes were clouded with pain, but she still managed to give him a taste of her signature, sweet smile. Grabbing hold of his jaw, she snatched a kiss just as her face tightened and the pain cranked up a notch. Clenching her teeth and bearing down, she gave it her all, only to fade fast when the contraction eased up. Breathing hard through her nose, she let go of a rag to grab his hand, giving it everything she had.

"I'm sure this one's a boy, a spitfire like your brothers." Jackson tried to give her a smile in return, but couldn't quite manage. "I caught that look between you and your mother," she said. "What's wrong?" The words spilled out in a rush. With contractions coming hard at less than a minute apart now, there was no time for dawdling. Her whole body tightened, the muscles standing out in her arms as the rags strained against her and started to fray along the edges, like his nerves. Panting when her body finally allowed her to, she blew her bangs out of her face and pinned him with bloodshot eyes. "Lord, I feel like I'll split at the seams. *Jackson Landon Henry, you tell me right now!*"

Applying the same techniques that he used with the animals they all loved so well, he stroked her hair and spoke in low, hushed tones meant to soothe her. "The baby is breech." At her look of horror, he projected a calm

he did not feel to steady his wife. "Mama's done this before, helping farmers' wives around here, and, heck, I've
done it plenty of times with the horses."

His wife didn't need to know how many times mothers and their babies had died. Resting his hands on her
belly, he closed his eyes to feel the outline of the little
one within. Beth's hands grabbed hold of his and he nodded. "Yes, I just felt a nudge from down there. Don't
worry, you can do this."

"Oh—Oh God help me, I've got to push—I've got to
push right now!" Her voice quickly rose in pitch and volume with a power that a football coach or drill sergeant
would envy. She grit her teeth and snorted, ending on a
hideous scream before her body went limp and blood
doused the towel set beneath her. He glanced up at his
mother, terrified, but she smiled reassuringly and
squeezed his shoulder.

"All right, Elizabeth, it's time, sweetheart. Jackson,
you hold onto her hands as tight as you can. I've oiled
mine and I'm going to slip them inside to try and ease the
baby out." Working quickly, but with great care, Ella
eased her hands into the birth canal. Beth emitted another
horrible scream when the tender, raw flesh was touched.

Looking on his wife's paper white skin and the dark
shadows beneath her eyes, torn apart by every scream,
Jackson could finally understand why the term labor was
used to describe the delivery process. He wiped her face,
her neck, and her shoulders, running his fingers through
her hair, and pressed his lips to her cheek. "You're almost
there. I'm so proud of you, Beth. You are an incredible
woman."

She was limp in his arms, her eyes closed when they
sprang open again. "Lord, it's coming. It's coming again!
I can't do this anymore! Lord help me, I can't!"

The tears were streaming down her face, and Jackson

pressed his forehead to hers once more. "It's going to be all right. You're in good hands, the best. Hold on. Just hold on." As another contraction rolled over her like a freight train, his mother placed her hands inside the birth canal once more. An instant later, she eased her way out, hanging on to two feet. "Yes, that's it, Beth! Come on, honey! The baby's part way out. I see some toes!"

Two more times, his wife bore down when the contractions had their way with her. Two more times, Jackson's mother plunged her hands in, Beth screaming in absolute agony as Ella gently shifted the baby to come more easily. "Please, for the love of God, please stop touching me there!"

Jackson pressed his head against his wife's shoulder, fighting tears, struggling not to break. All the while, his prayer was a litany. *Please God. Please save them.* The next scream tore through the room and nearly broke his heart and then there was a release. A final gushing poured out of her body, a small figure cradled in his mother's palms. There was an unnatural silence. Glancing over his shoulder, he could see the infant in his mother's hands, hands that were trembling, Mama's face a mask of fear. The baby was blue.

White hot terror stabbed at him as Jackson whipped around and took the baby from his mother who had frozen in shock. *A boy. It's a boy.* Pain and everything else forgotten, he flipped his son over onto his palm and began to tap at his still form, rubbing at the tiny back and shoulder blades. His hand seemed huge in comparison. He turned the tiny body again and laid him on the foot of the bed, falling to his knees. Beth was whimpering, a sound that scared him more than anything else.

Please God, don't do this to us. Don't do this to her. Jackson continued to rub the baby up and down, thinking of difficult births with foals over the years. He massaged his boy's chest and in a moment of inspiration, placed his mouth over the infant's mouth and nose, giving a little puff of air—and again. Not too much or too hard for such a little one. The third time, his heart a trip-hammer and the blood thundering in his ears, there was a cough and a thin wail rose up, the sweetest sound he'd ever heard.

Jackson turned the baby on his side to clean out his mouth and nose. With shaking hands, he accepted a warm, damp cloth from his mother. A quick wipe down and he wrapped his son in a blanket. He raised his eyes to see the tears streaming down Beth's face. One step forward and the baby was in her arms. "You've got yourself a fine boy, Mama." She bowed her head over her little one and cried her heart out.

Ella, saint of the woman that she was, prepared for the final stage of birthing. As if to make up for all of the trouble, the placenta came easily, passing quickly from Beth's body with an inconsequential grunt and a crease between her eyes. Jackson moved to help his mother, but she pressed his shoulder and urged him to stay put. While the new parents admired their latest blessing, a grace delivered to them by God, Mama tidied up the room and gave them a few minutes privacy.

Beth sat up with her back propped against the pillows, their son pressed to her breast as he suckled. Already, her color was returning and her eyes shone brightly. Jackson reached out with a trembling hand to stroke the smooth cap of the baby's fine hair, then laid his palm on the new mother's head. "You did it, little mother. Absolutely amazing. I thank God for you, for our little one, for all our blessings. I love you with all my heart."

She reached up with a hand that trembled to brush his cheek. "And I love you."

A ripple ran through him. Something nagged at him, something in her eyes as if she sealed herself off, barely grazing him with her touch. Had to be his imagination.

He took a deep breath and fought the urge to crumble, but couldn't hold back the tears as he looked down on the dark tuft of hair that stood up above the blanket. A tiny, scrunched face peeked up at them from inside the bundle, cheeks red, little fists waving. "Well, little mother. You did all the work. What do you want to call our little man?"

She stared at their son in wonder, her chin trembling, wiping away the droplets that hit the baby's face. "Wyatt. Let's make him Wyatt Landon." She glanced up at her husband for his approval, and he was humbled by the gesture.

"Sweetheart, you could call him anything under the sun about now and I'd say yes." Ella returned at that moment. "There's only one problem with Wyatt," he continued. "The next one will have to be Emmett—or Emily if it's a girl—otherwise Em will never let us live it down."

That set his mother to laughing.

Beth gave him a ghost of a grin. "That's fine, although I hope you won't mind if I take a break before working on that request." Her breath came on a sigh and she leaned back, eyes closed in weariness. He and Mama worked together to give the new mother a sponge bath, a clean nightgown, and fresh linens, installing her in bed with their baby who had been gently bathed as well. Mama kissed them all goodbye, insisting she'd go home and leave the little family some time to themselves.

Finally, Jackson changed and walked into his bedroom, fatigue settling down on him like a heavy blanket and the throbbing at the base of his spine hitting like hammer blows. He wasn't sure moving would be possible, even if the house was on fire, as he slid into his side of the bed. Beth must have been exhausted as well. She turned to face him, the baby lying between them, her hand resting protectively on his tiny body.

In a move that was pure habit, Jackson reached across to rest his hand on her hip. Her body turned to stone, every muscle pulled taut. He pulled back and met her gaze. The look in her eyes sent a shaft of ice through his heart and his head. It was as if a wall of fear came up, shutting him out.

Shivering with a sudden chill that had nothing to do with the temperature, he slid out of bed. "I—I know how tired you must be. I'm going to let you two be tonight."

She didn't make him stop. She didn't call him back as he walked out of the room.

CHAPTER 21

July 7, 1958:

No letter waited for him, not even a hasty note. Jackson could understand. Beth was beyond exhausted. That she had wanted to sleep alone, he could accept as well. After what her body had been through, it was only natural to need some time to herself, to get acquainted with the baby. It was her turning away from him for the first time ever.

He couldn't sleep. Lying in the guest room on top of the covers, staring at the ceiling until his eyes were dry, he finally pushed up off the bed—and his legs nearly gave out as a bolt of pain streaked up and down his spine. He grabbed hold of the wall for support with two hands and leaned against it. His head felt like cotton and throbbed. He had no right to complain, thinking about his wife, yet the fact remained. Between the labor and aftermath, Jackson had been up for forty-eight hours. He felt awful. His whole body ached, but that was nothing compared to his heart.

Feeling like a cripple, he fought to do the simplest tasks, his fingers fumbling to pull on clothing, make the coffee. With hands that shook, he choked down a double dose of pain pills, hoped they'd knock him out. He brought tea and a muffin, left by his angel of a mother, up to Beth. One foot in the door and she stopped his heart. Her hair was unfurled across her pillow, her cheek a healthy pink now that she'd had a chance to recover from the rigors of labor. She was turned toward Wyatt's bassinet, one hand resting on its side. Both were sound asleep.

Jackson set her breakfast on the nightstand and backed out on legs that suddenly went weak. He didn't want to wake her. Worse yet, he didn't want her to open her eyes and look at him the way she had the day before ever again.

Fighting his way back down to the kitchen, he choked down coffee, black. Everything tasted bitter. His stomach pitched so, he couldn't eat, actually ended up staggering outside and vomiting in the rose bushes. Jackson pressed his hands to his knees and took a few gulps of air. Fighting to stand up straight again, he went out to the barn just as the sun was waking up.

Wyatt and Emmett were already ahead of him, opening up the stable doors and letting the animals out into the pasture. Emmett caught sight of his older brother and his smile died. "God, Jackson, you look like death warmed over. Get back to bed. That's why we're here."

Wyatt gripped the new father by the shoulders and gave him a little shake. "Really, Big Brother. You're about to fall over."

Jackson mumbled a refusal and muddled through. Assuring the twins he was all right, they said a dubious farewell and headed home. He sat down on a hay bale for a spell, hanging on to his pounding head, wondering if he could get up again. The pain didn't ease. There was nothing for it but to force his way up. He wandered upstairs to check on the new mother and his son. The sound of splashing drew him to the bathroom.

Beth was kneeling by the tub and had Wyatt in a small

basin. She was cooing and singing to him softly, lovingly wiping him with a cloth. She didn't even acknowledge Jackson's presence, even though he'd made no efforts to be quiet. He turned on his heel, shaking, and left. He went down to the kitchen and made two sandwiches, only to throw his away. A plate and tall glass of sweet tea would be waiting for his wife when she finished the baby's bath.

So tired he could hardly see straight, the pain rolling over him in waves and threatening to take him down, he went back to the spare room to lie down. He must have drifted off because at some point, his room became darker. He barely managed to get out of bed and walked down the hallway to stand by *his* door, *their* door. With a hand that trembled, he pushed the door open. His wife sat in the rocker by the bed and Wyatt was nursing. Her golden head was bent toward their son, caught in the glow of light from the window. So beautiful she hurt to look on. Jackson pressed a hand against the door jamb to hold himself up. "Can I get you anything?"

His voice cracked, filled with pain and need, bringing her head up, her gaze meeting his. Something flickered, a fleeting shadow of the love that had always shone brightly, and then the shutters snapped shut again. "No, we're fine, thank you." A dismissal—and a stab to the heart.

He backed away and closed the door. Jackson didn't know how long he stood there, head pressed against the hard, unforgiving surface of the wood, the pain clamping him in its vicious jaws. Finally, he pushed off. Unable to remain so close to her and their son, the ache in his heart worse than anything else, he retreated to the couch in the living room. He sank down and held his head in his hands, unable to understand it, why he was sitting there while his family was upstairs. The most incredible moment of his life and he was left on the outside looking in.

Sunlight was streaming through the window, stabbing him in the eyes, bringing Jackson awake. A note waited for him on the coffee table. He sat with a jerk and gave a pitiful moan. Definitely not any better, but perhaps Beth's words could ease him.

Dear Jackson,
I'm just plain worn out and need some rest. I'm going to Mama and Daddy's for a few days. I'm sure you could use a rest too. Don't worry about us. I'll be home—when I'm ready.
Beth

He crumpled the paper and tossed it on the floor, certain his heart snapped clean in two. The pain bloomed at the base of his spine and he welcomed it. Jackson didn't care if he never got up again.

෴

Three days. Four? Jackson lost count, moving in a fog, unable to sleep or eat. He longed for his boy. He wanted to hold on to his son—hold on to his wife. Beth did not return, nor did she call. Somehow, he continued to do his chores even as his body began to unravel.

After another wakeful night on the couch, his back throbbing with every beat of his heart, and he sat up as dawn slipped through the window. A wave of dizziness made him sway and he started to cough. His nose was running and his head was too heavy to move. He pressed a hand to his forehead. It was hot. A dull sense of frustration came over him. Summertime colds were the worst.

He stood shakily, each step agony. His back—it wasn't getting better, only worse. Weaving like a man who had too much to drink, he rummaged in the medicine cabinet, choked down some aspirin. Finding that to be about as much as his body could take for the moment, he returned to the sofa and covered his eyes with his arm. He was hot one moment, shivering with cold the next, and hacking up a storm. Unable to stand himself, he pushed through the pain and forced himself to his feet to begin the trek to Mama and Pop's.

౿ఎఎ

"Get in here this instant!" Ella grabbed hold of her son's collar and gave him a gentle tug. "You look like you're about to faint. My Lord, Jackson!" She set her palm on his forehead and pulled it back fast. "You are sick! Go lie down in the living room for a little while and let me fix you up."

He nodded and limped past her, grabbing hold of chairs and the counter along the way, wishing he'd had the sense to bring his cane. It didn't even register when Mama whispered a curse behind him and ducked under his shoulder to offer her support.

Jackson had long since learned not to argue with the force of nature that was his mother. He slowly eased his way down, stretched out, and pulled the quilt off the back of the sofa. He was cold, so cold. It was wrong to feel like ice in the middle of a sauna of a summer. His mother was at his side, pulling back the blanket to put a healthy dollop of vapor rub on his chest. She rubbed it in thoroughly, went off to brew tea next with plenty of honey. While he drank it, she applied more vapor rub to his back as well as some of the liniment that did wonders since he'd been injured. The pleasant warmth began a thaw that worked from the outside in. "You are rundown and overdoing it, young man. You think you can do it all. Get that fool notion out of your head. The twins will take over with your chores tonight and tomorrow, longer if I say so."

When the tea was gone and he lay back down, Ella drew up a stool and started to massage his temples. "You are white as snow and the smudges under your eyes make you look like someone gave you a shiner. Not getting much sleep? I bet Beth could use a breather too. I'll have to give her a spell."

He shifted uneasily. Thinking about his wife only made his head hurt more. "I haven't slept at all. Beth went to her parents."

His mother paused for an instant, then continued to apply pressure, soothing him somewhat. "How long has she been gone?"

"I don't know. I've lost track of the days. A week maybe? She doesn't want me, Mama. I saw it in her eyes, the way she pulled away."

He swallowed hard, still raw inside from the memory.

His mother stopped and began to stroke his hair the way she did when he was a boy. "Jackson, Beth has just gone through a traumatic experience. Giving birth puts a woman through the wringer, leaves her feeling turned inside out and upside down. Add the fact that you came so close to losing little Wyatt, and she had quite a scare. You need to give her time. I want you to get the rest that you so badly need. When you wake, we'll go over together. You need to work this out."

On that note, she kissed his cheek and left him alone. He wanted to argue but he fell asleep.

തൽ

"Jackson! You look sick as a dog!" Beth moved forward, forehead creased in concern. Her palm rested on his forehead head and her eyes sprang wide. "You come with me."

His mother and father had come along, insisting on getting their hands on their new grandson for a while. They sat on the Masons' veranda, oohing and aahing. The little mother need only take a peek outside to reassure herself that Wyatt was all right, her parents on watch as well. There was no doubt that the baby was in good hands.

The only hands Jackson cared about at that moment were Beth's. As she stripped him down and pushed him into her childhood bed, her touch felt so good he nearly cried. She left him long enough to get their supply of vapor rub and applied a liberal coating to his chest before climbing into bed and wrapping herself around him. She was better than a pile of blankets, heating pad, or hot water bottle combined. The chill that had been consuming him finally went away.

Gradually, he stopped shaking and turned to face her. Her blue eyes were shadowed with worry, her mouth turned down in a frown as she rested her hand on his cheek. "Why didn't you tell me you were sick?" He shook his head, mouth clamped firmly shut. She threaded her fingers through his hair and gave a little tug. "Jackson, you talk to me."

"You didn't want me. There was a wall between us and you left me. I should've been the one to help you. I don't think anything has ever hurt me that much." He closed his eyes because otherwise losing his thin grip on control was a strong possibility.

She let out a long sigh, her breath kissing his skin. "I'm sorry. It—it wasn't you, Jackson. It's just—coming so close to losing Wyatt, too close, it scared me to death and when you touched me, all I could think about was locking myself up inside where nothing could hurt me, trying to keep the baby safe. If I let you in—I didn't think

I could hold myself together. What if we lost him? I don't think I could live with myself."

He fought the urge to cough, choking it down and concentrating, struggling to find words that would fit, to find words at all in a head that pounded. "We didn't lose him and you can't go through this world so afraid of dying that you forget how to live."

A sob rose up and she buried her head against his chest, letting out all of the pain and worry she'd carried for the past few days. For the past nine months. Gradually, her cries turned to soft hiccups and her body went loose. He rested an arm on her waist and she drew closer, exactly where his wife belonged. "I love you," she whispered.

"Always," he mumbled back and knew no more. When he awoke, the sunlight was streaming in brightly, heralding a new day. Jackson's head was better, although his body felt as he'd been run over with a steam roller. His throat tickled, bringing on a cough. Leveraging himself on one elbow, he drank from the full glass of water that had been thoughtfully placed on his nightstand, along with two aspirin. Swallowing both, he rolled over to see Beth sitting in a rocker in the corner, nursing Wyatt. On her pillow beside him, a note was waiting. Jackson watched her mouth turn up in a smile as her eyes met his, clear and open once more, better than any medicine. He began to read.

Dear Jackson,

I'm sorry this is late in coming, but congratulations, Daddy! You have been incredible, my rock from the first to the last. I know you were scared through it all, but you never let on. You knew exactly what to do and were such a help to me. I was in the best of hands—your hands, that are strong enough to hold up the world. I can never thank

you enough for helping our son to arrive—and live. For-
give me for shutting you out when I was afraid. I let you
down. Because of you, we welcomed Wyatt into this
world in our own home, his place in the world where
he'll grow roots and one day, stand tall, like his father,
and his father before him with a strong back, mind, and
heart. Because we worked together, Wyatt is here.

I keep pinching myself, wondering when I'll wake up
and find out this has all been a dream. I've learned a
valuable lesson. With you by my side, I can face anything.
I could not ask for more. I know I've said this before, but
can't say it enough. My cup runneth over. Let's go home.

Love,
Your Beth

☙☙☙

The barn and the house was buttoned up for the night.
The snow was coming down in sheets and showed no
signs of letting up. It was a blizzard in the making and
Emmett was exactly where he wanted to be, in the living
room, on the couch, his wife at the other end while he
massaged her feet and enjoyed watching what an effect it
had on her.

A smidgeon of fear ran down his spine as he watched
the wall of white falling down and glanced back at Casey's bulging belly. It couldn't happen tonight, could it?
Didn't bear thinking on. *Cross that bridge when you*
come to it, boy. His father's voice rang out in his mind.
Ever since they'd discovered the journal, Jackson seemed
closer than ever. Emmett smiled to himself. *You always*
did give good advice, Dad.

Casey let out a low moan that did funny things to his
insides, making the blood hum in his veins. He cleared
his throat and tilted his head to concentrate on her feet.

Facing her was not an option, not when she had stoked the fires. She chuckled. "Why don't you take a break and let me have a turn?"

He snorted. "Really? You think you can reach?" The woman was stubborn as all get out. She had to prove him wrong, clamping down on her tongue, focused on shifting this way and that, back propped against the arm of the couch, gesturing for him to rest his feet on her protruding stomach. Realizing arguing would not be a prudent move, he carefully set one foot down, then the other.

His wife's fingers went to work, making him mellow as molasses, turning up the heat that was always there, not far below the surface. "You are the devil in disguise, Case. It's just not right tempting me this way when I can't do anything about it." With a mischievous glint in her eye, she made it even worse by flicking her tongue over her lips. He squeezed his eyes shut and watched fireworks start to sizzle against his lids.

The phone rang. Once. Twice. Going on three. "Leave it," she murmured sleepily. "We've got an answering machine."

Reluctant to move, he fought his way to his feet and grabbed the call just as the recording began to play. "What? Wyatt? Wait a minute. Let me turn this blasted thing off." Anxious because of his big brother's tone, he ended up yanking the answering machine plug out of the wall in his haste. "All right. Hold up. Slow down, Wyatt. You're talking too fast. Okay. Okay. I'll meet you there."

The phone nearly slipped out of his hand. He couldn't breathe, a tight band wrapped so tightly around his chest it was squeezing his heart. Casey had managed to stand up after a considerable effort and stared at him intently. Emmett made for the front door before he could be placed under the microscope of his wife's scrutiny. Stay put and her doctor senses would spring into action—like Spiderman.

Besides, he knew nothing was wrong except a full-blown panic attack in the making and he didn't have time for it. He fought with his boots and laces, coming up to find her beside him. "What is it? What's wrong?"

He shrugged into his coat and grabbed a hat, crammed gloves in his pocket. "It's little Jack. You know how he's had that bad cold or whatever it was? It got worse, fast. He stopped breathing for a terrifying minute or two. They've bundled him up in the truck and they're headed to the emergency room. Figure the four-wheel drive will get them there faster than an ambulance. If only this damn snow would let up! I'm going to the hospital as soon as I can plow my way out of this mess."

Scraping her cheek with a kiss, he burst out into the snow, cursing at himself. *Should've plowed again. You know it.* He'd been too complacent, sitting there with Casey, starting to tumble off into sleep. An instant later and he cranked up the truck and turned it around, prepared to bully his way through the foot or so that had fallen to blast his way out to the road. He was forced to pull up short at the sight of a very pregnant woman waiting by the walkway, nearly stepping out in front of him.

Not now, Casey Henry. He kicked into high gear. Out of the truck, nearly pushing the door through to the other side, pulling up in front of her. She raised her chin and the flash in her eyes dared him to get in her way. "I'm going with you. Don't even try and argue. I'll climb up in the back of the truck if I have to."

"I'd like to see you try."

His body was an inferno, the heat headed straight for the top of his head, set on explode. A dull, familiar throbbing started at the base of his skull, threatening to migrate. *Don't even think about it!* his inner voice growled viciously, as if migraines responded to orders. None too gentle, Em grabbed her arm, brought her along to the passenger side, and boosted her up.

Back in the driver's seat, he glowered at her. "Hold on tight. We're doing this one time."

"At least I'll be at the right place if anything happens." She rested her hand on her belly, her eyes troubled. "Why didn't they call me?"

He reached out to thread his fingers through hers. "Probably because you're about to pop. Didn't want to stress you out. Remember what it was like for Sammie when she had little Jackson?" He set his hand on her rounded belly and told it firmly. "You stay put in there tonight, got it?"

She rested her hand on his for a moment before he let go to concentrate on the road. It was one hell of a ride, leaving them both tense and white-faced by the time they arrived an hour later. They walked in, as quickly as his very pregnant wife was able, to get the update. Jackson was in critical care, touch and go with a bad case of pneumonia.

やのやの

Casey held Sammie's hand, sitting quietly and listening as she babbled about the past few hours, everything her sister-in-law had tried to do leading up to the moment of crisis, releasing her pent up fears. Samantha Henry, was two years older and accustomed to the ups and downs that were a part of life.

She'd gone straight from being the farmer's daughter to becoming a farmer's wife. A good match for Wyatt, the skin on her hands was rough from joining her husband in the barn, her full lips chapped from hours spent in the bitter cold. Sunny hair was pulled back in a no non-

sense ponytail while her sky blue eyes were usually un-
troubled by whatever challenges were dished out on a
daily basis. That all changed when it involved their little
boy. She hit a roadblock.

"Come on, Sam. Let's walk, get a cup of tea or something. Sitting here worrying won't fix anything. Besides,
if I don't move right now, I'm not ever going to move."
Casey gave her sister-in-law a hug in encouragement and
accepted a hand up, using her strong, compact form for
leverage. The two women went in search of hot beverag-
es and a diversion, leaving the men behind. Watching
them go, Emmett was grateful his wife had been so in-
sistent on coming along. Between her time as chief doctor
in Albany's ER and as family physician at the Charlton
Medical Center, she was in her element. She missed her
practice terribly. At least her talents would be put to good
use tonight.

Wyatt leaned forward in the chair beside him and
threaded his fingers through hair gone dark as summer's
highlights faded away. His eyes slammed shut as he let
out a groan. "He's not even two yet, damn it!"

Emmett hooked onto his arm and gave it a hard
squeeze. "Don't you even think that way, you hear? That
boy will be here for his second birthday next month."

"How do you know, Em? Our family has had such a
good track record." His older brother shot a gray-blue
bolt of a stare his way and jumped up from his chair.
"That's it. I can't stand it. I've got to *do* something, pace,
hit a wall, anything. Send out an announcement on the
PA system if you need me." With that, the one with the
level head in the family on the brink of losing it completely, took off.

Tempted to do the same, Emmett chose another refuge. The chapel waited at the end of the hall, a small
room bathed in a soft purple light. A large cross hung on

the wall with a statue of Mother Mary standing below it, candles flickering at her feet. He moved forward to light one for little Jackson and slipped into a chair, thankful no one else was there. He gazed up at the wall and began to pray fervently. *Please God. Haven't we lost enough? First Ricky. Now*—He shut that thought down.

Footsteps sounded behind him and Casey eased her way onto the seat beside him, nudging him with her shoulder. Gazing into Mother Mary's serene eyes, she let out a pent up breath. "Listening to Sammie just now, thinking about ours on the way, I can understand Beth, why she closed up on your father after your brother was born. I—I think I'd go out of my mind if anything ever happened to you or Question Mark."

"I was thinking the same thing." Emmett tried to give her a smile, but just couldn't manage. "I wish Dad was here. Mama too." His voice cracked and he cut the words off.

She reached in her handbag and pulled out the journal, setting it on his knee. Emmett set his hand on the scarred surface, his tears splashing down, adding to the wear and tear. Casey rested her hand on his. "I think they are."

He nodded unable to speak. Closing his eyes, he prayed to his mother, father, God, and all that was holy above. *Please. Watch over Little Jack.*

At four in the morning, heavy footsteps came at a run and Wyatt grabbed their shoulders, giving them a little shake. "Jackson is going to be all right. He's past the point of crisis. Sammie's with him right now. I just saw him. He smiled at me and waved." His face caved in. Emmett rose to his feet and took his brother in his arms as he wept. *After all, it's what brothers do.* His father's voice was clear in his mind. The journal, pressed against his heart, was a tangible reminder of the man who built them.

Thanks, Dad. With a final glance at the cross on the wall, Emmett hooked an arm around Wyatt's shoulders, took Casey's hand, and they went to see his nephew.

CHAPTER 22

September 4, 1958:

Do you think he's all right?" Beth was nearly breaking her neck, craning so hard to try and look back at their son's bassinet under the shade tree in the backyard. Mama sat nearby, gently rocking the baby side to side. Catching their scrutiny, she lifted a hand to wave and gave them a big smile. The day was perfect, no clouds to mar a blue so bright one could get lost looking up, the air crisp like a fresh picked apple, and the trees wearing their fall finery.

Jackson couldn't have had a better day if he'd put in a personal request. There was no way that he'd let it get away from them. They would spend some time alone if he had to tie his wife up and drag her away, screaming and kicking. Hopefully, that wouldn't be necessary. *You'll catch more bees with honey.*

"Wyatt is fine. He's in the eat and sleep stage, remember? Not too much is going on right now. Besides, you're the one who's pointed out Mama is an expert after raising the three of us. She knows more than we do, all wrapped up in her little pinky!" At Beth's pout, he leaned in and kissed her cheek. "Relax. Enjoy the beautiful day God's given us. Happy Anniversary."

He gently nudged Ricky Ricardo in the ribs and the stallion set off at a trot.

His wife's laughter bubbled up, her hair whipping in the wind, and she leaned back against him, her arm snaking around his neck so that she could brush his jaw with her lips. "Happy Anniversary to you too, Jackson Landon Henry. Enough chat. Let's ride!" There was mischief lighting up her eyes brighter than a blue sky without end.

He was only too happy to fulfill her request. "Your wish is my command." Giving a shout, he let the horse have his head and Ricky Ricardo did not disappoint, putting on an exuberant burst of speed. His Lucy and Junebug, their young foal, were far out to pasture. The stallion's destination was obvious. The faster the horse went, the more Beth laughed, holding on tight to the pommel of the saddle.

Jackson wrapped an arm around her waist and kept her snug against his chest. Between the maddening scent of her hair and the heat of her body, pressed against a part of him that had been out of service for some while, he had quite a time keeping his seat. In one last glorious surge of energy, Ricky Ricardo finally met up with his family, snorting with his exertions. They greeted him affectionately and began to prance about, the couple's cue to dismount.

Jackson slid off the back of the saddle first, reaching up his hands to set Beth on the ground, pausing for a moment to savor the feel of her warm body in his hands. Finding her rosy cheeks and flashing eyes too irresistible, he cupped the back of her head and gave her a thorough kissing that nearly bowed her to the ground. Her arms wrapped around his neck and she gave of herself as skillfully as her husband. They only stopped when breathing became difficult, both panting.

"My, we sound like Ricky Ricardo," Beth murmured breathlessly, breaking free and setting off for the far boundary line of the pasture, marked by a white fence line that was continuous. She rubbed at her backside along the way, wearing a rueful grin. "My bottom isn't quite used to such abuse."

"Let me see what I can do about that." Jackson stepped in close and cupped her behind, giving her a massage that made her eyelids droop. Taking her by surprise, he picked her up and slung her on his back. She fought him, but there wasn't much that could be done about it. When a Henry set his mind to something, there was no stopping him.

They reached the fence and he let her off so she could shimmy her way over to the other side. Two giant steps and he was with her. Prone to being spontaneous, she took his hand and gave an enthusiastic tug. They ran side by side, into a wonderland of fall foliage. Thick and full, the trees closed ranks behind them, concealing them in a patch of woods that would be theirs alone with no interruptions.

His wife turned to face him, the flush rising from the opening of her collar and spreading full bloom in her cheeks. She raised her hands to thread her fingers in his hair, the sparkle in her eyes nearly blinding in intensity. "Jackson, make love to me."

His heart slammed against his ribcage, kicking into high gear. While he'd been looking forward to this moment since Wyatt was born, he had no intentions of rushing his wife nor did he have any expectations. He swallowed hard and licked lips gone dry. "Are you sure? I don't want to hurt you."

She took a step closer and her breath kissed his skin, making him close his eyes and begin to quiver, calling forth a groan that rumbled deep down in his chest. His thoughts turned inward, trying to ward off hyperventilation. "I want this. A little pain will be worth the pleasure. Please. It's been a long time." Her voice trembled on the end. She needed and craved this reunion of their bodies as much as he did.

"Then we'd best make up for it." He went slowly, giving thanks that his back did not act up, paying homage to the precious gift that was placed in his hands by the grace of God. Today was their anniversary, a time for romance, with no rushing or cares. Placing all of his focus on giving her the pleasure she asked for, Jackson began by stroking her hair, running his fingers from the crown to the luscious ends, twining his fingers in the heavy strands of gold and gently pulling her head back. His lips closed over hers in a kiss that carried them both on a wave.

Not content to stop there, he skimmed his way along her jaw, to her ear to take a nibble, and along her neck, stopping at the butterfly flutter of her pulse. Her blood had to be singing in her veins. Pressing her palm against his chest, he showed her that the same song was playing in his heart. His hands began to move, kneading at her neck, over her shoulders, down her back, and she let out a soft moan that was almost a cry, half agony, half joy. "Jackson—oh, how I've missed this."

"Me, too, darlin'." He kissed her again and his fingers fumbled with her favorite flannel shirt—*his* shirt—loosening the buttons and allowing it to drop to the ground. He inhaled deeply. She'd surprised him, wearing no shirt underneath, only a bra that revealed the fruits of a nursing mother. It was his turn to let out a low groan that came somewhere from deep within. "Beth, I feel like a man walking through the desert and finding an oasis."

"Then I guess it's time to dive in." She gave him a playful grin, rising on tiptoe to press her lips to his. Things started to move more quickly from there, restraint getting harder by the second, as they helped each other to shed their clothes and stretched out on a bed of freshly fallen leaves. The earthy scent rose up around them as he cradled his wife in his arms. He continued to go easy, trailing his fingers and his lips over her body, worshipping her. Rising above her, he stilled, marveling at the beauty of her hair fanned out against the explosion of reds, oranges, and yellows that carpeted the forest floor.

She looked up at him, lips parted and eyes heavy with passion. "What is it?"

He shook his head and pulled out a smile. "You are so beautiful. I want to hold on to you and never let go." Hands braced on either side of her head, he bent down to kiss her once more, trembling as his body was held in check, waiting for the right moment.

"Then don't. Take me with you wherever you go—all the way to the stars above. Take me *now*, Jackson." She nodded at him, answering with a smile of her own, and her body opened, welcoming him in a homecoming that nearly decimated them both as they tumbled into each other.

They lay in each other's arms until the sun was dropping low in the sky, heading toward the horizon in a blaze of glory. He stood first and offered Beth his hand, pulling her to her feet with ease, showering her with kisses once more and dressing her in between. His wife returned his affections and assistance until they emerged from the woods, fully clothed, holding hands once again. Mounting the fence first, he drew her up beside him. As they each straddled the top railing, he couldn't help himself. Another kiss was due.

A few minutes later and they crossed the field, climbed into the saddle, and began the journey back to the house as the sunset painted the sky in a mesmerizing palette of reds, pinks, and purples. Jackson was in a haze himself, his head clouded with the presence of his wife. Junebug and Lucy trailed behind them, following them into the barn. Habitual in nature, the horses knew that it was time to turn in. The others were not far away as Jackson brought them in to secure them for the night in their stalls.

Beth sat on a stool against the wall, her eyes following his every move. The heat of her gaze was like a physical touch, making his pulse beat harder again, pushing him to move faster and get through his nightly chores as quickly as possible. He was shutting the last stall when her arms wrapped around him, forcing him to set his forehead against the post.

Lord, give me strength. He knew the score. Wyatt would be waiting inside and any further celebrating would have to wait until bedtime, *hours* away. "What's wrong, honey?" There was laughter in her voice. His wife knew what she could do to him.

"You're—driving—me—crazy. I can't take waiting until later. I'm already in withdrawal." He turned around and gathered her in his arms. Pressing a kiss to the top of her head, he took a deep breath and attempted to steel himself. "Beth, you are something else and I would like nothing more than a repeat performance from the woods to happen right now, right here in the straw. There's only one problem. We have a little boy who is waiting for us."

Her smile was infectious, drawing him in as she laid a palm on his cheek and stared at him intently. "I have an anniversary present for you. Your mother is keeping Wyatt for the night." She nodded as the spark of excitement lit in his eyes and turned away from him, walking toward the door. Her hips wagged in an exaggerated fashion every step of the way. "Well? Are you coming or not?"

She didn't have to offer that invitation more than once. He caught up with her, snagging her around the waist and kissing her cheek. Beth nudged the door shut with her foot and they took the path to the house, Jackson's heart skipping every step of the way as his mouth formed some of the hardest words he'd ever said. "Are you sure about this? I know it has to be hard on you to be a night without him."

She turned to him as they stood inside the entryway of their home and looped her arms around his neck. "It is hard and I know that he needs me, but you need me too. Besides, *I* need a night alone with my husband. Accept this as part of your anniversary present."

"There's more?" He asked incredulously, receiving a nod in answer. They began to sway, dancing their way through the house, passing through the living room and ending in the kitchen with the last rays of sunset bathing them in a rosy glow. She hummed a sweet melody with every step, and he felt himself spiraling over the edge. Her lips caught his in a kiss that shook him to the core and he had to take a moment to center himself or be lost. "So what about this other present?" he asked in a throaty growl.

Beth smiled and gave him a push, seating him in a kitchen chair at a table that was already laid with their fine china and the dozen roses he'd given her first thing that morning when she woke up. "I want you to close your eyes, Jackson. No peeking." Having learned not to argue with his wife, a valuable lesson that all husbands should master sooner rather than later, he sat back and let his lids fall shut.

Music drifted his way first, something soft with a touch of jazz. Her perfume reached him next, something floral with a hint of citrus.

Her touch followed, her fingers running through his hair before her lips grazed his jaw and Jackson was certain he was going to come apart at the seams.

"You can open your eyes now. How do you like it?"

"I—love it." She made breathing, moving, or coherent thought nearly impossible, wearing a negligee of a deep blue that brought out the color of her eyes and intensified them. He found himself caught in her gaze, a ship cast away at sea, until she sat on his lap and gave him an anchor to hold on to. He buried his head in her chest and breathed deeply, allowing his hands to roam, ranging from the golden strands of her hair to cradling her hips. "Before we go any further, I have a present for you too."

Beth stood up with reluctance and propped her hip on the table. "You didn't need to give me another present. You already gave me my flowers, breakfast in bed, that wonderful horse ride, and the grand finale." She blushed prettily at the last and her mouth turned up in a bow.

Jackson shrugged, grinning at the shared memory of their time in the woods, and reached into his pocket for a velvet box. "I figure our first anniversary is something of an occasion. I'd best treat you special." He flipped the lid open, revealing a simple, gold band with three small stones in the middle.

His wife gasped and the tears came to her eyes as she fingered the ring. "That sapphire is for my September birthday. Since you and Wy are in July, I've got a ruby on each side. I'm stuck right in the middle, smack dab where I want to be for the rest of my life." He looked up and she was silently crying, smiling all the while.

"It's beautiful."

Jackson lifted the ring from the box and slipped it on Beth's right ring finger. She began to cover him with kisses while her hands gripped his shoulders and held on tight. "Did you know that sapphires and rubies complement each other and come from the same type of stone? Yours means purity of spirit. For me and Wyatt, it's happiness, beauty, love and passion." As he stared at her in incomprehension, she took his face in her hands and stared him in the eye. "Don't you see, Jackson? We're two parts of one whole. We complete each other."

He stood and picked her up in a move that had become his standard, taking the stairs slowly so that their lips could touch with every step. "I didn't need a ring to know that. I figured that out on that fourth of July before we were married." They crossed the threshold of the bed-room and he laid his wife down on the bed.

"But what about dinner?" She rose up to take hold of the lapel of his shirt. He stretched out beside her and let his fingers trail up and down her side, finally resting on her hip. She came in for a kiss and he nearly forgot the question.

"Dinner can wait. I'm only hungry for one thing right now." Jackson proceeded to give his wife his undivided attention. Sometime around midnight, they went down-stairs for dinner. With Beth on his lap, they shared one chair and the meal she'd carefully prepared, salad with diced chicken, strawberries dipped in chocolate, topped off with a sweet bottle of wine. He gave credit where it was due, finishing every morsel.

In the darkness, he trailed her upstairs and ran a bath, proceeding to take up a cloth and wash his wife from the soles of her feet to the strands of hair on her head. Beth repaid him in kind. They climbed back into bed and still, their passion wasn't sated.

"Jackson, what about sleep?" She was turned on her side and her eyes caught the moon's glow, flashing like starlight in the darkened room, her body cast in white like a statue from days of old.

He set his hand on her hip and moved closer until her breath warmed his skin. His lips brushed hers and he gave her a smile. "Who said anything about sleep?"

ભળભ

Good Lord. Not again! Jackson bolted out of bed. Somehow his body knew when Beth wasn't there. Those few days apart didn't help any, leaving him with a lingering sense of anxiety. Fighting to keep panic at bay, he searched the house, gasping in relief when he found Wyatt sound asleep in his crib. What if she'd taken him? There was no sign of her. He pulled on his coat, grabbed another for her, and slipped on his boots. Out to the yard, front and back, to the barn, staring out over the pasture. Nothing.

He rushed back inside and picked up the phone, glancing at the clock on the kitchen wall. *Two a.m.!* "Mama? I'm sorry to wake you, but I can't find Beth. I think she's sleep walking again. Will you keep an eye out for her? If she shows up, try and bring her in. Call me."

Stomach twisting so that Jackson thought he'd be sick, he choked it down and cranked up Belle. He had to hurry, couldn't leave the baby for long. Why couldn't Wyatt be at Mama and Pop's tonight? The thought hit him hard— what if Beth thought he was there, lost in the maze of sleep?

He pictured her stumbling through the darkness. All the way up their winding driveway, the truck inched along, fearful he might hit her. His heart was in his throat when he caught the figure of a woman in his headlights, all the way at the end, clinging to their mailbox. If she'd gone in the road—

He shuddered to think of what could've happened.

Leaving the truck running, Jackson climbed out and ran to her, his back flaring, but he ignored it. "Beth! Beth, wake up!" He grabbed her by the shoulders.

She turned to him and he almost cried out at the mask of pain that had replaced her beautiful face. "I've lost

Wyatt!" She moaned pitifully and dropped to her knees, wrapping her arms around her stomach. "I've lost him! I should have gone to the hospital. It's all my fault. He's dead because of me!"

Jackson didn't waste a minute, simply picked her up and set her inside the truck. Backing up as fast as Belle would go, he pulled up to their front door and came around. She was still sobbing, lost in her nightmare. He'd found that forcing her awake often made things worse, filling her with such terror that it would take him hours to soothe her.

He carried her inside, up the stairs, praying his back would bear the burden long enough. Into their son's bedroom, placing her in the rocker that had belonged to his great grandmother. He picked up Wyatt, hushing him as the baby began to stir and settled the warm, little bundle in his mother's arms. Jackson knelt beside her and stroked her hair even as she pressed the baby to her chest, silent tears still streaking down her cheeks. "Wyatt is fine, Beth. Wyatt's right here. Everything is all right."

Eventually, her crying stopped. She stopped rocking and met his gaze. She was back. "Oh, Jackson. It was so awful. I dreamt—"

He pressed his finger to her lip. "I know. I know, but Wyatt is okay, right here in your arms, healthy and strong." Letting go of his breath in a ragged sigh, Jackson leaned back against the wall and ran a hand through his hair. *Thank you, God.*

He didn't have the heart to tell her about her episode, of what a scare she'd given him, not yet. When she was settled, he set Wyatt back in his crib and led her back to bed. He wrapped around his wife spoon style and tumbled into an exhausted sleep.

Her moaning brought him awake. They'd overslept and the sunlight was peeking in, turning her hair to gold as it was strewn across their pillows. Her face was white, her eyes squeezed shut as she raised a hand to ward off the brightness. "Oh, my head. It's about to split open."

Jackson hurried to pull the shade and close the curtains, making it as dark as possible. He went to her side and started to stroke her temples. Sometimes after an incident of sleep walking, a migraine would set in, another remnant of that fateful day when she fell off of the porch. "Better?" He asked her hoarsely. How Jackson hated to see her hurting.

She shook her head and pressed her hands to her temples. If possible, she went whiter. "I'm going to be sick."

He didn't hesitate, simply picked her up and rushed her into the bathroom where she began to retch pitifully. She sagged to the floor, forehead on the cool tile, only to get sick again. And again. Jackson's stomach hurt watching her. He wet a towel with cold water and wiped her face and neck before pressing it to her forehead. "Just sit a minute." He went down to the kitchen to grab water and some of his pain pills. If they could take the edge off of his back, they should work for her. Wyatt started to wail, awake for the first time that morning and Jackson couldn't help but wince. Beth needed him.

There was a soft tapping at his door and Mama walked in. One look at his face and she gave him a hug. "I thought you might need a breather this morning. The boys have got the horses. I'll get Wyatt." Jackson had filled her in as soon as Beth was safe and sound in bed.

She was so welcome he almost unraveled. "Thanks, Mama. Beth's not doing well at all. She's got another migraine." At the sound of more heaving from the bathroom, he took the stairs two at a time, each step giving him a jolt of pain to remind him of what he wasn't supposed to do anymore. No time for his problems. His wife needed him.

He gave her the pills and held the glass for her, her hand was trembling so. She sagged against him, letting out a long slow breath. "I hope it works soon. My stomach is so topsy-turvy, I don't know if I'll keep it down." When nothing happened in the first few minutes, he scooped her up and brought her back to bed. All the while, she kept her eyes squeezed shut, head buried in his chest to keep the light out.

He set her in bed and covered her up. "Try and sleep. It will be better when you wake up." *Please God. Let it be better.* That evening, she was still pale and shaky, but thankfully her pain was gone. Jackson had learned a difficult lesson. He could take anything in this world— except Beth's pain.

The next morning, his note was propped on the bathroom sink when he stepped out of the shower. She'd even sprayed the paper with her perfume.

My Dearest Jackson,
After all you've done for me, you need a fancier greeting. Thank you for taking care of me and for the best anniversary a woman could ever have. I didn't get to tell you what with all of the upset yesterday. I don't need anything more when I have you and Wyatt. I'm only hoping we have at least sixty more anniversaries to share. That still won't be enough. A. A. Milne said it best, "If you live to be 100, I want to live to be a hundred minus one day so I don't have to live without you." I love you, Jackson Landon Henry, more than words will ever say. I guess I'll have to show you every day for the rest of my life.
Love,
Your Beth

CHAPTER 23

February 14, 1959:

Mid-afternoon and the chill in the air plummeted, snatching Jackson's breath away, making his toes and fingers hurt, taking the pain in his back to a whole new level. He learned to expect it with the cold and accepted it as par for the course. That didn't mean he had to like it. A strong gust began kicking up and then the skies opened, dumping hail of all things. He anticipated, even looked forward to snow in a New York wintertime, but hail, sleet, and freezing rain? No fun whatsoever.

There'd be no playing with Wyatt out in the snow today. Jackson loved being outside with the two people he loved more than anything, listening to the baby babble up a storm, all bundled up like a marshmallow in his snowsuit, watching his Beth turn rosy as her eyes glittered. Being cooped up would make her fractious. She hated being penned up. He tried to shake off his disappointment. Jackson had been looking forward to making a snowman, tossing a few snowballs, stealing a kiss or two. Getting a really good massage. Another glance at the sky gave him a sense of misgiving. Those clouds were ominous. Best to get bottled up for the duration.

Making a dash for the pasture, he had to scramble to get the horses out of the storm, balls of ice the size of a quarter pelting him all the while. No doubt there'd be bruises come morning. Only Lucy and Junebug, spirited creatures, gave him a run for the money. In a moment of inspiration, he saddled up Ricky Ricardo and rode out to meet the stallion's mate and offspring. When he started to gallop, didn't it beat all when the mare and colt started racing the stallion straight into the open door of the barn? Jackson buttoned everything up tight and headed back to the house.

One step inside and he thought about turning into a puddle. Nothing sounded better than thawing out, changing into flannel pajamas, and cuddling with his wife and son. They made a homey picture, burrowed under a pile of blankets on the couch, eating popcorn and watching a movie while a blaze snapped in the fireplace. Wyatt gave him a glimpse of his first tooth as he smiled and made a whole lot of nonsense noise for his father, waving his hands in the air. Jackson scooped him up off the sofa, ignoring the jab at the base of his spine, and his heart melted as he was surrounded by the scent of popcorn, oatmeal from breakfast, and baby powder.

His wife just about did him in when she joined in the mix, wrapping them all in the Wedding Ring quilt pulled off the bed. Her arms looped around his neck and Jackson dropped his face into a cloud of sunshine in hair that smelled like apples. "You do not know what you two are doing to me." Skimming his lips across hers, he forced himself to step back. "You need to save me some of this for later. I've got to go over and give Pop a hand before this gets any worse."

"Stay and have some coffee and soup first. You need to warm up some. It's nasty out there." Concern formed a line between her eyes as she pressed a hand to the nape of his neck, making it even harder to maintain his resolve. He snatched a kiss and ruffled Wyatt's hair, getting a belly laugh in response.

"I would love nothing more, but I don't want to leave Pop hanging. I'll be back as soon as I can. Keep that coffee pot going and that soup heated up on the stove." They followed him to the door as he pulled on a dry coat, hat, and gloves. He stopped long enough to give them a hug and press a lingering kiss to his wife's lips. "That will tide me over. Don't forget to save me some popcorn and a spot on that couch." His wife's smile was still burning brightly in his heart when he stepped out into treacherous weather.

Jackson cranked the heat up in the truck and spun the tires on his way out. He had a tough time getting traction as the conditions started to get slick. By the time he rumbled into his parents' driveway, the hail had ceased and freezing rain was pinging off his windshield. Wyatt, Emmett, and Pop were working hard to get all of the horses in, but there were still about twenty remaining.

Flipping up his collar and buttoning up to his neck, Jackson joined in the fray, slipping and sliding across a surface that was already turning into a sheet of ice. One good wrench of his back when he tried to catch himself and he couldn't breathe. He grabbed hold of Wyatt's shoulder to steady himself. At his younger brother's look of concern, Jackson managed to straighten up and keep going.

Twenty minutes passed before the entire herd was in and by that point, the trees were iced over, branches weighed down with a thick coating. Emmett and Wyatt worked their way to the front porch, holding on to each other, while Jackson did the same with Pop, struggling not to limp or let him know how much he hurt. Glancing at him from the corner of his eye, he didn't like the look of his father. His face had taken on a gray cast and his breathing was labored. "Hey, Pop. Are you all right?"

Landon waved him off, huffing and puffing with each step, nearly wiping out and clinging to his son's arm while they stood still a moment. "Fine, I'm fine. Just too old to be running all over the place, that's all."

They'd inched a little farther when a loud creaking and wailing had them looking back. At least a foot of snow had accumulated on the roof of the barn. With the added weight of the ice, the old structure couldn't take it. "Dear God, the roof—it's getting ready to cave in!" Heedless of the ice or his struggle to breathe, Pop sprinted toward the barn, scrambling over the slippery lane. All three of his sons joined him in an effort to bring the horses back out of the barn before calamity struck.

By some miracle, all of the animals were out just as the front section of the roof gave. With a horrendous noise, heave, and a shudder, the whole lot came crashing down. Landon stood a few feet from the entrance, leaning on Blackie when Jackson saw his face twist in pain. His father gripped his left arm, then his chest before tumbling to the ground. "Pop!"

All three Henry boys dropped what they were doing to gather around their father, kneeling on the ground beside him. Forgetting his own discomfort, Jackson loosened his father's collar and leaned in close. "He's not breathing! Emmett, go in and call for the ambulance. Wyatt, help me carry him up on the porch to get him out of this mess!"

Together, the brothers fought their way up the steps, nearly falling several times over. Jackson's back was screaming. They laid their father out on the floor boards, the tears streaming down Wyatt's face and Jackson was on the brink. "Run in and get blankets, Wy. We've got to keep him warm." His brother did his bidding while Mama and Emmett burst out the door. Jackson pressed his head to his father's chest. "It's his heart. There's no beat."

Emmett knelt down beside his brother. "Remember when I told you about Doc talking to us in Science class? He said you need to...to press on his chest or something. Right here." He gestured to the sternum. "Right, Wyatt?"

His twin had returned with a pile of blankets and was piling them up on his father, his hands shaking. "Right...I think. Why did we have to mess around like always?" He closed his eyes, forehead scrunched in concentration. "Doc Smith said to push a few times, I forget how many, and then breathe into the person's mouth."

Jackson had nothing to lose. Shaking so hard he was fit to fall to pieces, he found the center of his father's breast bone, just above the sternum and began to pump, alternating with forceful puffs of air into Pop's mouth by tipping his head back and pinching his nose. Mama knelt on the other side, holding her husband's hand, crying and telling him she loved him. Emmett and Wyatt gathered round as well, finding someplace to hold onto their father as they wrapped blankets around his still form. If sheer force of will combined with love could be a tether, Landon Henry's family would keep him with them.

Jackson tirelessly alternated between the pumps and the breathing, losing count and all track of time, when the wash of red and blue lights lit up the porch. He didn't stop until a paramedic gripped his shoulder and gently told him to back away. The young ambulance attendant leaned in close and looked back with a hint of a smile. "You did a good job. I've got a pulse."

Jackson sagged to his knees, his mother and brothers gripping him around the neck, sobbing their eyes out. Only then did he begin to shake hard enough that his teeth chattered, the fire at the base of his spine burning bright and spreading. Within minutes, the paramedics loaded Landon on a gurney and transferred him to the back of the ambulance, Ella climbing in to be with her husband. Jackson's brothers helped him to his feet, his back fighting him every step of the way, and they piled into his truck. He didn't know how, but they managed to get from point A to point B.

While Emmett and Wyatt gathered around their mother, Jackson stepped up to the receptionist. "Excuse me, Mam. Would it be possible for me to use your phone to call my wife? Everything happened so fast, I don't even have my wallet." The words poured out in a rush and he had to swallow hard to choke down the lump rising up in his throat. His stomach twisted in knots so tight, he feared being sick all over the pretty, young brunette behind the desk. *Don't think about it. Don't think about it. Think about Wy and Beth.*

She turned the phone his way and gestured to the seat. "Absolutely. Please sit down and take as long as you need." The woman gave him a smile of encouragement and patted his hand. "The doctors here do miraculous things. Your father is in the best of hands." Her kindness made his eyes sting and Jackson had to blink several times as he murmured thanks and fumbled with the dial.

On the first ring, she picked up, voice high with fear when she heard his greeting. "Jackson? What's wrong? I saw the ambulance pass on the road. Was someone hurt?" Beth was speaking so quickly, he could hardly understand her. His heart started tripping, aching with the news he had to tell.

"It's Pop. He's had a heart attack. We're at the hospital right now and the doctors are with him. We don't know anything yet. I'm sorry I didn't stop home, but—" He broke off, unable to say more. His fingers began to wind the cord round and round his hand, getting tighter by the second, until they hurt and the pain was welcome, anything to take his mind off his father.

"You had to get there as fast as you could, I understand. I'll call my parents and get there as soon as I can. I love you." Jackson softly told her the same before the phone disconnected. For a long moment, he sat still, staring at the receiver.

A hand pressed his shoulder and a steaming cup of coffee was held before him. The receptionist nodded at him. "Take this and drink it. You're shivering with the cold and half frozen, probably headed for shock too." Holding the cup with two hands that trembled, he managed to swallow the hot brew, thawing out some of the ice that had lodged in the pit of his belly. The hospital worker took the cup and squeezed his hand. "Did that help a little?"

Jackson stirred and rose stiffly from his seat. "Yes, thank you," a glance at her tag and he went on, "Nancy. I'd best go to my family." She resumed her place at the desk and he joined the others in the waiting area. There were a few people scattered about the large room, some holding hands, others flipping through a magazine or staring sightlessly at the television.

Ella sat in a corner, head bowed, the cross she always wore pressed to her lips. Wyatt and Emmett flanked her, holding on and praying alongside of her. Jackson did the only thing left to do—sink into a chair with his family and hand his father over to the Lord.

"Jackson!" Beth was running down the hallway, all out to get to him, holes in her old jeans, her shirt buttoned wrong, hair tugged into an untidy ponytail, two different sneakers on her feet. In his mind, she was the best thing he'd ever seen. She knelt in front of him and pressed her hands on his knees. "How is he?"

He could only shake his head. His arms wrapped around the warm, welcome body of his wife and his head dropped onto her shoulder. For the first time since his father dropped in his ice-coated barnyard, Jackson came undone at the seams, soundless sobs rising up until he had to take great gulps of air and the tremors shook his body. His wife held on tight and didn't let go, whispering his name all the while, giving her love, her strength and her faith.

Hamilton Mason sat beside his son-in-law and patiently waited, a firm hand on the younger man's shoulder. His own eyes filled, thinking about his old friend, but he cleared his throat and remained steadfast. When Jackson finally had himself under control once more, Beth sat in his lap and looped an arm around his shoulders. Her father nodded to them both and rested a hand on Jackson's arm.

"Jackson, there's something I need you to understand. As executor of your father's will, I've drawn up legal documents for him in the event of something like this. Landon signed a paper saying to let him go if there were any doubts. Your mother doesn't know this yet. He didn't want to upset her. However, God forbid there's a need, the doctors and your mother must know."

Jackson drew himself up straight, fighting the increasing ache in his back, and nearly started to shake once more. He felt like his head had been doused in ice water. "Are you trying to say my father doesn't want them to help him if his heart stops again?" At his father-in-law's nod, he gingerly stood and slowly walked away, down the corridor, away from prying eyes. A sign ahead marked the chapel. His feet found the way and he sank into a pew, lifting his gaze to a cross mounted high on the wall. The pain in his back rose up. It was nothing to the pain in his heart.

Dear God, please, please don't take him from us. We need him here. Pop is too young. Please. His plea ran through his mind again and again. He felt someone's presence and Beth took his hand. She slid in beside him and bowed her head. A few minutes passed and Jackson turned to her, his grip tightening until his knuckles were white.

"Beth, I watched the agony written all over his face, watched him fall. I can't get that out of my head. Every minute that I fought to keep him with us, I felt so hopeless. What if he dies? We need him, *I* need him." His eyes squeezed shut and he pressed his forehead to their clasped hands.

She smoothed his hair with her free hand and spoke very softly. "He's young and strong. All we can do is pray. No matter what, put your trust in God. Don't try to understand this. Believe that He holds Pop in His hands. Pray because we all love and need your father so."

Jackson straightened and looked her in the eye. Somehow his voice held steady. "What if God needs him more?" Her eyes filled and she shook her head, her face crumpling. She buried her head in his chest and he ran his fingers through her hair, over and over. Gradually, a feeling of peace settled in his soul. This trusting business, taking that leap of faith, wasn't easy. He took a deep breath. "Okay. Let's go talk to Mama."

When they returned to the waiting room, the doctor stood before Ella, wearing a smile that was answered by one of her own.

She fell into his arms and her youngest sons held her up. Jackson wrapped his arms around his wife and kissed her in the middle of the forehead. Landon Henry was awake.

Stepping into the dimly lit room, they found a stranger lying on the bed. Pop was whiter than the sheets or his pillowcase, impossibly small in the large bed beneath the blankets, connected to tubes and machines, with oxygen running through a mask on his face. Lights were blinking and blips sounded out, keeping track of each beat of his heart.

Jackson and his brothers hung back, letting Mama go in first. She sat on the side of the bed and rested her head on Landon's shoulder, her tears falling once more. His eyes did not open at first, but his hand lifted ever so slowly and rested on her dark curls. It was such a private moment between them that the others felt like they were intruding. Beth moved to step out and Jackson would have followed, but his father called to him. "Jackson. Stay."

He thought his legs would give, hearing that man calling his name. He found his way to the other side of the bed and bent his head to his father's. "Pop, I'm not going anywhere. Promise me you aren't either." His voice cracked on the last and it was Jackson's turn to feel his father's hand on the nape of his neck, pulling him in for a kiss on the cheek.

"Son, I'll do my best. Thank God for you doing what you did to keep me with you. I love you, Jackson." Landon's beautiful eyes filled with tears and he began to tremble. All of his family gathered in close, Beth and Hamilton as well.

Jackson lay his head on his father's chest and simply held on. There was no more pain in his back, no more fear, no room for anything else in this moment except the reassuring, steady thump of Landon's heart. "I love you too, Pop. We all do, so much." They all stayed as long as the nurses allowed it. Only one would not be leaving. Ella climbed under the covers and would not leave her husband's side. In nearly a quarter of a century, they hadn't spent a night apart. Mama wasn't about to let that happen now when she was needed most.

Hamilton drove Beth and Jackson back to the house, the twins taking the truck. They'd all wanted to stay, but Wyatt was home with Katherine and the horses needed tending come morning. The Masons didn't linger, everyone's exhaustion clear. The baby was sound asleep when his parents checked in on their little boy.

Comforted at some normalcy in a world turned upside down, Jackson practically stumbled his way to the bedroom, peeling off his clothes and leaving them in a heap, his mind set on one destination—bed. He crawled in first, eyes closing the moment his head hit the pillow, staving off a headache of monumental proportions. The aching deep down at the base of his spine settled in. He hoped for sleep to come swiftly, allowing him to escape it for a little while.

His wife followed soon after, sliding in behind him, spoon style. She pressed a kiss to his neck and began to stroke his hair, massaging his back and shoulders, anything to be soothing. "Beth," he whispered. "Just hold on to me and don't let go, will you please?"

"I can do that," she told him softly, one arm sliding under his body, the other coming over his waist to tighten around his middle. Locked in her grasp, maybe then he would be safe from the flashes of images cropping up in his mind, worse than any nightmare. Jackson slept poorly, waking often through the night, waiting for the phone to ring. Dawn couldn't come soon enough because that would mean that his father had pulled through. With each passing hour, there was hope that Landon Henry would be with them for the duration.

A week later, Pop came home with strict instructions to rest, avoid heavy lifting or hard labor, and go slowly. He'd also need to take heart medication for the rest of his life for the hidden heart condition no one had known about. There would be dietary changes as well. All in all, Landon was a bit ornery about his new limitations.

Getting him settled in his arm chair in the living room, Jackson sat on his heels and gripped his father's hand.

"Pop, we came too close to losing you. Follow orders. Doc Smith says you'll be strong enough come spring to get out there again, if you behave. Understand?" His tone softened and he had to look down to keep his emotions under control. "We're not trying to be hard on you. We love you and want you to stick around."

His father's palm rested against his cheek, making his eldest meet his gaze. "I know that and I'll be good. I promise." Ella came out at that moment with a cake and a candle flickering in the middle, Wyatt, Emmett, and Beth following close behind, Wyatt the second in his mother's arms. They all burst out into song, "For He's a Jolly Good Fellow," resounding through the house. Everyone had a piece, even Landon, although his was small, to celebrate his homecoming. It was a night that would burn brightly in their memories for years to come.

That night when Beth and Jackson went to bed, sleep was a long time coming as they made love with great tenderness, lingering in each other's arms, cherishing each minute. Pop's brush with death had reminded everyone how short life could be. Making the most of every minute, living while in it, was the best that they could do.

When Jackson headed to the barn the next morning, he found Beth's note tucked in the pocket of his coat.

Dear Jackson,

These past few days have been like riding on a thrill ride that makes you scared sick until all you want to do is scream, cry, and ask them to stop the world so that you can get off. I still cannot wrap my mind around the thought that your father had a heart attack. He is so young, the same age as my father. In a blink, we will be there ourselves.

Watching all of you with Pop, and especially your mother, I cannot help but think about what my life would be like without you. I know that because of Wyatt, I would have to keep going, to muddle through, but I know that would be very hard because the best part of me belongs to you. You give me a reason to live, to want to be here, to look forward to what is next. You are the colors in my life. Without you, every day would be a cold, cloudy sky and nothing but rain would fall. You're my sunshine, the air that I breathe, and the earth beneath my feet, keeping me grounded, letting me know where I belong. You're my compass, showing me the way home. You're my everything.

I hope and pray that I never have to live another minute of my life without you, Jackson Landon Henry. All I know is that while we're here in this place and time, I will do everything in my power to give you all the love this heart has to give for as long as I live. I love you more each day. How is that possible? Promise me. Promise me you'll never leave me alone.

Love,
Your Beth

෬ൈ෬

"Damn it all!" A war was being waged with a fence post. The jury was still out on who would win. Emmett had found the weak spot during a regular inspection of the pasture and couldn't take any chances. The horses could breach the opening and then he'd really have a mess on his hands. He'd been battling with the thing for the past few hours, getting the old piece out of the ground only with sheer bullheaded determination. Getting the new one in was proving to be the bigger challenge.

Covered in sweat and breathing hard from his exertions, plus a healthy dose of aggravation, he swung the mallet down again. As he tried to force the wood through the layers of frozen ground, the vibrations reverberated from his shoulders down to his toes with every blow. It was a disconcerting feeling. He wouldn't be surprised if a body part fell off. Another swing and *WHAM*! His thumb somehow got in the way. How many times could a man hit his own finger? Pulling his glove off with his teeth, blood dripping into the snow, he winced at the damage. *Say goodbye to that thumb nail.*

"How's it going, Little Brother? Making any progress?" Wyatt stood only a few feet away and curse him, he was laughing, his slate blue eyes twinkling. Of course, *he* wasn't fighting the post.

Emmett's breath rose up in a cloud as he exhaled from his nose—hard. "No." Gritting his teeth, he gave the stubborn piece of wood a good shove. "I. am. NOT."

"Let me guess. You figured you'd face this like anything else in life. When something gets in your way, just muscle your way through come hell or high water. Gotta do it by yourself, too. Can't trouble anyone else, right? Did you know that it is only ten degrees out here? Your nose is going to fall off if you stay here much longer. What possessed you to do this today anyway?"

Emmett pulled his glove back on over his throbbing thumb. It felt like his finger had a heartbeat. "I am cranky, ornery, and anxious as all get out. I figured it was best if I got out of Casey's hair. She's got enough on her plate, you know? It's just this waiting game is tough."

Wyatt reached out and pressed down on his shoulder. "I know."

With that, he picked up the mallet and took over. Calm. Collected. Deliberate. The way he'd always been for as long as Emmett remembered. It struck him hard. Wyatt was so much like their father. Together, they finally managed to get the post in place, strong and sturdy—as a Henry.

e/ɔe/ɔ

The football game created a dull roar in the background. Emmett didn't really notice. His beer had given him a dull buzz and his eyes began to droop. He jerked with a start and nearly upset the bowl of popcorn on his lap. Wyatt reached over and snagged it. "No sense wasting it. I'll finish that off if you're going to snooze on me."

Sheepish, Emmett scraped his hand over his face and shook himself. His brother's bottle was empty. He nodded to it. "You want another one?" At the shake of his head, he couldn't help but grin at his older brother. "Good, because I don't want to move, ever. Thank God you two came over. I am completely out of my element when it comes to that nursery. Sammie can help Case to move things, hangs things and all that."

"Don't I know it. You do not know what a headache she gave me when we did ours. She must have had me rearrange that room five times." Wyatt chuckled, glancing over at their son. Little Jackson had crashed and was out, sound asleep on a pile of blankets on the floor, his stuffed horse tucked under his arm.

He grew quiet watching the tyke sleeping so soundly. "He was worth it."

Watching his brother, Emmett couldn't help but notice again how similar Wyatt was to his father. Both were steady, solid—someone he could always count on. Thinking about Jackson Henry poked Emmett's conscience and shame washed over him. He had been selfish, keeping the journal to himself.

Standing slowly, his bones cracking along the way, Emmett crossed the room to pick up the book where they'd left it last. "Hey, Wyatt. I've been meaning to show you something Casey found in the old cedar chest in our room. I was going to bring it over as soon as we finished reading it, thought you might like to take a look too."

He set the leather journal in his brother's large, callused hands, so similar to his own. To their father's. Wyatt glanced up at him, questioning, then started to flip the pages, slowly at first, then faster. His breath caught when he came upon Mama's first letter and he swallowed hard. "Do you mind—is it all right if I read some now?"

Emmett nodded. "Take your time. The mother ducks will be a while." Unable to resist, he sat on the arm of the chair and leaned over his brother's shoulder, following along with him. He could never take his fill.

CHAPTER 24

March 12, 1959:

It took all Jackson could do to bring the last of the horses in. The simple act of lifting the latch on the final stall was nearly the last straw. He could hardly see straight, his whole body ached, and his back throbbed something fierce. One of the young stallions had given him a rough time in a battle of wills. He was really feeling it.

The pain, blossoming at the waist, radiated down to the base of his spine, making every move a challenge. Jackson took a few minutes—that's all he needed, just a few— to catch his breath, and bowed his head. He staggered, as an odd tingling traveled down his right leg, and grabbed hold of a stall, bracing his forehead on the door. A good cry might be in order, but that wasn't his way. *You buck up and press on.*

The barn door creaked behind him and the scent of Beth's perfume surrounded him. That was enough to give him the strength to lift his head, square his shoulders, and stand tall—until she touched him and he was nearly reduced to a quivering mess. Her hand was soft and warm as she gently rested her palm on the nape of his neck.

"Jackson, it's time to call it a day. It is seven o'clock.

Wyatt's already eaten, been bathed, and is sound asleep. If you don't come in now, I'm bound to find you curled up in a stall with straw for a bed."

Turning and looping his right arm around her shoulders, he brushed her cheek with a kiss. They slowly made their way in the house, each step killing him. Easing himself down at the table, Jackson could hardly dredge up the energy to chew. As for an appetite, forget about it, what with the pounding in his back. He picked at the meal without really tasting anything, forcing himself to focus on his wife. "How was your day?"

She tapped her fork on her plate, her eyes flashing. "Fine, like always. Too easy compared to yours. Never mind about my day." She set her silverware down and ran her fingers through his hair. His eyes drooped closed and his chin nearly dropped.

"Okay, that's it. Before you fall out of that chair, I'm going to run you a bath and tuck you in." He was painfully slow and couldn't hide his grimace as he stood up. Beth wrapped an arm around his waist, her mouth turned down in a frown, her eyes dark with worry. "Jackson, it's too much for you, taking care of your father's horses plus your own. You're getting up earlier and staying out later night after night. You're burning the candle at both ends. You're only one man. Tell Wyatt and Emmett. They can help."

Jackson inched his way down on the side of the bed and set his head in his hands, elbows propped on his knees. "No. I don't mind. They've got a full plate and I don't want Pop to worry. If he hears about any trouble, he might try to do too much. I don't ever want to see Pop like that again."

A shudder ran through him as a glimpse of that terrible, icy evening flashed in his mind, one he would carry with him the rest of his life. "If it means I have to work a little harder and hurt a little more, then, by God, I will."

She kneeled on the floor before him and set her hands on his knees. "All right. You hush now. You do for everyone else. It's your turn to let me help you." She rose up and pressed a kiss to the top of his head. He held her close for an instant and found the strength to stand again even though each time it was harder, following her into the bathroom. With utmost tenderness, she helped him to ease his way out of his flannel shirt and T-shirt. Any sharp movements, twists, or bends brought tears to his eyes.

Beth shook her head and winced. "I saw you struggling out there today. Stubborn as a mule, that's what you are. Get in that tub and let me tend to you." She let his pants and underwear drop on the floor. "I thought you might throw in the towel, but you just pushed on and got the work done. I don't know how you do it."

Jackson stepped over the side and sank down in the glory of hot suds, his head falling forward as he let out a long sigh of pure pleasure. With the heat came long-awaited relief, bringing the aching down to a tolerable level. "Some of the horses are more hard-headed than others, but none are a match for a Henry. They always come around."

His eyes were closed, but he heard the whisper of fabric sliding against skin. A second later, his wife climbed in behind him. She looped her legs around his and started running her hands over his poor, tired body. Taking up a cloth and lathering it with soap, she devoted extra attention to his back, continuing her ministrations everywhere that was within reach. Her touch was pure heaven as muscles gone tight finally loosened for the first time that day.

She saved his hair for last, running her fingers through the thick strands, adding shampoo and massaging his scalp, pouring water over his head next. He nearly came undone, letting loose a deep groan. She set the wash cloth aside and covered his shoulders, neck, and cheek with kisses. "How does that medicine feel?"

"The best." She pulled the drain and the water gurgled on the way out. His wife climbed out first, giving him the pleasure of looking at her treasure of a body, lending him a hand to get up and out. She had a surprising amount of strength in that little frame. Beth slipped a nightgown over her head and applied a soft, fluffy towel to his skin, drying him from head to toe, finishing by holding his pajama bottoms so he could step in.

Jackson pulled her flush against him and propped his chin on the smooth, shining cap of her hair. "Thanks for taking such good care of me." His mouth, never too tired for a grin, tipped up at the corners. When she looked up at him, he found enough energy for kisses as well. Good. The well hadn't run dry.

"I'm not done with you yet." She gave a tug and led him back to the bed where he unceremoniously dropped down on the side of the mattress, swaying a little as he did. It wouldn't take much to make him tumble over. She went to the bathroom and returned with her tried and true canister of liniment. It had a strong, spicy scent, perking him up some as her fingers dipped in and rubbed the concoction between her palms. For a moment, his back was on fire when she first started rubbing the ointment in around the bones, joints, and muscles, running from the site of his original injury, honing in on the long scar left from his incision, all the way up to his waist.

The pain turned to pleasure as the medicine, and her thorough rubbing, made the aching go away. For the second time that night, he couldn't help but moan. Her eyebrows shot up. "Am I hurting you or making it better?"

"Better," he murmured, leaning over to graze her jaw

with a kiss. She handed him pain pills, next, with a glass of water. One hearty swallow and they went down the hatch. The covers were pulled back and he found himself tucked in crisp, cool sheets that smelled like sunshine. *Must be hanging clothes on the line already. I love it when she does that. Feels like I'm sleeping on a cloud.* Patting her side of the bed, he smiled up at her. "You get in and I'll be cured. Love you, Beth." His words began to slur into each other as sleep came for him.

The mattress gave beside him and her lips touched his, one hand resting on his hip. "I love you too, Jackson. Good night. If you need anything, you tell me." Drifting off in her arms, he knew—his wife was the only thing he would ever need. All the rest? Fluff.

૮🜚૮🜚

Something was wrong. Coming to in the morning, he tried to figure out what was different, his head in a haze from a combination of being tired and the medicine.

Jackson hardly ever took anything. When he did, pills threw him for a loop. Cracking one eye, he moaned long and low. The sun was streaming in the window which could only mean one thing. It was late. Way too late. He made to sit up and gave a wild shout.

Beth came running from the bathroom, Wyatt wrapped in a towel in her arms. "Jackson! What is it? Is the pain that bad?" She was shaking with fear.

One more try to pull himself up and his breath came out in a rush. He met his wife's eyes, but couldn't hide his mounting panic. "I can't feel my legs."

૮🜚૮🜚

Doc Smith stepped into the room, carrying his black

doctor's bag. "Let's get you on your stomach, youngster, so I can see that back."

About the same age as their parents, he was a fatherly figure in the community, beloved by all. His salt and pepper hair and vibrant green eyes were always a welcome sight, unless you were scared out of your mind. As soon as he heard Beth's frantic plea for help, he dropped everything and hurried to the Henry House.

With Wyatt settled in his playpen in his room, Beth was free to assist the doctor. Between both of their efforts, they rolled Jackson over. Doc ran his hands up and down the spinal column, paying special attention to the area surrounding the incision that had taken on an angry red cast. It was swollen, the skin pulled taut. A bit of prodding with no reaction and he gave a nod.

"That's what you get for being obstinate and doing too much. You're dealing with some major inflammation at the site of your injury. It's caused swelling that has pressed in on your spine, cutting off feeling. I'm going to give you cortisone by injection—it's an anti-inflammatory. With rest, time, and patience, the feeling *should* come back."

Beth was holding Jackson's hand while he closed his eyes and held his breath. '*The feeling should come back.*'

"You might feel a pinch."

The doctor's tone was hopeful. Four times, he went in. Four times, Jackson felt nothing and his fingers tightened around Beth's until his knuckles cracked. His wife was white around the lips, her face gone tight, but she would not look away from his eyes.

Doc Smith rounded up his things and rested a hand on Jackson's shoulder. "I'll continue this treatment for the next few days until we get some results. Until then, the only thing you can do is rest up and take a break, Superman."

The doctor paused at the door and cleared his throat. "Don't worry. No one told your father a word. Your brothers took care of their duties and headed over here. It's a mighty fine thing, what you boys are doing for Landon. I think I'll check in on him next. There's no need to tell him about your condition when I'm sure this is only a temporary situation." With that, the kind Samaritan left them in silence.

Jackson closed his eyes and fought to catch his breath. A temporary situation. It *had* to be a temporary situation. Beth rested her hand on his head. She could not hide its quivering. "We simply have to have faith. It will be all right. I told you. You've been working too hard. Time to rest."

Rest? What else could he do? He stopped eating and sleep was elusive while he became a player in the most intense waiting game of his life. He had no choice but to lie flat on his back while Beth gave him sponge baths in bed. Even harder to swallow—three times a day, Wyatt and Emmett came to carry him to the bathroom. If Jackson pressed on his stomach, he could relieve himself. The trips had them all sweating with the strain by the time he was back in bed.

Three days in and Emmett sank into a chair, head in his hands while Wyatt sat on the side of the bed, a hand on his brother's shoulder. "Jackson, you've got to tell Pop. You think he won't notice something's up?"

Jackson shook his head at that one and gripped the twin's hand. "Not a word, not yet, you got that? This is all Pop needs. Beth and I've agreed. If it's not better in a week, we'll have no choice, but not now."

His younger brothers didn't like it, but they agreed.

Lying on his side, staring into the darkness night after night, Jackson envisioned a life imprisoned in his body. Beth held on tight and calmed him when he began to pan-

ic. She refused to give up on him. He wasn't as sure of
himself.

~*~

His wife pulled up a chair next to the bed and took his
hand in hers. "Jackson? Jackson Landon Henry, you look
at me? What's going on in that head of yours?"

There was no escaping her. He couldn't get up and go.
His only choice? To shut her out by closing his eyes. He
couldn't let her see the desperation—the downright despair.

He'd thought dealing with the constant pain was bad,
but this? So much worse. He could deal with the hurting,
work his way through it, push on. But this numbness?
There was nothing to do except think, think about a lifetime of helplessness. A lifetime in a wheelchair. A lifetime of sitting on the sidelines while someone else took
care of his home and horses, while he was useless.

"I think you and Wy should go to your parents." Day
in and day out, listening to her bustling around the house,
singing, humming, playing with the baby, Jackson knew
it was an act. In the middle of the night, when she thought
he was sleeping, he heard her muffled sobs from the bathroom. They'd vowed *In sickness and in health,* but Beth
didn't deserve this.

She moved to the bed, pulled up the covers and slid in
beside him, wrapping her legs around his, pressing her
palm to his cheek. Getting as close as she possibly could.
Nowhere to hide and his thin grip on control began to
crumble. He was shaking, fit to fall apart, and his Beth,
bless her, wasn't far behind. "I'm going to forget you ever said that to me."

"Why? What kind of husband can I be to you? What
kind of father to Wyatt? You need someone who can take

care of *you*. Not the other way around. You need some-one like Clyde Peabody. Dear God, what do I do?" For the first time since he woke up and could feel nothing, he broke down, great, awful sobs rising up, threatening to shatter him.

"Jackson Landon Henry, I have never wanted some-one like Clyde Peabody and I never will. I wouldn't care if you could only move your pinky finger because I love you!" She held on tight, shushing him, running her fin-gers through his hair, crying with him. When he finally stopped, hiccupping for breath, she kissed him tenderly. "Our biggest mistake any time before was trying to take on life's troubles by ourselves. We will figure this out together. I'm not going anywhere."

He took a shaky breath and gave her a smile, even though the sense of futility was barely held at bay. "Me neither." That startled a laugh out of her, and they both cried again.

గూగూ

On the eighth day, he waited for Doc Smith, on edge, hope crumbling. A baby's babbling took his attention away from himself when Beth stepped out of the bath-room. Her cheeks were rosy, her hair curling around her face, her blouse damp. Wyatt waved at his father and gave a grin of such infectious proportion, Jackson couldn't help but join in. He held out his hands. "Let me hold this beautiful boy."

She gladly obliged, tucking their boy in the crook of his father's arm and sitting beside them. Wyatt chortled as he was tickled from head to toe, covered with kisses next. His mother couldn't resist getting in on the act. Jackson reminded himself. *Count your blessings.*

Beth smothered their son with kisses and blew on his

neck, making him shriek with laughter, before moving on to her husband. Her lips touched his and she smiled somewhat anxiously. "How are you feeling? Any change?" Her face fell at his expression. A knock sounded on the door. "I'll be right back. You'll be okay with Wyatt?" Wiping at her eyes on the way out, she turned and blew her husband a kiss.

He grinned even though his heart sank. He played with his son's toes, listening to the musical sounds the baby made and closed his eyes. *Be grateful. You have her and your boy. It is enough. More than enough.*

"Oh, sure. Here you are lazing about." Doc Smith stepped in, his footsteps spry, his smile firmly in place, but the concern was there, more marked with each visit. "Your wife says no change still?" They'd all expected results by now. "Could you pick up that sweet boy, my dear?" he murmured, already concentrating on his patient.

Beth stepped in and scooped Wyatt up. His giggles spread grins all around and lightened the mood, if only for an instant. Prepared for his daily inspection, Jackson heaved himself onto his stomach. It wasn't pretty, but he managed. The doctor ran his hands from the waist down, starting at an area of sensation, ending with nothing.

"Well?" Jackson asked in trepidation.

Doc Smith exhaled hard. "We'll keep doing what we're doing. I consulted with a doctor in the city. He told me to try a higher concentration of cortisone and more injections. We'll try six today and keep going until we see progress. As always, you may feel a pinch."

Five times—nothing—and then Jackson was on fire. He reared back, gasping as a hot poker jabbed him in the spine and kept digging in deeper. "Sweet Jesus!" he called out before burying his head in the pillow.

Unnerved, Doc Smith dropped his syringe, the needle

clattering on the floor. "What is it? Did you feel something?"

Jackson's fists clenched around the edge of the mattress as every muscle in his body tightened. "Good Lord, *do* I feel something. It's worse than the day this all started in the hospital—and it's the best thing ever."

Beth was sobbing. He wasn't far behind, and even the doctor's eyes filled.

He ran his hand along Jackson's spine once more. The effect was electric the instant he touched the area around the incision. A ragged scream from his patient made Doc Smith pull his hand away. Fishing in his bag, he pulled out a cold pack and set it down low on Jackson's back. "Does that help?"

Jackson needed a moment before he could speak, the air hissing through his teeth. "Yes. I've got that horrible pins and needles in my legs now. They're coming back. It feels awful, but thank God, they're coming back!"

They all had a good cry together. Doc Smith left orders to continue rest for another week to avoid undue strain. He also recommended a regimen of ice and heat for the next few days to ensure the inflammation did not return. That night, Jackson was sitting up for the first time in over a week, riding wave after wave of pain. He'd never been so happy to hurt. A quiet knock came at his door. "Come in."

Landon Henry walked in and crossed the room slowly. Pale and gaunt, he was a far cry from the healthy, vigorous man he'd been before the heart attack, but he was alive. "Why didn't you tell me?"

No niceties. No beating around the bush. Straight to the point, that was his way. The Henry way.

Jackson shifted, wincing as he did and his father's face softened. He reached out and took his son's hand.

"I didn't want to worry you, Pop. You and Mama had

enough on your plate. I didn't want Em and Wy to know either, but I had no choice. I needed help, someone to help Beth and Wyatt." That one was still hard to swallow.

His father gripped his oldest boy at the nape of his neck and gave a hard squeeze. "I understand you trying to ease my load, and you don't know how much that means to me, but never again, you understand? As long as I draw breath and this ticker keeps ticking, I'm here for my sons—in the good times and times of trouble. Are we clear?"

Jackson nodded. "Yes, sir." He choked down the lump that rose up in his throat as his father pulled him into a hug and he heard that great heart beating.

Landon pulled back, wiping at his eyes. "All right, now that we've got that out of the way, I brought you something I thought you'd need." He reached behind him and pulled out the cane that had been left behind on Jackson's wedding day. "You'll use it again." It wasn't a question.

Jackson smiled at him sheepishly. "Any time I need it. I promise." He met his father's eye and caught his knowing nod.

Both of them had been thrown a curve ball, and they'd pulled out a catcher's mitt. They were Henrys.

That night before bed, Beth gave Jackson another massage with that incredible ointment, bringing him to the brink of heaven, but better yet was the moment she climbed into bed and he could feel her hand on his hip. He rested his head on her shoulder, inhaling the sweet scent of her, and let out a great sigh. "I've got to tell you something. You'd better be careful with all of this spoiling me or I'll get used to it. Just the feel of your hands on my body is an addiction."

She turned out the light and rolled toward him, rubbing her palm in circles on his stomach. "You are worth every last bit of attention you get. I wish I could do more. As for being an addiction, I feel the same way about you. Go to sleep and be well. I can't stand to see you hurting." Her voice became choked and she buried her head in his good shoulder.

He kissed the top of her head and began to stroke her hair, sending up a prayer of thanks to God above for his health and for this incredible woman. "Now you know how I felt when you had Wyatt." She fell asleep first that night and he used the time wisely, memorizing everything about her beautiful face before being next to drift away.

The next morning, he eased his way out of bed with the help of his cane. Jackson felt weak as a kitten and his legs nearly gave out once or twice, but he made it to the bathroom and back. Downstairs, he could hear the homey sounds of water running, something crackling and popping on the stove, the coffee percolating. Wyatt giggled and something banged, probably his cup or spoon on his tray. They were the best sounds Jackson had ever heard because soon, he'd be a part of them once again. He took his pills at the side of the bed, thoughtfully left there by his wife. She'd left a folded piece of paper with his name on it as well.

Dear Jackson,

Such a scare you gave us all. You frightened me the most when you tried to shut me out. Don't ever do that again. You need to learn how to slow down, listen to your body. You've got to take care of yourself before you try to take care of the rest of the world. Please don't make me call Doc Smith again. I don't think that my heart could take it.

I can't tell you how much I admire you. Such a strong man I have married, with a good heart, one with a love so pure and deep. I have never seen or known such devotion. You keep taking on more and you never complain, just keep on—until it almost broke you. Never again. I want you to know that I'm always here for you, to listen, to hold your hand, to give you a shoulder to lean on if you should need it. I'm stronger than you know. I've had a good teacher, the best, in you. I love you. Be well.

Love,
Your Beth

CHAPTER 25

May 20, 1959:

Jackson pulled the fish out of the water and held it up high for everyone to marvel at. "Oh, the one that got away. When Wyatt can talk, he will have a whale of a tail to tell."

They were rocking gently on a large pond at one of the neighboring fields. Stan and Gloria Jacobs gave free access to their property, able to relate well to the Native Americans because they believed no one could truly own a patch of the earth and the elderly couple should share what they have. That included the rowboat tied to the dock. No one had abused their kindness and generosity as of yet in fifty years of following an "open door" policy.

The young Henry family was taking their fill that day, out for fishing and a picnic lunch for the afternoon. Everyone had a pole, even Wyatt with a tiny Mickey Mouse pole that Landon picked up during his last shopping trip. Since he was still on light duties on the farm, Pop had been indulging Mama in drives, outings, and even a few overnights here and there at bed and breakfasts.

As long as Jackson held on to his son and the rod, there was no chance of losing either. They'd had great cause for celebration with Wyatt's first catch, a tiny sunfish catching the light as it dangled in the air. The baby giggled and clapped his hands while

Beth snapped a picture. She laughed with their son and tucked the camera away for safekeeping. "Tell me again. What made you decide to come out for the afternoon today? You've got a long day ahead tomorrow. I thought you might want to rest up and take it easy."

Jackson snagged an arm around his wife and slid her in close to him. "This is taking it easy and why do I need a reason to spend the day with my family? There hasn't been enough time in the day for anything lately and I know you two have been at the bottom of the list. I aim to do better."

He kissed her on the cheek, the neck, and the sweet skin of her shoulder, exposed once again on a mild day in a sundress he loved, one covered with daisies. "Besides, there is nothing easier on a body than spending it with the people you love. Have I told you lately how beautiful you are? You look prettier than the flowers I used to pick in Mama's garden."

"You tell me every morning when I wake up, every night when I go to bed, and many times in between." The color rose up in her face, reminding him of the perpetual bloom in her cheeks when she was carrying Wyatt. He couldn't help but wonder when that would happen again. She turned to him and threaded her fingers in his hair. "Do I tell *you* enough how much I love you?"

He smiled and dusted her lips with his. "Every time you look my way." The wind drifted across the water, making her golden hair unfurl behind her, ruffling Wyatt's soft brown locks. Staring into his son's slate blue eyes, Jackson gave his boy a loud smacker as well and hoisted him up into the air, making him giggle again. "Such a happy guy you are."

"Why shouldn't he be? Wyatt has us." Beth took their

boy next and sat him on her lap, wrapping her arm around him and holding him close. They stayed out on the water until their stomachs started to rumble. Jackson rowed them back to the dock, pulling hard on the oars, relishing the ability to move, to feel, to be whole again after that horrible week none of them would ever forget. The sun was shining overhead, the day was fine, and his family was all his for a whole afternoon, a true luxury.

Beth climbed out first, catching Wyatt in her arms. Jackson tied up the boat and set the cooler on the dock. His wife gave him a hand up and his cane. He still felt weakness from time to time and found that the pain was more manageable with extra support. He was confident that it wouldn't be needed soon, but he wasn't complaining. With a little bow, he let his wife lead the way, enjoying the view before him. She noticed his attention. She kept glancing over her shoulder with the smile of the cat that stuffed itself on a fat canary casserole and had a pronounced swing to her hips that would try a saint. Jackson could only shake his head and let out a long, low whistle.

A turn off of the lane and the woods closed around them until they emerged by the swimming hole. Jackson pulled off his boots and poked his feet in the water, holding up his arms. "Hand Wy over. He needs to dangle his feet." Beth obliged, kicking off her sandals and sitting beside them, giving a little cry at the chill.

Summer might be around the bend but the water temperature hadn't caught up yet. Holding their boy over the water, Jackson's muscles bulged each time he plunged his son's feet in and picked him up again, glorying in the spray of droplets, Wyatt's vigorous kicking, and his peals of laughter. Jackson chuckled with him. "It's so easy to make him happy!"

Beth rummaged in the cooler and handed over a sandwich, taking one up for herself, and setting cereal with

sliced bananas in Wyatt's hand. He hungrily ate everything, reaching for more from the bag on her lap. When
they'd all stuffed themselves on a sumptuous lunch that
left no room for even a morsel, Jackson and Beth
stretched on the grass and sat Wyatt down in between
them.

At ten months, he was on the brink of walking, but not
there yet. That didn't mean he wasn't mobile. At home,
he'd been crawling up a storm, getting into one thing or
another. Today, he nearly wore a strip of land bare, heading to the barrier of his parents' feet and back up to their
heads over and over again. Jackson took up a tall piece of
grass and tickled the baby's neck with it, getting that
toothy smile and a belly laugh in answer. Both parents
doted on him, watching Wy's every move until he suddenly ran out of steam like a toy winding down. Their
little boy simply rolled over on his back, closed his eyes,
and the Sandman carried him away.

Beth turned on her side so that she could study her
husband and Jackson did the same. Their hands linked on
the green carpet beneath them and her smile lit up her
features, making her eyes shine brighter than fireworks
on the fourth of July. "You don't know how much this
means to me. Today. Coming here of all places, that you
remembered. I just can't get enough of you lately. I know
it's not your fault, but it doesn't make it any easier. I'm
selfish. I want you all to myself."

He reached out to tuck a strand of hair behind her ear
and his hand lingered on her cheek. "I feel the same way.
Sometimes, I wish I had a normal job, something I left
behind when I came home every day on a normal schedule. You know, nine to five, something like that." He
shook his head and began to chuckle. "I couldn't give up
the horses. They're in my blood and God, but I love those
animals." He leaned in close and kissed her gently on the

lips. "Yet I love you and Wyatt more. I'm sorry the farm takes up so much of my time. Do you regret choosing a horse farmer?"

The thought had crossed his mind many a time. Beth never complained, but was she truly happy?

"Jackson Landon Henry, I don't want to ever hear such words come out of your mouth again! Do I regret you? You are the most amazing thing that could have ever happen in my life. I have a beautiful home, this precious boy, but most importantly, a man who cherishes me. I understood what I was getting into when I married you. What I didn't realize was how much you could love me or how wide my heart opens every time I think of you." She slid in closer and rested her forehead against his. "No matter what life throws at us, I can manage if you're there beside me to help play catch."

He couldn't help but smile at her, the blush creeping up in her cheeks with her agitation. He proceeded to give her the full kissing treatment, starting with her forehead, then her nose, her cheeks, and finally coming to a standstill at her lips. Stopping to breathe, only because it was necessary, he told her hoarsely, "I'm glad we got that established. When it comes to how I feel, I know without a doubt, I'm the luckiest man alive."

They devoted some more time to kissing and simply holding each other, because chances to do so were far and few between. Overhead, the clouds drifted by as the leaves waved in the wind, birds singing in the branches. Only when the sun dipped down toward the horizon did they make the journey home, Wyatt tucked in his mother's arms or alternating on his father's shoulders.

Jackson brought the horses in for the night while Beth prepared a simple meal. They both shared bedtime rituals with Wyatt, bathing him, covering him in a cloud of baby powder, dressing him in fuzzy pajamas, and tucking him into bed. Leaning in the doorway, head tipped against the jamb, Beth whispered softly. "Night, night, little Wy. Mama and Dada love you." She turned to her husband and smiled. "Who is going to get me ready for bed?"

He smiled and cupped the back of her head with his palm. "I think I could be persuaded." They crossed over to their bedroom, hand in hand. He did the honors of lifting his wife's sundress over her head and replacing it with a cotton nightgown, the white fabric floating around her when she walked. Gesturing to the bed, he sat beside her and began to run a brush through her hair, working his way gently from her scalp all the way to the golden tips that nearly touched the blankets, her hair had grown so long.

She closed her eyes, a smile playing at her lips and Beth began to hum, setting off a completely different kind of humming in his veins. When he couldn't take it any longer, Jackson set the brush aside and his lips found their way home to hers.

"Jackson," she murmured breathlessly. "I think it's time for you to get to bed." Her hands trailed through his hair, over his shoulders, and to his chest, working at the buttons and pushing his shirt to the floor. The t-shirt went next, followed by his jeans, and he climbed in beside her. No need for a cane now. A turn of a knob and the light was extinguished, replaced by a pale streak of moonlight dripping through their window. It was enough to turn his wife into a goddess.

"As long as you don't plan on going to sleep just yet." Her answer? To sidle in close and hold on tight. His head dipped to hers and they continued to tune up their kissing skills, a job that would never be accomplished. That didn't mean they wouldn't enjoy trying.

He woke up the next morning feeling loose and mellow, prepared to take on the long day ahead. Resting a hand on his wife's shoulder, he gave her a kiss and slid out of bed. Her eyes fluttered open and he kissed her again. "Stay put. It's really early and you've got a busy day ahead. Catch a little more sleep. I can manage coffee." He showered, poured himself a mug, and headed out to the barn.

She brought him his second cup and a smile later in the morning. Still in her bathrobe and slippers, her hair pulled up in a knot on the top of her head, with sleep in her eyes, she looked impossibly cute. "Thank you for a wonderful night, Mr. Henry. You keep up with more like that and we could have another Wyatt on our hands. We must have worn him out. He's still sleeping!"

Jackson accepted her offering, his free hand catching her at the nape of her neck, kneading the tender spot and making her eyes slide closed. Perfect timing to steal a kiss. "Oh, I could've stayed in bed sleeping with you all day long. I'll be in another couple hours and we'll get ready to go, okay? Thank you for giving me pleasant dreams."

She winked at him and practically skipped back to the house, her step was so light. She turned back and blew him a kiss. "You're a dream, Jackson. The only one I've ever really wanted." That gave him enough giddy-up and go to finish his chores in record time. When he headed in for one more cup of coffee, his wife was ready for him. With an imperious point to the living room, she made him stretch out and gave him a good rub down with liniment, followed by some of his pain pills. He'd be putting in a hard day. Best to be prepared. Keeping his hands off of his lovely wife was a challenge to say the least and her teasing smile proved she knew it.

Come ten o'clock they were ready to walk over to Mama and Pop's. Beth's mother would pick up the cake later on. By the time they emerged at Jackson's parents' place, the beehive of activity had already begun for a barn raising that would make the Amish proud. Giving his wife and son a kiss, Jackson immediately joined in. He paced himself and was careful in his movements, his trusty cane never far from his reach. He left the heavy stuff for the others. He'd learned his lesson well.

The women made sure the workers were fed and stayed hydrated while a hot sun blazed overhead. Everyone worked tirelessly and by sundown, a new barn stood in place of the old. There was some finishing work yet, but the bulk of the job was done, many hands making the load easier to bear.

The tables were laden with food for dinner while Landon and Ella were ushered to a place of honor. They stood and raised their drinks in a toast. "I am so humbled and grateful for all you've done for us today. I don't know what I did to deserve such good people in my life, but I'm forever in your debt. Thank you for all you've done, every one of you here. If I can ever help you, you need only ask." He hooked an arm around his wife's neck and kissed the top of her head. Ella was crying and could only smile at everyone, waving a napkin.

Jackson and his brothers chose that moment to step away. Momentarily they returned with Beth's cake between them, a beauty of a confectionary creation, a tower of layer cakes diminishing in size, topped with a horse at the top. They set it on the table before their parents and Jackson cleared his throat. "Mama and Pop, everyone is here for one reason—because we love you. They're here to help you when you need it, but they also want to celebrate with you. Happy twenty-fifth anniversary!"

That had the water works going throughout the place, Mama worst of all. Both Landon and Ella pounded their boys on the back and gave kisses while the crowd applauded and whistled. A receiving line of sorts began as townspeople stopped by their table to wish them well. The food and drinks began flowed and a local band struck up some music in the background.

The first love song they played, Landon stood and held out his hand to his wife. Ella accepted and they moved to a space in the middle of all of the tables, turning it into a makeshift dance floor. Round and round they went, kissing from time to time, staring into each other's eyes with a love that had only grown stronger over the years, smiling so hard it must have worn their cheeks out.

"Just look at them." Beth swayed with Jackson, but she couldn't tear her gaze away from his parents. "Do you think we'll be like that?" He pressed a palm to the side of her face and turned her eyes his way. Bending his head, he kissed her slowly and completely, bowing her back toward the ground, getting applause when her hair skimmed the grass.

"We already are. I expect we'll have at least twice as many years as Mama and Pop. We're off to a good start. I love you, Mrs. Henry, more and more each day." He kissed her again and the rest of the world went away for the space of a song or two. There were only two, young people in love and two hearts beating as one.

The next morning, when he found it hard to sit up after all of the hard labor from the day before, Beth's note on his nightstand gave him a reason to get out of bed.

Dear Jackson,

I can't stop thinking about your parents and the love light shining in their eyes. I want the same for us all those years down the line. I hope you can feel my love burning in my heart. It is a torch that grows bigger and brighter each day.

Your mother and father seem stronger than ever after Pop's scare. I can only imagine that nearly losing him would make them appreciate each moment even more. I want you to know how much every minute with you—in sickness or in health—means to me. I don't need any reminders to know that your love is everything. I love you more than you can ever know.

Love,
Your Beth

ℰↄℰↄ

"Nothing fits!" Casey stood in their closet in her bra and underwear, staring at a selection that was totally inadequate. She actually wanted to cry. All of her nightgowns were in the wash, a fact that had slipped her mind until now when all she wanted to do was crawl into bed. Her back hurt. Her feet were so swollen that none of her shoes fit anymore and the baby was pressing on her diaphragm, making it hard to get a deep breath. All in all, she was miserable.

Emmett was lying on the bed in his flannel pajama bottoms and T-shirt, an arm pressed to his eyes. *He's probably trying not to strangle you.* A rush of air and he unfolded himself from the bed, his body making a few more creaks than usual. There'd been a load of shoveling and plowing that day, not to mention the regular barn chores and he was flat out.

Pushing his own needs aside, he stepped up behind her and wrapped his arms around her. She leaned back against the solid wall of his body as he rested his chin on her head. "You could wear your birthday suit." His voice wore a smile.

That irritated her to no end. "I can't do that! I'll get cold and my skin is hypersensitive. It will make me feel even more like a whale. Why is it that at the most amazing time of my life that I feel so ugly?"

A rumble of a chuckle ran through her and her husband kissed the sweet spot beneath her jaw. "You're beautiful."

He reached around her and grabbed an old flannel shirt, one that was frayed and soft with wear. "Here. Let's try this." Several sizes too big so he could wear layers on the coldest of days, it worked. As Casey watched him fasten the buttons, she remembered one of their first mornings together. She'd chosen the same shirt. The urge to cry finally won, the tears running down her face and trickling into his hair. That was the way of it these days, running the gamut from incredible peaks to terrible valleys in a heartbeat.

He looked up at her and his face softened. Emmett gathered her in close, her ear pressed against the steady, reassuring beat of his heart. He started to sway, humming old-time Christmas songs, the kind that never grew old, carrying her back to childhood. Round the room they went until he gently picked her up and set her on the covers. If she was lucky, she might even get a bedtime story.

෴

"Emmett?" Sometime in the middle of the night, she awoke shivering. Her heater was missing. Casey lumbered out of bed and went to the bathroom first, because she had no choice in the matter. What she wouldn't give for a night without feeling like her bladder was about to burst. That mission accomplished, she waddled her way down the stairs. The kitchen light was on.

She padded on stocking feet into the kitchen. Her husband didn't hear her coming. He sat at the table with his head in his hands. His cane, stashed away since he regained his sight, and his father's cane, held on to all these years, were lying before him. He reached out to stroke the horse's head on the handle, jerking up when she touched his shoulder. "Good Lord, woman! What are you trying to do to me?"

She ducked around him to press a kiss to his cheek. "I woke up when you were gone. What's wrong? Do you have another headache?"

He shook his head, standing and pulling out a chair for her. Emmett poured a glass of milk and slid a plate of half-eaten cookies across the table. She began to nibble. She was always hungry these days. Letting out a long sigh, her husband sat back down and scraped a hand over his face. "I couldn't sleep. I keep thinking about what's coming soon and sometimes I get a little panicked. I wonder if I'll be any good at being a father."

She munched thoughtfully on her cookie and ran her hand over both canes. A good swallow of her milk and she stood, moving to her husband's side to loop her hands over his neck. "I'd say those canes on the table can answer that question. You and your dad have a lot in common. Both of you have been made from some pretty tough stuff and both of you made it through really tough times. I think you'll do all right. Now take me back to bed, Em. I'm too tired to make it back up those stairs."

He cleaned up the table and picked her up, giving her one of those endearing grins that made her melt time and again. "I guess I must be tough if I can carry you now." Emmett faked a stumble on his way to the stairs and got a whack on the back for that one. All the way up, not even breathing hard, and he set her gently back in bed, pulling up the covers. He dropped a kiss on her mouth and wrapped himself around her. "Thanks for always saying the right thing, Case. Love you."

"You make it easy. Love you back." She stroked his hair and felt his body finally go loose. Watching him sleep, she couldn't help but love him more. *It's easy knowing what to say with a man like you. A man of few words, like your father.*

CHAPTER 26

July 5, 1959:

The day was a cooker for Wyatt the Second's special day. Mama and Pop had a feast planned, cake, ice cream, presents, the works. The table and chairs were set in the shade for the meal, but everyone was hitting the pool first. Wyatt the First and Em were horsing around in one end already, secretly keeping their eye on Pop and the birthday boy in the shallow end.

The one-year-old was spinning in a little float, Pop throwing his head back and laughing in great barks that could be heard all the way to the house where Mama was taking care of last minute odds and ends. Katherine and Hamilton Mason sat beneath an umbrella on the patio blocks next to the water, sipping cold drinks and taking great pleasure in watching their grandson's enjoyment. They couldn't help but join in Landon's enthusiasm, chuckling along with him.

That laugh was something Jackson was glad to hear. Seeing Pop with a healthy glow was even better. The gaunt, strained look that had stayed with him the first few months was gone. He'd gone to see the Bradleys the day before and stayed to the end, walking Mama home. The walk was nothing. They went every day, a little farther each time. Pop had resumed duties around the farm for half the day.

He'd take on the rest soon. Landon had made major milestones in his recovery thanks to the medicine and doing as he was told. Part of following orders meant not taking on too heavy of a load. As a result, half the herd would stay with Jackson, something Pop had wanted anyway, but knew his mule-headed son wouldn't accept as a gift. A health crisis was another matter entirely. Hard to believe Landon had been suffering mini heart attacks for years, brushing them off as a pulled muscle or indigestion as he ignored what his body had to say. Now he'd learned how to listen. Jackson had learned the same lesson. He didn't push too hard, rested more, and leaned on his cane when necessary, although those times were far and few between. He also leaned on others to lend a helping hand when his body was pushed to the limit. Temporary paralysis was quite a wake-up call.

Beth stepped up beside him, smiling at the antics of her son and father-in-law, only to get a long whistle from her husband. "Woman, you look amazing. When did you get that suit?"

Attractive didn't cover the way his wife looked in a sky blue bikini with white polka dots, her blonde hair piled on top of her head and tied with a bandanna to match. She gave him a little wink and spun in a circle, receiving claps from the youth in the pool.

"Never mind the Peanut Gallery and their foolishness. You let *me* have a gander."

She headed toward the pool, wagging her hips and making her pony tail bob. "Oh, I have my sources. Are you coming in or what?" When Jackson broke into a jog to catch up, grateful beyond measure that he could, she entwined her fingers with his. They were nearly to the side of the in-ground pool when she told him in a low voice. "I'm thinking it's time Wyatt had a brother or sister."

Jackson bent his head to give her a kiss that would leave no doubts as to his feelings concerning the matter. "Only too happy to help. I've got this horse business down. We can make some time to work on this, regularly I might add." That made her blush.

To cover her crimson cheeks, she dove into the deep end of the pool with a loud splash. Taking his cue, he shucked his shirt and shoes, plunging in next with a clean jackknife. Wyatt waved and splashed at his parents, babbling happily like a chattering chipmunk. Beth waved back at him and blew him a kiss. Jackson dunked underwater, came up by his father and son, and tugged on Wy's toes. That only made him laugh harder until everyone thought he'd roll out of his float.

"I've got him, Jackson. Go give that beauty of yours some attention." Landon nodded with an appreciative smile. "Yes sir, that wife of yours gets prettier by the day. You certainly got a winner of a catch in her."

Jackson smiled from ear to ear. "You'd better believe it and I won't ever let her go." To prove his point, he gave a powerful kick and surged out of the water next to Beth, catching her up in his arms and making her squeal. His brothers found this to be great entertainment and took turns tossing her up in the air until she finally landed back with her husband, coughing and sputtering. Her eyes glittered in irritation and she gave a mighty tug, pulling him under.

Jackson came back up, gasping for air and her lips sealed on his. "I can handle mouth to mouth. I've got loads of experience. Stay calm." Calm? Impossible when his heart was tripping and his head was spinning from her undivided attention. He wouldn't have been surprised if the pool vaporized around them. Clapping, whistling, and a whole lot of throat clearing finally broke them apart. Beth grazed his cheekbone with one more kiss, whispering in his ear, "I'll give you some more of my first aid tonight when we go to bed."

Mama stopped at the side of the pool and gave a shout. "All right, all of you sea creatures. Lunch is ready. Let's all eat so we can get to the most exciting part of all— Wyatt's cake!"

Ella wore a red dress that fit snug on the upper half of her body and belled out at her waist, flaring around her when she moved. Perched on red heels with a crimson flower tucked in her curls, she made for an extremely eye-catching sight. As Jackson climbed out of the pool and helped his wife, his eyes wandered to his father and he saw a look pass between his parents with enough heat to set a forest fire. Life-threatening incidents could really set a blaze that was hard to put out.

Beth smiled as she followed his gaze. "Your father and mother are so in love. Can you blame them? She is absolutely gorgeous and your father is as handsome as they come—with the exception of you of course. I think they appreciate each other now more than ever before. They won't take each other for granted, that's for sure."

Jackson tucked her in against his side and kissed her cheek. "I could never get too full of myself with you. Every morning I pinch myself to make sure you're real and every night, I thank God that you're mine." They walked together to the house to change. Behind them, they heard Wyatt's laughter and turned to see him propped on Landon's shoulders. He didn't keep his throne long, though. The twins had to take turns next. Watching his son, holding onto his Beth, Jackson knew. He was head over heels for the both of them.

Before you could say boo, Wy was running clumsily across the lawn, chasing his uncles and a ball they'd picked up especially for the little man. The boys were shouting that nickname to him as Wy tumbled over, climbed up again, and fell again. All the while, he smiled, laughed and got up again, reaching out for two more grown-ups that were in love with the little boy.

Landon took big strides to break even with his wife and another shout rang out as he picked her up and headed to the house. "Landon, you put me down this instant! Remember your heart!" Mama was truly distressed, her voice trembling as she held on to his neck and stared into his eyes.

Pop didn't falter or slow his pace and his smile was brighter than the sky on a Fourth of July firework-filled night. "Ella, I'd rather have my life cut a bit shorter and know I grabbed hold of every minute with you than drag it out and not live at all. Besides, I'm all right. I feel good, strong. You're not too heavy on this heart of mine. If anything, you make it feel lighter."

She buried her head in his shoulder as they passed through the front door, murmuring, "How I love you," on the way. Jackson took one, long look at his wife and mimicked his father. Beth's eyebrows nearly landed in her hairline, her grin contagious.

He shrugged. "If Pop can do it, I've got to prove I've still got it in me." While his parents stopped at the foot of the stairs and were taking a moment to hold each other, forehead to forehead, he took his wife all the way to top, his back barely giving him a twinge. All the way into his old bedroom until he laid her down on the bed. Her arms hooked around his neck and drew him down for a kiss that burned away the last of the chill from climbing out of the water. "Hmm. Guess I've got a lot in me."

"Enough to make another baby?" She teased, snatching another kiss on the corner of his mouth. He lay down beside her and pulled her on top of him, allowing him to thread his fingers in her hair to draw her in like a second skin.

"I'll give you the best that I've got. Right now, we'll have to take a rain check. It's our son's birthday, remember? One year old? Kind of a big deal. Wy's waiting for us and we've entrusted him with my brothers."

She shot up like a bullet. "If we don't get down there he could be bald, have a tattoo, or learn how to curse a blue streak like a trucker. I wouldn't put it past either one of those mischief makers." The couple dressed in record time, but Mama and Pop beat them, his arm looped around his wife's shoulders as they stood by the buffet table and waited for everyone to fill their plates.

Hamilton had little Wyatt's hand and was speaking gibberish to his grandchild until the guest of honor saw his parents and his smile grew. "Dada!" He called out, his fingers up in the air, grabbing for his father. Beth covered her mouth, tears filling her eyes while Jackson lifted his son high overhead and kissed his belly, making him laugh hysterically. Everyone they loved was there to hear Wyatt speak his first words. What a present!

They all ate their fill, stuffing themselves until moving was near impossible. The family caught up on all of the latest news, finding room for more food when Ella carried out her confectionary delight, a large sheet cake, half chocolate, half vanilla, frosted and decked out with a mini version of their farm. Wyatt would be able to play with the figures and buildings after. He clapped his hands and blew at his candles, finishing the job with some help from his mother and father. The presents came next.

By evening's close, there was another generous pile of gifts. They left some things at Mama and Pop's to spread the wealth for the times Wy came to visit and the little family went home, tired but content.

Beth changed the birthday boy and set him down in

his crib. He was out in an instant. Smoothing his hair and bending over to kiss his cheek, she didn't even start when Jackson shadowed her every move. Leaving his own kiss on his son's head, he followed her into the bedroom where she unceremoniously shed her clothing. Jackson's came next and they held each other in the moonlight. They began to dance until their footsteps slowed and Beth pushed her husband on to the bed.

She moved on to give him a massage and he did the same until they were both about to liquefy. "Are you sure this is how babies are made, Mrs. Henry?" His voice was deep and throaty, rumbling deep in his chest. If she touched him again, he'd be past the point of no return.

"Even if we're wrong, we'll have such a good time trying." Her laughter washed over him and her head dropped to his chest. He joined in her merriment, but things grew serious soon after. Time to get down to business. He was still thinking about their night when he stepped out of the shower and found a letter on his clean change of clothes first thing in the morning.

Dear Jackson,

I don't know if anything happened last night, but you sure did light a spark inside of me. Every time with you is absolutely amazing, beautiful, incredible, wonderful...I could keep going with a river of words and they still wouldn't be enough.

I look at our Wyatt, light of my life, and I can't wait to have more with you, a baker's dozen even! I hope and pray that God will fill our house with little ones. What better way to have an everlasting testament of our love. They will go on, long after we are gone, and our love will burn brightly inside of them. Thank you for being the father, husband, and son that you are. I couldn't ask for more, except more of your babies. That is my prayer—

day in and day out—to have another piece of you that will live on.

Love,
Your Beth

CHAPTER 27

December 14, 1959:

I t was Jackson's favorite time of year. He didn't like being cooped up on the worst of days and the work could get harder, especially when there was two or three feet of snow to clear before the horses could get out, but like all the Henrys, he loved everything else about winter. With the cold, the ache in his back set in deeper, shaking him to the core at times. When it was too much, Jackson called his brothers. Together, they managed without mishap.

There was nothing like filling his lungs with that breath of cold air that made him feel alive, watching the cloud of steam around his head that proved it was true. When a fresh snowfall came down, it was like magic. Beth called it a winter fairyland. With a gift like her and Wyatt to wake up to every day, Jackson half expected she was on to something.

Christmas was the icing on the cake. He couldn't wait for all of it. The big feast. The tree. The lights. All the trimmings. Wy would understand it more this year. Jackson had spent hours working on a wooden hobby horse, just his size. He couldn't wait to see his little boy's face.

As for Beth, she was like a little girl, so excited, ready

to pop. She'd gone overboard with everything, decking the halls, shopping, baking, and freezing all kinds of goodies. Jackson found some earrings for her, really delicate gold ones, shaped like hearts. Perfect because the girl had his heart and always would. He didn't want or need anything. All the same, Jackson thought his wife might have something extra special tucked away for him. *Whether she knows it or not.* A smile bloomed with the secret hope that had taken root in his heart.

Thinking on his wife, as he so often did, filled him with a longing that pushed him to hurry with the morning chores and get inside. Shivering hard enough to make his teeth chatter, he peeled out of his outer gear and went in search of Beth's warm arms and a large cup of coffee in that order. The familiar sound of retching pulled him up short. It had become a regular occurrence for the past week or so, either first thing upon waking or at some point during her morning chores.

Not one to shy away from an uncomfortable situation, he strode into the bathroom and patiently held her hair away from her face while she faced another bout of vomiting. "Whew, this is not how I planned on getting ready for the holiday season."

She sagged on her knees, palms resting on her lap while taking a few restorative breaths. She let loose a puff of air, running a shaky hand across her lips. With Christmas only two weeks away, his wife's agenda of things to do was long. Throwing up daily was not on the list.

Drawing her to her feet and stepping behind her to rub her shoulders, he pressed a kiss to her cheek. "Have you noticed something about this? Seems like the last time around when Wy was on the way. When was your last cycle?"

She stepped to the sink and rinsed her mouth with cold

water, splashing her face next. Beth stood stock still, eyes grown wide, staring up at her husband. "I—I guess I lost track." Closing her eyes, she swayed a little and he caught her. Leaning against him, a hint of a grin made an appearance. "I'd have to say mid to late October." The comprehension dawned as her blue gaze began to shimmer and the color crept into her cheeks. "Do you really think—"

Jackson wrapped an arm around her waist and set a palm to her belly. "Most likely so. What do you say we drop Wyatt over at Mama and Pop's? What with half of his herd here and the twins taking care of the rest, my father is going stir crazy. You and I will go see Doc Smith, confirm our suspicions, and do a little shopping. I'll even take you to lunch at the Olde Inn and Tavern."

He gave her a wink and a kiss on the tip of her nose. They took their time going down to the kitchen.

She broke away to start the coffee pot, hands resting on her middle as her gaze turned inward. "I can't believe I didn't even think about this. What if Doc can't see me?"

Jackson took the mug from her hands and led her to a chair. Fixing his own cup of her strong brew, he prepared tea for his wife and set the steaming mug on the table. Toast duty was next. As soon as the first slices popped, he slathered on a light layer of butter and slid the plate to her to stave off any lingering nausea. "Don't you worry about that. Doc is sweet on you, has a soft spot, you know that. Let me finish my toast, take care of the horses, and we'll get going."

An hour later, Wyatt was in his grandmother's arms and they were headed toward town.

Jackson's confidence in the doctor was well-founded. As soon as they walked into his waiting room, the town's doctor found room in his schedule.

"This so happens to be my lunch break, but we'll con-

sider this a working lunch and a pleasure when it comes
to two of my favorite people." The doctor had delivered
Beth, making him especially partial to her.

He ushered them into his office, brushing salt and
pepper strands of hair from his eyes. The salt was coming
in a bit more heavily, the pepper growing scarce. The
years were beginning to catch up to him. While that
might be true, time could not diminish the brilliant gleam
in his green eyes, partially hidden by wire-frame glasses,
or his obvious pleasure at seeing the young couple.

Waving a hand to the examination table, he gestured
to Beth to sit, Jackson moving in by her side, the only
place he'd ever be when it came to his wife. "So, I saw
Wyatt the Second the other day, see he's doing quite well
moving full speed ahead. How about your father, Jackson?"

"He's doing well. We still can't believe he had that
heart attack at forty-five. It's really thrown us all for a
loop. Pop doesn't like the restrictions either, watching
what he eats, going slower and taking care with how
much he exerts. He's chomping at the bit to do *everything*
like before, even though Pop is managing a full day most
of the time now. Mama's keeping him in line, and Wyatt
and Emmett are backup." Jackson closed his eyes, trying
to shake off the images that still crowded his mind from
that terrible day. "I don't ever want to see him go through
that again."

Beth squeezed his hand, her voice trembling a little.
"None of us do. He's still so young. You're sure I don't
have anything to worry about with Jackson, Doc Smith?"
Her eyes were on her husband the whole time. There
might have only been the two of them in the room.

"Now Beth, I told you that I'm healthy as a horse. You
were here with me when Doc put me through my paces.
I'm still recovering from the workout he made me do. He

took blood work, chest x-rays, and EKGs. I don't have
any hint of what Pop has." Shortly after his father was
released from the hospital, she'd demanded Jackson have
a full check-up, pulling out all of the stops and Doc Smith
was only too happy to oblige. Landon's health crisis had
scared them all.

Doc Smith stepped forward and patted her hand in fatherly affection. "Beth, you know I wouldn't keep anything from you. Landon's heart condition appears to be
hereditary, that's true, but that doesn't guarantee it will
happen to Jackson. His brothers show no signs either.
Luckily, your father-in-law is responding well to the
medication and changes in diet. If he continues to follow
orders—" His words had a bit of an edge. "—which I
know you all will help him to do, he'll lead a long, productive life with many years ahead."

Looking up, the doctor patted Jackson on the shoulder
and gestured for him to turn around. "That reminds me.
Before I give this young lady my full attention, let me get
a gander at that back of yours."

Jackson grumbled, but did as he was told, sliding up
his shirt while Doc Smith's capable hands ran up and
down his spine. Pressure on the incision made him snap
his teeth together and tighten up. He got a noise of disapproval in answer. "You watch yourself, youngster. It's
much better than last time, but I see you moving stiff.
Hang on one minute." He went to the counter and pulled
out a needle. A quick alcohol swab followed, cold
enough to make him jerk when it swept across the skin at
the base of his spine. The doctor murmured, "Now hold
steady."

Jackson pressed his palms against the wall while the
needle gave a quick stab in and out, leaving a burning
sensation behind. "Man, that stings, Doc! Was that really
necessary? This is Beth's appointment."

The good doctor gave him a smile and patted his shoulder. "That's just to hold off any inflammation. Got to stay ahead of it, you know? Tonight, you take a good soak and let Beth give you a nice rubdown, understood?" He returned his attention to his other patient. "Now young lady, I believe you are chomping at the bit to talk about *your* health. Your color is good and those beautiful eyes are sparkling. They're like a blue sky on a perfect summer day, aren't they? You look about the same weight as always, give or take. What seems to be the problem?"

Jackson jumped in, unable to contain himself. "We think there might be another bun cooking in the oven!"

His wife gazed down at her feet, her mouth turning upward as her skin flushed even more brightly.

Doc Smith's smile nearly split his face in two. "A new, little Henry toddling around? Now that would be a sight I'd like to see. Take this hospital gown and get changed so I can take a look at what's going on down there. I'll take a quick blood sample now so Lila can check it out in the lab while you wait." He drew a tube of blood, shaking his head. "My, my. Such excitement around the holidays. I'll be back in a moment. You two kids behave." The door closed as the doctor stepped out.

Beth turned her back and started to undress, glancing over her shoulder at her husband, blushing all the while. He moved in close and set his hands on her shoulders as she unbuttoned her dress. "Need any help getting changed? I do know what to do. I've had a little experience." His voice dipped down low and his grin set off a shy smile.

"I can manage quite fine, thank you." She began to hurry, shimmying out of her pants and underwear, slipping her arms into the thin gown. His fingers skimmed along her body and rested on her waist as his mouth found the way to the soft, tender skin just behind her ear. "*Jackson!*" She hissed breathlessly. "Just tie my robe, will you? You're going to have my pulse going off the charts!"

Chuckling at the distinct possibility, he made bows down her back and turned her to face him. Locking his gaze with hers, his head tilted her way. He stole a kiss and her hands rose up to press against his chest, the only barrier between them. "Jackson Landon Henry, we have got to stop! Doc Smith will be back any moment!"

He smiled and his palms cupped her beautiful face. "Do you know how sexy you are, all in a tizzy? As for Doc, I don't think there's anything we could do that he hasn't seen before." One more kiss, this one slow and easy, made his wife's body go loose, drooping against him. Finally. Surrender.

"Hmm. I guess I should have given you two lovebirds a little more time." Doc Smith laughed softly as he returned, closing the door softly behind him. The couple broke apart, both red in the face. Beth climbed up onto the table and Jackson took her hand. She gave him one of her prettiest smiles, holding nothing back, as her hair fell in a full and glorious tumble around her. She positively glowed. That was proof enough for Jackson.

Doc set up the stirrups and a light with a little finagling. Once all of his instruments were in order, he pulled on his rubber gloves and patted her knee. "All right, young lady. Put your feet up here and scoot your bottom down. Relax while I get a gander." He slid the light closer and rubbed some gel on his gloves. "All right. I'm going to put the speculum in. It's a little cold and might be a tad uncomfortable. I'll be as gentle as I can, sweetheart."

The doctor eased his way in with the tools, so adept that she didn't even flinch. He peered intently at the area in question and his smile, part of his daily wear, grew beyond proportion. " Oh yes, there is definitely another bun tucked inside your sweet, little oven. Your cervix has a bluish tint to it and is closed nice and tight. I'd say everything looks good down here. When was your last cycle?"

Beth put her feet down and sat up straight, the roses in her cheeks blooming with her excitement. "Mid to late October, I'd guess. To be honest, Doc, we've had so much on our plates, what with more horses, Wyatt growing in leaps and bounds, and the holidays, I plumb forgot about it." Her tongue was truly wagging in her excitement.

Jackson couldn't blame her. His heart had started to skip the moment Doc confirmed his suspicions. "It doesn't matter, just that we take good care of you now. What do you think, Doc? The way I reckon, we'll have another July baby."

Doc Smith peeled off his gloves and nodded his head. "Yes, just like their mother, too. I still remember the day you were born, Elizabeth. It was the hottest day of that summer and the sweat was pouring off of me. You really made your mama work hard for you, too. I've got your baby picture on my desk yet, with Wyatt's beside it."

He threw away his gloves and moved forward to pat Jackson on the back, shaking the expectant mother's hand at the same time. "Now, I expect you to treat yourself well, young lady. No overdoing it, no heavy lifting. If you're tired, rest. Eat well and make sure you drink plenty of fluids. Limit your coffee and no alcohol or smoking. Not that I have to worry about you. How's the morning sickness?"

Beth stuck her tongue out, making both men grin. "Like clockwork. It hits me the moment I get out of bed each morning. The rest of the day I'm a little queasy or light headed now and then, but first thing?" She closed her eyes and shuddered. "Sometimes I expect to see my kidneys or my shoes coming up!"

Jackson's hand moved to knead her neck and he kissed the top of her golden head. "Anything you can do about that, Doc? I hate to see her sick. Sometimes, she seems liable to turn herself inside out."

Doc shook his head with a small frown. "I'm afraid it's a burden mothers must bear. Here are a few things you can try that might help. Have water and crackers next to the bed each morning. Sit up real slow, not even all the way, and have a few nibbles and sips before you get out of bed. Take your time standing up and crossing the room. You might keep the nausea at bay. If you feel that way anytime during the day, have a few more crackers and water. Sometimes, it helps. You can also lie down until the feeling passes."

He took a step closer and gave the expectant mother a hug. "If you have any problems or questions, you know where I am, Miss Elizabeth. Any time, and I do mean that. I expect to see you back in this office once a month." He gave Jackson's shoulder a squeeze and a smile. "You make sure she behaves, young man. Congratulations."

The doctor left them to their privacy, giving Jackson the chance to truly show his appreciation. He picked his girl up in his arms and swung her around, letting out a whoop. His mouth touched down to seal hers. "Well," he asked in amusement. "Are you ready for round two?"

The tears rose to the surface and the dam broke, spilling down her cheeks. "More than ready. I can't wait! I should have felt something, seen the changes. I still can't believe I didn't know."

His eyes began to sting as he gave her one more kiss. His voice dropped to an awed whisper. "I knew it all along. I can't wait either." Saying anymore wasn't possible. His heart was too full. He helped her dress and they headed back out into winter's chill. The afternoon passed quickly and pleasantly enough in Saratoga, picking out odds and ends for the holiday, admiring all of the finery that gave everything a festive spirit.

The young couple savored the opportunity to spend an afternoon alone. Such moments were far and few between what with the demands of running a farm and raising a family. Jackson felt like a kid in a candy shop with every second he stole with Beth. She certainly wasn't complaining either. As the day grew late, the truck took them homeward bound until they found themselves in Charlton. "How about dinner at the Olde Inn and Tavern?"

Beth had slid across the bench seat and her head was resting on his shoulder. Jackson thought she was snoozing until she perked up and her hand gripped his knee. "Oh really? I'd love that. It's been so long since we've been here." Or *anywhere* except home or their parents' homes.

Jackson pulled into a parking spot, walked around to open her door, and helped her from the truck. His hand rested on the small of her back, protective as always. The hostess brought them to a table in the corner, discretely pouring ice water with lemon for each before slipping away. He raised his glass to his wife and they clinked in a toast. "To the most beautiful girl in the world and the next little Henry on the way. Do you remember that this was where we sat on our first date?"

"How could I forget?" Beth gazed around the room, finally propping her chin on her palm and staring into Jackson's eyes. He could feel himself losing his footing, getting ready to tumble overboard into the sea of deep blue that carried him away every time. "Look. The white lights are still here, like fireflies. It's nice to know there are certain things I can count on to be there for me, like you."

He didn't care who was watching or that they were in a public place. He leaned across the table, his hand cupping the back of her head, and gave her a kiss that intoxicated them both without a drop of alcohol.

∽∾∽∾

"Stop playing with your food, Wyatt! Eat!" Beth actually snapped at the little tyke, a true rarity. At nearly a year and a half, their boy was feeling his oats, exploring his world, getting into a bit of mischief. Finding some amusement with his breakfast wasn't out of the norm.

Jackson picked up the baby spoon off the floor, rinsed it, and set it back in his son's hand. "Come on, Wy. Try some of that oatmeal your mama made. Mmmm!" He took a big spoonful of his own and crossed his eyes as it went down. The sound of Wyatt's chortles made him melt inside every time.

Beth shook her head, her smile creeping up as she pushed a strand of hair from her face. "Oh Jackson! You are something—"

Her words broke off as she went white and scurried out of the room. The painful sounds of retching came next. She was having a rough morning. When she returned a few minutes later, eyes watering, a tad shaky, he had the table cleared, the remains of breakfast cleaned up, and Wyatt on one arm.

"All right, Mrs. Henry. You need a break." Jackson hooked an arm around her waist and led her to the bedroom. He pulled back the covers and gave her a nudge. "Get in and get some shut eye. I know you were up before me today, getting sick, like now. Maybe a little rest will help you find your sunshine." He pulled up the covers and planted a kiss on her forehead. "Sleep well. I've got Wy. He'll make my chores go easier."

She reached up to snag Jackson's collar and reel him in closer. She gave him a long, lingering kiss, then one for the baby, capping it off with the gift of her smile. "You're a godsend, Jackson Henry. I love you."

Threading his fingers through her hair, his mouth closed on hers, hungry for more and his eyes squeezed shut. "You do not know how hard it is to walk away right now, but if I stay, you won't be getting any rest. Take all the time you need. Wyatt and I will be fine."

Jackson carefully bundled his son up in all of his winter gear until the poor baby could hardly move, his slate blue eyes crinkling up at the corners as they stepped into the bitter cold. Even pressed close against his chest, his son's cheeks were still beet red by the time they hit the barn, but his smile was wide. He was a happy, little fellow who tagged along after his father and mother like a shadow and rarely gave them a lick of trouble.

Settling his little tyke in a pile of straw, penned in by several bales, Jackson handed him some toys that were kept in the barn. It wasn't the first time he'd created an impromptu playpen. The morning chores went quickly, giving the horses their oats, mucking their stalls; filling them with straw; putting fresh, sweet hay in the hay bags; keeping tabs on his son all the while. As he finished the last one, his back started talking to him. He stopped and reached above his head, giving a good stretch to relieve the pressure down at the base of his spine. The pain eased some. Relieved, he devoted his attention to his son.

Jackson returned to the straw play area to find that Wyatt had toppled off to sleep, his dark hair brought to a high gloss by a shaft of sunlight poking through the window. "Hmm. Don't mind if I do."

Unable to resist, he stretched out in the straw and

tucked his son in under his arm. The position of the sun had changed when Jackson felt someone poking him.

Wyatt was only a nose away, staring at his father, jabbing him with a piece of straw. "Dada. Dada!"

The moment Jackson opened his eyes, his boy started laughing. God, how he loved that sound.

Rising to his feet in one smooth movement, he caught Wyatt up in his arms and swung him around. "Well, that's a fine how do you do, Wy! What should we do now?"

Set on giving Beth a well-deserved break, he took a glance around when inspiration struck.

ℰↃℰↃ

"Jackson Henry, you take him off of there right now!" His wife stood at the other end of the barn, framed by a blazing afternoon sun. She set off, nearly at a run, coming head on. One good look at her snapping eyes and Jackson knew she wasn't joking.

"Beth, calm down. I've got a good hold on him. Pop said I was practically born in the saddle. I figure Wy is overdue." Their son was perched on the back of Ricky Ricardo. The stallion stood munching oats calmly, totally unperturbed by the frazzled woman before them.

She stepped up next to them and jabbed Jackson in the chest, her face gone white. "I mean it, Jackson. You take him off, *now!*"

You shouldn't argue with a pregnant woman. He attempted to mollify her, speaking softly, wearing a smile even as he kept a firm grip on Wyatt. "Beth, I would never let anything happen to him. If Wy is going to be a horse farmer, he needs to get to know them, the sooner the better."

"Maybe Wyatt won't be a blasted *horse farmer!*"

She might as well have slapped him. It wasn't so much what his wife said, but how she said it.

Jackson pulled their son off of the horse's back so swiftly that Wyatt began to cry. Fire crackled up and down Jackson's spine with the sudden movement, and he welcomed the pain. He jammed his boy into Beth's arms. "So you want him to be a lawyer or some such? Maybe you agree with your father about me, after all! You should've married Peabody!"

He turned on his heel and stalked out of the barn, giving the door a good slam on the way out.

❧❧❧

For the first time since they'd been married, he didn't go in for dinner. He had to find a way to deal with the knife wound of her words, cutting deep, had to put it away. He couldn't do that sitting across the table from her. His feet knew where to go, taking him to the woods and the path between his house and his parents. Almost to his destination, he turned around. This was his pain and he didn't want to share it with anyone. To make matters worse, his back started throbbing with every step. All he wanted was to go to bed and start this day over.

They said wounds took time to heal. It would appear that Wyatt's difficult birth was still fresh in Beth's mind, making her want to keep their son in a protective bubble. What Jackson couldn't wrap his mind around was the lash of her tongue, slicing him to the quick.

He emerged from the forest under the cover of darkness with a canvas of starlight overhead. Focusing on one blazing star, he inhaled deeply. Let it out. Did so again, struggling to restore his equilibrium.

Beth sat on the steps, wrapped in a blanket, shivering. "Jackson, come here."

Who knew how long she'd been sitting there? A
while, judging by the dusting of snow that shimmered on
her hair. He swept a hand over his head, realized they
must look the same. One, slow step followed another, and
he stood below her.

She rose up and opened her blanket, wrapping it
around them both, shaking. "I'm sorry, so sorry. It was
stupid, what I said. I'm just so scared,. I can't lose him,
but I can't lose you either."

"You won't. Trust me." He picked her up and carried
her inside, even as the pain stabbed at his back harder.
She'd lit candles and laid blankets by the fire, a pitcher of
steaming cider waiting on the table. He didn't question it,
simply strode forward and set her down. With trembling
fingers, Beth helped him to shed his boots, his coat, and
the layers of his clothing. As for the wonder that was his
wife, she wore nothing under the blanket, making his
brain hit a road block.

She couldn't help but see how stiffly he moved and
she frowned. "You're hurting." She went off to the medicine cabinet and returned with his ointment. She gestured
for him to lie down and put her fingers to work, kneading
the muscles and rubbing the liniment in until she got a
groan in answer.

He took the canister from her hands and pulled her
down beside him. She wrapped her legs around him, her
hands running over his body, latching on to his hair. "I
didn't mean a word of what I said earlier, and get it
through your head once and for all—I *do not* want Clyde
Peabody! I want Wyatt to be a horse farmer, to be exactly
like you, to be a man of few words who speaks with his
actions and his heart. Talk to me now, Jackson, with
those incredible hands of yours."

He obliged, learning the map that was his wife once
again, finding his way home. When they were spent, a

tangle of breath, hair and limbs, he buried his head in the mess of her curls. One thought pulled him from the brink of sleep. "Beth? Where's Wy?"

Her laughter spilled out, making him feel light. "Your mother has him and that means you have me—all night." A tug of her teeth on his earlobe made him snap to attention.

"*All night*? We might not get another chance for twenty years or so. Best make the most of it." Jackson proceeded to love his wife and love her well, her warmth, her touch, and her body healing the wounds of her words. All was forgiven.

തൽൽ

He found his letter the next morning. A tad stiff and sore from sleeping on the floor, getting up took a little longer than usual, his chores dragging out a bit as well. When he finally came in, blowing on his hands to try to get some feeling back from the frigid air, breakfast waited on the table with a note propped on his glass of orange juice.

A glance in the bedroom proved Beth had taken to their bed, her eyes closed, the rhythmic rise and fall of her chest evidence that sleep had come for her. Their night had been anything but restful. He remembered how it was with Wyatt. She was growing a person inside of her for Lord's sake. Being tired was to be expected. Slipping into bed, he quietly opened his note so as not to disturb her.

My Dearest Jackson,
A million times over, I'm sorry for tormenting you so yesterday. I don't know what is wrong with me. This fierce protective streak rises up in me whenever I think of

anything hurting Wyatt or you. I guess it's because I love you so much that it makes me crazy. I hope you'll forgive me and accept that I am a bit emotional right now. I feel like I'm on a roller coaster ride at the fair!

This morning, when you left our makeshift bed, it finally hit me that God will bless us with another little one soon. I feel like Wyatt only got here yesterday. I'm still getting to know him and all of his secrets. I still haven't learned everything about you! No matter. I will enjoy spending every day, traveling all of its twists and turns on this journey we take, and I promise I won't hurt you like that again.

I will do my best to be a good wife to you and a good mother. Sometimes I feel like surely I do not do enough, that I need more of me to go around, but one thing I know for sure. I have enough love inside of me to fill the world's oceans and sweep you all away with me. It is a great tidal wave rolling in, day after day, tossing me up, filling me with such happiness and contentment. I am so blessed.

You asked me what I wanted for Christmas. I thought I already had it all, two gifts that you gave me—your love and Wy. Now I know that I was wrong. The new member of our family, a seed that has just been sewn, you have given me this as well. Thank you for all of my gifts beyond measure, more precious than any jewel, silver, gold, or money. Those are things that come and go. Your gifts are a part of me. You are mine and I am yours—forever, time without end.

Love,
Your Beth

e∕3e∕3

"I'm a hippo!" Casey stood at the mirror in the doctor's office and turned to the side, running her hands over her stomach. She was glowering at her reflection. "This gown might as well be a tent and look at my feet! They're balloons!" Nearing the end of her pregnancy, her appointments were weekly at this point. Emmett would go daily if it would get them to the finish line. Anything to make her feel better.

He stopped his pacing, clamping down on the case of jitters that had been under his skin since he found out she was pregnant. Stepping up close, his mouth turned up in a grin and he turned her to face him. "Well then, you are the cutest hippo I ever saw. Besides, don't mirrors add like a hundred pounds or something?"

She stuck out her tongue. "You need your eyes checked."

He skimmed his hands over her body, threading them in her hair. "My eyes are fine. You're beautiful." He couldn't help it. He had to have a taste. His head tilted and his lips touched down on hers. So good. She always felt so good in his arms.

"Okay, kids. Break it up. This is a doctor's office here. No hanky panky." Sharon Matthews was a pixie of a woman with a cap of short blonde hair and cornflower blue eyes that didn't miss a trick. A wag of her finger and she gestured to the examining table. "You know the drill. Let me get a look, see how that baby is percolating in there."

Still forehead to forehead and breathing hard, Casey rested her palm on Emmett's chest, sure to feel the hammering of his heart. He swallowed hard and told her hoarsely. "I guess I'll have to take an IOU." He gave her hand a squeeze and led her to the table, helping her to climb up, then standing back. He had to stamp down the urge to retreat, get out, be anywhere but here. A strong dislike for doctors' offices had developed since he'd been

seriously injured nearly two years before. Casey glanced
his way and smiled, giving him a lifeline.

The two women chatted about his wife's pregnancy,
the practice, and other inconsequential matters. After
working together for a year or so, they'd become good
friends.

The niceties out of the way, Sharon got down to business. She started with the baby, checking the heart beat
first, running her hands over Casey's belly. "Good, everything is good. The heart sounds healthy and your question mark has gone head down, exactly where we want
the little peanut to be. Now, how have you been feeling—
besides pregnant?"

Casey's face twisted in a grimace. "Everything aches,
I can't breathe half the time until the baby shifts, and then
I feel like I'm going to puke. There's not enough room in
here for the both of us. I'm tired of being landlord. When
can I kick my renter out?" She'd been patient, but Emmett knew that it was getting harder. Casey was just
about at the end of her rope.

The OB/GYN pulled out her stethoscope and applied
the blood pressure cuff, a line forming between her eyes
as she did, a pointed glance directed at her patient's feet.
Emmett winced at the sight of them. Casey wore his slippers that day. Nothing else would fit.

"I really want you to take it easy and keep an eye on
your blood pressure. It's a little high and could make you
a candidate for preeclampsia." At the expectant mother's
look of alarm, Sharon patted her arm. "I'm not worried,
just being cautious. You know the drill. Check it a few
times a day. If it's one-forty over ninety or more at least
two times, four hours apart, you need to go to the hospital
and we'll see about inducing or a C-section. All right,
let's take a look down below. Feet in the stirrups."

"Hmm. Sounds sexy." Emmett wiggled his eyebrows

suggestively. Casey's hand reached out as if by reflex and he took it, entwining his fingers with hers.

"More like a medieval torture device. Feel free to try it when I'm done." She leaned her head back and closed her eyes while her doctor did some probing. A flush crept up her neck all the way to her hairline. He wondered about her blood pressure now.

Sharon stood back and eased Casey's feet out of the stirrups, gently giving her belly a pat. "Well, little Mama, you're dilated three centimeters. You could go today. You could go next week. I'd like you to rest as much as you can, do your best to stay calm, and don't overexert. Remember to keep tabs on that blood pressure. I'll see you next week or in the delivery room. Whatever comes first." A bright smile, a peck on Emmett's cheek, and she breezed out of the room.

He turned his attention to his wife and saw an upset on the way. She'd hoped today would be the day her doctor would tell her, "Let's do it." He leaned over her and cupped her face in his hands. "Let me buy you breakfast."

෴

Food couldn't fix everything, but it helped. At Sonny Side Up, Emmett tucked away some bacon and eggs, leaned back against the booth, and watched his wife picking at her omelet. Finally, she pushed her plate away with a sigh. "Not hungry?" He asked her in sympathy.

"No. Whatchamacallit is pushing on my stomach with one end and my bladder with the other. If I go to the bathroom one more time—" She grimaced, rubbing her belly. There was barely enough room for her to slide in. "That's it. I've got to go again. Sorry, Em. I wish I could enjoy this more."

He stood and helped her to her feet, touching down for

a feather kiss. "It's okay. You've got a lot on your mind—and in here." His hand patted her stomach. "I'll pay and meet you at the counter."

He was catching up with the owner, Sonny Olsen, when his wife waddled their way. *Kind of like a penguin. Better keep that one under wraps.* She glanced up and her eyes glowed, brighter than emeralds. "Hey, Sonny! You staying out of trouble?"

The big, bald man pulled her into a hug, his dark eyes warm as always. "I try. As for you, you are amazing. You'll name your first born after me, right?"

She laughed and kissed him on the cheek. "I don't know yet, Sonny. You're in the running!" They took their leave, walking slowly to take heed of icy patches on the sidewalk. Emmett boosted her up into the truck and walked around to the driver's side.

When he climbed in, Casey had her head back and eyes closed, her face more flushed than usual. He reached across and took her hand. "You okay?"

She nodded even as she winced. "I just have a headache. Can we go home, Em? I want to lie down."

He was easy on the drive home, going slow through the curves, watching the bumps. She drifted off five minutes in. He parked by the walkway, scooped her up, and carried her in. Her arms trailed up to his neck and held on. "You're so good to me."

"Bed or couch?" He asked once they were inside. He set her down long enough to take off their outer wear, then picked her up again.

"Bed." That made his heart jump a little. She often rested on the couch, but avoided the bedroom, insisting pregnancy did not make her an invalid. Not about to argue, he took his time going up the stairs and set her down, pulling up the covers.

He bent over her and rested his hand on her cheek. "Can I get you anything?"

"Just you." That was all she needed to say. Emmett slid in next to her and held her close, reassured by her warmth, the even rise and fall of her breathing, and the thump of her heart when he rested a hand on her chest. Shift his palm to her belly and he imagined that tiny fluttering against his skin was the baby. "Em?" It was the softest of a whisper, practically a sigh. "Read me a story."

He knew there was only one story they wanted to hear right now. He gave her a squeeze and got out of bed, on a quest to find his father's journal.

CHAPTER 28

July 2, 1960:

Beth, you've sprung a leak." She was lying in Jackson's arms and it was late, sometime around midnight.

Her eyes fluttered open, her hand traveling down to feel her wet nightgown, the sheets. Her face flushed with embarrassment. "I'm sorry. It's my water." She was groggy, just coming up out of sleep when she inhaled sharply. He took her hand, gave it a squeeze. Slowly, she let the air out through her nose. "Mmm. Guess it's time."

"Do you want to go to the hospital?" he asked with a flicker of hope, but should have known better. His wife wouldn't choose easy.

"No. Here at home." Her chin lifted and her eyes met his, clear and focused. He couldn't help getting pulled in to that pool of blue.

"Do you remember what happened the last time?" He was already moving, sliding out of bed, stripping out of his clothes and tugging on clean pajamas, grabbing a nightgown for her next.

She took his face in her hands, making him go still. "You taught me, Jackson. You're here and I'm not afraid."

He was. Heart hammering, he quickly went about the business of stripping her wet clothes and the sheets, projecting an air of calm. He slipped a fresh nightgown over her head and settled her in the rocker in the corner, tugging out fresh linens from the cedar chest at the foot of the bed. All the while, the sweat was pouring off of him. It would have to be one of the hottest blasted nights of the summer.

"Jackson. I want to walk."

Just like the mares when their time came, having that need to move, to help the baby work its way down the birth canal. He whipped the sheet in place on the bed and took her hand, marveling at the strength in those delicate fingers when she squeezed her eyes shut and shut her mouth, nostrils flaring.

"Remember to breathe. Let it out nice and slow." When the pain eased and Beth's sweet smile was back, he helped her to her feet and they began to stroll from one end of the bedroom to the other, back and forth, stopping when another contraction hit. She'd grab whatever she could get her hands on—the wall, a chair, the dresser, Jackson—and wait it out. In the first hour, the pains dropped from every ten minutes to five. In the next, they were down to two. By the third, they were a minute apart.

"I need—I need to lie down—now." She panted, gripping the bottom of her belly. He nodded, piling up the pillows and helping her to prop herself up to nearly a sitting position. She grabbed the quilt and buried her face in it, smothering her scream, fearful of waking little Wyatt. "Lord. It's like someone is pounding me with a hammer, way down low in my back." He could sympathize. He knew the feeling well, was feeling a bit of it right now what with all of the back and forth and his body tensed into knots. He pushed it down. This was not about him.

The next pain hit, harder and faster than the last. Jack-

son squeezed her hand. "I'm going to call Mama. Pop
will bring her over in no time."

"No! Don't leave me, Jackson!" She grabbed hold of
his shoulder and tugged him down next to her, so close
their foreheads touched. "I'm scared."

"You can do this. *We* can do this together. Just let me
get ready. It's nearly time." Something had made him
gather things together and lay them all out on the dresser.
Call it premonition or just an overactive case of the
nerves. His hands clenched into fists as he left her side,
his eyes slamming shut. *Please God. Keep her safe, her
and the baby. Help me to help them. Let this one come
easier.*

His hands shook as he grabbed towels, scissors, twine,
and oil. He set them all on the cedar chest at the foot of
the bed. Moving to the head, he tied rags to the headboard and set them in her hands. "You pull on these when
you need to, hard as you can. Break the bed if you have
to, I'll build a new one. I just need to wash my hands and
fill a basin with hot water. I'll be right back." An ungodly
groan, barely contained by a pillow, came next, making
him move faster.

He pulled up a chair and sat at the foot of the bed, ignoring the sharp stab down low in his back. *You just pipe
down!* He pushed Beth's legs back and threw her nightgown over her knees. His eyes sprang wide, the sight
sucking the breath from his lungs. "Honey, you're crown-
ing already! When the next pain lets up, try and go easy.
I'm going to rub some of this oil on you, try to keep you
from tearing. I'll try not to hurt you."

She cried out when he touched the inflamed, swollen
and stretched skin, making his own eyes begin to burn.
With utmost tenderness, Jackson rubbed the oil over her
poor body, marveling as the baby's head slid back for a
moment. Amazing, absolutely amazing what a woman

could endure. Another pain hit and Beth clenched her jaw, grunting as she pulled on the rags so tightly that the wood began to creak. A deep, hard breath huffed out as the contraction eased up and she bore down. *POP!* The head was out, just like that.

"Sweet Jesus! The head's out! Give me another push, sweetheart, give me all you've got!" This time, she didn't care about the scream of victory as the baby made it all the way, into his father's waiting hands, a loud, healthy wail rising up with his arrival.

Jackson swiped the back of one arm over his eyes, wiping away the tears, and quickly cut the cord, tying it off and wiping the baby—*his baby*—with an extra towel. "It's a boy, Mama! You've got yourself another beautiful boy!" He was laughing and crying, as he wrapped the bundle up and set him in his mother's waiting arms.

The tears were streaming from her beautiful eyes but her smile was bright enough to blind a body as she reached out to set a palm on Jackson's face. "You did it. You did it, all by yourself. How I love you."

"I love you too. I did have a little help. I'd say you did all the work." He sank down on the side of the bed and simply took them in, enjoying the pleasure of seeing his new son and wife together. A ripple of pain flashed over her face and he remembered. They weren't done yet. Using his experience with the horses and memories from Wyatt's birth, he massaged her belly as gently as possible. A little grunt and the placenta slid out onto a waiting towel. He wiped Beth down with a damp, warm cloth, setting a clean towel between her legs to absorb the blood. He was tidying up when Wyatt came scampering in.

"Mama! Mama! You have baby?" His eyes were wide with wonder at the sight of the dark-haired bundle in his mother's arms.

She reached out for their oldest, the tears running down her face even as her smile threatened to split it wide open. "Yes, he's here, honey. You have a baby brother." Wyatt stood close to her, marveling at the new addition to their family.

Feeling like he ran around the world and back, Jackson propped a hip against the bed and simply looked at his family. "So, I guess this is Emmett. Nice to meet you, buddy. You sure did get here fast. Guess you couldn't wait. Thanks for going easy on your mother."

Jackson's voice was practically gone and he kept having to dry his eyes, so happy to meet his son, so relieved that his wife was all right. He bent his head to gently brush the baby's soft cap of hair with his lips, dropping a butterfly kiss on Beth's mouth next. "We knew from the start about his first name. How about a middle name?"

She ran her finger along the baby's cheek, practically vibrating with joy. The pain was already an echo of the past. All that mattered was the adorable fruit of her labor lying in her arms. "Oh, that's easy. It's Jackson of course."

She looked up at her husband, her eyes bright, chin trembling. Birthing babies meant riding a roller coaster of emotions. One moment, Beth would be laughing; the next, she'd be crying. Clearing her throat, a finger wagged at him in warning. "Don't you try and argue with me either. I have my reasons and I think you should humor me, especially after what I've been through tonight."

Chuckling, he tucked her in against his chest, she, Wyatt, and the baby fitting perfectly at his side. "Darling, I have completely run out of steam. You won't be getting any trouble out of me. What do you say we get you cleaned up, in some nice fresh sheets, and sleep for a week?"

She tipped her head his way like a sunflower raises its

petals to the sun, nearly blinding him with her smile and the light in those deep blue eyes that pulled him in time after time. "Only if you'll sleep with me." She kissed him and his heart started to do a little dance, the one part of his body that could respond no matter what state the rest of him was in. There still remained a tiny part of him, afraid that Beth would shut him out again. That fear could finally be laid to rest.

Pressing a palm to her cheek, he gave a kiss back to her and stretched it out for good measure, one that would surely tide her over during a good, long sleep. "I wouldn't be anywhere else but next to you. How about we start right now?" The bed shook with her laughter as she pressed her forehead to his chest. He rested his arm on hers, holding both his wife and sons close to his heart, a place they'd be as long as he lived.

The next morning, Beth tapped him on the head. "Jackson?" She whispered, her throat scratchy, eyes heavy with fatigue. He mumbled something incoherent, reluctant to face the sunlight beating on his eyelids. He drew up the wedding quilt snug round them and froze for an instant, his back talking to him. Moving a bit slower, his breath eased its way out, the pain ebbed, and he tucked her in closer against him with a sigh. Her hair was tickling his nose, but he didn't have the energy to do anything about it. "Jackson, it's nine! What about the horses?"

He shifted slowly, his body heavy with fatigue, overcome by an unusual bout of laziness. Not inclined to move after their ordeal, he doubted that she was either. He reached out and stroked her hair, admiring the bloom in her cheeks. She looked tired, but a good tired. "I think we've earned a morning to sleep in. I know you have. I called over to Mama and Pop's early this morning. Em and Wyatt are taking care of the animals, Pop has Wy, and Mama's here to keep an eye on Little Emmett. Relax, Little Mother. Take a breather while you can. You'll be on double duty soon enough."

She rested her head on his shoulder and he felt her body loosen as she drifted from wakefulness to sleep. He planned on taking advantage of the opportunity and joining her until he heard a squawk from the next room.

His mother padded in quietly in her slippers with a tiny bundle wrapped in a soft, blue blanket. Beth was instantly awake, holding out her arms for their son. "He's been good as gold," Ella said softly as she handed the newborn over, "but I think he's hungry now." Mama's dark eyes were warm as melted chocolate as her hand skimmed little Emmett's head. She left the new mother to nurse him for a few minutes, eventually returning with a tray laden with food, tea, and coffee. "If you need anything, you just call me."

Jackson caught his mother's hand before she left and reeled her in to plant a kiss on her cheek. "Thanks so much, Mama, for everything." The tears sprang to her eyes instantly and she flapped her hands, disappearing before she was overcome. That left him more time to watch the marvel of his wife and child. "Beautiful," he murmured, taking pleasure in the suckling sound of that tiny, hungry mouth. He couldn't help feeling another kind of hunger, watching the glory that was his Beth.

She gave him a smile and her cheeks flushed. "He is, isn't he?" Jackson pulled her in closer, resting his chin on her head and his hand on the warm cap of fine hair on his son's head. No there was no better place on God's green earth than right here, with this woman, in the bed they shared. The only thing missing was Wyatt and he'd be home soon, making everything right in their world.

"I was referring to you, but yes, he's absolutely gorgeous." Beth sighed, smiling at the compliment, waiting patiently until Emmett nodded off. Jackson had the perfect opportunity to feed his wife, holding the cup for her, sharing a plate between them. All the while, they intently watched God's great wonder, their son.

"Where did your Mama get the name Jackson for you?" she asked sleepily as she pushed the plate away, full and mellow. She rested her head on his shoulder, waiting expectantly for an answer.

There was nothing for it but to tell the tale. He set the dishes on the bedside table and relished the opportunity to cuddle with his wife. "Oh, she's a romantic. Mama has always loved the story of Stonewall Jackson and the way men would follow him to the ends of the earth. Those confederate soldiers marched barefoot, through the worst conditions, for miles. How they carried on when he was killed. Did you know one of his own men shot him and he died because of it? They were heartbroken."

He fell silent, picturing that long ago time and such devotion. Would they have won the war if Stonewall lived? "She thought I should have a name with potential, one I could grow into. Guess we're connected to Stonewall somehow on my father's side."

Beth laid a hand on his cheek, entwining her fingers in his hair. "I'd say the name fits you. I'd follow you anywhere." The heat flooded his cheeks in a rush, at her touch, at her attention, at her words. Talk about devotion.

"The same goes for me. What's the history behind your name? Anything special or did your parents choose Elizabeth because they liked it?" His hand ran through her hair and he marveled at its shine and softness, like fine silk. He played with a handful, for a heartbeat or two, glancing up to see her grinning at him, waiting patiently. He shrugged and focused on her.

"Oh, my name's not nearly as exciting. It comes from my grandmother, Elizabeth Hamilton Mason. When Daddy was born, Grandma Mason insisted that he be named after her maiden name. She never quite got over the fact that women couldn't keep the name they were born with. Quite a stubborn, opinionated woman. It turns out there were a lot of strong people in the family. On my mother's side, she can trace her relatives back to Revolutionary days." Beth yawned, her words trailing off at the end, her eyes beginning to droop.

Jackson leaned over to give her a kiss, and the corner of her mouth turned up in a smile, even though she was on the brink of falling back to sleep. "I'd say our son has a good foundation to stand on. He comes from a family made of pretty strong mettle."

Her eyes opened wide and she slid in closer to her husband. "Want to find out how strong? I know we can't do much, but there's always kissing to test out our theory." Jackson willingly obliged, finding her affections and enthusiasm to be an experience that made them both go weak. He knew that when sleep came for him again, there would be some really nice dreams waiting for him.

Sometime in the late afternoon, when the sun came from another angle, he woke up alone, actually shivering without his wife's warmth and company. She sat in the rocker in the corner, softly singing to Baby Emmett, rocking slowly. He propped his head on one hand, watching them, not wishing to disturb them and break the spell. While he waited, he found a letter on her pillow.

Dear Jackson,

Finally, the long wait is over. I think it was harder waiting this time, knowing what we had to look forward to after all of the excitement with our Wyatt. What a feisty, little bugger Emmett was! He sure was in a hurry. Hardly gave either one of us a chance to breathe. I wasn't sure I could do it. Then you'd be right there, look-

ing me in the eye, holding on tight and I knew—you would never let me go. I'm so proud of you, bringing Emmett into this world all by yourself, with a little help from me, of course, and God above.

You asked me why I picked Jackson for his middle name. I chose that perfect name because I can think of no other man that is as worthy to share his name with our son. I would choose it as his first name, but your brother would never forgive us. Through all of the craziness, not once did you show any fear. Not once did you leave my side. Not once did you let me down.

If our little Emmett can have the same qualities, I couldn't ask for more. He will be a fine man indeed. He'll have big shoes to fill, but you'll let him try them on for size with a little help from Wyatt, the best big brother he could ever have. Thank you for being the husband and father that you are, partner and guide. You humble me every day and make me kiss my lucky stars every night. I'm sure that this little boy is going to be amazing—like Wyatt. Like you. I love you.

Love,
Your Beth

CHAPTER 29

October 30, 1963:

I can't find Emmett!"

Beth, Wyatt clinging to her hand, had made her way out to the pasture, walking out in the middle of the field where Jackson was working with a few of their yearlings.

One look at her face and he dropped what he was doing to follow them inside. This time, it was for real, not one of her nightmares and her fear was contagious.

"Emmett? Come on out, son. That's enough playing. You've got your mother and brother scared," Jackson called out as soon as he hit the door.

If there was one thing Emmett responded to every time, it was his father. He'd do anything to avoid his disapproval.

Beth was close on his heels, Wyatt now on her hip, his lip beginning to tremble as the tears threatened to fall. His kid brother was his whole world. "He was trying to snitch cookies from the cookie jar. Wy caught him in the act and came to get me. By the time I reached the kitchen, the little dare devil had climbed up on a chair and was teetering on the edge of the counter. The cookie jar smashed on the floor. Emmett would've been next, the little stinker, if I hadn't snatched him when he fell."

"I didn't mean to make Em run away!" Wyatt wailed and buried his face in his mother's shirt. She rubbed his back consolingly while Jackson patted his head.

"It's not your fault, baby! You kept him from getting hurt and did right." She leaned down to kiss him on the top of the head, her forehead creased in a worried frown. "I gave him a swat on the bottom and sent him to bed, said he needed some time to think about making good choices and a nap. I know I gave him quite a tongue lashing. It wasn't because of the cookie jar, even though he *should* mind me. I thought he'd break his neck!"

She was close to hysteria by this point. Jackson pulled her into his arms, keeping his oldest snug against him as well. "He's probably just playing hide and seek." Their youngest loved the game and could play it for hours, indoors or out.

He let them go and picked up the phone. "Hey, Mama? Could you round up Pop and the twins? Emmett took off and I need some help looking for him." He nodded with a grin that he didn't feel. "Yes, I'm sure he'll be the death of me."

He turned to Beth and gave her a hug and kiss on the top of her head. "You stay put, in case he comes back here. Mama's doing the same over there. Don't worry. We'll find him." Jackson spoke firmly, leaving no room for doubt to work its way through the cracks.

He was at the door when he felt a tug on the tail of his flannel shirt. Wyatt stood before him, lip thrust out, shoulders set. "I want to help."

God love him. He knelt down to his oldest boy's level to stare into steady blue gray eyes that were stormier than usual today. He set his hands on Wyatt's sturdy shoulders and gave him a gentle squeeze. "You're a big boy and I wish you could help me, buddy, but I need you to be man of the house. Your mama is scared and needs you to watch over her, keep her company, okay?" He gave his little one a hug and a rough kiss on the cheek, then went out.

Thankfully, it wasn't too cold for a day in late October, but the air had a bite to it, the wind sending the leaves skittering by his feet. They made a mournful sound that sent a shiver own his back. Hopefully, the boy hadn't gone far.

He started with the barn and outbuildings, then moved on to the woods between their house and his parents' home, running into his brothers along the way. Landon was searching his own farm thoroughly before getting in the truck and heading out to talk to the neighbors. They joked and laughed a bit early on in the day, keeping it light. As the sun sank toward the horizon, all humor was gone from the situation.

When darkness fell, Jackson headed inside for a flashlight. Wyatt was in the living room, drawing pictures on the floor. Beth was pacing from window to window. An untouched dinner waited on the table. She whirled around to face the creak of the opening door, hope lighting her eyes, then she squeezed them shut, a hand to her mouth.

He gathered her in. "He's just being stubborn. You know how he is."

"Eat something before you go out." He shook his head and grabbed his coat off the hook, thought twice and draped a blanket over his arm as well. "At least take a thermos of coffee?"

"No, I don't want anything. I'll be back soon." Jackson fervently hoped his words were true. At around eleven at night, he paused his search long enough to bring in the horses, frustrated to no end to have to stop. As he held the barn door open to guide the horses in, his eyes followed the beams of light that passed back and forth around him in the woods, and nearby lanes. The twins, his father, and more of their neighbors had joined in the hunt and the thought squeezed his heart.

The last horse was in his stall when Jackson pressed his hands to the hard wooden gate and prayed. *Please God. Please let me find him. Guide my path.* It had dropped to below forty degrees and there was a frost advisory. Emmett had left his coat behind. If he didn't find shelter—

Jackson shuddered at his imaginings.

The scrambling of the barn cats overhead pulled him from his thoughts, and he went stock still, his eyes pinned on the ceiling. His youngest loved the wild cats, probably thought they were kindred spirits. He'd spend hours playing with them, begging his mother to bring them into the house on a daily basis.

Hoping against hope, Jackson climbed the rungs of the ladder and swept his light over the loft. His heart sank to the pit of his stomach. Nothing. Unwilling to give up, he traveled the entire length of the barn to the far corner. He was on his way back, the heavy load of dejection settling in on his shoulders, when he caught sight of a small sneaker.

A step closer and he found his boy sleeping in a pile of straw behind a stack of bales, a black kitten curled up against him. His face was streaked with dirt, the tracks of his tears running down his cheeks. Leaves and straw were in his dark hair, and he'd ripped his jeans, revealing a glimpse of a badly scraped knee. It would appear Emmett's adventure hadn't been uneventful.

Jackson was torn between desire to shake him or cry. As relief flooded through him and pushed aside the rush of adrenalin, he knelt down and the latter nearly won out as his eyes filled. Hand on his boy's head, he told him hoarsely, "Em, wake up son. Time to go in."

"I'm sorry about the cookie jar, Daddy." Emmett looked up at his father, his big golden eyes beautiful enough to hurt, even with fear flickering in their depths. The charmer. He didn't even know it, but with that gaze like honey and his smile, there would be big trouble with the girls down the line. *All in due time.* Jackson leaned in and hugged his boy, thankful that for now, he only had to worry about tonight.

"It's all right. It's not about the cookie jar, really. You disobeyed your mama, but more than that, you could've been hurt. Plus you've had Grandpop, your uncles, and our neighbors worried sick about you. You really scared your mama, me, and Wyatt."

His baby's eyes were filling as he started to whimper. Maybe *this time* it would get through to him.

Jackson knelt down and set his hands on Emmett's shoulders. "Promise you'll never run away when you're in trouble again. You need to face what you do. If you get punished, it's because we're trying to teach you. No matter what, we'll always love you. Running away won't ever fix anything. Understand?" At Em's nod, he swept him up in his arms and wrapped him in the blanket. The escapee didn't even ask for a kitten this time.

They walked inside to find Wyatt asleep on the couch with Em's favorite bear tucked in his arm. Beth sat at the table, a cross, the family bible and a candle flickering in front of her. She was praying. She looked up and let out a small, strangled cry.

Em streaked across the floor, sobbing and apologizing at the same time. Wyatt woke up and joined in the fray.

Jackson was last, gathering them all in close. He was thankful to hold his family together, under his roof, safe in his arms. If only he always could.

For the first time that day, he remembered how to breathe.

c/sc/s

The power went out the second Jackson hit the door, followed by an ungodly shrieking from above and his heart went into overdrive. Between Emmett's recent escape and the eventful life of fatherhood, Jackson was quite sure he'd be old before his time. Fortunately, he had the presence of mind to fumble under the kitchen sink and grab a flashlight before taking the stairs two at a time. "Beth? Wyatt? Emmett? Are you all right?"

Another screech and he burst into their bedroom to see a mountain of blankets on their bed, illuminated from underneath. He wilted by the door for an instant and his heart resumed its beating. His wife was playing with the boys, entertaining them and distracting them at the same time. Might as well join in the fun. Tiptoeing across the floor, Jackson lifted the blankets with a giant roar, making both boys squeal. Beth made plenty of noise right along with them, sending a wink his way to show she was playing along.

They were all decked out in their Halloween costumes in a western theme. Wyatt loved anything to do with Tombstone, the OK Corral, Wild Bill Hickok, Buffalo Bill, and Billy the Kid. When he heard about the famous lawman that shared his name, it only made sense that Jackson would be Wyatt Earp. The boys had chosen to be the James brothers. Little rascal that he was, Em would be the infamous, younger brother. The role of Jesse suited him, the little wildcat. Thank God he had Beth's firm, gentle hand to keep him in line, that and a heart of gold.

Beth was Annie Oakley. She'd modeled her costume for Jackson the night before. He thoroughly enjoyed removing it, one item at time. *Wouldn't mind doing it right now.*

"We're telling ghost stories, Daddy, and we're dressed

to be tough for any storm." Wyatt smiled up at him, his eyes, dark blue clouded over to slate, big as a full moon. Jackson wrapped an arm around him and gave his oldest a squeeze, ruffling his hair as an added bonus.

Em, wearing a fierce expression and gleam in his eye to rival his namesake, grabbed his father and hollered, "Boo!" With a pounce, he threw himself on top of the glowing flashlight, trying to snatch it.

"Oh, it's like that is it?" Jackson laughed and began tickling the boys, effectively pinning them on the bed. "Say Uncle Sam and I'll stop! Do you surrender?" Wyatt gave in first, then a reluctant Emmett. That left Beth. There was only one thing to do with a woman who wouldn't surrender. Jackson set his hands firmly on her shoulders and his mouth on her lips. She started to wriggle beneath him and he pulled up. "Well, are you going to say Uncle?"

"Not yet." Her face was flushed, eyes glittering more brightly than blue gemstones as she panted up a storm. Jackson came in for another long, lingering kiss, determined to get her to wave a white flag. He nearly got his way when the tables were turned. Somehow, Beth flipped him with her leg tangled around his and the boys pinned his feet. She sat on top of him, legs straddling his chest, her golden hair tickling his face as she kissed him senseless.

He broke off the kiss, turning his head to the side, breathless. "Uncle Sam," he whispered hoarsely. Jackson found himself fighting a stirring in his belly. He wanted her right then and there, boys or no boys.

Closing his eyes, he swallowed hard, trying to accept the need to wait. No easy task. He could never get enough of his wife.

Beth nodded and kissed his cheek, understanding in her eyes and a hunger to match his own. She climbed off of him and scooped up the covers in one arm, giving him a tug with the other.

He stood and handed his flashlight to Wyatt. "You take your brother's hand going downstairs. We don't need anyone falling and getting hurt."

Emmett thrust his lip out in a pout. "But Daddy, *I* want to hold it!" He stomped his feet angrily and crossed his arms.

Jackson squatted down and rubbed between his youngest boy's shoulder blades. "I know, but you tend to get carried away. You might leave your brother in the dust—until you really think he's in trouble. Wy's the responsible one."

Beth rested her hand on Em's head as he stared up at her with a mournful expression, the flashlight catching the gleam of honey in his eyes, too sweet to resist. How either of them managed to keep their resolve concerning discipline was a minor miracle. "When you get downstairs, you can take the lead, *if* your brother decides to tag along."

Wy might tend to be cautious, but he was not a coward. While Jackson took a flashlight, some covers and Beth's hand to navigate the dark stairwell, the boys forged ahead. As soon as they hit the first floor, Em grabbed the flashlight, still tenaciously clinging to his big brother. He wasn't about to let him go. Wyatt was game and off they went.

Their parents waited for a crash and other evidence of destruction, but only heard giggles, thumping feet, the occasional screech, and Wy shouting, "Cut it out, Emmett, *or else!*" They had been known to flatten each other on occasion before parental intervention. Jackson was a firm believer of allowing the boys to solve their differences as much as possible, based on his own experiences. As his father said, it built character. There might be moments when they fought like the lawless barn cats that were always in abundance on a farm, but they loved each other and would always make up.

Jackson chuckled to himself and built up a fire, warming the room with a cheerful crackle while Beth set up a nest of covers and pillows on the floor. Aiming to create a homey nest to ride out the storm, she scrounged up candles and placed them out of harm's way and potential mishaps brought on by two playful boys. Jackson rustled up some supplies from the kitchen and called out, "Boys, we're doing hot dogs, s'mores, and hot cocoa on the fireplace." Scampering feet pounded their way with two boys wide-eyed and wreathed in smiles, eager for a treat usually reserved for campfires.

For the rest of the evening, the whole family stuffed themselves silly, topping off the goodies with popcorn. The boys loved taking turns hanging on to the handle of an antique popcorn popper left over from Jackson's great grandparents. They shook the metal basket over the flames, giving little squeals, jumping with every pop. Their little hands and faces were soon covered in butter, salt, chocolate, and marshmallow goo, but no one cared that night. Camped out on the rug, watching the flicker of dancing flames, they sang songs until no one could think of anything more.

From there, Jackson and Beth started taking turns telling stories, a departure from the books that were read to them as a bedtime ritual every night. She recalled the day that their father put a frog down her shirt, making her fall in love on the spot. He had a goldmine of tales about his brothers' escapades and scrapes, and how he used to come to the rescue most of the time. One of the best was the day he had to grab Pop's red bandanna and run out in the middle of a field to get a mean, ornery bull's attention so the twins could escape.

His voice was growing hoarse with the telling when his boys finally gave in to sleep, their faces looking even younger when they closed their eyes. He pulled their wedding quilt up to their necks, feeling a tug on his heart to see his sons wrapped up together in a tangle of arms and legs. God, there was no way they could love each other more. A kiss to their foreheads, a stroke of their dark heads shining in the firelight's glow, and he had to step back, clearing his throat as he did.

His wife patted his cheek before ducking down to give her goodnight peck on the forehead and the sign of the cross over their sleeping forms. One thing was certain. Between Beth, Jackson, and Almighty God, someone was always keeping a close watch on the Henry boys. She turned away and took hold of his lapels. "You did such a good job tucking them in. What about me?"

"Well, Mrs. Henry, you need to get into your nightgown first. Let me help you." Moving ever so slowly, stretching the moment out, he lifted her blouse over her head, unbuttoned her jeans, and watched them fall. Her bra and underwear hit the floor next, leaving him staring in awe at the wonder that was his wife.

"Mmm…Mrs. Henry, you are so beautiful, more so every day." Jackson took her hands and turned her this way and that, enjoying the play of light and shadows on her body. It was the body of a mature woman, no longer a mere girl, with a little extra softness and roundness that came with motherhood twice over. She was incredible. "What's your secret?" He asked, stepping in closer and pressing his lips to hers.

"It must be the way my husband takes such good care of me. Now let me help you." She started with his old standby, his flannel shirt. One button at a time, with her tongue pinned between her teeth in concentration, driving him to distraction. The shirt was discarded and his T-shirt went next. He groaned as her hands rested on his belt. "What is it?" Concern darkened her eyes and made that dent on her forehead go a little deeper.

Jackson shook his head. "Just a little sore. I think I pulled some muscles in my shoulders and my back. I had to fight to get those horses in and shut the doors in the wind. I'll live." Her smile lit up her features, and she moved behind him, her hands running over his body, from the sturdy column of his neck, all the way down to his waist.

She pressed, kneaded, and ran her lips over his skin, bringing forth another moan, one of absolute pleasure. He turned and caught her up in his arms, bringing her flush against his chest. "I feel much better. Why don't we lie down now? You must be tired."

"I'm not that tired, Jackson."

Her head bowed as her hands moved to his belt buckle, loosening it and letting his pants fall. Looking up at him again, the gleam in her eyes pulled him flush against her.

In an easy tumble, they dropped onto the blankets, warmed by the fire, each other's arms, and the heat that always burned between them.

When sleep came, Jackson forgot all about the hurting. He was so far gone, his body didn't feel anything at all except his Beth's arm wrapped around his middle and her breath on his cheek. Sweet dreams.

He woke up to the sound of the coffee pot perking, the strong brew's scent wafting its way into the living room. The boys were sound asleep, cheeks flushed, hair tousled. *Snug as a bug in a rug.*

Jackson couldn't help but grin at the sight of them. Propping himself up on one elbow, he saw an envelope propped up on the coffee table and snatched it up, rubbing sleepy seeds out of his eyes as he read.

Dear Jackson,
Last night was the best storm of my life. I wouldn't mind waiting out a few more, as long as we're all tucked in close together, here in our home, with everyone I love the most beside me. I couldn't ask for a better way to go to sleep either. Maybe we'll finally have that next baby we've been trying for.

I'm really looking forward to trick or treating tonight, showing off our costumes with you and the boys, watching them light up each time a door opens and someone puts something special in their goodie bags. The best part will come last, after they're sound asleep, and you are all mine. I can't wait to play dress up with you, Jackson. I know I say it every time, but I love you. More and more, every day.
Love,
Your Beth

⊂⊃⊂⊃

The old house shuddered as the wind made a mournful howl, effectively snuffing the lights out. Emmett set his father's journal down and grazed his lips across Casey's cheek, giving her a reassuring squeeze. "Hmm, talk about timing. I'm not surprised the power is out. The snow is really coming down out there and that wind is whipping around like all get out. Stay put and I'll get a flashlight, okay? Promise you won't go anywhere."

Her voice was slow and lazy in the darkness. "Are you kidding? I'm so sleepy now, I don't think I could move if I wanted to. Hurry back." Somehow, her hand found his and she gave him the kind of kiss that left him begging for more.

Ignoring the tripping of his heart and the tightening in his belly that was par for the course with his wife's affec-

tions, he forced himself to feel his way through the bedroom to the bathroom, squashing the rising panic that
threatened to choke him. He'd spent roughly a year in
perpetual darkness thanks to a severe head injury. There
were many times since his sight had been restored that
nightmares had shaken him awake, dousing him in a cold
sweat, making his breath come in gasps, pitching him
from the bed as he grabbed at his eyes, fearing the blindness had returned. His wife was always there, holding on,
proving otherwise, filling his eyes with her.

A bit of fumbling in the vanity and he snatched up the
flashlight. Instantly, a welcome beam of illumination held
the shadows at bay and he could breathe again. Stepping
back in the bedroom, he offered his hand for leverage and
raised his wife to her feet. She grabbed some blankets
and pillows off the bed and they headed for the stairs, his
arm wrapped protectively around her waist. "Easy. Take
your time and don't miss a step."

"For Pete's sake, Em, I'm not going to break!" She
blew her bangs from her face with one forceful puff of
air, but humored him, inching her way forward as she
peaked over the heap of bedding in her arms. They hit
the ground floor and she got herself situated on the floor
while Emmett stoked up the fire and moved the coffee
table out of the way. With the pillows propped against the
couch and a few blankets for a cushion, they had a cozy
spot to snuggle up. She glanced up at her husband and
found him spreading candles throughout the rooms. "This
feels like déjà vu, right out of your father's journal."

He sank down beside her and nuzzled her high on her
neck, glorying in the play of firelight on her flushed
cheeks. "I wish our night could end the same way as
theirs." His hand skimmed over her body and rested on
the sweet spot of her rounded hip. Holding onto her was
always a pleasure, one he'd grown to love long before the

lights turned back on when it came to his vision.

The phone rang, making them both jump. After their last call that came in late at night, they were a little paranoid. Casey stretched for the receiver on the end table by the couch and pressed it to her ear. "Hello? Emily, is that you? I can hardly hear you."

Emily Richards was their eighty-year-old neighbor who lived a couple farms down the road, next to Wyatt's. There was a faint exclamation and the sound of a crash on the other end.

Casey hung up and dialed with fingers that shook. "Hello, operator? I need an ambulance for Emily Richards, number twenty on the old Charlton Road. Tell them to hurry! I think she might have had a heart attack." The phone slipped from her hand and she turned to face Emmett.

He tried staring her down. When it came to being obstinate, they were pretty evenly matched. "You've done your part. You can't go. Remember what Sharon said about taking it easy. You don't need the stress, Casey!"

Her eyes filled and her lip trembled. "Don't you get it, Em? I'm a doctor! I have to try. Even with Daddy—" Her voice broke on that one. "I had to try."

Being a doctor wasn't the sole reason for her urgent need to respond to the call for help. Emmett knew that her father's death had a major impact on his wife. That and the journal entries about his grandfather were all too fresh in both their minds. She raised her chin and faced him head on. "I'm going." Her eyes said, *Just try and stop me, Emmett Henry.*

"Then I'm going with you. Let me get the truck." He hurried out, fired up the farm truck, and cranked the heat. He pulled the pick-up to the door, got out, and helped Casey to get in.

As they gunned it out of the driveway, he inwardly

cursing the weather, the hour, the distance to the nearest hospital then remembered the reason for their late night excursion.

He began to pray in earnest for a woman who had been like a grandmother to him. His wife bowed her head, fingers clasped, and she whispered under her breath. There could never be too many prayers.

In less than five minutes, they were in Emily's driveway. Emmett helped Casey and tried the door. No luck. Running around back, he kicked at it in frustration. Locked. With no other option, he picked up a rock and broke a window. With a heave over the sill and a mad dash to the front door, Doctor Henry was in.

Stumbling through the dark house with only the light of one flashlight to guide the way, they found the elderly woman sprawled on the kitchen floor, the phone next to her.

Casey struggled to get down by her side with Emmett's help, frantically checking her vitals. "She's not breathing and I can't find a pulse." Shifting, she fought to give their neighbor CPR, but her pregnant belly kept getting in the way and she simply couldn't get enough air to share it with her neighbor. Her eyes filled in frustration. "I can't reach her!"

"Tell me what to do." Emmett hit his knees and followed Casey's tearful directions, first the forceful chest compressions, then the puffs of air, trying to ignore the tide of memories as he captured the scent of powder and lemon verbena. Five minutes in and Emily took a breath. And another. Her pulse was a weak flutter, but she had a pulse.

The wash of blue and red lights flashed against the walls. The cavalry had arrived.

కావు

The power was still out when they returned home. Emmett settled Casey in their nest of blankets and kept a close eye on her. She'd gone from pale to scarlet and back again since their neighbor called, her palms cupping her belly. He didn't know if she was being protective or in pain. He laid his hand on hers. "I know you must be really tired after all of this tonight. Why don't you go to sleep?"

She smiled at him and dropped a butterfly kiss on his jaw, then his lips. "I am tired, but I'm wound at the same time. It's like electricity is crackling through me. You, too?" At his nod, she took his hand. "I'm never too tired for some hugging, kissing, and holding on to you, not to mention feeling the touch of those oh-so capable hands. My back is really killing me. I could use some expert attention."

Her expression turned into a pout, one that could make him walk the plank. Lord, the woman had him wrapped around her pinky.

Emmett ran his hand over her hair, ending at her neck and kneading muscles gone tight, reveling in the moment they loosened as she fell into him. "I think I can do something about that. Stretch out and I'll give you a good rubdown."

He started with her shoulders, working at each one with a firm, masterful touch, then inched his way ever so slowly down to the middle of her lower back. This was the place that needed the most attention, bearing the brunt of her weight day after day. Forming a fist, he drove his knuckles into the midpoint and pressed until her body bowed. She let out a low moan. His fingers splayed at the thought that he might have hurt her until she turned and her eyes begged for more.

"Oh please don't stop, Em. You do not know how good that feels. That is the first time in days that the ach-

ing has gone away. It's been like a toothache, a dull
throbbing that dogs after you. Not anymore." Her breath
came out in a sigh and her eyes drifted closed. He continued his competent ministrations until her body finally
went loose.

He lay down beside her and they both stared into the
dancing flames of the fireplace. Emmett was about to be
washed away when Casey's warm voice rolled over him.
"You were wonderful tonight, Em."

"No, *you* were. I couldn't have done it if you didn't
tell me how." He rested his hand on her belly and
wrapped a leg around her legs, wishing he could always
keep her safe.

"Now you know." That was one lesson he never wanted to repeat. "Em?" She tugged at him again, keeping
him awake a little longer. "Read to me, will you? Your
dad's journal really soothes me, that and your mother's
letters."

He fought to shake himself fully awake. Another kiss
from the beautiful woman at his side helped. She handed
him the small, leather-bound book and hitched herself up
on the pillows. "I notice your dad's entries are far and
few between toward the end."

Emmett couldn't help but chuckle. "I think they had
their hands full, what with two kids, a farm, and a herd of
horses. We can kind of relate, don't you think?" At her
nod, he flipped through the pages, skimming over his father's neat writing to pick up where they left off.

Outside, the wind continued to screech like a banshee,
but inside the Henry Homestead, all was well. They were
warm and dry, sheltered from the elements. Best of all,
they had enough body heat generating between them to
tide them over for as long as they needed. The rest of the
world could go away. Emmett Henry didn't need anything else in life except for his wife.

CHAPTER 30

May 8, 1964:

The water was boiling over on the stove, dishes were heaped in the sink, and a pile of clothes was tossed on the couch. No lunch was waiting on the table. Wyatt and Emmett were plopped in front of the television, both of them fighting back tears. Beth didn't like them spending too much time in front of the TV. If she had her druthers, they'd be outside from sun up to sundown.

Jackson pulled off his barn boots, turned off the burner, and knelt down beside the boys. Automatically, they stepped into his waiting arms. "Where's Mama, boys?"

"She's up in bed, Daddy. She told us to be good boys and watch a television program quiet for a little while, said she didn't feel good. Do you think Mama's real sick?" Wyatt's lip was thrust out, his eyes red. He was trying as hard as he could to be tough.

"No, I don't think so, fellas. I just think she's tired. Let me go check on her. You two stay put." He kissed them both on the top of the head and took the stairs two at a time.

Jackson was worried about Beth. Usually, she'd come out to see him in the barn or pasture, bring him sweet tea and an extra sweet smile, the boys tagging along to have some rough and tumble time. The past few weeks, she'd been absent. He'd catch her crying, sitting motionless, other times praying. When he asked what was wrong, she pressed her hands to her stomach, told him nothing was wrong. Beth had wanted another child when Emmett was two. Their youngest would be four soon. What if something *was* wrong?

Jackson's stomach was churning by the time he pushed their bedroom door open. She was under the covers and didn't move. For the past few days, he'd found her in their bed more than not. She'd overslept for a week. Each time, he came in, cooked breakfast for himself and the boys, and brought up a tray. Beth didn't touch it.

He sat down beside her and laid a hand on her back. "I think you should go to the doctor. This has been going on too long."

She rolled over at that one and pulled herself out of bed. "No, no. I'm fine."

A trip to the bathroom and she walked out, smoothing her hair. Absently, she skimmed Jackson's jaw with a kiss and went downstairs. She made more of an effort the rest of that day and the next, but it was the look in her eyes that scared him the most. The light had gone out.

Frustrated by her refusal to get help or talk to him, he called Doc Smith. If he couldn't bring Beth to the doctor, Jackson would bring the physician to her. He sent the boys off with Uncle Wy and Uncle Em. Taking up his post at the pasture fence, he stared out at his horses and tried to find the peace that they usually gave him. Worry for his wife kept getting in the way.

A half hour later, the doctor walked out and draped his arms on the post. "It's not serious, Jackson, but it's a problem, nonetheless. Elizabeth has a serious case of depression. Some of it could be lingering effects from that time she hit her head. Has she been sleepwalking lately?"

A shudder went through Jackson as he gripped the fence, thinking of the worst of it, that night she made it all the way to the road. "Not like before, nothing bad. I've found her in the nursery, standing over the crib, acting as if there's a baby there. She insisted we set up that room, so sure we'd have one soon." He ran a hand through his hair, picturing Beth's face, filled with longing and wonder as she stared at the landscape of her dreams.

Doc Smith rested a hand on his shoulder. "What about the migraines? She said no, but that one is stubborn and might not be completely honest with me."

Jackson slid the doctor a grin. "I know what you mean. No, she hasn't had any migraines, not in a long time. Headaches from time to time, like anyone else, but she doesn't complain."

The older man shook his head. "Sounds familiar. How about you? Been using your cane?"

Jackson shrugged. "It's there when I need it. I haven't. I've learned to pace myself, take breathers. I get my brothers to lend a hand if my back is troubling me. This isn't about me, Doc. My wife wants a baby in the worst way and is worried about running out of time. I keep wondering. Could there be something wrong with her, or with me? The last two were so easy."

Doc Smith smiled and wiped off his glasses with his hanky. "Silly woman. Such a young thing. She's just worrying too much. Here's my prescription. You two get some alone time, you hear me? Take the pressure off and enjoy each other. Making babies isn't something you control. It will come in God's sweet time. This visit is free of charge. Just ask that peach of a girl to send me over one of her raspberry pies next time she makes one, all right?" With a pat on the back, Doc Smith walked away, his car leaving behind a cloud of dust along the way.

The first thing Jackson did was to call his parents, asking them to keep the boys until that evening. He proceeded to go upstairs, lift his wife from their bed, and carry her to the tub. He ran the water nice and warm with plenty of bubbles and knelt down by her side.

She didn't talk, simply watched him as he washed her body and her hair.

When he was done, he kissed her hand, her arm, and traveled all the way to her cheek, earning a flicker of a smile in return. He raised her out of the water, dried her off, finally wrapping her up in a new robe and slippers that he picked up a few days before. Jackson brushed her hair and braided it like his horses' tails. A trip back to the bedroom was as far as he could make it before he kissed her one more time, settling in, giving her all he had—and she was a torch in his hands. "Sit tight." He told her, heart pounding in anticipation.

He returned with a dinner tray and a dozen roses. She giggled. "Soup, grilled cheese, *and* roses?"

"Comfort food. It works on hearts too." She gave him a little smile, but the tears were hovering as she picked at her food. He caught her hand and held it in both of his. "You have to eat, Beth. Can't have a baby if you aren't strong and healthy."

She nodded and ate everything. Jackson moved the tray aside when she was done and stroked her cheek with his thumb. "I want you to stop fretting about this. Have faith. It will happen when it's meant to. Until it does, I'd really enjoy trying again." She fell into his arms with a soft sob. Very tenderly, he made love to his bride, and she opened to him like a blossom opening its petals to the sun.

⌒⌒⌒

"Do you think the boys are all right? What if they're too much for Pop?" Beth's gaze was trained out the window. She was fighting tears and didn't want Jackson to see. He could hear it in her voice. He knew she'd been chewing on something, not talking to him until they nearly crossed the Canadian border.

Pulling her across the seat, he tucked her under his arm. "Pop is fine now, really. He just has to watch himself, not go hog wild or anything. Between Mama and the twins, our sons are covered." Seeing the gleam in her eye and the beginning of a grin, he nodded. "Yes, even Em, wildcat that he is." He brushed the top of her head with his lips. "Will you please relax and enjoy this? Remember why we're doing this."

He felt her body go loose beside him and her palm pressed his thigh. "You're right. I'm sorry. You must think I'm so ungrateful." She fell silent for a few minutes until they crossed the bridge and saw one of nature's most incredible marvels in all its glory. A spray was tossed into the air as massive amounts of water tumbled far below over Niagara Falls. He nearly ran off to the side, the breath sucked out of him. He'd never seen it before. "Oh my. Jackson, this is my first time ever. Isn't it simply amazing?"

Slowing for the customs booth ahead, he let the truck idle and caught her chin in his hand. "Yes, *you* are. How many times do I have to tell you that?" His grin was playful, his heart light, as he leaned in close and took her sweet lips in a kiss. They didn't stop until someone behind them honked the horn.

Three days were over in a blink with no time to catch their breath, think about anything, or miss anyone. They rode a boat that brought them close to the base of the falls, walked the cliff walk by the water, and headed into a little cave. Jackson took Beth to fancy restaurants each day, bought her trinkets at the shops, and helped her to pick out things for everyone back home.

They made good use of their room as well, calling in room service on two mornings for breakfast, allowing them to laze about and sleep in. The hot tub saw plenty of use, as did their balcony overlooking the falls, a true favorite in the evening when the lights splashed the water with colors. Jackson held his wife in his arms and they danced, getting drunk on each other, finding their way to bed late at night. With no distractions and no obligations, they devoted all of their attention to each other.

෴

He came awake instantly, shivering, feeling like someone dumped a bucket of ice water on his head. *No, no. Not again. Sweet Lord, please not again.* His heart was thudding so hard, it made the blood thunder in his ears and Jackson was gasping like he'd run a marathon. A glance at the door and he wilted in relief. Still chained and bolted from the inside. The bathroom was empty as well. But the balcony—

"Oh, dear God!"

He lunged out of bed, oblivious to the poker jabbing him in the back, and made it through the open sliding glass door in a heartbeat.

Beth was at the railing, climbing up, reaching out toward the raging water below. Even as he reached for her, he cursed himself. *How could you choose a waterfront hotel?*

"My baby girl! I've lost my baby girl!"

She let out a pitiful wail, stretching even farther, her foot slipping as the wind swept a blue scarf he'd bought her from her hand. It floated out and away and she shot forward, still screaming for her baby.

Jackson grabbed her just in time and wrapped her in his arms. On legs that shook so hard he could barely walk, he made it to the side of the building and slid down, holding on tight to her. He began to rock, telling her to hush, trying to calm her—and thought his heart would explode.

She didn't wake this time, simply slid off into a deep sleep. He carried her inside and locked the glass door. He pulled the covers up around them in bed and held on tight, waiting for the tripping of his heart to slow down. It hurt to think there was such a pit of despair inside of his wife. He prayed his love would be enough to fill it and perhaps by the Grace of God, he could give her a child. He did not go back to sleep that night, keeping watch until morning when she awoke and gave him her sweet smile. He almost broke down right then.

Their second night put them both through their paces. Jackson didn't tell Beth, *couldn't* tell her about how close he came to losing her, only that she'd had a nightmare. She didn't remember it, but they made love with an even greater sense of desperation as if both were aware of how fragile life was. Both were a little sore, a bit bruised, and a tad tender. He climbed back into bed after getting a drink of cold water, his throat parched. Sliding closer to her, his body was pleasantly loose and heavy. He rested his head on his pillow and took great pleasure in his favorite pastime—studying his wife. Her hair was fanned out on her pillow, gleaming as bright as sunlight, a full bloom in her cheeks. A smile tugged at the corner of her lips and he couldn't help but chuckle. "You are too beautiful. How do you feel?"

Her blue eye opened, dazzling in its intensity, and her hand reached out to rest on his cheek. "Like I've been turned to butter." She dropped her hand to her belly and grinned. "I *know* we made a baby last night."

Jackson leaned in and his lips grazed a trail from her shoulder to her neck to her jawbone and mouth. "Which time?"

"I lost track. Maybe the fourth or the fifth?" Her eyes closed and she practically purred, stretching and running a hand along his side. His blood began to hum and his heart kicked into overdrive.

"Maybe we should give it one more go, just to make sure." Her hands threaded into his hair and her sweet lips were on his. That was answer enough.

His note was long in coming, arriving a week later. She tacked it on the barn door, one of her favorite spots for sentimental reasons from the time when their love was born. Leaning against a stall with Ricky Ricardo nuzzling at his neck, searching for a juicy apple, Jackson's smile grew. Their love still felt shiny and new, putting a spring in his step and song in his heart every day.

Dear Jackson,

I had to wait until I had something concrete. I saw Doc Smith yesterday afternoon when I finished up shopping, just dropped in out of the blue and he cleared his calendar for me. We did it. I'm pregnant again. I think it will be a girl this time. Thank you for Niagara Falls, for your strong arms, your beautiful smile, and big heart. You remind me time and again—my cup runneth over. I hope yours does too. I love you.

Love,

Your Beth

He had to see her, to tell her that instant. He ran to the house, even forgot to pull off his boots in his haste, trucking mud across her clean, kitchen floor. She was washing up the breakfast dishes, her arms plunged deep in the suds. From upstairs, the sounds of the boys playing in the tub traveled far, what with the splashing, squealing, and horsing around going on.

Two giant steps across the room and he swept her into his arms, spinning her around like those old-time romance movies before setting her down. His hands threaded through her hair, effectively pinning her in place. "My cup? It's full, a hundred times over. No, make that a thousand. You think it's a girl?" He freed one hand and splayed his fingers across her belly. Closing his eyes, Jackson pictured the wee pixie blossoming inside of his wife.

Beth rained kisses all over his face, her laughter bubbling up. "Yes, I'm certain of it. Come next March, she'll be here. Another addition to the Henry family. I couldn't ask for more." He looked into her gaze and found himself transfixed. The thought crossed his mind of carrying her off to bed that instant to give the mother of his children her due. Another kiss would have to suffice, but left him wanting more.

"God, I love you, Beth. I never thought I could be so happy it hurts, right here." He thumped a fist on his chest, over his heart, then gently placed his palm over hers, thrilling to the steady beating beneath his touch. His voice dropped down to a whisper. "I hope she looks just like you, with the sky in her eyes, sun in her hair, and enough joy in her heart to light up the world."

Beth smiled at him, the tears trickling out of the corner of her eyes. "I wouldn't mind ten more that were the spitting image of you."

She pressed herself against him, wrapping her arms around his neck as he bowed her down as low as she could go. The sink began to overflow, water gushing on to the floor. Neither of them remembered to care.

CHAPTER 31

July 4, 1963:

Jackson's mind was clouded by his family as he took care of the horses about an hour earlier than normal, eager to spend as much time with his wife and boys as possible. There were never enough minutes in the day and they seemed to slip through his fingers like sand. He'd made a resolution to himself not to waste any opportunities. Might as well start today.

The first round of work done in record time, he hit the door to be met with the mouthwatering scents of his wife's cooking and the woeful stare of his youngest son, perched on the wooden, milk stool that had been renamed the quiet seat. Jackson poked his head in the kitchen to find Beth manning the stove while Wyatt stood with his head down, studying his feet. "What's he done now?" Jackson jabbed a thumb in the direction of the living room.

His wife gave him a smile on the tail end of a sigh. She generally doled out the discipline, being on the front lines, but he always offered his support, intervening and laying down the law when his boys wouldn't toe the line. This did not appear to be one of those occasions, but he knew the job could wear on their mother and her soft

A MAN OF FEW WORDS   371

heart. She was fair and could be firm, but didn't always like it.

"Em decided to try and be Superman. He had a towel around his shoulders and was about to jump out the attic window. If Wyatt didn't come and get me, we'd probably be calling the ambulance or crying our eyes out right now." Shaking her head, she reached out and gave Jackson's arm a squeeze. "He's done his time. You can tell him to get up now. I swear, that boy is going to be the death of me," she murmured under her breath.

He snagged Beth around the waist for a pick-me-up kiss and headed into the next room. Wyatt had moved to the couch, scuffing his feet on the floor, wearing a hangdog look. The boy hated it when his brother was in trouble and didn't like to rat him out. The two were inseparable. An impulsive soul, Em was his sidekick in every escapade, usually running pell-mell, head on into scrapes with his big brother generally saving the day.

The guilty party sat with his jaw poking out, bulldog stubborn, his arms crossed across his chest. The devil was at war with the angel in his glare. While the angel always won out in the end, his youngest had a hard time fighting temptation. Jackson knelt down in front of him and laid a hand on his son's knee. "Emmett, do you know why you're here?"

Em looked up and glared at his brother. "Because Wyatt told on me. Tattletale!" He scrunched his nose up and stuck his tongue out before gluing his eyes to the floor.

Jackson pressed a finger beneath his boy's chin and made him meet his gaze. "It's not tattling when it's something really bad or you could get hurt. Trying to jump out of a window is both. Your brother did right."

He looked over his shoulder to give his oldest a wink, staring into somber, slate blue eyes with a jolt. Wyatt was so similar to his father, taking the role of being the eldest to heart, being serious enough to make up for his little brother's lack of good judgment. How many times had Jackson done the same with the twins? "Remember what I told you after we watched the Superman show. Heroes aren't real."

"But *you are*, Daddy," Emmett piped up and climbed onto his father's lap, wrapping his arms around Jackson's neck. The angel was shining in his eyes, golden as honey gleaming in a jar, so bright they were nearly blinding.

Jackson hugged him hard enough to squeeze the stuffing out of him and gave Emmett a reassuring smile. "I'm glad you think of me that way, but I don't have any super powers. Remember when I stumbled over that hole in the field last week?" He pushed his sleeve aside, revealing a nasty bruise that covered his entire shoulder. "It still hurts like the dickens. I couldn't fly that day to save my life and neither can you." His boy didn't need to know how much his back hurt—all the time, day in and day out.

Tousling Emmett's unruly mob of dark hair, Jackson turned and opened his arm for Wyatt. "Come here, bud." His oldest obeyed, allowing his father to hook him around the waist and draw him in close. "I'm proud of you. When you were younger, you told on Em every chance you could get. Now you've learned the difference between tattling and averting disaster. You did a good thing." He kissed Wyatt on the cheek and turned his attention back to his youngest. "I want you to apologize to your brother. If anything happened to you, he'd be lost. Look how bad he feels."

Wyatt's eyes had darkened to a stormy gray, wet with tears that he was determined to hold back. He might be soft at heart, but his oldest boy was tough as nails. Emmett took one good look and his lip started to tremble. "I'm so sorry, Wy."

He reached out and hugged his brother, stealing his

breath away, but Wyatt's grin from ear to ear showed forgiveness had been granted.

Jackson kissed both of his sons on the back of the head and gave them a gentle push. "All right then. Go sit down and get ready for Mama's breakfast. She's been working hard for you." A race ensued, two boys scampering across the house in their bare feet and pajamas. They climbed up on their chairs and propped their chins on their hands, watching their mother do her kitchen dance.

Jackson gave them a wink and tiptoed in behind Beth as she moved swiftly between the pans on the stove, turning bacon, smiling at sunny side up eggs, and popping toast on plates. She was humming something chipper and tossed a wink at her boys. The bow on the back of her apron was tempting, making his fingers itch to untie it and sweep his wife into his arms as a prelude to a trip to the bedroom. He'd have to satisfy himself by snaking his arm around her to snatch a piece of bacon. *Whack!* She snapped the spatula across his backside, setting off peals of laughter as two little boys headed toward hysterics.

"Jackson, you cut that out, you hear? I need something to put on the table! Don't you see those starving children over there? They're beginning to wither!" She was effectively silenced when he put one hand on her shoulder, the other on her waist, and bent her backward until her ponytail skimmed the floor. He shook his hair out of his eyes and pressed his lips to hers, breakfast crackling on the stove all the while.

She slapped at him half-heartedly, giving in and threading her fingers in his hair. *"Jackson!* The boys are watching!" Her voice was weak and she was out of breath, as if she'd been running uphill for a long time. Fighting her husband was a losing battle as he rained kisses all over her face.

"Now Elizabeth, we live on a horse farm. They're

bound to learn about the birds and bees sooner or later."
His laughter rolled out and carried her with him until they
were a wheezing tangle of limbs on the floor, quickly
joined by two, impulsive imps, and the bacon started to
burn.

Somehow, they managed to collect themselves and
share a large meal, Emmett chattering like a jaybird, Wyatt quietly basking in the warm, golden glow of his brother's eyes. He was crazy about Em. Jackson caught Beth
from time to time, watching them all with such affection,
her arm resting protectively on her stomach. The woman
was born to be a mother. Her eyes turned his way, their
soft gleaming drawing him in and he couldn't stop grinning. *Correction. She was born to be a mother and my
wife.*

The family worked together as a team, putting the
kitchen to rights. Mission accomplished, Jackson propped
his shoulder on the door jamb and crossed his arms. "All
right, everyone. I've got work to do. I need two farm
hands. Any takers?"

Wyatt and Emmett whooped with excitement and ran
upstairs, returning in seconds, dressed in boots, T-shirts,
and jeans, miniatures of their father. Jackson put Wyatt
up on his shoulders and swept Emmett up onto his left
arm. Leaning in to give Beth a kiss, he whispered. "I'm
looking forward to having another one on my right arm."

Striding out into the sunshine of early July, the warm,
moist air pressed in on them, heavy like a wet towel.
Jackson shrugged it off, followed by two tagalongs. He
took care of a few duties in the barn and grabbed a saddle
and bridle, gesturing to his boys to keep up.

Unlatching the gate, they stepped out into the pasture.
In only a matter of minutes, a large, chocolate stallion
approached from the middle of the field.

At four years old, he was practically a baby, but remarkably calm and completely devoted to Wyatt.

"Hi, Curious George," his boy called out, pulling an apple out of his pocket and letting the horse munch on it in one big bite.

Jackson had given the colt to his oldest as a present when he was two. They'd been inseparable ever since. Both boys fawned over the gentle giant while their father heaved the saddle in place, tightened the girth, and put the bridle in the horse's mouth. Eager to ride, the brothers were itching to get started, but waited patiently even if it was killing them.

Jackson picked up Wyatt first and set him in the saddle, putting Emmett in place next. He pressed a hand on his youngest's shoulder. "You mind your brother." Lifting his chin at his oldest, he smiled up at him. "Go easy, Wyatt. No showboating."

"But, Daddy, I can do it," Em protested, cranking up for a good whine. Wyatt reached around him and took up the reins while Jackson gave the impatient boy a hard stare, cutting off any more complaints.

"I know you can. When you are six like Wyatt, you'll get to be in charge. You need to be patient. If you're not ready, you could hurt George, Wyatt, or yourself and someone watching us would really kick my butt." He reached up and patted Emmett's cheek. "One other thing. I'd feel really bad. Don't disappoint me, son."

Glancing up one more time, filled with pride at the sight of his oldest sitting straight and tall in the saddle, completely at ease, Jackson gave him a wink and spoke hoarsely, "Steady as he goes, Wyatt."

He let them go, watching them like a hawk, staying close in case they needed him. There was no need to look to know Beth was there. He could feel her pull. Eventually, the boys began to walk along the fence line and Jackson turned around to see his wife in a shaft of sunlight, the glory of her hair a golden cloud shimmering around her and falling to her waist. It swayed when she walked, making him stop and stare. Caught in her deep, blue eyes, George's nicker was the only thing that could shake him from her spell, her soft laughter following him as he ran to catch up with the boys as they headed to the barn.

By the time they dismounted, took care of the saddle, and rubbed the horse down, Beth stood in the barn door-way, pretty as a picture. She wore a sundress in a pale pink that accentuated her coloring, bringing out the roses in her cheeks and shine in her eyes. She carried a picnic basket in one hand, a lawn chair in the other.

"Let's go, boys. The Bradleys are waiting for us, along with everyone else in town!" They piled into the pick-up truck, the whole family squeezing in on the front, bench seat. Beth started singing nursery rhymes and their sons chimed in, only too happy to join their mother in any en-deavor. A short drive later, they found themselves in the middle of all the festivities, neighbors oohing and aahing over the Henry boys. Uncle Wyatt and Uncle Emmett made sure to have some fun as well, even though they were older and wiser than they used to be. They hadn't completely given up their wild side.

The Fourth of July festivities were a smashing suc-cess, as always. A day of laughter, catching up with friends and family, stuffing themselves with good food, ending with fireworks as Jackson, Beth, and the boys shared a blanket with his parents and brothers. Watching the colors splashing over those he loved, the starbursts in their eyes, and the smiles on their faces, Jackson knew he was blessed beyond measure.

The clock ticked to ten o'clock as they rolled into their driveway, both boys and their mother yawning as they climbed out, but their tiredness was forgotten when they laid eyes on the tent in the front yard. "Daddy, Daddy, you 'membered!" Wyatt chirped and dashed across the lawn, Emmett close on his heels.

Beth wrapped an arm around Jackson's waist as they followed at a more sedate pace. "Jackson Landon Henry, you are something else. How did you manage this?" She waved a hand, encompassing the tent, a small ring of stones with wood laid out for a campfire, and a cooler.

He shrugged. "I have my ways. I promised Wy that he could camp out and wake up as a six-year-old big boy. Figured that was a simple enough request." She shook her head and kissed his cheek, leaning in close, the scent of summer, barbecue, and her shampoo drifting up and making him weak in the knees.

He had to get another dose of her. Cupping the back of her head, he pressed his lips to hers and didn't stop until two giggling boys cleared their throats and waited expectantly with a jar in hand. Their parents couldn't help laughing along with them, but before Jackson joined them in the pursuit of fireflies, he stole one more kiss and whispered, "Elizabeth Mason Henry, it's *you* who's something else."

An hour later, a fire was crackling in the pit, casting sparks up into the darkness to join the stars in the sky. Wyatt and Emmett, snug in a sleeping bag together, were sound asleep, marshmallow coating their faces. Jackson was stretched on another sleeping bag, biting off a groan, Beth tucked under his arm, staring at the flames through the open tent flap. He knew it would have to be put out, but was reluctant to move, especially since his back was talking to him. "You are going to be so tired tomorrow," she murmured softly, playing with his hair, firelight and shadows dancing across her face.

He shrugged. "I'd rather be tired now then look back when I'm old and kick myself for missing this." She turned over and he rested his hand on her hip, fingers splayed to touch the slight swelling of her stomach. "How about you? You've got to get enough rest for two. You're building a person in there."

"I feel the same way as you—can't bear to miss a second with all of you. You know what they say—I'll sleep when I'm dead."

Her words sent a shiver down his spine. *Someone's walking on* her *grave.* The old wives' tale frightened him and he pulled her close, pushing superstition away. Such a thing did not even bear thinking about. His wife responded, threading her fingers through his hair and giving him that sweet smile that always made his heart beat faster.

He kissed her, the hunger for her stirring deep within. Jackson buried his face in the crook of her neck, breathing in the blend of smoke and the scent that was undeniably hers. "You are definitely *not* dead, Mrs. Henry. The boys are sound asleep. Can you stay awake a little longer?"

Her soft laughter and willing arms were answer enough.

The birds' chirping, quite a ruckus after a scant five hours of sleep or so, woke him as the tent began to glow in the early light of dawn. There was a rock digging into Jackson's back and, good Lord, he was stiff. He might not be old, but his body didn't take as kindly to the ground at twenty-seven like it did as a boy.

Shifting slightly, he glanced down and had to smile. Two ruffled, tufts of hair poked up in the middle of the sleeping bag, only noses poking out, his boys curled up like wooly bears. Wyatt and Emmett had joined their parents in the middle of the night, frightened by the cry of a hoot owl.

Beth lay beside them, hair mussed, cheeks flushed, her arm stretched across her sons and resting on their father's hip. She grinned and cracked an eyelid. "Morning, sunshine."

His lips began to twitch and he leaned over to give her a kiss. "Good morning, beautiful." Her eyes drooped shut again and he lay still, simply watching the glory that was his Beth. When her breathing fell into a normal rhythm and her body went loose, he slipped out of the covers and inched his way up to his feet. Outside the tent, he took a deep breath and stretched out the worst of the kinks to build up a fire. Jackson had made a promise to cook bacon and eggs over an open fire for Wyatt's birthday. He kept his promises.

Soon enough, the flames were flickering, the bacon snapping and crackling in the pan. He stood tall and listened to his bones pop, scraping his hands across his face in an effort to wake up. Tired. He was so tired. Soft arms wrapped around his waist and a warm body pressed against him, bringing about a remarkable revival. Turning around, he caught his wife up in his arms and gave her a kiss to write home about. "Good morning again."

She hugged him hard and stood still a moment, her head leaning against his chest. "Good morning, I think, though I feel like I should sleep another day or so. How about I sneak inside for some coffee?"

He let out a groan and kissed her shining hair. "Woman, you are truly heaven-sent." She gave his hand a squeeze and ventured off to the house. A few minutes later, Wyatt and Emmett emerged, hair poking up like hedgehogs, their eyes squinting in the bright light of day. "Good morning, boys. Happy birthday, Wy!" He swept his boy up in the air and swung him around, fatigue forgotten as his oldest son's eyes opened wide and a grin stretched across his face.

"Me too, Daddy! Me too!" Em stood off to the side, eager to have a turn in one of their favorite games. Jackson obliged, taking the little tyke by the hands and whipping him out in a circle until his chortles rang out across the yard. Their mother joined them, carrying a tray with coffee, tea, and her standby, crackers to get past the nausea that greeted her each morning. Glancing at her face, Jackson could see that she'd gone pale and was a little shaky. He set Emmett down and pressed a hand to the nape of her neck. "You all right?"

She let out a deep breath and nodded, the sparkle in her blue eyes giving him peace of mind. "I'm fine. The little one just has to remind me she's there." Funny. The both of them were convinced this baby was a girl. Hopefully they were right or someone might be confused.

She dished out breakfast plates and they all sat cross-legged on the ground, the morning dew making their clothes damp, but no one cared. Beth nibbled at her crackers and managed a bit of her husband's cooking, while the boys cleaned their plates. Jackson cupped his coffee in two hands and closed his eyes, savoring the scent and taking his time drinking the sweet, dark brew.

A kiss on the cheek made his eyes snap open. His wife stood beside him, gesturing to his lap. No arguments there as he gathered her in his arms and settled her on his knees. They sat quietly, the heat of the sun warm on their backs, watching their boys' antics as they poked marshmallows on sticks and stuffed themselves some more. "I think that's enough, fellas, or you'll have a bellyache and won't be able to eat Nana's cake."

There were grumbles, but Wyatt and Emmett listened to their mother, tossing the sticks in the fire and watching them burn. Occupied only for a few minutes, their sons moved on, taking up their jars of fireflies and examining their prisoners. "Daddy, they're just sitting on the bottom and they won't light up."

Wy held the jar up to the sunlight, his forehead

creased in concentration. Emmett began to shake his own container, but stopped when he received a glare from his big brother. "You'll hurt them." Contrite, Em set the jar down and stared at the contents.

Jackson reached out to hold his son's shoulder. "Wyatt, sometimes when you really love something, you have to let it go. Fireflies aren't meant to be kept. They'll die in there and won't shine anymore. Set them free."

A set of serious, smoky blue eyes met his father's, joined by a gaze of golden amber, a full blown pout not far off for either one. It was clear that both boys wanted to keep their treasures, but they knew their ten commandments well, especially obey thy father and mother. Wyatt was first to open the lid and Emmett followed suit. They stood and watched the tiny creatures take flight, ending the peaceful moment when Em poked his brother, yelling, "You're it!" and scampered across the yard.

Beth leaned against Jackson, her body gone heavy as if asleep, but her eyes were open as she gave him a lazy smile. "What about me,? Are you ever going to let me go?" Her eyes were playful and she glanced at the empty tent, mischief in her gaze.

He stood up in one fluid movement, surprising both of them after a night spent on the ground, and carried her inside, closing the flap behind him. Laying her down on the sleeping bag, he wrapped his arms and his legs around her, holding her tight. "I will never let you go, Beth Henry. To the ends of the earth, until time stops, you are mine."

She smiled at him, the color rising up in her cheeks, and proceeded to kiss him thoroughly. There was no telling what else might have happened if two masculine voices didn't call across the yard. Uncle Wyatt and Uncle Emmett were there to lend a hand so that the entire Henry family could celebrate with the birthday boy. Jackson gave his wife one more kiss and pulled her to her feet. "We'll have to take a rain check."

She smiled at him and tossed him a wink. "You've got that right, getting me all hot and bothered. Rain or shine, we've got some catching up to do *tonight*." Any other words would have to wait when Emmett opened the flap and swept Beth into his arms, making her shriek and carrying her across the yard. Jackson could only laugh. *Brothers. God love them.*

The three Henry brothers made quick work of what had to be done with the horses while Beth showered, scrubbed the boys, and packed up their campsite. The uncles grabbed hold of their namesakes and put them up on their shoulders, carrying them as they walked the quarter mile path that ran between the two homes. Jackson and Beth followed, holding hands.

She made him feel like a teenager on a date, looking so pretty, his heart hurt. She wore clam diggers and a bright blue, button-down knotted at a waist that was still trim, her braided hair forming a golden rope that swung back and forth, tantalizing him to grab hold and reel her in. Thinking back to that distant afternoon when he walked her home from quilting, his eyes cast a glance at the sky above and he held out his empty palm. At her quizzical gaze, he shrugged. "Checking for clouds. I wouldn't mind getting caught in the rain with you again."

Planting her feet in front of him, she looped her arms behind his neck and rose up on tiptoe. "We don't need rain to get in some loving." His head bowed for easier access to a kiss that was so sweet and ripe, he needed to sample another—and another.

They eventually stopped, both flushed and breathing as if they'd run a marathon. She licked her lips and stepped back with an effort. "That's enough for now. Remember that catching up I promised? Now I'll owe you some more. You'd better take it easy today because I am going to wear you out tonight."

"Don't you worry about me, darling. You'd better save up some energy of your own." Taking her by surprise, he boosted her up on his back and began a slow jog to catch up with the others, her laughter bubbling up along the way.

∽∾∽∾

Mama and Pop were sitting on the patio out by the pool, lounging in chairs side by side, their hands linked. They looked relaxed and happy, making Jackson's eyes sting at the sight of them and the memory of the heart attack that almost stole his father away from them. They blew kisses and shouted birthday greetings to Wyatt. The boys waved and called back to their grandparents from their high vantage point. On top of their world.

Their uncles, by no means completely mature or having outgrown their mischievous stage, raced up the deck by the pool and launched their nephews into the water. Jackson set Beth down and threw his brothers in next, but he was unprepared for their lightning swift response. They grabbed his ankles until he tumbled in, with a helpful push from his wife. Traitor that she was, he climbed out, scooped her up kicking and screaming, and jumped in with her. They stayed in the pool until everyone looked like prunes and the boys' teeth started to chatter.

The rest of the day was a blur. Pop broke out the barbecue and outdid himself with heaps of hamburgers, dogs, sausages, and ribs. Mama topped off the meal with sweet corn, salads, and home-baked bread. A cooler chock full of sodas, all of Wyatt's favorites, gave the boys a chance to indulge in a sweet treat that was not the norm. They drank grape, orange, and lemon pop until they were nearly sick, stretching out in the grass and tracing cloud shapes in the sky with the help of their uncles, waiting for their small stomachs to settle for the grand finale.

The cake was a beauty, dressed with sparklers, trimmed in red, white, and blue. Wyatt puffed his cheeks up and blew so hard, the candles almost tumbled off the cake. Once everyone had their piece, frosting covering both boys in unbelievable places, Jackson swept his oldest boy up onto his shoulders and the group serenaded him with their old standard, "He's a Jolly Good Fellow."

A perfect day ended with a perfect night. Even though they were beat, Jackson and Beth carried their boys up to bed. Dropping kisses on their sweaty heads that smelled of sunshine, barbecue smoke, and chlorine, the two proud parents stood in the doorway, watching their sons' faces bathed in moonlight. A sigh escaped his wife and she leaned against him, drooping at the end of a long string of full hours.

As if by a will of their own, his hands trailed through his wife's hair, ending at her waist and turning her to him. A small sound, of pleasure or surrender, escaped her and she fell against him. "It's time to say goodnight, Jackson."

He got the message loud and clear with one look at the light in her eyes. Sweeping her up in his arms, he performed the duty of a husband, carrying his wife to bed, even as his back stabbed at him and snatched his breath away. They helped each other to undress, worshipping the gift of their bodies, taking their time, taking their fill. Before they could slip away, Beth took his liniment from the bedside table and gave him a massage he'd never forget.

If Jackson wasn't so tired, they would have spent the entire night making love. When they finally tumbled off into dreams, sleep took them down fast, and he knew no more.

∾∾∾

"We can cancel, really. I'll call Wy." Emmett stood by his wife's side, hand resting on her neck, kneading the muscles that had tightened into knots. Casey had a rough morning, starting out with a pounding headache and throwing up. She'd checked her blood pressure and almost got sick again. It was high—but that could be due to a bout of retching strong enough to take her breath away and set her heart to hammering.

Breathing out hard through her nose, she shook her head and offered him her hand. It filled her with gratitude when he didn't hesitate to lift her up, lending her his strength when she needed it most. "No, I'm all right. Everything is cooking and the table is set. I want to have a nice family dinner with your brother while I still can." She crossed her eyes and stuck her tongue out at her husband. "Now go out and find me a party tent that I can wear."

He laughed at that one and snatched a kiss. Taking her cue, he went off to forage in the closet while she fiddled with her hair, finally forming a braid down her back. Even that simple act had her breathing hard, the color rising up fast all the way to her roots. She gripped the dresser with one hand and pressed her hand to the base of her spine with the other. *Soon. Please let it be soon.*

"Let me do that." Strong hands had her around the waist, taking her and leading her to the bed. Emmett sat her down and started to massage her neck and shoulders, devoting extra attention to her poor, bowed back. "Better?" he asked softly.

She nodded and released the breath she'd been holding

the entire time. Mouth tipping up in a grin, she offered her hand again. "Help me get dressed?" Infinitely patient, he raised her to her feet, took off her nightgown, and slipped a long, loose dress in sky blue over her head. The fabric was cool against her skin and swished when she moved. A peek in the mirror proved she *almost* didn't look like a house. She caught her husband's eye and could only shake her head. "When? When did *you* have time to go shopping? It's perfect."

Emmett shrugged. "I have my ways. Now, are you sure you're okay? If so, I have a few things to do in the barn, then I need a shower, and I'll get dressed." She released him with a kiss.

Humming softly to herself, Casey finished their dinner preparations, a full turkey dinner. It was her traditional Christmas Eve dinner, but she didn't expect to be cooking then. Either little question mark would be here by then or she'd be so miserable no one would dare come near her.

Nearly everything was ready when her husband appeared, washed and dressed for company. She stopped her preparations and grabbed hold of the table. He looked so good she was dizzy. Alarmed, he sprang forward. "Case, what is it?"

She shook her head and took hold of his shoulders to steady herself. "It's just...you. You look incredible." Strange how jeans and a soft brown sweater, perfectly molded to that honed body, could make her heart flutter.

He grinned playfully and nuzzled her neck, burying his face in her hair. "I know what I'll wear when you're ready for some fun again."

She groaned at that one and gestured to her belly. "Lord knows when that will be. I think I might be the only woman to be pregnant for a year!"

He could only chuckle. A knock sounded at the door, making him light up. "That would be the rest of the Henrys." Dropping a kiss on her nose, he snitched munchies and made for the door. Soon, the house was filled with a lively commotion, what with a fully recovered toddler on the verge of turning two, an exuberant Wyatt, and bubbly Samantha. Casey was grateful to have a diversion. When she checked her blood pressure again, it had dropped considerably. *Thank God.*

❧❧

Emmett bowed his head and said grace. Everyone sat with their hands linked, a visible reminder of the ties that bound them together, the river of Henry blood running strong. They enjoyed the meal immensely, but it was the stories that were the best, of Wyatt and Emmett as boys, of Sammie and Wyatt when they met in elementary school, the many scrapes that had happened over the years.

Watching Sammie talk, and the way Wyatt was a bee to her honey, it gave Casey a start. The couple was so similar to Beth and Jackson. Find a picture of her brother and sister-in-law from high school and she'd bet they were almost the same as the young couple in that birthday photo that tumbled out with all of the bits and pieces from the past. It was a comfort. *True love never dies.*

Blinking hard to hold back the sting in her eyes, she felt a nudge under the table. She looked up and Emmett took her hand, leaning in close to graze her jaw with his mouth, finally taking her lips with his. His simple gesture was filled with a sweetness that made her heart thump faster. Yes, it was surely true. A Henry love was strong enough to overcome all obstacles.

After dinner, the men took to the living room, the roar of a game carrying into the kitchen, along with some horseplay with little Jack. Giggles bubbled up as Casey listened to the ruckus. "Em is going to be such a good father."

Sammie took the plate from her hand and stretched up high to put it away. "Absolutely. He's had good teachers." She smiled wide and kept on plugging away, accustomed to being on full throttle.

As for Casey, she felt like her clock was definitely winding down. If she didn't sit soon—"Oh." It was a small sound as the glass slipped from her hand. Sammie caught it and grabbed her sister-in-law's hand as the expectant mother held on to her belly.

"Are you having pains?" At Casey's nod, the smaller woman, tough and wiry, guided her to a chair. She knelt down beside her and took her hands. "Breathe. Yes, that's it. Breathe again. Try not to tense up. Don't fight them."

Casey somehow managed a grin. "And to think, you had to do most of this all by yourself." She closed her eyes and waited. Another ripple shot through her, like bands tightening around her belly and squeezing hard. Her hands gripped Sammie's until both of their knuckles went white.

"Do you want me to get Emmett?" Miraculously, her sister-in-law was the picture of calm. She spoke softly and soothingly with no signs of panic. If Casey could take her pick of a support system at this moment in her life, the right person was here now.

Her mouth went dry at the thought. After the mall incident, she wanted to be sure before all hell broke loose. "No...just...just let's wait a little bit." It seemed to be a wise decision as the pains fizzled out once again. Casey tipped her head back and growled in frustration. "I wish it would just be done and over with."

Sammie smiled and gave her hug. "Soon, chickadee, and then you'll wish you could just put it back." She returned to the dishes. "You stay put. I can finish."

A few minutes later and Casey had a decidedly uncomfortable feeling. She struggled to stand up, wrinkling her nose. Something was *slimy* in her nether region. *That can't be my water.* "Hey Sammie, will you help me up to the bathroom?" She felt a little woozy and didn't want to take a header down the stairs. With a sturdy arm around her waist, Casey made it without mishap.

Patting her sister-in-law's arm in reassurance that she was all right, Casey closed the door and sat down on the toilet, exhaling hard. Her eyes widened at that one. She hadn't been able to do that the day before. Running her hands over the contour of her belly, she realized the baby had dropped—considerably. Thinking about what that could mean, she glanced down at her underwear and made a face. There was a brownish-pink jelly type substance staining her underwear. *Ew!* Things were definitely happening.

"Casey? Case, let me in. Are you okay in there?" Emmett's voice was loud and clear on the other side. He must have given Sammie the inquisition. "Casey, say something or I'm coming in."

"Just a sec." She stripped off the underwear and threw it away, washing her trembling hands next. The face in the mirror stopped her. She held her palms to flushed cheeks and nodded to the woman with glittering eyes. *You know what's coming, don't you?*

Her husband was sitting on the floor, back against the wall, head in his hands when she opened the door. He looked up at her and let out a ragged breath. "I've got to tell you. You're driving me crazy."

"How do you think I feel?" She held out her hand. Instead of coming up, he settled her in his lap. He began to run his hands through her hair. She suspected that it soothed him as much as it calmed her.

"Nothing?" he asked with trepidation. Shifting her in

his lap, his hand drifted to press under her chin, forcing her to look him in the eye. "Don't lie to me."

She shrugged and patted her belly. "Not yet, although Question Mark has dropped and I lost my mucous plug."

Thanks to the many foals that he'd delivered in a lifetime, Emmett knew what that meant. "All right then. Not much longer." He bowed his head and pressed it against her shoulder. "Please don't let it be much longer. I can't take it."

They sat there for a while, breathing each other's air, soaking up the warmth of their bodies, He continued to stroke her hair while she focused on little it. *Ollie, Ollie, Oxen Free. Ready or not, here you come.* She snorted at that one and caught Em staring at her. "What is your family doing down there? We're being quite rude."

"They sent their thanks and cleared out. Jack was getting tired and they thought we could use some alone time. Wyatt said just call if things start moving." He sized up her stomach with a critical eye. Apparently, nothing was happening yet.

She nodded. "Okay. I'm too tired to be upset that they didn't stay for dessert. Could you help me to bed, Em? I just want to crash."

A deep breath came out in a rush and he pressed back against the wall, coming up to his feet with a grunt, his wife still in his arms. Impressive. Emmett didn't even stagger, his steps sure, as he carried her in and set her on the bed. They both changed into pajamas and he settled in next to her. Eying her as she stared up at the ceiling, wide eyed, hands moving round and round on her belly, he blurted out, "Mind too busy?"

"Yes. Yours, too? How about we finish the journal. We're almost at the end." That gave her a little pang. Casey would be sorry when it was over. She could see the aching in Emmett's eyes as well, but he didn't argue.

Once you started something, you had to finish it. That was part of the Henry code.

CHAPTER 32

July 5, 1964:

Jackson woke with a start, sunlight streaming through the window, making him squint in the brightness. He was accustomed to rising before the dawn, when his room was still cast in darkness or a dim light.

Rolling over, he gazed on his wife and grinned from ear to ear. Beth had overslept, a rare occasion indeed. Who could blame her after the busy schedule they'd kept on Independence Day? Usually, she ran their household like clockwork and never missed a beat. She looked so content, he didn't want to pull her away from her sleep. Instead, he took pleasure in something that seldom happened—the opportunity to simply watch his wife.

Her mouth curved in a small smile, as if she kept a secret. Her hair, full and glorious, fanned out on her pillow, tempting him to play with it and pull her close. Finally, unable to resist, he skimmed her cheek with his lips, just a feather of a touch, pulling back with a jerk as if bitten by a snake.

Cold. She was cold, like ice. His heart started to thump painfully in his chest.

"Beth? Beth!" he shouted hoarsely in her ear, feeling like a great weight had settled on him, smothering him.

He grabbed hold of her shoulders and shook her, but could not wake her.

Stumbling away from the bed, trembling fingers dialed the operator and the receiver dropped from his hand twice. All the while, he stared at his wife, frozen in shock. "Yes. Please. Could you please. Help. Please help me. This is Jackson Henry...Yes, yes, Louisa, yes, it's me...Please send an ambulance right away and call Doc Smith for me. It's Beth. Something's wrong with Beth."

The phone slipped from fingers gone numb. He turned to his wife, his life, and took her face in his hands, willing her to open her eyes. To pin him with that patch of sky once more. To hear her laugh, asking him what all the fuss was about. To find out he was dreaming. Nothing. Shaking fit to fall to pieces, he kissed her once more and walked away on legs that wobbled.

The boys were sleeping. He scooped them both up, wrapped a blanket around them, and wove his way to the truck like a drunken man. Wyatt stirred, but Emmett slept like a rock.

"Daddy? Where we going?" his oldest asked fuzzily, sleepy seeds gumming his eyes, only a glimpse of slate blue peeking out.

Jackson rested his hand on the shining cap of his son's hair and brushed his cheek with a tender kiss, soaking in the warmth of his skin. Both boys were flushed from sleep, bundled in their one-piece pajamas that had been left at his parents, perfect for warding off the chill of evening. "Going to Grandmama's and Grandpop's, baby. She's cooking a big breakfast, said she was missing you boys."

Wyatt accepted his answer and slipped back into sleep.

Not even five minutes passed and they rolled to a stop by his parents' place. His father poked his head out of the barn, taken by surprise by such an early visit, seven a.m.

being an unusual hour for socializing. Jackson's parents
didn't get much company in the wee hours of the morning around these parts, what with all their neighbors running some sort of farm. Pop must have seen something in
his son's face because Landon started a slow, easy jog,
picking up the pace the closer he came. The doctors may
have told him to go easy on his heart, but the look in his
oldest boy's eyes must have made his blood run cold.

"Son? What is it, boy?" Boy. The term was fitting
what with the stark terror that must have marked Jackson's face. His father reached out and hooked him at the
nape of his neck, pressing down hard and giving him a
little shake. "*Jackson?*"

Jackson's throat closed up, a lump rising from the pit
of his stomach, the pain in his heart such, a heart attack
couldn't hurt as much. He shook his head, eyes burning,
and nodded to the door. His father opened it and allowed
him to pass. A few steps carried him to the living room
and his boys were snug on the couch. He grabbed another
blanket off of the back, tucking it around them gently. He
prayed they'd sleep a little longer. Let them go on believ-
ing all was right in the world, just a little longer.

His mother met him in the kitchen, smelling of coffee
and bacon, pancakes, the big breakfast Beth loved to
cook for him and her boys. Ella stepped in front of him,
raised his chin, and took his face in her hands. "Jackson,
you're scaring us. What is it, honey?"

"Can you keep the boys a while, Mama?" Cold. He
felt so cold, as if he was freezing from the inside out.
"Something's wrong with Beth. I—I couldn't wake her
up this morning."

The incomprehension, the fear, rose up in his mother's
eyes and she wrapped him in her arms, her heart fluttering madly against his chest. If only he was a boy again,
when Mama's hugs and kisses could fix everything. His

father clamped an arm around his shoulders and Jackson could feel Landon trembling.

He didn't know how the truck found the way back home or how his feet carried him inside, his heart thumping sluggishly in his chest. Jackson walked into their bedroom and began to shake. A wave of nausea rolled over him at the sight of his wife's cold, lifeless body. On the verge of being sick, he ducked inside the bathroom, frozen by the image on the mirror. In bright, red lipstick, his Beth had managed one last message inside a heart:

Beth loves Jackson
Forever and Ever, Amen
Thank you for a perfect July Fourth

He could picture her standing at the sink in the middle of the night, smiling, sleep in her eyes, tilting her head to the side as she yawned. Always thinking of him and their boys, even at the last. His fist slammed against the glass, making it splinter. Letting out the howl of an animal in agony, he fell to the floor, clutching his hand, heedless of the blood dripping down. The hurt was nothing to his heart being torn in two. He began to rock back and forth, a river of tears joining the pool of red on the floor. That was where the paramedics found him when they came to take his Beth away.

CHAPTER 33

Jackson didn't even remember getting in the truck or driving to his parents. He shouldn't have been behind the wheel in the state he was in. Complete and utter shock and bereavement.

His brothers met him on the porch, caught him when his legs gave out, allowed him to smother a great sob against their broad chests. "Jackson? What did they say?"

He didn't call when the doctor broke the news, couldn't find the words without falling apart and wailing inconsolably, so he held everything in, bearing the burden alone, crushing him with the weight of a boulder. Hooking an arm around their necks, he pulled Wyatt and Emmett close.

"She's gone. Beth is gone." His voice cracked and the tears couldn't be dammed any longer. His brothers, God love them, joined in with him. They did not sob or carry on, unwilling to scare his boys, but their hearts were broken all the same. Letting them bear him up for a few precious moments, Jackson straightened and prepared to shoulder the load once more. "Where are Wy and Em?"

"The pool. Mama's watching them. Pop's in the barn."

He nodded, scraped a hand across his eyes, and took his time crossing the yard. He went to Landon first, because a father could make everything right or pick up the pieces and hold him together. He was standing at the open door and Jackson was right. Landon caught him when he fell.

"Pop, remember when you said people should send all of their lost and hopeless causes to me? What do I do now that I'm one of them?"

The sobs came then, those of the broken hearted, shaking both men to the core. His father held on tight, his tears mingling with his son's, and he did not let go.

❧❧❧

Jackson sat in the living room, hands threaded in his hair, ready to pull it out of his scalp. Maybe that would drown out the pain. Being torn limb from limb couldn't hurt this much.

The boys were still blissfully unaware. The twins were keeping their nephews occupied in the pasture while Jackson attempted to pull himself together, an impossible task. His mother sat down on one side, his father on the other. "Explain it again, son. I don't understand how that sweet girl could be gone." Landon's voice broke, but small mercy, he gripped his son's thigh. Steady as a rock.

Jackson's voice was flat and lifeless as he repeated the words that had run through his mind like a record all the way home. "The doc says she had an aneurysm. I'm still trying to wrap my head around that one. He said it was like having a ticking time bomb in her brain, a weak spot that suddenly exploded without any warning. He said it was a blessing that she wasn't in pain, that most go through terrible suffering. If they live, a coma is likely or they're damaged forever."

His body was shaking, so hard he didn't think it would ever stop. He shot up from the couch and began to pace, a hand raking through his hair. "A blessing. A *blessing*? She was twenty-five! We were supposed to have a houseful of babies, share a patch of porch in rocking chairs years down the line. The only thing that gives me a little peace—knowing she went quiet. At home, in our bed, next to me, lying under the wedding ring quilt that she made with her own hands. With her babies down the hall, the other safe and warm inside of her. Dear God—I will never know the other. Was it our little girl? I do not think that it hurt. She wore a smile. Please God, don't let it have hurt her."

He went to the window and yanked it open, trying to get some air. Jackson felt like he was going to suffocate. His hands pressed against the frame hard enough the wood should have cracked, the only thing that was holding him up. "Lord help me. What if this is because of me, because of that day we argued and she fell? This could be *my fault!* I want to go with her."

His words, spoke in barely a whisper had an effect like lightning, bringing his parents up off the couch with a jolt. His mother reached him first, wrapping her arms around his waist, her cheek against his back. "Don't you *ever* talk that way again. Beth's fall was an accident and you can't blame yourself or think of hurting yourself! You have one thing—make that two—to make you hang on. You have your boys—and you have us. You will always have us."

His boys. Dear Lord, he had to tell his boys. Jackson's legs gave out, and he crumpled to the floor.

ↄ෨ej

"What's wrong, Daddy?" Emmett piped up first, sitting on the guest room bed, the one he and Wyatt shared whenever they slept over at their grandpop's and grandmama's house.

Jackson felt like he was moving under water as he

walked in and shut the door behind him. Darkness had fallen. The rest of the Henrys had muddled through the day while he took care of arrangements, then stumbled along the path between the two houses, putting off this inevitable moment. He'd hoped the earth would swallow him up along the way, but he was still here.

Wyatt, standing in the corner, his face serious, stared at his father with eyes that had gone a fearsome gray. He didn't move, only whispered. "Something's wrong with Mama." It wasn't a question. He was old enough to understand that the grown-ups were upset even though they kept their emotions bottled up tight. There'd also been no sign of Beth. Neither of his boys had gone a day of their lives without seeing their mother, except for the vacation to Niagara Falls. Jackson's heart gave a spasm at that one. *At least you gave her Niagara Falls.*

He knelt down on the floor. His legs wouldn't carry him farther and he didn't think his back could bear this burden, but he would have to try. "Boys, come here." His voice cracked. Emmett ran to him and flung his arms around his neck, rocking him on his heels. Wyatt hung back. "Wy. Come here. Now." That was enough to make his son move, but his oldest was reluctant. His first born didn't have it in him to throw a tantrum, but it was obvious. Everything in him was trying to avoid this moment.

Jackson sat down, cross legged, and settled them both on his lap, arms hooked around them. He pulled them in close, absorbing the heat of their sturdy bodies. Inside, he was a block of ice. "Wy—Em—I've got to tell you something bad. Something hard. I know it won't make sense to you. It doesn't make sense to me. Boys—Mama was sick and we didn't know it. The angels in heaven came to get her last night to make her better. I guess—" He choked down a sob, but the tears were coming on fast, raining down on their heads, mingling with theirs. "I guess God needed her to be another angel, to watch down on us from up there."

"But, Daddy, we need her down here!" Wyatt cried out at the top of his lungs. "I need her now. Daddy, go get her!"

Emmett simply started to bawl, so hard the whole town would be sure to hear him. Jackson wanted to join right in.

He held on even tighter to his boys. "I can't bring her back, Wy. I want to, but can't get to heaven. We can only go when God says so."

"No, Daddy! No! No! No! Bring Mama back! You bring our mama back!" Wyatt started to punch at the wall of his father's chest and his arms, small blows that shattered him nonetheless.

Jackson took it without a word and when his son finally collapsed, sobbing and exhausted, he tucked him in tight against his chest, Emmett too.

"I'll take care of you, boys. *I'll* be here. Uncle Wy, Uncle Em, Grandpop and Grandmama too. We're all here for you. I love you. Don't forget that." Jackson stood up slowly, so weak he didn't know if crossing the room was possible. How he wanted to take the words back, to keep the pain from their eyes, watching as their faces crumpled and they began to cry.

He laid down on his old bed from his growing up years, wanting nothing more than to go back to his childhood, heart too sore to go home.

Jackson stared at the ceiling, holding his boys close in a pile of blankets and tangle of limbs after Wyatt and Emmett cried themselves to sleep. As the big, fat tears rolled down his face and his throat closed, their father did the same.

❧❧❧

He hadn't eaten in three days. Couldn't then, couldn't now. Today, they would put her in the ground. His stomach was a churning mess that stabbed at him, made him bend over and spit bile into a handkerchief when no one was watching. Standing in the shower, the tears running down in a steady stream, Jackson couldn't stop crying and buried his face in a towel when he started to howl. So many things he couldn't do. He was a man who had been so capable, but losing Beth wrecked him.

"Jackson. It's time." Wyatt stood beside the tub, holding out a robe. He helped his big brother to shrug into it, reached in and turned off the tap, giving him a shoulder to lean on when he stumbled. Weak. Jackson felt as if all of the strength had gone out of him, trickling away like the water gushing down the drain.

His clothes were laid out on the counter. He stared at them dumbly, the will to move gone. His brother stepped up, gently drying him with a towel, handing him each piece of clothing one at a time, dragging a comb through his hair until he was presentable. Standing at the mirror, a stranger stared back, a man with no light in his gaze and dark shadows under his eyes, his cheeks sucked in with hollow spaces. Jackson's head bowed down and he gripped the sink as his body began to tremble. "I can't. I can't do this. Can't let her go."

Wyatt gripped his shoulder and gave it a hard squeeze. "She's already gone with the angels and you *can* do this. Remember what you said that day in the truck, when I hit Hamilton's car? You told me you'd be right there if I needed you. It's your turn now and I'm here for you."

"Me, too." Emmett's voice cracked, but held from his post, leaning against the door jamb. He stepped forward and took his big brother's arm. "We're with you every step of the way."

The twins flanked Jackson and held on tight. Together,

they made their way out to the funeral director's car waiting in the driveway.

The wake and funeral were a blank spot in his mind, his thoughts turning back to that party with the Bradleys on the Fourth of July six summers ago, to their wedding that September, to all of the precious moments in between. Strung together like beads on a necklace, but now the chain was broken.

Once the service was over, Wyatt and Emmett were back at his parents' house, his in-laws going with them as well, shell-shocked. Jackson and his sons hadn't gone back to their own home since Beth died. They'd have to do that soon, but right now, his boys looked the way he felt, like a Mack truck ran over them. The one thing he could give them was a little more time.

He had to be there for them, would be soon, but right now, Jackson waited for the grave diggers to fill the hole, shivering all the while even though he wore a suit on a day that broke ninety degrees. Somehow, it didn't seem right that the sun could be shining on such a horrible morning. The workers plied their shovels quickly, uncomfortable under the widower's intense stare. Arranging an ocean of bouquets last, they patted him on the back and quietly slipped away.

He waited until he was completely alone and lay down on the bed of flowers over his Beth's grave. He stretched out, breathing in deep, imagining the scent of the blossoms was hers and the petals were her cool touch after she stepped out of the bath and lit his blood on fire. Time passed and the sun dipped lower in the sky.

"Beth," he whispered brokenly, "I know that you're not here right now, but I hope you can see me and know what I say. This isn't goodbye. A love like ours can't end. I'll see you—in a while. I love you, baby, with all of my heart." The tears were raining down once more when he sat up and pulled a letter from his pocket. He'd found it in her dresser drawer while looking for clothes to lay her out. With trembling fingers, he unfolded the paper and the tears splashed the page.

July 5, 1964
To My Henry Boys,
I'm writing you this letter because when really important things have to be said, it's best to put it down in writing. Words can be like water, slipping between your fingers. Try to say them and they get away or time gets away and I forget to tell you what's on my mind. I want you to know right now—all of you are always on my mind.

When I put my thoughts on paper, I have time to mull them over, really get it right, make them permanent. Words in a letter—they're meant to last forever. You'll always have this present from me. When you're old and gray, you can pull this letter out and know how much I love you.

I want you boys, my sons and my man, to know how much you mean to me. You are my greatest gift, the best thing that could ever happen to me. My Wyatt and Emmett, it gives me great satisfaction to know I had a part in making you, in bringing your light into this world. As for my Jackson, I have loved you with all that I am, the greatest man I have ever known—and that's saying something. You know my favorite line from the Bible: my cup runneth over. Nothing could be more true. I have been so blessed in this short lifetime of mine, been given more blessings than most could have in a hundred lifetimes. I love you with all of my heart—always have, always will, time without end.

Love,
Your Beth, your mama

തെൻ

Rising to his feet, letting out a scream that tore at his throat, Jackson was tempted to rip the letter into shreds. His hands were poised to do it, but he couldn't, had to save her legacy for his boys. Someday, he'd read it to them, someday when he was alive again. He thrust it in his pocket and began to run. He couldn't outrun the present, his reality or the past.

He had a stitch in his side and was gasping for air when he finally came to a stop by the swimming hole. Bending over, he gripped his knees and a hot, bitter stream of bile shot out, followed by the dry heaves. They brought him down, where he knelt there, with his head pressed to the ground. Time ticked by, the sun moving through the sky, his thoughts tumbling like a kaleidoscope. Snippets and images, of Beth, the boys, his family. The grief rose up inside him with the force of a tidal wave, choking him, coming out in great, harsh sobs until he was sick again and quivering.

Jackson fought his way to his feet, rage coming with him as he confronted Beth's ghost in that bikini on that first meeting here after the Bradleys' party. "Why, God? *Why?*" He picked up a rock and threw it at the water, at the rock in the swimming hole, at the tree where he carved their initials in a heart, at nothing in particular— one after another, until he fell to the ground, spent. He didn't weave his way home until the moon came out.

CHAPTER 34

September 2, 1964:

Aweek? Two weeks? He'd lost track of time. The herd. Jackson was supposed to take care of the herd. *And the boys. Don't forget the boys.* His head was fuzzy. He couldn't concentrate, couldn't hold a train of thought. *This must be depression.* Only now did he understand how his Beth felt when she'd wanted another baby so badly. That thought was a dagger so sharp, cutting so deep, that he actually clutched at his heart. Pushing away from the prying eyes of his parents and his brothers, he mumbled, "I'm going home," and wandered out the door.

The place was a ghost house. He hadn't been back inside since they took her away. He went into their closet and buried his face in her clothes. His arms came up to hold them close and he imagined that she was there. The sobs tore through him again when a hand clamped down on his shoulder. "Son—son, you've got to pull out of this. It's been nearly two months. Please Jackson. If not for your mother and me, or your brothers, do it for your boys. They need you."

"But, Pop, *I* need *her*." He turned and his father opened his arms, holding on tight.

"I know that, but she's gone and Beth would never want to see you this way. You and the boys were her whole world. She'd want only the best for all of you. This is not even a fraction of your best. Remember who you are. You're a Henry. Start out by taking care of her blessings the way your wife would expect from a Henry. Help them mend and you will heal too." His father didn't let go. Landon would be his son's rock for as long as he was needed.

Jackson took a deep shuddering breath and pulled away. "I need to do something and then I'll go get the boys, all right?"

Pop gripped his arm, his eyes bright, then walked away. Jackson listened for the sound of his retreating footsteps and the closing of the front door. He turned around and gazed at their bedroom. How easy it would be to turn this room into a shrine, but he couldn't. He wouldn't be able to function, be there for his sons, if he didn't put away the past. He set to work, his emotions under a tight rein. Otherwise, he'd break. Pictures, the locket with their wedding picture, a sachet that Beth had made, soon accumulated in a pile. He gathered up the wedding quilt next, folding it carefully. One last thing.

He sat down to pen his final entry in his journal, the book that had followed the journey from the day Jackson met the girl he would marry to the afternoon when her memory would be tucked away. Taking his time, getting those few words right, he wrapped everything up in the quilt.

He tied it with a ribbon and set it at the bottom of the cedar chest, under a board that had been set there to keep important papers private. He sat back on his heels, hands on his knees, as the dust motes danced around him, glittering in a shaft of sunlight.

Feeling their warmth, Jackson imagined it was Beth,

comforting him with her touch and her presence. He rested a hand on his heart and felt its steady beating. She was there.

CHAPTER 35

I'm wrapping her pictures, mementos, locket, letters, and this journal in the quilt she made for our wedding night, the one that covered her when our babies were born and the last night that she was with us. There are still many reminders of her for my boys. I would not want them to forget her, but these things belong to Beth and me.'"

Emmett had to stop, the hurt too deep to swallow, lodged in his throat. He brushed at the tears, but it was no use. He couldn't turn off the tap.

Casey took the journal from him and continued. "'I pack them away for two reasons. One—If I can get to them, I won't be able to resist temptation to cross over and be with her. I understand Poe and *Annabel Lee*. When you lose your heart's content, how do you go on? Two, my boys need me here and now, not in the past. I have to be a true father for my Wyatt and Emmett. She wouldn't forgive me if I was anything less. For her, for them—I will do my best. I have to put the pain away. Just because you can't see it, doesn't mean it isn't there, a pain so deep and dark, I will drown if I let myself go under. God give me the strength to stay afloat, trusting that she is in Your hands and one day I will see her again.'"

Casey rested her palm on the words as if that could stop

them. She was crying so hard, she couldn't see the page anymore.

Emmett took up his courage. He owed it to his father and his mother to see this through to the end. He didn't know if he'd be able to have the strength to read this book again. It would go to his brother next, then perhaps little Jack, and one day to his own child. Right now, it was in his hands. He swallowed hard and continued on, brokenly, pausing many times, but he finished. "'No matter. Every letter she ever wrote, every word she ever said, every moment we shared is written on my heart. When I want to be close to Beth, all I have to do is press my hand to my chest and feel that steady beating. I loved my wife, with all that I am, all that I'll ever be. What else is there to say?'"

The journal slipped from Emmett's hands and he wept. The last time he cried that hard, they'd put Jackson Henry in the ground.

❦❦❦

Eventually, he became aware of Casey's soft sobs, her hand resting on his head, stroking him like she would a child. He straightened his shoulders and laid a palm on her swelling belly. He kissed her tears away and scraped his hand across his cheeks. "I know what he means. For a man of few words, he said it all."

He sat with her, arms cradling his wife and their un-born child, rocking them both back and forth. Wrapped in the quilt made by his mother's hand, they were surround-ed by Jackson and Elizabeth Henry's love. Darkness had fallen. Well past dinner time, they'd lost track of time, trapped in the pages of the book. "I hope I can be half the father that he was."

"Well," she told him breathlessly, her eyes glittering

with excitement, tinged with a little fear. "You're going to find out soon. My water just broke."

His eyes popped wide and he sprang up from the floor, bringing her up with him. Her stretchy pants and the bedding was wet from a puddle of fluid that continued to trickle down her legs.

She glanced down and stuck her tongue out. "Ew! I have to change." Letting go of his hand, Casey waddled across the room, grabbed the flashlight, and started upstairs, her husband shadowing her every move. As they approached the top, a flood of light nearly blinded them as the power came back on after yet another outage, her cue to step inside the bathroom and close the door.

He stood outside waiting, forehead pressed to the door. "Casey, you listen right now. I don't care that you're a doctor. Don't get any ideas from that journal or my brother and Samantha. We are not having this baby at home. I'm grabbing your bag, warming up the truck, and we are going to a nice, sanitary hospital that is full of equipment and people who know what they're doing." He finally ran out of steam and began to sag, his heart pounding so fast, fit to leap from his chest.

She pulled the door open, nearly sending him tumbling inside. Her cheeks were rosy, her eyes bright, and she rose on tiptoe to kiss his nose. "Emmett, will you calm down? I don't want to have the baby at home either, but it's not time yet. I haven't even had a—" She suddenly cupped her belly and exhaled hard, closing her eyes a moment. When she opened them, he felt like all the blood drained out of his body. "Okay then, there's my first contraction. When they're five minutes apart, it's time to head to the hospital. For now, we wait until they get closer together. This could take hours. Let's help it along. Walk with me."

"What if it doesn't? What if you're Speedy Gonzalez,

like my mother with me?" Emmett asked her. She stuck
her tongue out in answer. Taking hold of his arm, she
gestured for him to lead and the pacing began. Back and
forth, up and down, they roamed through the rooms of the
Henry House. Ironic how similar it was to the day he and
his brother were born. Stopping by the living room window to stare out at the wintery wonderland, he squeezed
her hand tightly. "This time it's for real?" Her nod, followed by another instant when she was brought to a
standstill, was answer enough.

In the beginning, she talked and laughed. However,
around three in the morning, her knuckles were turning
white every time she gave his hand a squeeze and the
pains were down to seven minutes apart. "All right, Case,
this is it, no turning back, no false alarms. We've got a
half hour drive to the hospital. Let's get you in the truck."

She didn't argue. Emmett bundled her up, grabbed her
overnight bag, and led her down the walkway. When another contraction hit, he simply picked her up, letting her
bury her head in his chest until they finally made it to the
truck. Belting her in securely, he went around to the driver's side and gunned it. They'd never gone that fast down
the winding lane before. Thank God for small favors, the
storm had ceased hours before and the road was plowed.
Wyatt had thought of everything, giving the driveway a
sweep to help the young parents-to-be and smooth their
path.

"Hey! Try not to kill us on the way, okay?" Casey
smiled at him with a wink, breathing in pants and gripping the dashboard when the next wave rolled over her.
Swallowing hard, she glanced at him out of the corner of
her eye and grabbed hold of his hand. "I can't believe this
is it. The wait is over. Finally." Another forceful breath
and she clamped her jaw shut, squeezing her eyes tight.

Em wrapped his fingers around hers and smiled, even

if he didn't feel like it. "Almost. Don't have it here. A little bit longer, all right? You're going to be okay."

Thank the heavens above, the weather cooperated, cold and clear, the stars shining brightly. He made record time getting to the Women's Hospital, the best in the area. Good timing too because things really started to get moving. By the time he wheeled her up to the receptionist in a wheelchair snagged in the entranceway, his wife was at two minutes apart.

ల్యేల్య

The hospital staff kicked into action, quickly ushering them to a birthing suite. Casey was stripped down and given a hospital gown for easy access while Emmett was covered in scrubs. If she wasn't in labor, they'd be living out some fun fantasies with her husband playing the role of the incredibly handsome doctor. Even in the throes of labor, she didn't miss the appreciative looks nurses were giving the daddy to be.

Filing away her imaginings for later, it was time to face reality with her husband climbing up on the bed behind her, massaging the small of her back like she'd envisioned only a short while before. A half hour later, the maternity nurses suggested she climb into the birthing pool to relax and make the whole process easier.

With her husband's strong arms to hold her, she slid into the warm waters that felt like heaven. He climbed right in with her. "Em, you don't have to do this," she told him when the pain let up long enough to let her breathe.

"I'm not made of sugar, no matter how sweet I am. Besides, you were with me through everything with my eyes. The least I can do is get wet." He sealed her mouth with his and her body went loose.

"I don't think I've ever loved you more than right now." She leaned her head against his chest, beginning to drift, when the next pain rolled over her in an intensifying wave and the pressure down below began to build. "Oooh—I want to—I've got to push!"

Her voice rose up in a pitch that was not hers. Emmett took her cue and turned her over, cradling her body, allowing her to press her back against his chest. She gripped her legs, gritted her teeth and bore down with everything she had. There was a sense of something shifting, breaking loose within, and the water became first clouded, then pink with blood.

"That's it, baby. Almost there. You're doing everything just the way that you should." All traces of earlier panic were gone and her husband became her rock, stroking her hair, kissing her cheek, taking her hands in his, lending her his awesome strength. When her body started to tighten and she arched her back, he pressed a fist into the bowed point at its middle, driving his knuckles in hard. "Come on, Case! Let's go! Make this one count!"

A grunt ended on a scream and she was sure all of the blood vessels in her face popped, but an instant later, a tuft of hair emerged between her legs. Seeing the finish line in sight, she took a deep breath and gave one more monumental push. There was a stinging and a rush, followed by euphoria as the doctor took up her son—*my son!*—and set the squirming, pink bundle in her arms. His healthy wails could be heard throughout the floor.

Casey couldn't stop crying. Looking at Emmett's face, a sheen of tears coated eyes like golden honey with the sunlight streaming through, making them glow brightly. He pressed a kiss to her lips, then the baby's. "Beautiful, the both of you are absolutely beautiful."

Later, when everyone was cleaned up, all needs attended to, and they were covered in a pile of blankets, the three of them sharing the bed, he grazed her hair with his lips and asked softly, "Well, what do you want to call him? You did the work. You should get first dibs." They couldn't help but smile, remembering his father's journal.

"Emmett Jackson Junior." He raised his eyebrows in surprise. "Our son needs a name with loads of potential, one he'll grow into, like his father, and his grandfather before him. It's a name as strong and wonderful as the mighty oaks, like you."

Em nodded, his eyes filling once more as he pulled his family close and kissed them both once more. Clearing his throat, he finally managed to speak his mind. "Emmett Jackson it is." Glancing up to the night skies through the hospital window, he whispered softly, "Meet your grandson, Pop. I hope he'll be a man of few words and choose the ones that matter, just like you. I love you. You too, Mama." Turning his gaze back to his wife and newborn son, he couldn't forget to add, "And I love the both of you, more than words can say."

About the Author

Heidi Sprouse lives in upstate NY in historic Johnstown. She attended college at St. Rose in Albany, knowing all along her two loves were teaching and English. It took four years before she landed the teaching job of her dreams, but twenty years later she is still nurturing little ones in pre-K. She loves the privilege of watching brand-new little humans as they discover and begin to shape their own worlds.

Knowing what she wants and going after it in relentless pursuit is Sprouse's gift. Deciding to become an author can be downright unnerving, but Sprouse bit into the challenge, took off, and never looked back. Her perseverance proves success is not a matter of luck. It's a matter of finding what speaks to your heart and committing to do that thing until it makes a difference.

When she isn't busy teaching or with her husband Jim, her son Patrick, and her canine kids Chuck and Dale, she's cooking up her next novel. She dabbles in sweet romances, historical fiction, and suspense thrillers, depending on what pleases her reader's eye at any given moment. Sprouse is always in search of the extraordinary in the ordinary, writing about strong men with old-fashioned values and the women who pick them up when they fall. She'll tell anyone it's never too late to chase after your dreams, no dream is too small or insignificant, and any mountain can be moved with a proposal and a good plan.

Her past works include: *All the Little Things, Lightning Can Strike Twice, Aging Gracefully, Sunny Side Up, Against the Grain, Adirondack Sundown, The Edge of Forgiveness on Blue Mountain, Sunrise Over Indian Lake, One Last Adirondack Summer, Whispers of Liberty and Liberty's Promise.* Stay tuned for more to come!